The Jacobite Grandson

The
Jacobite
Grandson

T. J. Lovat

Matador
9 Priory Business Park,
Wistow Road, Kibworth Beauchamp,
Leicestershire, LE8 0RX
Tel: 0116 279 2299
Email: books@troubador.co.uk
Web: www.troubador.co.uk/matador
Twitter: @matadorbooks

ISBN 978 1800461 949

British Library Cataloguing in Publication Data.
A catalogue record for this book is available from the British Library.

Printed and bound in Great Britain by 4edge Ltd
Typeset in 11pt Adobe Caslon Pro by Troubador Publishing Ltd, Leicester, UK

Matador is an imprint of Troubador Publishing Ltd

ACKNOWLEDGEMENTS

As with all novels, there is one named author but many unnamed helpers. I acknowledge here those family members, friends and colleagues, especially Stephen, Amy, Tracey and Di, who played some part in shaping this book. Whether through reading the entire manuscript, simply a part of it or providing feedback on my earlier novel, I could not have done it without you. Also to Tom for the graphics. Thank you.

FAMILY TREE

Edward Lovat _____ Emma Simpson _____ Will Hartshorne

b. 1725   (m. 1744)   b. 1728   (m. 1773)   b. 1723

d. 1746

Eliza Harding _____ Thomas Lovat _____ Sarah Harding

b. 1750   (m. 1775)   b. 1746   (m. 1784)   b. 1748

d. 1776

Edward Lovat

b. 1776

I

Tommy Harding glanced over his shoulder. Cecil Greenham had reached the top of the long staircase, pistol in hand.

Tall and ungainly, Greenham looked past Harding. His undersized body in the doorway was of no significance. Harding saw the fury in Greenham's eyes. He was intent on one thing, killing his nemesis, Thomas Lovat.

Thomas, back turned and tending to Sarah, Greenham's wife, was a sitting duck.

Harding struggled to take in what was playing out before him. His wits returned as Greenham was about to shoot. Mustering all the strength this spindly man could, Harding made his move.

'NO! NOOOO,' he shouted, grabbing the pistol hand and using his other arm to throw Greenham backwards.

'Let me go, you fool.'

Harding continued pushing against a now off-balance foe. Greenham's heels hovered over the top step. He made a final attempt to steady himself and aim the pistol. Harding pushed him backwards. Greenham tumbled backwards, head over foot, all the way down the long, immaculately lacquered stairwell. His lanky body lay immobile at the bottom.

Harding clung to the top of the balustrade to steady himself. He looked back to see Thomas standing at the bedroom doorway.

'Ye saved my life, Tommy.'

'Perhaps,' Harding said, struggling for breath, 'but how's Sarah? Is she…?'

'She's alive, thank the Laird, but we need help. She's nay breathing so braw.'

Harding raced down the stairs. He quickly checked on Greenham who had not moved. Outside, he jumped on his horse and galloped the half mile or so to the local constable's house.

While the constable was on his way, Harding went to the doctor's house, secured a cart and driver and returned to the house with the doctor in tow.

The doctor confirmed that Greenham was dead. He had broken his neck on the fall. The doctor ascended the stairs to find Sarah cradled in Thomas's arms. He was leaning against the badly ruffled four-poster in the middle of the vast bedroom. Sarah was barely conscious. The doctor did what he could on the spot, then ordered the cart driver to help in carrying her down the stairs.

'Take her to my surgery. And be quick about it, man.'

Thomas and Harding followed. The constable advised they would need to report to his house later in the day to make a statement. He might have arrested them was Harding not so well known to him as a prominent lawyer in the town of Burnley, in northern England, where this event unfolded.

II

J*ust forty-eight hours beforehand, Thomas had been sharing his* concern about Sarah with his mother, Emma.

'Try and be patient, lad. Ye dinna ken what harm might come to Sarah if ye interfere. Especially if ye were to go there in yer current state.'

Emma took the opportunity to chide Thomas about his drinking. The problem was escalating again. They were sitting by the crackling fireplace in the Pemberton home they shared with Emma's second husband, William (Will) Hartshorne. Thomas was staring into the fire, whisky-filled glass in hand, greying, unwashed and uncut hair falling over his eyes.

'But I have to do something,' he blubbered, downing the remains in a single gulp.

Emma agonised over her only child, born on the day of her first husband's death at Culloden thirty-five years beforehand. It was the last day of the Jacobite Rebellion that had silenced the Scottish push to overtake English rule. She pondered on how much like his father Thomas was, in looks and disposition. That lick of jet black hair hanging loosely over one eye that had first

3

attracted her to his father could still be seen through the greying wrought by too many tragedies. Thomas's determination to right all of life's wrongs, especially those that affected his loved ones, was also so familiar to her.

At the same time, she reflected that she had never seen his father looking as dishevelled or lost as she now viewed her son.

'Well, lad, the truth is ye canna do anything the way ye are, so ye'd best be *comhla*. Get yerself together and be quick about it.'

—⋘—

The year was 1781 and the American War in which Thomas had been badly wounded six years earlier was still running its course. His wounds were physical and mental. The former included a bullet that rested too close to one kidney for a safe operation. The mental scar was the wracking guilt that he had led eight young men to their death in his last act as a British officer.

Worst of all, soon after his return to England, his wife, Eliza, died giving birth to their only child, Edward. Eliza was the younger sister of Sarah, with whom Thomas had had an on-again, off-again relationship from their early teens. During an extended off-again period, he had travelled to the Middle East and married a Persian woman. Mahdiya was a few years older but many years more mature. They had conceived a child who died, along with Mahdiya herself, on a tragic sea voyage home to England. While Thomas was grieving, Sarah had married Cecil Greenham, a lawyer friend and colleague of her brother, Tommy Harding. Soon after, Thomas married Eliza.

The match between Greenham and Sarah quickly manifested as an unhappy one, with Greenham moody and violent. Especially after Eliza's death, Thomas and Sarah had slipped into an unhealthy obsession with each other. They both fought it for propriety's sake but Sarah's miserable situation continued to stoke the obsession.

—⋘—

'I promise I'll nay go to her house,' Thomas said to his mother the morning after the fireside chat. 'But I *am* going to see Tommy. He needs to ken what's happening to his sister.'

Tommy Harding, Thomas's old school friend, lived in Burnley, about thirty miles from Pemberton and only a few miles from the Greenham house.

Thomas rode on horseback from Preston, a town about twenty miles from both Pemberton and Burnley. He had been teaching there through the day, a Friday. He arrived at Tommy and Margaret Harding's house in the early evening. Tommy greeted him warmly with some "good news".

'Sarah and Cecil'll be joining us for dinner. When I knew you were coming, I thought what a grand idea it'd be.'

'That'll be braw,' Thomas said, his face paling.

Tommy seemed oblivious to any complications or troubles in his sister's marriage. This did not surprise Thomas. Tommy was a fine human being but not the sharpest of wits when it came to human relations. He was smart with facts and figures and a very competent lawyer, by all accounts. Nevertheless, he was one of those people who never looked much beyond the surface of human interactions.

So different was he in this respect from his two sisters. Which is no doubt why he was the last one to know that Sarah had been carrying a candle for Thomas for years, the very last to know when Eliza began her tilt towards Thomas and now, it seems, among the last to notice trouble in Sarah's marriage.

Least of all did he suspect that it might have been wiser if he had not invited her, nor Cecil, especially, to join them for a relaxing evening meal.

'I'm surprised they were available at such short notice,' Thomas said.

'Oh, Sarah simply jumped at it and apparently Cecil was delighted too,' Tommy replied, his eyes popping with excitement.

Thomas wondered at what might really have occurred at the Greenham household.

Thomas was in one of a number of ample guest bedrooms, each with a four-poster bed bedecked with the finest linen, pillows and quilt and surrounded by immaculately polished bedside tables and a tallboy. The Hardings had no children and Margaret's full-time occupation was in keeping the house at the standard expected of one of Burnley's most prominent lawyers.

Thomas laid out his best clothes, a black suit, bronzed waistcoat and bow tie, on the bed, knowing that nothing less formal would suffice at the Harding establishment, even for a casual dinner.

He heard the visitors arrive, earlier than expected. The studied calm left him. He could feel the sticky sweat around his neck as he tried to move the top shirt button through its accompanying hole.

'Damn,' he said to the uncooperative button.

He tied the bow tie, hands fumbling and the sweat increasing. He caught a glimpse of himself in the full-length mirror that stood in the corner of the room. The hair he had spent some time brushing was messy and that annoying cowlick had surfaced again. He attended to these giveaway signals of discomfort and finally donned his coat.

He realised he had been listening to Greenham's and Tommy's loud banter for some time. But he had not heard Sarah. His concern for his own appearance was gone in an instant. Surely she had come. If not, the worst of evenings lay before him.

He hurried down the marble stairs. Any intimidation at meeting Greenham was overwhelmed by concern to know that Sarah was there – and well.

Their eyes connected. She was standing quietly to one side while her husband and Tommy carried on with their ribaldry. She flickered a smile, one that disappeared as quickly as it came when she noticed her husband's eyes upon her.

Greenham turned to Thomas, now almost at the foot of the stairs.

'Greetings, old friend. How jolly wonderful to see you after all this time.'

'Braw to see ye too, *auld friend*,' Thomas said, extending his hand. 'How bonnie ye could come at such short notice.'

'Oh, I *insisted*. I knew Sarah wouldn't want to miss the opportunity to catch up. I do know how much she values your friendship; as do I … as do I.'

His voice trailed off at the last three words.

'Sarah, how bonnie to see ye again,' Thomas said, approaching her.

He offered no emotion beyond what protocol would demand, giving her a cursory peck on the cheek as he pressed her hand. He hoped the flush he could feel in his cheeks was not too apparent.

'Lovely to see you, Thomas,' she replied, giving no more away than him.

They were both conscious of Greenham's persistent gaze.

Throughout it all, Tommy was like the cat that ate the cream. He seemed delighted to see his "two best friends" getting on so well and his sister looking so happy.

Margaret, another good but guileless soul, popped her head in from the dining room.

'Dinner will be served soon, ladies and gentlemen; oh, I should say *lady* and gentlemen,' she said, letting out a snorting guffaw.

Thomas saw in an instant how things were here and why Sarah would get no support from her brother and sister-in-law. Their lives were "all the little ducks in a row" – career, marriage, fine house and carriage. That was what mattered; no complications, please. Greenham played beautifully into this space and Sarah suffered for it.

Thoughts of rowing Sarah down the Thames at Oxford in their teens flooded back. That magic day that finished with a mutual squeezing of hands that contained a promise, so they thought then.

—∽∾—

Tommy and Margaret went to one side of the table, Sarah and her husband to the other. The sole seat at the end of the table was where Thomas was placed. Sarah moved to the farther position.

'Darling, why don't you sit next to Thomas?' Greenham said. 'I'm sure you have so much to talk about. Is that alright with you, old man?'

Thomas could see he was looking to gauge his reaction.

'By all means.'

Although it was awkward for both of them, Sarah and Thomas took some comfort in being close, even if for a short time. There were moments when a nearest ankle or knee seemed magnetised and drawn to its equivalent part in the other. The sublimated pleasure was something they conceded to each other with the occasional glance, both carefully choosing the moment when the attention of the other three was elsewhere. This was rare, especially on the part of Greenham who maintained a beady eye in their direction.

Thomas was reminded of the many times he and Mahdiya had to resort to those kinds of nuanced communications in the Shiraz Consulate and how much better at it she was than him.

—∿—

The dinner was held by dim candlelight and it was a large table so Thomas could not see Sarah's face so well. They moved into the hallway and passed under the brighter lamp over the stairs. Thomas noticed for the first time the slight blackening under one of Sarah's eyes.

'Sarah, what've ye done to yerself? Have ye been fighting it out with anyone lately?'

Sarah blanched.

'Oh come now, old man,' Greenham said. 'You know women don't like talking about their appearance, do you my darling?'

'No, I *suppose* we don't.'

Tommy and Margaret had taken in the exchange. While Tommy was prepared to take Greenham's lead, Margaret exhibited her customary level of discretion.

'Sarah, you look like you've been nursing a black eye.'

'No, it's not a black eye; it's just the last stages of a nasty cold I had. It got right into my eyes; they were an awful mess a week or so ago. Now, let's go to that port Tommy was boasting about.'

She led the way, grabbing her husband's arm and virtually carrying him with her.

The penny had dropped in Thomas's head. He now knew the extent of what Sarah was enduring, and it was killing him, and killing this evening. He became sullen and confused, not sure he could survive another half hour in the same room as this cad without doing to him what he had done all those years ago to Tommy in the Stonyhurst school playground, namely beaten him to a pulp. Oddly, the event had marked the beginnings of their friendship, something Thomas was quite sure would not ensue were he to do the same to Greenham.

He sat on the rose-coloured leather chair, slightly apart from the twin matching two-seaters on which the other four were conversing. Sarah was doing her best to pretend she was interested in their meaningless chit-chat and to ignore Thomas's stares.

Thomas stood up, gulped down the last of the whisky and placed the glass on the table more loudly than intended.

'If ye'll pardon me, I'm rather tired and probably should go to bed.'

'By all means, old man,' Greenham said. 'I imagine teaching those bally children must be awfully exhausting; blowed if I know how you do it, I must say.'

Thomas took it as a snobbish putdown. The alcoholic effect was not helping in steadying his emotions. Sarah could see the fury in Thomas's eyes.

'It *is* an exhausting job, teaching,' she said before Thomas could speak, 'I know well from my sister's experience of it. It's way more demanding than many of us realise. Isn't that so, Tommy? You remember how exhausted Eliza would be at the end of a week, especially when she was starting out.'

'Ah, yes. I think I remember that.'

'Good night, then,' Thomas said. 'And thank ye for yer hospitality and graciousness, Margaret, Tommy. Good night, Sarah.'

'Good night,' Sarah, Tommy and Margaret echoed.

He looked in Cecil's direction, a stare suggesting he knew what was going on between him and his wife.

'Good night, *auld man.*'

'Good night,' Cecil said, looking away.

III

Thomas *rose early to avoid a communal breakfast. He had slept* badly.

Sarah sensed he was up. She slipped out of bed and stole down to the kitchen. Thomas was cutting a loaf of bread and making coffee.

Both sets of eyes welled up. They rushed together and embraced.

'What're we going to do?' Thomas whispered. 'What *are* we going to do? I canna bear to see what ye're putting up with. I fear I'm going to kill that *rocaid*.'

'Don't talk like that. You *mustn't* talk like that. I don't know if I can stand it much longer but you must be careful. Cecil's a vicious man. He could destroy you in so many ways.'

'I'm nay worried about what he might do to me – but I *am* worried about what he might do to ye. What he *is* doing to ye.'

'Oh, I'm strong, my darling; you must know that by now.'

'Strong in spirit, nay doubt, but nay strong enough if what I ken's happening *is* happening. He's beating ye, is he nay?'

Sarah was silent for a moment.

'Oh only now and then and only when he's at the end of his tether. Frankly, it's not the worst of it; it's more his moods. He cuts me right out; won't talk to me for days.'

Sarah faltered. She tightened her hold.

'I've never known anyone so surly. I really don't know what causes it; I've tried so hard to work around it, make myself the smallest of targets, but it's no use.'

She faltered again.

'*And*, you know, in a strange way, when he does, it's a bit of relief. At least he's acknowledging I exist; for a while after, he's actually nicer than normal. It's very strange.'

'Oh *fear gaolach*, what've I done to ye? You should've been mine all along. If I'd nay gone on that *damnadh* trip to the East, I ken we'd be together. It was all I wanted. And then …'

'And then destiny took over. If we'd come together then – and it's all I wanted too – you'd have never known your Mahdiya and made my little sister the happiest woman in the world and Edward wouldn't exist. Mind you, there might be some other tiny people who we'll never know – but no Edward. Think of that. What will be, will be, my darling!'

There was a tell-tale sound of someone racing down the stairs. They sprang apart, gave one last look that said it all and she rushed to the back door.

Thomas returned to the knife that sat halfway through the slice.

'*Where* is my wife?' Greenham asked.

'As far as I ken, she's having a wash,' Thomas replied without looking up.

Greenham rushed past him and out the back. Thomas could hear him banging on the wash room door.

'Where *were* you? *Why* did you leave the room without telling me? *How long* have you been down here?'

Greenham stormed back in, ignoring Thomas, and raced back up the stairs.

Tommy and Margaret rushed out of their room, asking Greenham if everything was alright.

'*Yes*, everything is fine, thank you.'

His door slammed shut.

Tommy came down the stairs.

'Thomas, do you know why Cecil's so upset?'

'Tommy, we have to talk about Sarah. Now's nay the time but we must talk; I'll stay until Sarah and Cecil have gone home. We *must* talk; is that clear?'

'Of course, of course. I believe they'll be going after breakfast.'

—⟶⟵—

The pair left without any breakfast. Greenham's foul mood persisted. Sarah maintained the calm necessary to get him out of the house before some irretrievable event occurred. Tommy and Margaret flapped around trying to get their little ducks back in a row.

'Please stay and at least let us get you something for breakfast.'

'I'm afraid we really do have to go, dear ones,' Sarah replied. 'We'd completely forgotten we have guests coming for lunch.'

She was first down the stairs with her apparel. Thomas approached her, offering to become involved if it would help.

'No, leave it with me,' Sarah said.

In a quick exchange, Thomas asked for reassurance she would be alright.

'Yes,' she sighed.

'I'm coming to see ye. Are ye home alone on Monday?'

Sarah's eyes welled as she nodded. Thomas squeezed her hand and then disappeared before Greenham came down the stairs.

They were gone within minutes, barely a goodbye to anyone, least of all Thomas.

—⟶⟵—

'Oh my,' Tommy said. 'I've never seen Cecil like that.'

'Oh dear, I hope I didn't cause it all by talking about Sarah's black eye,' Margaret said. 'But it did look like a black eye, didn't it?'

She looked from Tommy to Thomas and back again.

'I'm afraid it was,' Thomas said. 'Tommy, that's what I wanted to talk about and I suppose there's nay any better time than now. My apologies, Margaret; I was nay going to bother ye with this, ladies' sensitivities and all, but I ken the time's come to call a *sluasaid* a *sluasaid* and see what we can do for Sarah. D'ye ken Cecil's beating her?'

'Oh, my Lord,' Tommy said. 'Are you sure? I just can't believe it. Cecil?'

Margaret blanched and hastened to a seat.

'Aye, I'm sure. Ye ken Sarah; when she says something like that, ye ken it's true. What can we do? Tommy, ye're the lawyer. Should we go to the constabulary? Are there any legal avenues?'

Tommy now needed a seat. Margaret reached over and held his hand.

'I just can't believe it. Cecil can get riled if things don't go his way. I had to step in once when he was rousing at this young girl who'd put some papers in the wrong cabinet. His reaction seemed more than the misdemeanour warranted and the poor girl was visibly distressed. But he's by and large an affable fellow, and damned good worker, I must say. Excellent lawyer; extraordinary. Why, we once had a case...'

'Nay doubt, Tommy,' Thomas interrupted. 'But what about Sarah? What can we do? *Should* we go to the constable?'

Tommy and Margaret looked at each other for guidance.

'Perhaps I should go and talk with them,' Tommy finally said. 'I get on well with Cecil; he's my best – I mean second-best – friend, after you, Thomas, of course.'

'*Tommy*, for the Laird's sake, listen to me; answer my question. Is there anything the law can do? *Can* we go to the constable?'

'Oh – no, I don't think so. The constable would say it's a family matter and the law's equivocal, to say the least, about violence in the home. Even if he did intervene, no magistrate I know of would touch it; it'd be thrown out and Sarah could be in an even more vulnerable situation.'

There was a moment of silence.

'Yes, I think I'll go and speak with them,' Tommy said again.

'Well, I'll come with ye then.'

'I don't think that's a good idea, Thomas. I don't know why but Cecil seems not to like you. Perhaps it's because of yours and Sarah's past.'

'I'm just worried for yer safety, Tommy, that's all.'

'*My* safety? Cecil and I are the *best* of friends; I'm sure whatever's going on here is just a disruption, something they'll get over in time.'

'Aye, if ye insist,' Thomas said. 'When will ye go?'

'I think I'll go right now. Is that alright, darling?' Tommy said, looking over at a still pale and confused Margaret.

She nodded.

Tommy set out for the Greenham house, not more than five miles away. Margaret had taken to her bed to recover while Thomas pretended to go to his room. Only five minutes after Tommy left, Thomas was saddling a horse in order to follow him. He knew he could catch up with his less able friend.

—⁓—

When Tommy arrived at the house, he could hear Greenham shouting. He knocked, then banged loudly on the door.

Silence. He banged again.

'Please let me in; will one of you please let me in?'

Greenham appeared at the door. Tommy noted the ruffled hair falling over his sweaty brow.

'Why Tommy, old fellow, what a surprise. Did we leave something behind?'

'No, Cecil, I'm concerned for Sarah. Thomas says you've been beating her. Please tell me that's not true.'

'That's absurd. What nonsense! *Do you know* that Sarah and Thomas have been having an affair behind my back? What do you think of *that*?'

'I really don't think that's the case, Cecil, but let me speak with Sarah about it – *Sarah*, are you there?' he shouted into the open door, glaring at the top of the staircase.

No response.

'She's not well; she's sleeping. It'd be far better if you came back later.'

'No, Cecil, I need to speak with her now. Please!'

Tommy attempted to push past him. Greenham blocked his way and pushed him back.

'I'm telling you to go away.'

The two men, neither of them built for battle, began to tussle in the doorway. Thomas, a battle veteran, sprang from the bushes. Before Greenham could take steps to avoid it, Thomas had landed a full fist to the side of his head. Greenham fell backwards, struggling to find his feet. Thomas bounded up the stairs with more agility than he had displayed for years.

'Sarah, Sarah, are ye here?'

Once atop the long staircase, Thomas went straight to the closed door of the main bedroom immediately opposite. He opened it to find Sarah on her back on the floor next to the four-poster. She seemed to be unconscious.

Tommy arrived in the doorway a split second behind.

'Sarah, *Sarah*. Oh my God,' Thomas cried, rushing over and kneeling next to her.

He could see the fierce red marks around her throat. He placed his hand near her nose, feeling for her breath.

Tommy was frozen on the spot in the doorway. He heard the clambering up the stairs behind him but was fixed on what was in front of him.

—∿—

And so, the events unfolded that culminated in Cecil Greenham's death. Sarah was freed of her marriage but at a terrible cost, one that would put even further strain on the perennial confusion around her relationship with Thomas.

IV

'So, are you saying you were regularly beaten by your husband, Mrs Greenham?' asked the magistrate.

'Yes, Your Honour.'

Sarah wore a long black dress with a discreet silver necklace and her slightly greying blonde hair tied back tightly. Her face was pale with reddened brown eyes atop dark circles. The magistrate noted her appearance.

'But you told no-one about these beatings? Is that correct?'

'I did eventually tell Mrs Hartshorne, Your Honour.'

'And Mrs Hartshorne is who exactly?'

'Colonel Lovat's mother, Your Honour.'

'And Colonel Lovat is who to you, Mrs Greenham?'

'A friend of my brother, Your Honour.'

'This is the same Colonel Lovat who was present on the day Mr Greenham died; is that correct?'

'Yes, Your Honour.'

'And why was Colonel Lovat present in your bedroom at the time of Mr Greenham's death?'

'The Colonel had accompanied my brother to our home.'

'And why was your brother at your home at that time?'

'He was concerned for my welfare, Your Honour.'

'And why was he concerned for your welfare if he knew nothing about your husband's abuse?'

'I believe Colonel Lovat had told him shortly before.'

'So, Colonel Lovat knew of the abuse?'

'Yes, sir.'

'How did he come to know if you had told no-one?'

'I believe Mrs Hartshorne may have told him, Your Honour.'

'So Mrs Hartshorne told her son who then told your brother; is that what you are saying, Mrs Greenham?'

The heavy questioning about Thomas's knowledge of the abuse resulted from rumours spread by the Greenham family about an alleged affair between Sarah and Thomas. His family was adamant that Greenham was the victim of a lovers' tryst, now covered up. Sarah's demeanour was not aided by knowing the family was in the courtroom urging a murder conviction.

'Mrs Greenham, I'm sorry to ask this so forwardly, but have you and Colonel Lovat slept together?' the magistrate persisted.

'No, Your Honour.'

Thomas was next to take the stand.

'Colonel Lovat, have you ever been intimate with Mrs Greenham?' was the magistrate's opening question.

'Nay, Yer Honour.'

Thomas and Sarah had spoken about the best way for each of them to answer the inevitable questioning.

The magistrate concluded that Tommy had acted in self-defence. The death was deemed accidental. He also judged that neither Thomas nor Sarah had played any deliberate part in it.

—⚬—

'But we *did* sleep together, Thomas,' Sarah said. 'We *did*. We slept in the same bed. And we put our hands on the Bible and denied it.'

'Sarah, sleeping together means having sexual relations and we've nay had them; being intimate means having sexual relations and we've nay had them. From memory, we nay even slept that night, much less had relations.'

Thomas had needed to stress that any hint of an affair could have led to them both, and perhaps Tommy, being found guilty of murder.

—⁂—

Sarah's concern related to an incident on Thomas's birthday some months beforehand. They had seen little of each other in the five years since Eliza's death. The odd meeting had been awkward and painful.

When Sarah received an invitation to join the family for his birthday, she accepted, running the gauntlet of her husband's objections. She was the only invited guest to make it, partly owing to one of Lancashire's worst mid-Spring storms. She arrived late, dripping wet. Emma took her to her room to dry off and change.

By the time they got back to the table, Thomas and Will were fighting over how best to handle Edward's tantrum, one of his worst. He wailed, throwing anything he could lay a hand on, thumping the table, red-faced and breathless.

'Now, little fellow, what can I get you?' Will said. 'Look at your little bear; he's wondering why you're unhappy.'

'Stop now or else,' Thomas shouted, raising his striking arm.

Will intervened to stop him from hitting the child. Emma and Sarah re-entered the room to find Thomas shouting at Will and Edward distraught in his chair.

'Stop it, Thomas,' Emma ordered. 'Ye're terrifying the bairn.'

She lifted the boy out of his chair, caressed him and whispered in his ear.

'Now what's the matter with my favourite laddie in the whole world?'

With the whisper blending into a lullaby, Emma took the boy out of the room and headed for his bedroom. Will followed.

Sarah and Thomas were alone.

'I'm sorry, Sarah.'

Thomas sat at the table, placing his head in his hands. Sarah came up behind him and placed her hand gently on his back.

'Thomas, I can't bear to see you like this.'

Thomas turned his head and placed his arms around her. He buried his head in her chest.

She held one arm around his neck and ran her fingers through his hair.

Thomas was digging his fingers into her back so much it began to pain her. Her clothes were concealing a number of bruises.

As she moved to ease his grip, Thomas looked up at her. She would tell herself later that she intended only to kiss him on the forehead or perhaps on the cheek. She had not intended her lips to meet his but she was also not resisting.

The blood came back to her head and she pulled away.

'I can't; Thomas, I *can't*.'

'Aye, I ken. *Thalla*; please just go away. Why did ye come anyway?

He stood up and strode out of the room.

She sat at the table, tears rolling down her cheeks.

'What's wrong, Sarah?' Emma said, walking back in. 'Where *is* that lad of mine?'

'Oh, I don't know; I'm a fool for coming.'

'Ye're *nay* a fool! *Ye* are nay the fool. What on earth happened?'

'Oh nothing. I think I just need to go.'

'Well, ye canna be setting out tonight. Let me get ye something to eat.'

Emma went to the kitchen and came back with a large bowl of broth and some bread on a plate. She placed it in front of Sarah and went and sat opposite.

'Thank you,' Sarah said. 'You've always been so kind to me.'

'Sarah, I'm sorry to be so *maol* but what about ye and Thomas? I ken ye still have such intense feelings for each other. If that was ever proven, it's tonight that ye'd come here in this atrocious weather.'

Sarah was silent, spooning her soup, before she spoke.

'I know, I know. I admit when you told me he wanted me here I felt more alive than I have for years. I've been so miserable but…'

'Well, what are ye going to do about it then?'

'What can I do?'

'I ken, I ken. Ye're married. But there are times when ye have to take yer life in yer hands and I sense that's nay what ye're doing. Ye're barely surviving and I'm worried ye'll nay survive. Cecil *is* beating ye, is he nay?'

The words stung. This was the secret of secrets. Sarah would have sooner told about the passionate kiss with Thomas than admit she was being abused.

'It's alright. Ye dinna need to answer; although I think ye already have. Sarah, ye have to do something. Does anybody else ken this?'

'No-one knows. And please don't tell anyone. Especially Thomas.'

They spoke for hours and then went to bed.

Thomas meantime had been in Edward's room, sitting next to the sleeping boy in his bed.

'I'm *duilich*, wee laddie; I'm so sorry.'

The boy had stirred at one point and looked up. Thomas was sure he had smiled and mouthed *Da* before falling back to sleep. Thomas then lay on the floor next to the bed, curling up and falling asleep.

He woke with a start in the middle of the night, recalling his words to Sarah.

'…just go away, will ye?'

He hurried to her room, tapped on the door and opened it.

'Thomas?'

'I'm so sorry,' he said as he sat on the side of the bed. 'I nay should be here but I was frightened ye might've gone.'

'Oh, I probably *should* go for all our sakes but I can't. I'm too unhappy without you.'

He lay on top of the bed and she pulled an outer quilt to cover him against the cold. They lay there for hours, holding each other and talking as they never had before. They resisted anything that might complicate things even more.

'Let's be patient, my darling,' she said. 'Promise me you'll be patient.'

'I promise.'

—⚬⚬—

But Thomas's patience ran out. Thence followed the chain of events that led to Cecil Greenham's death. While they were acquitted, Sarah's guilt persisted. She accepted an invitation from her aunt to go and stay in Bordeaux.

—⚬⚬—

'There's nay need for ye to come,' Thomas said to Emma and Will. 'I'm perfectly capable of getting Sarah to the port. And I *dinna* care what people think.'

'I ken ye dinna care but perhaps ye should, lad,' Emma replied.

'Your mother's right, Thomas,' Sarah said. 'We *do* have to be careful.'

'I agree,' Will said. 'Any sniff of new evidence and who knows what the Greenhams might try?'

Hence, Emma, Will and Thomas escorted Sarah to Scarborough to board the ship to France. The night before the ship sailed, they stayed together in a guesthouse. Emma and Will went to bed early.

Thomas and Sarah held hands on the two-seat sofa facing the crackling fire.

'How long will ye be gone?'

'I don't know, Thomas. I just need to get away from everything for a while. You do understand, don't you?'

'Aye, of course. It's just that we're nay getting any younger.'

'I know that, my darling. Just give me some time.'

'Of course I will. Just ken I'm here. However long it takes, I'll be here. I've let ye go too many times and I'm nay lettin' ye go this time – even if that's what ye want right now.'

'I *don't* want that, Thomas. I *just need time.*'

He looked into her deep brown eyes, the ones he had dreamt of so often over the years. They were now ringed with even deeper circles.

'Then do what ye must.'

He touched her lightly on one cheek. She grabbed his hand and held it to her chest.

'If it takes a lifetime, Thomas, if it takes a lifetime. You know it's *all* I've ever wanted.'

'Maybe not a *whole* lifetime. Just until we're eighty perhaps.'

'I love you, Thomas Lovat. I've known that forever, perhaps even from a past life.'

They kissed as they had on the night of Edward's tantrum. Confusion and guilt were fading. Determination was taking its place.

V

'Oh, it's my favourite Redcoats,' Mrs Prendiville said, greeting Thomas and Edward at the door. 'Come in, my lovelies, come in. Look 'o's 'ere, everyone.'

They stepped through the door into the warmth of the Prendiville home. It seemed smaller than Thomas remembered it. He forgot to duck and hit his head. Edward laughed.

'Ye shouldn't laugh at yer poor Pa,' Mrs Prendiville said as she lifted Edward into her arms and planted a wet kiss on his cheek. 'So, this is yer li'l Redcoat, is it Thomas? I'm so pleased to meet him at last.'

'Oh, 'e's so cute,' Mary, one of the daughters said as she pulled him out of her mother's arms.

'Don't 'og 'im, Mary,' Louise, the other daughter said. 'Ye always 'og everything.'

The girls ran off, fighting over who could give Edward the greater attention. Edward seemed happy to be fought over.

'Don't forget 'is Pa's 'ere too, girls,' Mrs Prendiville called after them. 'I'm sorry, Thomas. The girls've been so excited to 'ave a li'l one in the 'ouse.'

'That's perfectly alright, Mrs P. I'm sure my lad'll nay be complaining.'

'Wonderful to see ye again, Thomas,' Liam, the older son, said, shaking his hand.

Mr Prendiville waved from his chair in front of the fire. The fireplace was in the corner of the small room that served as kitchen, dining and loungeroom in one. Three small bedrooms ran directly off this central space, the parents' room on one side and two for the children on the other. The smell of broth filled the air.

—꙳—

The Prendivilles had befriended Thomas during his assignment as a Sub-Lieutenant in Tralee, Ireland, many years before. It had been his first army posting as a British "Redcoat", supposedly there to keep the Irish under control. Thomas had helped Liam when he was thrown into prison for breaking the nose of a British soldier. It had happened on one of the nightly rounds that Thomas led through the town.

Lieutenant Sutherland had been in charge of the barracks that night. He had Liam thrown into a cell. Thomas had come to his rescue, challenging Sutherland's authority in the process.

It was one of many situations that challenged Thomas's comfort as a British officer. He came to realise how deeply Highlander Jacobite blood flowed through his veins. He found it easier to identify with the suppressed Irish than with the occupying army he was representing.

On his several stints in the Americas, Thomas felt the same about the American patriots. He bemoaned the fact that their just cause failed to resonate among Britain's leaders, be it King or Parliament, and least of all with the occupying army. His wounding just before hostilities began had saved him from having to fight against a cause for which he had increasing sympathy.

It was in Tralee that Thomas first experienced the dilemma so it had a special place in his heart. He had particularly enjoyed the time he spent getting to know the Prendivilles. He kept up a correspondence with them throughout the intervening years. Liam had sufficient schooling through the local parish to be the correspondent but Mrs Prendiville was never far behind the pen, instructing him with what to say.

Tell my favourite Redcoat he's always welcome in our home and to make sure he brings his little Redcoat with him. And tell him to please come back anytime and take over from the current batch of Redcoats.

Sutherland was still there, now a captain and in charge of the barracks.

Thomas felt good to be back in their midst for the first time in years. He could breathe here and get some respite from his constant fretting about Sarah.

—ɷ—

'So, how's my bonnie friend, Captain Sutherland?' Thomas asked.

'Same old Sutherland,' Liam replied. 'I presume ye'll be going to see 'im to renew acquaintance.'

'With nary a doubt,' he smiled. 'What *did* happen in the cell that night? Ye were bashed, weren't ye?'

'Yes.'

'Who was it then?'

'Pringle.'

'*Pringle*? The one whose nose ye cracked?'

'The selfsame.'

'How on earth? I ken he was in the surgeon's ward getting his snout fixed.'

'Not the 'ole night. It must've been a couple o' hours after I was flung in there. I was out to it so the first I knew was when a bucket o' cold water was bein' thrown over me. I woke and there's

Sutherland standin' there, shoutin' at me. Two o' the soldiers 'aulin' me up by the arms and pinnin' me against the wall. Sutherland's callin' me Irish scum and this is what ye get when ye attack one of 'is Majesty's men. Next thing, Pringle appears from nowhere, bandaged snout an' all, and starts whackin' into me with somethin' really 'ard. No idea what it was 'cause my 'ead's down tryin' to protect myself. All I know is it took three or four whacks before I was out to it again. When I woke, there was blood everywhere and my breeches were full o' ye know what.'

'I ken what,' Thomas said. 'I had to clean it up if ye remember. So, Sutherland was there the whole time?'

'Yes.'

'And ye've never reported it?'

'No, what'd be the use?'

'Would ye now?'

'No.'

'Even if I came with ye?'

'Where to, Thomas? Sutherland's the law 'ere. D'ye seriously think 'e'd give me the time o' day?'

'What about if we went to London, to Army HQ?'

'No, Thomas. Ye don't understand. Sutherland'd get 'is own back one way or t'other. If it was just me, maybe, but there's Ma and Pa, and the two girls, and Paddy.'

Paddy, the younger son, was now a priest in an adjoining parish.

'Paddy? Surely they'd nay go after a priest?'

'Oh, Thomas, my lad, ye don't know what these people are like.'

Thomas had assumed things were fairly settled in Tralee. The Irish Jacobite resistance had been quelled and the army numbers halved. He shared these thoughts with Liam.

'Yes, that's true. And things were quiet for a while but the worse it's all gone for the British in the Americas, the more they take it out on us. Since fancy-pants Cornwallis came back with 'is tail between 'is legs, things've become even worse. It's as though they want to do to us what they couldn't do to the Americans.

Arrogant bastards, the English; they just can't believe they're not able to control everything.'

Thomas knew that Marquis Cornwallis, who had been assigned to teach the Americans a lesson, had been defeated by George Washington in October of that year, 1781. Unlike most of those around him, Thomas had been pleased to hear of it. By this time, he had lost respect entirely for the British cause and only hoped the Americans would win quickly so to minimise the loss of British lives, already far beyond what this battle was worth. For all the loss of respect, he had not figured on the army being so low as to take out their defeat on the already subjugated Irish.

'When will they ever learn?' Thomas said, shaking his head.

'When 'ell freezes over, p'rhaps,' Mr Prendiville called from his spot in front of the fire.

'And speakin' o' such things,' Liam said. 'The church and its priests seem to threaten 'em like no others. Probably because they've all the respect the army'll never 'ave. So, all a priest 'as to do is say one word that sounds a bit disloyal and the army comes and does a search o' the presbytery or even disrupts Mass on Sund'y. No-one knows what it's all about. Even when they don't find anythin', that doesn't stop 'em doin' the same the next Sund'y. And Paddy's a real target, I think 'cause 'e's my brother and...'

'And what?' Thomas asked.

'Ah, 'cause 'e's *yer* friend, if ye must know.'

'Oh, my Laird. I'm so sorry, I'd nay idea. And to ken I once wore that uniform.'

—⁂—

'Li'l Redcoat. 'ow are ye, this mornin'?' Mrs Prendiville asked as Edward took his place at the breakfast table.

'Bonnie, thank ye, Mrs Pendible.'

'Don't call 'im a Redcoat, Ma,' Mr Prendiville said. 'Ye don't want to lay a curse on the boy. No offence, Thomas.'

'Nay offence taken, sir, I assure ye of that.'

'I dinna like red,' Edward said.

'There ye see, Ma,' Mr Prendiville said, laughing. 'The boy's a Jacobite; 'e wouldn't be caught dead in red, would ye, Eddie?'

'Don't call 'im Eddie, Pa,' Mrs Prendiville said.

'Reddie Eddie,' Mary laughed as she tickled Edward in his side.

Mary was sixteen years of age, tall, thin and with dark brown hair that perfectly matched her eyes and fell neatly over her shoulders. She knew what no-one else in the family knew, that she had a male admirer in the parish. She was thinking ahead and interested to nurture her maternal skills.

Her sister, Louise, was fourteen, short, plump and with light brown hair that was no match for her hazel eyes. It was normally pulled back because she could never get it to fall like her sister's. She knew what everyone in the family knew, that she wished desperately to have an admirer from the parish, or anywhere for that matter. She was also looking to a future as a mother.

Both sisters relished having a five year-old in their midst.

Edward loved the attention, especially the teasing. He had not experienced much in the way of young girls fawning over him.

'Oh, Mary, don't be foolish,' Mrs Prendiville said. 'Paddy's comin' for dinner, Thomas. I 'ope ye can be 'ere. I know 'e wants to see ye.'

'Aye, surely, Mrs Prendiville. I'm looking forward to seeing him again.'

Mrs Prendiville delivered the final plate of bacon and eggs. She sat down at the opposite end of the table from her husband.

'Now, let's say three 'ail Marys and a Glory be.'

Edward looked up at Mary next to him.

'Hail Mary,' he said, chortling.

Mary and Louise broke into laughter, Liam and Thomas smiled while Mr Prendiville mimicked a scolding look and Mrs Prendiville called everyone to order.

'Now, Edward, my darlin', we mustn't make fun of Our Lady, must we?'

The three children bowed their heads. Edward wondered what was going on. He had not grown up with such piety.

—⚹—

Father Paddy Prendiville came to dinner. He was only fifteen when Thomas had last seen him. Thomas was finding it difficult to imagine him as a priest until he walked in with his black suit and clerical collar filling the doorway. Unlike Liam who was tall and thin, no doubt the thinness owing much to his work as a field hand, Paddy was shorter and decidedly over-weight.

'*Give him a brown habit and he could be Friar Tuck,*' Thomas thought.

'Paddy, darlin', look 'o's 'ere,' Mrs Prendiville said, giving him a motherly hug.

Thomas followed in her step.

'Lovely to see ye Paddy, or should I say, Father?'

'Paddy'll be fine, Thomas. Lovely to see ye too after all these years.'

'And this is our li'l Redcoat, darlin'. Why don't ye give 'im a blessing?'

Edward's eyes were fixed on the over-sized black figure staring at him.

'Ah, to be sure I will. Hello, Edward, I'm Father Paddy.'

Edward froze in his tracks, not sure what a blessing entailed. He was expecting Paddy to offer his hand for a handshake. Instead, it extended upward, pointing to the ceiling as he began to mutter something in a language Edward had only ever heard from a distance.

'*Benedicat te omnipotens Deus, Pater et Filius et Spiritus Sanctus, Amen.*'

Paddy waved his arm up and down, then from right to left.

Edward was stunned. He was half expecting the ritual to end with a slap in his face, so wildly were Paddy's gestures moving around his head. The girls began giggling. Mrs Prendiville remonstrated with them for their sacrilege and Thomas moved to reassure his son.

'That was braw, Father, thank ye so much. Laddie, thank Father Paddy now for blessing ye.'

'Thank ye, Farver.'

They all laughed and moved to prepare for dinner.

It was a roast, as was customary whenever Paddy came around. He had lashings of the lamb and several more spuds than anyone else, all washed down with the fine wine Thomas had managed to bring from home. Thomas could see why Paddy had put on so much weight.

—◊—

After dinner, the girls were assigned to the happy duty of putting Edward to bed with a story prior to joining their mother in the kitchen for the washing up. Meantime, the men got to talking about serious matters. Mr Prendiville stayed for a while but when he realised the talk was moving to British mistreatment of the population, he excused himself and went and sat in front of the fire. He lit up his pipe. He had lived through more than enough of British bastardry and now just wanted to stay out of trouble.

'So, Liam tells me the army's bothering ye,' Thomas began.

The details of army abuse shocked Thomas who thought himself unshockable by now. At the same time, Paddy was at pains to caution him against doing anything that might make things worse.

'I hear ye, Paddy, and I ken yer concern but surely ye dinna ken we can just turn a blind eye to it all. As a man of God, ye've a keen sense of justice and ye ken the army behaviour's unjust.'

'As a man of God or a man of the world, I've no doubt about that. But, Thomas, we've learned the hard way to be realistic about what can be done and what's best to accept.'

VI

'Colonel Lovat to see Captain Sutherland,' Thomas said to the young Redcoat guarding the familiar gate.

'Do you have official business with the captain, Colonel?'

'Aye, it's an army matter.'

'Please wait here, sir.'

The young soldier stepped inside the gate and summoned the corporal. He came forward to check Thomas's credentials before calling the Officer of the Watch. Soon afterwards, a well-dressed lieutenant came to the gate.

'Colonel Lovat, sir, I wondered if it was ye.'

Lieutenant John MacAdam had been a young associate of Henry Coolidge, Thomas's great friend among the American patriots. Thomas had met him at a Franklin Society event in Boston in the early 1770s. Both being Scottish born, they had warmed to each other.

'There's nay need to salute, John. I'm out of the army now. It's good to see ye again.'

'And ye, sir.'

'Call me Thomas, please. What brought ye here?'

'Things went bad with my business once the war began. It was getting harder to get materials in and out of New York and, unfortunately, my Scottish brogue had many Americans ken I was the enemy. Not all Americans are as tolerant as our friend, Henry.'

'Indeed, I saw that when I sat in on one of Thomas Jefferson's courtroom defeats. He was fighting to free a slave of mixed race with his white family fully supporting him. Jefferson was brilliant but the jury and the judge, all Americans, found against him. Nay an Englishman in sight. Even if the Americans win this war, which of course they will, I dinna ken their fight's over.'

'Agreed, sir. I mean, Thomas. Anyway, I came home and felt I needed a steadier job so here I am. The army wanted to send me back to America but I put in a request nay to and told them why. They were nay happy so my punishment was to be sent to the last outpost of the British Empire.'

'Is it really that *dona*?'

'Nay, I actually like the people but … anyway, I'm sure ye're nay here to hear my life story. What can I do for ye?'

'I'm here to see yer commanding officer if he's free.'

'Captain Sutherland?' MacAdam said, raising an eyebrow. 'Is he a friend?'

'Nay really. We were here together though back in '69.'

'Really? He's nay ever mentioned ye, which is unusual granted yer fame. Strictly between us, I'd nay have imagined ye as friends.'

'Aye, is *that* so?'

'Nay. I'll tell him ye're here, will I?'

'Please.'

They walked together towards the commanding officer's quarters. Thomas remembered it as belonging to Major Grant, the kindly commander who had written such a positive report on his posting in Tralee. He was sure it was the reason for his quick promotion as Captain of the Guard in Boston.

The thought of Sutherland sitting in the same chair horrified him.

When they arrived at the door, MacAdam asked Thomas to wait while he went inside. There was no movement or sound for twenty minutes or so when MacAdam finally came out.

'Captain Sutherland will see ye, Colonel.'

Thomas moved inside, following MacAdam to Sutherland's office door. MacAdam knocked and opened the door. There sat Sutherland behind a lavish desk, one at least twice the size of Grant's. There was a range of expensive looking furniture and equally costly artwork on the wall.

'He has made himself at home,' Thomas thought. *'I suppose when ye have nothing else ....'*

Sutherland was busy with paperwork, or pretending to be. He ignored Thomas's presence before finally lifting his head with a look of annoyance.

'Sub-Lieutenant Lovat, how *lovely* to see you.'

Thomas noted the avoidance of recognition that his own rank now far exceeded Sutherland's.

'Good to see ye too, Captain.'

He was sure Sutherland showed a flicker of annoyance that he had failed to rile Thomas as he once did.

'What can I do for you?' Sutherland said.

'I'd like a word in private, if I might, Captain.'

Sutherland hastened MacAdam and his adjutant out of the office.

'So, to the point, Mr Lovat?'

'I wish to caution ye, Captain, that I've detected some dissatisfaction in sections of the population about the heavy-handed ways the army's treating them. I'm sure ye'd be sensitive to the Government's need to keep things quiet here, granted the resources being expended in the Americas.'

Thomas was still bristling from the accounts he had heard from Liam and Paddy, most especially Liam's finally admitting that Sutherland himself had overseen his beating in prison. Nonetheless, he managed to say what was needed in a way that betrayed no emotion. Sutherland was aware that Thomas's cousin, Simon Lovat, was a senior General and member of the House of Commons and that he had other close relatives in the diplomatic corps.

'I don't know what you're talking about but I'll certainly look into it. Could you provide me with some details?'

'Nay. There's nay need for details. I'm sure ye ken what needs to be done.'

Thomas turned and walked out without as much as a goodbye.

MacAdam was waiting in the courtyard when he came out.

'Is there any more I can do for ye, Colonel?'

'Aye, join me for dinner sometime if ye can. I'll be here for another three weeks.'

Thomas gave him the Prendiville address and suggested he let him know by note when he would be free to take up the invitation.

'Thank ye. I'll look forward to it.'

As Thomas walked away, he mused on the consternation in the Prendiville household when they found out yet another Redcoat was coming to dinner.

—⁊⁊—

MacAdam's next evening off was the following Sunday. Messages were exchanged discreetly with Thomas, signalling that he could come for dinner that evening. Thomas had done the spadework to ensure he would be well received. Mr Prendiville and Liam were hesitant about the idea but Mrs Prendiville would have given the shirt off her back for Thomas so another Redcoat for dinner was fine by her. Mary and Louise were excited that a male, whatever colour his coat, was coming to their house.

'What about me?' Edward asked at the end of the negotiation.

'What about ye, Teddy?' Louise said.

'I'm nay Teddy,' Edward said, his big smile betraying his delight at the banter.

'Yes, what about ye, Reddie Eddie?' Mary added.

'Dinna I get a say?'

They looked at each other and smiled.

'Ye're absolutely right, my li'l Redcoat,' Mrs Prendiville said. 'Ye should 'ave yer say too. So, what do ye think about another Redcoat comin' for dinner?'

'It's braw.'

'Well, that's that then,' Mrs Prendiville said, rollicking with laughter. 'The boss's spoken, 'aven't ye my darlin' boy?'

She reached across the table and grabbed him by the hand.

'And I'm goin' to give my li'l Redcoat the biggest kiss when I can reach 'im properly.'

'And me too,' Mary said, reaching down to kiss him.

'Me too,' said Louise, moving in from the other side.

'Yuk, yuk, yuk,' Edward said, ducking and weaving.

—⁊⁊—

The following Sunday evening, John MacAdam stepped through the doorway in a civilian suit and tie. The family had gathered, including Paddy, as arranged.

'Mr and Mrs Prendiville, please meet my friend, Lieutenant John MacAdam, a Scotsman I hasten to say.'

'Any friend of Thomas Lovat's is a friend of ours,' Mrs Prendiville said. 'Welcome, Lieutenant.'

Liam and his father came forward with a notable hesitancy. The girls bounced forward in their Sunday dresses, hair out and well-brushed. They giggled as they greeted him with their warm smiles. Edward held back until called forward to do his duty.

'I'm delighted to meet ye, Master Lovat. Oh, and aye, how ye do look like yer Da.'

'And I'm delighted to meet ye, sir. Welcome to our home,' Edward said, mocking an adult-like voice.

They all laughed. Thomas took note of how secure and happy his son appeared in this place.

Paddy had been in the backyard praying the Divine Office when MacAdam arrived. He stepped in the door and moved towards MacAdam to greet him.

'And this is my son, Lieutenant,' Mrs Prendiville said. 'Father Paddy Prendiville.'

MacAdam turned to greet him. His face dropped, as did Paddy's.

'Why, *halo*, Father,'

'Hello, Lieutenant.'

'So, ye two ken each other, I take it?' Thomas asked.

'We do indeed,' Paddy replied.

MacAdam stood silent.

'The lieutenant and I've met at church, let's just say,' Paddy said. 'Including this morning.'

Thomas pondered the wisdom of inviting MacAdam.

The rest of the family went silent. Mr Prendiville took himself off to his customary spot in front of the fire. The girls hurried Edward off to their room to play. Liam stood his ground, ready for any eventuality. Thomas was trying to find the words to steer things back towards the pleasantries.

Mrs Prendiville spoke first.

'Well, ye two must 'ave lots to talk about then. Always best to do that over an ale. Would ye care for one, Lieutenant? Actually, do ye mind if I call ye John?'

'If it's alright with Father,' MacAdam said. 'About the ale, I mean. Aye, please call me John.'

'Liam, pour the Lieutenant, John, I mean, an ale, would ye dear?' Mrs Prendiville said.

Paddy came forward with an extended arm.

'I suppose we do, Lieutenant. Have things to talk about, I mean.'

'Good,' said Mrs Prendiville. 'Then why don't ye boys sit at the table and 'ave yer talk while I finish off the dinner?'

Liam poured the ales and sat at the dining-room table with MacAdam, Thomas and Paddy. Mrs Prendiville walked to the stove in the corner, pretending not to listen. Mr Prendiville stayed where he was at the fire, staring into it, sucking on his pipe.

'So, the lieutenant and I know each other because he's the one who's led the raids on our church,' Paddy said. 'And I don't apologise for describing them as raids.'

'Is this true?' Thomas asked, looking in MacAdam's direction.

'I'm afraid so.'

'Well, why are we all sittin' around like we're one big 'appy family?' Liam asked.

'Shhhh, boy,' Mrs Prendiville said. 'Ye'll scare li'l Edward.'

'Sorry, Ma. But really, why don't we just 'ave Sutherland to dinner and be done with it?'

'I understand yer feelings, Liam, and I'm truly sorry, Father,' MacAdam said. 'There are things about the army I really dinna like and, between us, I've made my feelings apparent to my superiors but then, orders are orders. I've nay ever ken why yer church has been targeted for this kind of treatment – and it is *yer* church, particularly, and indeed *ye* yerself who seems to be the main one being targeted. I'd assumed initially that ye must be under suspicion for some reason but then the complete lack of evidence left me feeling ye were just being intimidated for the sake of it. I still dinna ken what that's about.'

'I'll tell ye what it's about,' Mr Prendiville called from his chair. 'It's about bein' a Redcoat. It's what Redcoats do. That's why the Lord made 'em. Just like 'e made snakes. They do no good; they're in this world to do evil.'

'I really think I should go,' MacAdam said.

'Now, ye can't be so rude, John, as to walk out without 'avin' yer dinner,' Mrs Prendiville said. 'I'm sure yer Ma brought ye up better than that. There's no excuse for rudeness – *from any of us.*'

She looked sternly at her husband who had sunk back into his chair and his silence.

'Thank ye, Mrs Prendiville.'

'I think we all ken what this is about,' Thomas finally found his voice. 'Well, probably not ye, John, and I apologise for nay filling ye in earlier about the history of this braw family.'

Between them, Thomas, Paddy and Liam filled MacAdam in on those events that had made the Prendivilles particular targets of Sutherland's ire.

'I ken the final piece of the puzzle is for Liam to tell us,' Thomas said. 'It's something I always suspected but was never sure about 'til a few nights ago.'

Something about MacAdam's manner and words had restored a measure of trust among the Prendivilles – apart from the old man. So, Liam filled in the final piece by recounting how Sutherland had overseen his bashing in the cell those many years ago.

'This was a direct violation of orders,' Thomas said. 'Major Grant had given strict instructions that we were nay to do anything to incite the locals – and these were orders that had come directly from London. Because of the growing American War, we were told there'd nay be any reinforcements should there be an uprising in Ireland and so to be careful about being overly heavy-handed. I only wish I'd ken about it back then. I'd have told Major Grant and had Sutherland run out of town, if nay out of the army.'

'I'm sorry I didn't tell ye then too,' Liam said.

'It would've done no good,' Mr Prendiville said without looking away from the fire.

'Well, what can we do about it now?' Thomas asked the men around the table.

'I'd be 'appy to tell 'oever ye think should be told so we could be rid o' the cad and teach any other Redcoat 'o wants to 'arass us a lesson,' Liam said.

'That's braw, Liam, but it'd take forever,' Thomas replied. 'By the time the army investigated, the Secretary to the Army deliberated and Westminster decided, we'd all be dead.'

'Would ye go and speak with him, Thomas?' Paddy asked.

'I did, Paddy. Just the other day. Which is nay doubt why ye got a visit from the Redcoats this morning. John, when were ye ordered to Paddy's church?'

'Just yesterday,' MacAdam replied.

'So much for speaking with him then,' Thomas said.

'I told ye not to bother, boy,' Mr Prendiville called again from his chair.

'I'd be prepared to confront him with ye, Thomas,' MacAdam said.

They all stared at MacAdam. Mrs Prendiville turned to see the look on his face. Mr Prendiville took the pipe from his mouth and, for the first time, turned his gaze from the fire.

'Are ye serious, John?' Liam asked.

'That would indeed be a blessed thing to do,' Paddy said.

'And foolish.' Thomas said. 'It'd be the end of yer career, John. It's nay that we're dealing with an honourable man in Sutherland. Nor indeed an honourable system in the army.'

'To be honest, I dinna really mind. I've nay been at ease with army life, especially since coming here to Tralee. I find I have more time for the Irish than for the English. Perhaps it's because I'm a Scot.'

'I understand what ye're saying, John. It's exactly what I suffered all those years ago, both here and in the Americas. All the same, ye could be putting yerself at too much risk. Sutherland could even have ye court-martialled for insubordination.'

'I dinna think so,' MacAdam said. 'There's something about Sutherland ye need to ken. He's a miserable *coot*, nay doubt, but he does have some reason for being like that. His whole family was wiped out when he was small. I'm nay sure just how it all happened but I ken he talks about it when he's had too many ales. I stumbled on him talking with Pilgrim one time. He was actually crying; I could nay believe my eyes. He tried to hide it when I walked in and then later he confided in me – just a wee bit. I ken he thought I might tell someone at Army HQ. All I'm saying is the *coot* has a weak spot and he ken I ken it.'

'Oh, the poor man,' Paddy said. 'Perhaps I should go and speak with him myself – just as a priest, I mean.'

'I dinna think so, Father,' MacAdam said. 'I ken he hates Catholics. I'm nay sure just why but he's always talking about the treacherous papists.'

'Well, I've another idea,' Paddy said. 'What if I were to get a delegation of influential people together, including a Protestant or two, and we go and see him together?'

'Who would ye be thinking of, Paddy?' Thomas asked.

'Well, the mayor for a start. He's Irish Church but doesn't like the army because it causes more trouble than it's worth. He and I get on quite well. And then there's Alan Brodrick up in Cork. He's the Whig member, also Irish Church. He just wants to keep the peace. I've met him once or twice. And he and my bishop, James Kenny, are quite good friends.'

'Paddy, ye need to be careful o' these Protestants,' Mrs Prendiville said. 'Ye can't trust 'em. And Bishop Kenny should know better.'

'We have to work together, Ma,' Paddy replied. 'They're good men. Better than some Catholics I know.'

'Oh, go on with ye, Paddy,' she said. 'I sometimes wonder about that seminary training. Ye were more of a Catholic before ye went.'

'So, that'd be five of us then?' Thomas said. 'I still dinna think it's wise for ye to be part of it, John.'

'Or ye, Thomas,' Paddy said, 'It's our fight.'

'I want to be involved. I feel responsible. It's largely because of me that all this is happening. If I'd just let things be back then, he'd probably nay be bothering ye now.'

'Ye mean let me die in the cell,' Liam said. 'Because that's what would've 'appened.'

'Yes, ye mustn't blame yerself, Thomas,' Mrs Prendiville said. 'Ye saved our son and we'll be forever grateful. Besides, if ye 'adn't stuck yer nose in our business, we'd 'ave never gotten to know ye – or our li'l Redcoat – and 'ow would that've been?'

'Are ye talking about me again?' Edward called, racing in ahead of the girls.

'Yes, my li'l Redcoat, and just in time for dinner,' Mrs Prendivlle said.

Mrs Prendiville began serving the roast. Mr Prendiville, finally away from the fire, was asking MacAdam about his business in America. The girls fussed over Edward while Liam, Paddy and Thomas took their places. When all was settled, Mrs Prendiville asked Paddy to say grace.

'And give the lieutenant a blessing,' Edward said.

—⁊⁊⁊—

Late the following week, Thomas led a delegation to meet with Sutherland. MacAdam was not part of it but advised Sutherland he should meet with them. Apart from Thomas, there was the mayor, Paddy and Bishop Kenny who had a letter of support from Whig Member, Brodrick.

One by one, the men made their point about the need to desist from the harassment that was being felt in sections of the population and especially the church.

Sutherland listened, then quietly read the letter from Brodrick.

'I'm sure ye ken how important this is for *all* concerned,' Thomas said.

'Be assured, I'll do what I can,' Sutherland replied. 'Thank you for coming, gentlemen.'

As he was ushering the delegation out, Paddy took his hand and shook it.

'Bless ye, Captain. We all know ye're a good man.'

—⁊⁊⁊—

On the ship on the way home, Thomas braved the frosty elements on the forward deck, a rugged-up Edward on his lap and snuggled into his chest. Every now and then, they would chat, Thomas pointing something out or answering one of his son's persistent questions.

He had seen another side of Edward in Tralee. The wholesomeness and warmth of the Prendivilles had brought him alive, and father and son together, like never before.

Thomas was feeling better than for a long time. He thought of Mahdiya and the baby he never knew, as he always did when out to sea. He thought of Eliza, that very different but equally strong love of his life. He thought of Sarah and wondered if there would be a letter waiting for him.

VII

'Nay, my darling. Sorry.'
Thomas had asked his mother if there was another letter, one that had not made it to the pile on his bedside table.

He had written to Sarah three times in Tralee so hoped at least one reply would be waiting.

It was several months since she had left for France. The pace of letter writing had slowed, especially from her end. He had noted it before the trip to Tralee but had kept his spirits high. The lack of any missive now, after several weeks away, threw him back to those old feelings of despair.

'I'm certain she'll write,' Emma said.

'Aye, or perhaps nay. How can a Highlander compete with Parisian charm, after all?'

'I dinna believe Sarah'd be susceptible to Parisian charm, darling. She loves ye. My God, she's always loved ye. Surely ye ken that by now.'

'Aye, well, we'll see. We'll see.'

—〰—

Christmas came and went and still no word. Emma saw the disappointment written on Thomas's face. But she also saw how much more time he was spending with Edward. They were both the better for their trip to Tralee.

'There must be something in that Irish water,' Emma whispered to Will one night in bed.

'That's generous, coming from a Highland lassie.'

They chuckled, snuggling closer on that bitter winter's night.

—⁂—

Thomas went back to his teaching post in mid-January of 1782. He was no sooner settled in when they received word that Simon, his father's cousin and best friend, had suffered a suspected heart attack. Like his father, Simon had fought the English at Culloden, been wounded but recovered to forge a career with the British Army. He was also the House of Commons Member for Inverness and *de facto* Lord Lovat, Head of the Clan, though the title had been suppressed after Culloden. He had been a mentor for Thomas, especially in his army career.

Thomas was distraught. He had declined the invitation to spend Christmas with Simon and the Lovats at Castle Dounie in Beauly, Scotland. Their last communication had been an unpleasant reprise of their many differences over British foreign policy, especially in the Americas. Nonetheless, the minute he heard about Simon's ill health, he knew he must be there by his side.

Emma accompanied Thomas and Edward on the trip to Beauly. They were shocked to see Simon brought so low. He was only in his fifties.

'The doctors don't hold out much hope,' Catherine, Simon's wife, said on their arrival. 'He stirs into consciousness now and then but, for the most part, he seems resigned to the long journey home.'

'Thank you so much for coming, Thomas. I know he wants to see you.'

Thomas was reminded of Catherine's perpetual warmth towards him. She had been a mother figure when she lived at Pemberton before her marriage.

They stepped into Simon's room to find his siblings, Georgina and Archibald, sitting on one side of his bed. Archibald had been crying. Thomas had never seen him like that. It took him by surprise because he had never regarded the two half-brothers as being especially close.

'It's so wonderful to see ye, Thomas,' Georgina said. 'He's been asking if ye were coming.'

'He has indeed, Thomas,' Archibald said, rising to greet them. 'He was awake just a few moments ago and was asking after ye. And thank ye for coming too Emma. *Halo*, young lad.'

'*Halo*, sir,' Edward replied, daunted by the emotion in the room.

It dawned on Thomas how remiss he had been in keeping these people out of his life in the past few years. They truly did love him and were so much part of his own story. Georgina was the matriarch of the Lovat Clan. She had kept things together as best she could after the horrid events of Culloden and the Clearances that the English foisted on the Highlanders after the Jacobite Rebellion. Archibald had been Thomas's stand-in father after his own father had been killed at Culloden, later seeing him through the Middle East and those most significant parts of his growing up. And Simon, of course, who should have been Lord Lovat other than for English punitiveness, had been his father's most trusted friend.

'How is he?' Emma asked.

'Very weak,' Archibald replied, choking on the words. 'The next few hours'll be crucial, the doctors say.'

—∞—

They were taking it in turns to sit with Simon. Thomas was seated next to his bed, dozing on and off. Catherine was sleeping on a sofa near the window. It was close to dawn on the day after they had arrived when Simon stirred.

'*Halo*, Thomas.'

'*Halo*, Simon. I'm so pleased ye're awake. I was frightened …'

'I ken, I ken. It's alright. We all love ye, Thomas. I want ye to ken that and never forget it. I've wanted so much to say that to ye face-to-face. And I'm so sorry for our differences. They're of nay importance. I want ye to ken that.'

Simon's eyes had been partly open but they now closed. Thomas reached over and held his hand.

'Thank ye for everything. I'm so sorry for being like a spoiled bairn at times. I ken ye were my Da's dearest friend and I've nay ever forgotten that.'

He fell over Simon's outstretched arm. He felt Simon's other hand gently stroking the back of his head.

Catherine had woken and was quickly standing behind Thomas, her hand on his back and leaning over him, peering at Simon.

'Darling, you're awake. Isn't it marvellous that Thomas is here?'

Thomas felt the hand on his head go limp. He sat up to check. Simon's eyes were closed but his mouth was open. He let out a guttural sound that Thomas had heard all too often. He turned to see the distressed look on Catherine's face. He stood up to let her sit closer by the bed and raced to the door. He shouted down the hallway for anyone who could hear to come quickly.

Archibald was the first in the room. Georgina was close behind.

—◊◊◊—

Simon was given a State Funeral with full military honours. It was held in the Church of Scotland's Saint Stephen's, the largest church in Inverness. There was no representation from the Catholic Church or recognition of Simon's Catholicism. The long cortege took his remains to the Mausoleum at Kirkhill outside Beauly where his coffin was laid in the crypt.

The Wardlaw Mausoleum had been built by Simon's father, the Old Fox, to honour his own father, the 10th Lord Lovat. It was widely believed to be the final resting place of the Old Fox himself, though a brass plate in the Tower of London suggested otherwise. The legend was that members of the Clan had stolen the Old Fox's headless body from the Tower and brought it to Kirkhill where it belonged. In that case, three generations of the Clan nobles now rested there.

The day before the State Funeral, family, friends and residents of the Lovat Estates had gathered at St Mary's Catholic Church in Beauly for a quiet memorial ceremony. There was no recognition given to it from the State. The Catholic Emancipation Act that endorsed the Catholic Church's legitimacy in the British Isles was still half a century away.

—m—

'He and I were never close but I miss him already,' Archibald said.

'Me too,' Thomas replied. 'Apart from my Ma, I always felt closest to Da when I was with him.'

'He used to say the same about ye, d'ye ken?'

'I'd nay idea. Why would he've nay told me that?'

'He was an army man and a politician. Have ye ever ken either of them to be honest?'

'Well, aren't ye a politician?' Thomas laughed.

'Nay, I'm a diplomat. That's different. But aren't ye an army man?'

Their laughter broke the sombre mood and reminded them both of the bonds they shared from earlier times.

As it was, Archibald would soon become a politician. He would inherit the seat of Inverness left vacant by Simon's death. It was a popular move among the electors of Inverness. His erstwhile pompousness had mellowed through having to deal with the complex challenges of Algiers. He had done so well in this post that the Foreign Office prevailed upon him to remain there as Consul-General, albeit one who would be absent more often than present.

Archibald had also mellowed as a person. Thomas pondered that fatherhood might well have been the cause, with Archibald clearly a fond father to his three surviving children. He and Jane had lost a child at birth and then George, just an infant, had died the year before. Jane could barely bring herself to mention it.

'Fatherhood agrees with ye, Arch,' Thomas said.

'Aye, well it was ye who taught me how to be a Da, do ye ken?'

'What d'ye mean?'

'I was an unhappy wee lad when ye came into our lives after yer Da's death at Culloden. I might be an unhappy *mor* lad now but I learned the joy in forgetting yer own worries and caring about someone else. I learned that because of ye.'

'I'm happy I played that role for ye. Ye were certainly important for me. There was nay any other real Da in my life.'

They were silent for a time.

'Losing George must have been awful for ye then,' Thomas said.

'It was the *as miosa* time in my life. People offered token sympathy. I ken they thought a Consul-General must be so hardened by the job that a loss like that'd be a wee burden. Some'd say, *oh, thank heavens ye have the other three children*, as though that would console us in losing someone we adored. Jane used to get so angry with that kind of comment. I used to say, *they just dinna ken what to say, dear*. And she'd say, *then they should say nothing*. She's right but of course that's nay going to happen. It's been so *duilich*.'

VIII

'N ay, darling. Still nothing,' Emma said

Emma and Edward had travelled home from the funeral a few days before Thomas. He had become resigned to the disappointment of hearing nothing from Sarah. But he still quietly hoped for something whenever he had been away.

It was the day before his birthday some months later that a letter finally arrived. It was handed to him at dinner-time by Will.

'Thank ye,' Thomas said, shoving it in his pocket.

Once Edward was safely in the hands of Emma's nightly ritual, Thomas hurried to his room and tore it open.

Dear Thomas, please do have a very happy birthday on 26th instance. I will be thinking of you on the day. I'm not yet sure when I can come home but will be certain to let you know with plenty of time to spare. Please give little Edward a big hug and kiss from his loving aunt. Affectionately, as ever, Sarah.

He read the letter over and over, trying to decide what code was waiting to be deciphered. It was good that she had remembered his birthday and would be thinking of him on the day. But what of her needing to stay longer? Why would that be? *Affectionately, as ever* was pleasing but why hugs and kisses for Edward and not him? He tried to sleep but woke an hour later, lit a candle and read the letter again.

—⁂—

Spring turned to summer turned to autumn and the cycle repeated. Two years had passed since Sarah had left for France. Only a few stilted letters had passed between them of late, mainly for birthdays and Christmas. Thomas's gradually became as non-disclosing as Sarah's. He was losing hope though the occasional flirtation with any other woman left him missing her ever more.

There were plenty of distractions, apart from his teaching. As the American War ground to a humiliating end, making bad foreign policy all the more obvious, Thomas's wisdom on the event became important, for some at least. Archibald, now a House of Commons member, had him speak with the Government's Foreign Committee about ways in which the new American Government might be coaxed into an alliance. There was now genuine fear that the Americas might become a French stronghold.

Thomas was even asked if he might join a future delegation to the new republic once hostilities had ceased. It was an exciting prospect but he wondered how his body would cope with the travel and strain.

In October that year, 1783, the British finally withdrew all forces from the Americas.

Thomas had maintained some contact with his former commanding officer in Boston, General Eastley. Eastley had retired from active duty but was now involved in officer training. He met up with Thomas in Preston one evening after school to discuss ways in which the lessons learned from the American War could be integrated into training.

—⁂—

There were further distractions of a different order. Thomas was back in Tralee twice more in those two years, each time with Edward in tow. Mrs Prendiville would not hear of him coming without her "li'l Redcoat". Nor would the girls.

The first trip was to serve as best man for Liam at his wedding to Therese Kelly. The service was at Saint Brendan's Catholic Church where Paddy was the curate. The wedding date was the 19th of September, 1782. The second trip was for the baptism of Liam and Therese's first child, Denis (named after Liam's father), born on the 19th of June, 1783, nine months to the day from the wedding.

'My brother was never one to sit on his hands when there was a job to be done,' Paddy said as he began the ceremony.

The congregation tittered until Mrs Prendiville spoke.

'We'll 'ave none of that talk in God's 'ouse, Father.'

Priest or no priest, Paddy was still her little boy who needed a scolding from time to time.

Hence, Denis Prendiville was baptised into the Catholic faith in orderly Roman fashion. One of Therese's unmarried sisters was the godmother. Thomas was the godfather.

'So, I hear the Redcoats are all withdrawing,' Thomas asked Paddy at the morning tea.

'They are indeed; and how we'll miss them, Mr Sutherland especially.'

'Did he ever change?'

'No, the poor man. There are rumours that he got into some trouble but then we heard he was promoted and sent to some lost outpost. But at least the army laid off the church after yer intervention, so thanks be to God – and Thomas Lovat – for that.'

'Let's just leave it as the Laird's work.'

'Ye'd always be welcome here, Thomas, ye know that.'

'In spite of my Redcoat past?'

'Of course; there's Redcoats and Redcoats, just as there's Irishmen and Irishmen. The good and the bad all mixed in.'

'Well, thank ye, Paddy. I must say my wee Redcoat always seems happier here than anywhere. But what would I do here?'

'Anything ye wanted. There'd always be a job for ye teaching in one of our schools. Or ye could take over the constabulary. Glory be. Much as I despise the Redcoats, I dread to think of my countrymen running themselves. We're better at running revolutions than law and order.'

'And ye ken an ex Redcoat Scottish Highlander's the answer?'

—⁘—

Winter was closing in that year. Thomas found a letter waiting for him one evening on his return to Pemberton. He recognised Sarah's handwriting.

Dear Thomas, I am coming home and hope so much to see you. I am due in Scarborough on December the 2nd at about 4pm. The ship is SS Broadmeadow. It being a Saturday, I was hopeful you might be able to meet me there. There is no need to write. If you are not there, I will understand. My love, as ever, Sarah.

It was as if an angel of mercy had passed by.

'Of course I'll be there,' he thought.

The six days between receiving the letter and being in Scarborough were among the longest of his life.

—⁘—

In the carriage on the way to greet her, the thought crept into his mind that Sarah might only want to see him to tell him personally that she had decided to end their relationship. Perhaps she really had fallen in love with a charming Parisian. Perhaps she had decided she wanted to be free to explore more of the Continent. Perhaps she had found the pain of their relationship too much to bear.

All the doubts that the excitement of the past few days had suppressed were there with a vengeance. By the time Thomas alighted in Scarborough, his head was swirling. He almost decided against taking the last few steps to the dock. By the time he saw her walking down the gangplank, he was ready for the worst.

'Oh, Thomas, you've come. It's *so* wonderful to see you. Thank you, thank you, *thank* you for being here.'

Thomas had noted her eyes welling up as she rushed towards him and threw her arms around him.

'It's so wonderful to see ye, Sarah. *So* wonderful to hold ye again.'

All the resolve to be distant vanished in an instant. If she had bad news, he would just have to bear it.

'I love you, Thomas. I love you *so* much – and I just hope to God you love me at last.'

'*Love* ye? I *adore* ye. I *want* ye. Please be mine; *please* be mine.'

'Yes, yes, yes. I'll be yours, Thomas Lovat. For better, for worse, in sickness and in health. Is that really what you're asking?'

'That *is* what I'm asking. Will ye be my wife?'

'I do,' she said – and they laughed, and they kissed – a lingering kiss with a ship's full complement as their witnesses.

—⁊⁊—

Thomas had booked the same wing in the guesthouse where they had stayed with Emma and Will the night before Sarah left for France. It had three bedrooms so it was a discreet place for them to spend the night. For appearance's sake, they deliberately disturbed the beds in two of the rooms.

Thomas drew on Mahdiya's understanding of marriage as something that happens when two people commit to each other under God's watchful eye. Ceremonies can come later. He shared the idea with Sarah as they snuggled together on a bitter wintry night that required lots of snuggling to stay warm.

'What an amazing woman she must've been,' Sarah said. 'So wise.'

'Ye dinna mind me talking about her?'

'Not at all. I've actually thought about her a lot and wondered how it is that she had so much influence over you – perhaps looking for clues as to how I could have that sort of influence.'

'Ye dinna need any clues, my darling.'

'I'd love to have met her. I feel in a sense that I have. And I agree with her. You and I *are* married, aren't we? In a way, we've been married for years; perhaps even since that day you rowed me down the Thames in Oxford. Do you remember the way we held hands at the end of the day as we waited for Tommy and Eliza and my parents to come out of St Oriel's?'

'How could I forget? I nay thought of anything else for weeks afterwards.'

'Me too. Well, for me it was more like years. I knew then I'd never be happy unless I was with you.'

'And then I went to the Middle East and…'

'Don't. Don't. Not tonight. Tonight's our wedding night, remember.'

She snuggled in even more tightly as Thomas held and kissed her. The kiss lingered even more than on the dock. He moved his free hand over her clothed body and then through any opening that allowed access to her nakedness. Sarah was helping and they were soon giving themselves to a pleasure anticipated for too many years.

They were married. The ceremonials could wait.

—◊◊—

Thomas had alerted Will that it was possible he would be absent from school the following week. He asked if he could let the headmaster know.

'I hope you're absent,' was Will's response.

—◊◊—

'So why did ye nay write?' Thomas began on the third night in the guesthouse.

They were cuddling on the two-seater, mesmerised by the fire.

'I did write – so many times – but...'

'Truly? But what?'

'Oh, Thomas, so many words, so much grief, guilt, desire, hopefulness followed by hopelessness. I couldn't begin to describe the mixed feelings, the agony, the confusion. It was as though all the stresses and strains of a lifetime ganged up and charged at me like one of your army – what do you call them – platoons?'

'Aye, or regiments.'

'Regiments. That's it. As though the whole vile army was out to destroy me.'

'Oh, my darling. How awful. I'm so sorry. I'm such an *amadan*.'

'Why are *you* a fool? I'm the fool.'

'Well, when I didn't hear from ye, I thought perhaps ye'd found it all too hard, so ye'd stay away forever – or perhaps ye really *had* found someone else – after all, the only Frenchmen I've ever ken seemed like womanisers.'

'That's what you think of me is it, Thomas Lovat?' Sarah chuckled. 'I'm the type of woman to be lured into the first womaniser I come across. Is that right?'

'I suppose nay.'

'You *suppose* not?'

'I mean I ken nay. Of course, I dinna ken ye like that but I was just so anxious. I was nay sure how I'd cope if I lost ye now. I'm sorry.'

'Oh, my Thomas. I'm the one who's sorry; sorry for putting you through all that. I've known I've wanted you since I was twelve years of age – and the feeling's never left me. That's why it was so wrong to marry Cecil. Poor Cecil. I was such a wretch to him because I couldn't get over my love for you – and there was no-one to share my feelings with, especially after you and Eliza

... Poor Eliza, my darling, darling sister. She knew about my feelings but I had to keep them from her, pretend I was happy, be happy for *her*.'

'So these are all the things that were going through yer mind and preventing ye from writing?'

'Well, I did write but nothing I said worked – and the more I tried, the more I felt I was going mad. Truly, when I read back on some of them, I sounded like a mad woman. And I'd think, *how can I send that to him? He'll never want to see me again*. So, I'd put them aside or scrunch them up or ... and then try and write something more normal but then it'd sound as though I didn't care, so I'd set that aside. I meant to tear them all up but something stopped me. I was just so confused and tired...'

'I'm so sorry, my darling. I *am* an *amadan*.'

'*Amadan* or not, I love you and I'm so happy right now.'

They snuggled together, holding tightly, and eventually fell to sleep where they were.

—ww—

'Would you like to see any of those letters?' Sarah asked the following evening.

'If ye'd like me to.'

'I think I would. In their own way, they're part of our history – even the bond between us.'

Sarah went to the bedroom and came back with the pile. She untied the blue ribbon.

'They're in order, believe it or not.'

'I'd nay expect anything else from ye,' Thomas said, smiling.

They spent the next couple of hours reading through them, Thomas in silence with Sarah, head on his shoulder, looking over the same script. Now and again, he would ask a question or she would re-live a particular moment.

'What do ye want to do with them?' Thomas asked.

'I don't need them. Now that you know what I was going through, I don't think I want to see them again.'

'Shall we, then?'

They spent however long it took stoking the fire with paper whose time had come.

—⚹—

On the following Saturday, they made their way back to Pemberton. They re-inhabited their old bedrooms, in different parts of the large house and on separate floors. Will had questioned Emma about this arrangement.

'They're nay married, darling. I'm sure this is the way they'd both want things to be.'

Will pondered on things she had forgotten.

For the next ten days, a late night and early morning ritual saw Thomas slip out of his room and make his way to Sarah's. Only once was he caught when he ran into Will who was up earlier than normal.

'Lost your way?' Will asked, grinning.

'Aye, where *is* that room of mine again?'

Gradually, through the course of the ten days, Thomas and Sarah shared the news that they were engaged to be married. Will smirked. Emma's glance questioned why.

'We've decided to settle in the Highlands,' Thomas said.

'Oh darling, why? Ye can be here as long as ye like,' Emma said.

'Is it because ye'll miss *me* or my *wee laddie?*'

'Both of ye, of course.'

'Well, we were wondering if ye'd like Edward to stay with ye for a while, at least until the end of the school year. I'd then like him to experience Highland life but I'd also like him to go to the Stonyhurst school when he's twelve. So ye could be his close carers then as well. How does that sound?'

'Of course, darling. We'll be here whenever ye need us. And for Edward as well.'

Thomas knew his mother would be happy with any arrangement that gave her maximum care of his son. She had after all been effectively his mother from the beginning, the only mother he had really known, except for Mrs Prendiville and her girls during those magical times in Tralee.

'What will you do there?' Will asked.

'My auld commander from Boston, General Eastley, is now in charge of the Inverness Military College. When I found out, I wrote and congratulated him. He wrote back and said if I was ever interested to take up a position there, to let him ken. So, I wrote back and asked what it would involve. It'd mean taking up a commission again but just for teaching purposes; no active duty beyond that. I've been thinking of it for a while and now it fits perfectly.'

'How d'ye feel about that, dear?' Emma asked Sarah.

'I think it's a wonderful opportunity for Thomas and it'll give us a new start, well away from Burnley and the Greenhams.'

'Are they still bothering you?' Will asked.

'I've had letters from Tommy saying they're still spreading poison about me. They seem convinced that Thomas deliberately murdered Cecil, so having us settle anywhere around there would be difficult.'

—⟪⟫—

On the 20th day of December, they began the four-day journey north to spend Christmas at Castle Dounie, in Beauly, with the extended family. Thomas shared his memories of earlier Christmases at the castle, of its snow-capped turrets and window sills, of the family huddled around the largest fireplace he had ever seen. Sarah saw the excitement of a little boy as he spoke about it, the boy she had fallen in love with all those years before.

Thomas and Sarah stayed on in Beauly to prepare for their wedding scheduled for the 26th of January, the same day as Edward's eighth birthday.

Emma stayed as well to help them prepare while Will returned to re-open his school after the break. The day before the wedding, he returned with Charles Thewell, his Jesuit friend, who was to perform the ceremony. Charles had also performed Thomas's wedding to Eliza, as well as Edward's christening.

On the appointed day in 1784, Edward had to share the excitement of his birthday with his father's wedding.

'What a lucky laddie ye are,' Emma said. 'Only special bairns get to go to their Da's wedding on their birthday.'

She hoped her enthusiasm would work on a boy clearly struggling to accommodate the sharing. Edward was unimpressed.

A quiet family wedding ensued in the same small church in Beauly where Emma had married Thomas's father almost forty years beforehand. For Emma, these were the memories that filled her head as she gazed, mesmerised by the flickering candles on the altar. She could have sworn they were the same candles she remembered gazing at during her own wedding. The memories were all the more vivid for the fact that Sarah was wearing her dress, a simple white satin one with lace adorning the neck and a matching lace veil. She was even carrying a single pink rose, just as Emma had those decades before.

—m—

The newlyweds retired after a small celebration to the dwelling in Eskadale set aside for them. It was the same logged cottage, nestled in the woods by the river, where Emma had spent her first nights after that wedding forty years before. Thomas and Sarah would live there for the next few years while Thomas took up his appointment as a non-active full Colonel at the Inverness Military College where he had trained those many years ago.

Sarah, meantime, followed her sister and husband into teaching, helping to set up a new Catholic school, St Mary's, at Eskadale, just down the river from their home. It was one of the first Catholic schools to open in the Highlands after the Clearances.

Edward continued to live with Emma and Will, though he came to Eskadale often to stay with Thomas and his "other Ma". At other times, Thomas and Sarah would come to stay at Pemberton and, on several occasions, would pick up Edward to accompany them on a holiday in Tralee.

'Dinna ye ever go there without me,' Edward ordered.

'As if we would,' Thomas would reply. 'Ma Prendiville'd nay let us in the house without her wee Redcoat.'

It was the happiest time of life for both Thomas and Sarah.

'I'm delirious,' Sarah said when Emma asked about her happiness.

'And how's my bairn?'

'He's happy too. Very happy, he tells me, and I believe it. But his health is coming against him more and more.'

'He nay talks much about that, does he?'

'No, he's the classic Highlander, and army trained to boot. It's a deadly combination.'

They smiled at each other.

'But I can see his difficulty in moving around. It's definitely getting worse. He finds even the small manual jobs around the house more and more taxing. Getting on and off a horse seems to be an increasing challenge and even getting out of a chair. I hear him groan, especially when he thinks I can't hear. I'm not sure how long he'll be able to keep up the College job. '

'Oh nay. He loves that so much.'

'He does. The classroom work seems manageable but it's the field training that he finds so difficult. Along with the travel in and out of Inverness every day, it's wearing him down. I can tell.'

'Oh, the poor lad. I'm just so thankful he has ye to support him.'

'It's the easiest thing I've ever done, believe me. I love your son so much. He's such a good man. I feel blessed – at last.'

'Ye did say delirious, dinna ye?' Emma asked.

'Delirious!'

IX

'*I have to go back to Persia.*'

Sarah had just arrived home from school when Thomas made the announcement.

'What on earth for?' she asked. 'You struggle getting out of bed some days. How on earth would you cope with that?'

'Can I come too?' Edward asked, excited beyond anything they had seen from him of late.

—·ɯ·—

The year was 1789. Edward, thirteen years of age, had moved to Eskadale two years beforehand to be with his father and stepmother. He took the final years of primary schooling at St Mary's, where Sarah taught.

Edward relished his time in the Highlands, sensing the presence of his grandfather, the famous Jacobite by the same name. He loved walking and running through the hills, rowing along the river and especially going to Culloden where he would imagine being the original Edward, this time vanquishing the execrable

English. He would regularly go to Beauly, just a few miles away, and wander through the ruins of the Old Priory destroyed by the Reformers two centuries earlier. He also liked going to the Wardlaw Mausoleum at Kirkhill where he remembered Simon being buried. He came to believe firmly in the legend that the Old Fox's headless body had been buried there, stolen from the Tower of London after his execution. It took way less than two years for him to know who he was, what he wanted to be, a Highlander first and foremost.

Living in Eskadale was good for Edward in all ways, except for school.

—⚹—

'Aye, it might be good if ye do come with me,' Thomas replied to Edward.

'Wait a minute,' Sarah said. 'This is all going too fast. Why on earth would you be going to Persia?'

'I'm sorry, my darling. Look at this, will ye? It's a letter from Mahdiya's parents. Completely unexpected. The Consulate in Shiraz sent it onto the Foreign Office and they've contacted the army. It was on my desk at work today.'

Thomas handed Sarah the letter.

Pleas dear sir, we belove Mahdiya mere et pere. We so sad an broke-heart lose our chil. We told yu marry our chil and have bebe befor she go Allah. We giv anyting meet yu know mor bout her die an her bebe. Her mere is grieve. Soon she die. Can help us pleas? Your mere et pere Ahmadi.

The "English" translation had been written roughly below each line of the Farsi original. Thomas remembered being told by Mahdiya that none of the rest of her family spoke English. It was now over three months since it had been written.

'How remarkable,' Sarah said. 'So they live in Shiraz, do they?'

'In Sadra, not so far away. It's where Mahdiya grew up. She used to say how frustrating it was that they were so close but she felt she could nay visit them. Nay so long before we fled Shiraz, she had contact with a relative that gave her some hope but, in the end, we had nay time to do anything about it. She even spoke about going back someday to see them; she talked about it several times on our *seolta* journey.'

The "crazy journey", to which Thomas referred, was well known to all in the family. He and Mahdiya had fled Shiraz via the arduous route to Bandar Abbas on Persia's south coast. They then sailed on several ships until she and their unborn child were killed during a sea battle between a French Man o' War and their Royal Navy vessel.

'You feel you owe it to her then?' Sarah asked.

'I suppose I do. Is that alright?'

'Of course. It's frightening, though. It's not an easy journey, even for someone in the best of health.'

'Aye, and that's why I have to go too,' Edward said. 'When do we leave?'

Thomas and Sarah looked at the boy, then each other.

'He's so like the boy I fell in love with,' she said.

—⁓—

It took some months to organise the travel. Archibald's assistance through the Foreign Office was invaluable. He arranged for the Shiraz Consulate to maintain contact with the parents and let them know Thomas was coming.

Thomas's rank as an Army Colonel assured passage for himself and Edward aboard a Royal Navy ship, *HMS Stirling*. It would take them as far as Gibraltar. The *Stirling* was a 3,900 ton "ship of the line" with eighty-four cannons on three deck levels, twelve at the stern and the rest on its port and starboard sides. Its full complement comprised over seven hundred men, including officers, crew and marines principally. There were also a few select passengers, such as Thomas and Edward.

On sighting the *Stirling* at Portsmouth dock, Edward leapt from the carriage.

'Goodbye, darling boy,' Sarah called after the disappearing figure heading to the gangplank.

'Wait up, Edward,' Thomas shouted. 'Ye have to wait until we're invited on board. Come and say goodbye to yer Ma.'

Edward trudged back and gave Sarah a quick kiss. He struggled out of the bear hug she was trying to give him.

'*Mar sin leat*, Ma. Can we go now?' he said, turning to run towards the ship again.

'Just wait,' Thomas said.

He turned to Sarah and gave her the hug she had attempted on Edward.

'Goodbye, my darling. Make sure you do as the doctors told you. The medicines and the exercises. I don't really fancy the idea of having to come and rescue you from Persia.'

'Truly? Are ye saying ye'd nay come and get me?'

'You know I'd follow you into Hell if that's where you were. I love you so much, Thomas Lovat. Please come back in one piece. And make sure your son's in one piece too.'

Their lingering kiss was one rarely displayed in public.

'Come on, Da. We dinna have time for that.'

Thomas and Sarah peeled away from each other and the Jacobite son and grandson made their way to the foot of the gangplank. They were invited aboard where the captain, Commodore Angus MacGregor, greeted them.

—ɷ—

As the ship sailed down the French coast, it passed within fifty or so nautical miles of the spot where Mahdiya and her unborn child had been buried at sea. When Thomas could get Edward's attention away from the minute by minute happenings of a military ship under full sail, he would take the opportunity to fill him in on this part of his life story.

'So, there's a little brother or sister of yers down there with my first wife.'

Edward found all this a little puzzling and hard to imagine. On the other hand, he was fascinated to know everything there was to know about the sea battle that had preceded these events. Every night before they fell to sleep, he would ask a little more.

'Will we get to fire at a French ship, Da? I really hope so.'

'I hope nay but if we do, I'm sure we'll win.'

'I love ships. I ken I want to be a sailor, or maybe a captain even.'

—⚓—

Commodore MacGregor was a few years older than Thomas and so had childhood memories of Culloden. They had both lost fathers on that dreadful day but, unlike Thomas, MacGregor could remember his and the devastation wrought upon his family by the loss. It was a talking-point at the dinners held each evening at the Captain's Table.

'Of course, everyone kens the legend of yer father, Colonel,' MacGregor said. 'Edward Lovat's name's synonymous with Culloden and Highlander resolve.'

'Ye're a very lucky wee lad to have such a famous grandfather and to share his name, d'ye ken?' MacGregor said, turning to Edward.

'Did ye ken my Grand Da?'

'Nay lad, but my Da certainly did and he spoke so highly of him, how brave he was and how braw a soldier.'

Thomas could see Edward's chest puffing out as McGregor spoke. For himself, it brought home the feeling of loss he had carried all his life. He envied MacGregor that he had at least some traces of memory of his father.

'So what do ye want to do with yer life, laddie?' MacGregor asked.

'I wanna be a soldier or a sailor.'

'Well, if ye do become a sailor, I hope ye'll get to sail on my ship. I'd be proud to have an Edward Lovat on board. I ken it'd be an omen of braw luck.'

There was then some silence as they tucked into their shipboard fare of chicken soup, fresh pork and potatoes. Edward had no idea then how different it was from the watery stew and hard tack being fed to the rest of the crew.

—⚹—

Thomas and Edward disembarked the *Stirling* in Gibraltar. MacGregor repeated his invitation to Edward to consider a future at sea.

'He's a remarkable lad,' he said to Thomas as they departed. 'Cherish him, will ye nay? I lost my own laddie when he was about the same age. I only wish I'd spent more time with him while I could.'

'I'm so sorry to hear that, Angus. And thank ye for yer advice. I'll heed it *gu cinnteach*.'

—⚹—

The clipper sailing to Alexandria was delayed by a few days. This would give Thomas's aches and pains time to heal.

'I can go out on my own, Da,' Edward said.

'Nay, ye canna, lad. Just give me a wee while to rest up.'

The responsibility of being sole carer for an eager thirteen year old was wearing Thomas down more than he had anticipated. For Edward, constant curiosity could only be satisfied immediately. Waiting quietly for a father to take his "wee rest" was impossible.

On one occasion, Edward slipped out of their guest house room while Thomas was dozing. Thomas woke to find him gone and unresponsive to his shouting. Panicking, he defied the pain and hurried as fast as he could down the street. He found him in a nearby market, haggling with a seller of Spanish sweets. Thomas quickly finished the exchange by handing the seller some cash and dragged Edward back to the guest house.

'Ye paid too much, Da.'

'I dinna care about the price, lad. Just dinna do that again.'

'Do what?'

'Leave the room without telling me, lad. Gibraltar around the docks is nay a good place to be for an *oganach* on his own.'

'But I did tell ye and I ken ye said it was alright. Perhaps ye were just snoring. And I'm nay an *oganach*. I'm thirteen.'

'Well just dinna do it again, d'ye hear?'

Edward did do it again but only when he was convinced his father was asleep and that he could get back before he woke. He made a daily visit to the market and the Spanish sweet cart and got a better price each time.

—ɯ—

They sailed out of Gibraltar heading for the port of Alexandria. Their ship, a mere 700 ton barque with two large and one smaller mast, was quite boring in Edward's eyes compared with the *Stirling*. If he was to be a sailor, it had to be with the Royal Navy, he decided.

Nonetheless, he was back on his beloved sea. Edward was more and more confident he could find his way around, especially on this smaller vessel. He had little to no need of an infirmed father. Thomas tried to engage him in the story of how, twenty years before, he had sailed on *HMS Hood* in the dead of night to bring the President of Corsica into exile. Edward was more interested in what the sailors were doing on the deck and atop the sail masts.

'This was why the French ship attacked us, ye ken?' Thomas said in a last attempt to gain his son's attention.

'Aye, ye've told me all that before, Da.'

With that, Edward would run off to assist some of his mates among the sailors. Many of them were not much older than him. One was even younger.

Charles Talcott was two months younger than Edward. He was an orphan and a vagrant who had grown up the hard way. His ruddy, pock-marked face and cauliflower ears told the story. His long, ragged hair, hardly ever out of his eyes, seemed never to have seen a brush or comb. But, in his own words, he had been fortunate to secure a post as a cabin boy.

Charlie, as he became known to Edward, would run the length of the ship doing any and every job for all on board, from the captain to the cook. To the onlooker, his was the lowest of the lowly roles on the ship. But Charlie knew life could be far worse than having a place to lay one's head at night, food twice a day and a guaranteed income, however paltry. Add to that the chance to see the world and what could be wrong with being a cabin boy?

That's how Charlie saw it, and so increasingly did Edward. The two boys quickly struck up a friendship.

'Sorry, Da, Charlie needs some help.'

'Edward, it's nay yer job.'

'I wish it was, Da.'

He would be out the door before Thomas could think of another way of constraining him.

After the third day, Thomas hardly saw his son. He spent from dawn until dusk and beyond racing around the ship learning the many arts of cabin boy work. As much through this as his own natural way with people, he got to know everyone on board. He was even choosing to eat the watery stews and hard barks that the crew had to endure, rather than risk being seen as the "toff's son" who would be eating officer meals that the likes of Charlie would never have known.

Thomas was reminded of how he had seen Edward come to life on that first trip to Tralee. With the Prendivilles, his "wee Redcoat" played the court jester, charming all in the family, most especially the two young girls. Here, on board, he was much more the self-assured and energetic young man, charming everyone by his willingness to engage in all manner of work. Nothing was too hard, nothing too menial. No-one was too lowly with whom to engage respectfully. Thomas could see in all this that Edward was his father's son but he still wished he would take more care.

—◊—

They were six days into the Mediterranean when the storm hit. Charlie had been dragooned into helping the sailors steady the ropes hanging from the mainsails while other sailors were climbing the masts. They were replacing the mainsail with trysails more appropriate for the big blow. As ever, Edward was there assisting his newfound friend. No cajoling or even rousing from Thomas could drag him away from his self-imposed responsibility.

Thomas was making his way unsteadily across the rocking, slippery deck to keep an eye on his son. A huge gust of wind threw one of the sailors, high atop one of the two main masts, clear off it. But for the rope he managed to cling to, he would have been deposited in the ocean. It happened to be the same rope that Charlie and Edward were hanging onto on the deck.

As the sailor was falling, dragging the rope with him, the other end of the rope jolted upwards, throwing Charlie clear but carrying Edward with it. The sailor and Edward smashed into each other about halfway up the mast, forcing the boy to drop the rope and fall back towards the deck. As he was falling, a massive wave hit the ship, forcing it to lurch to the side and, as a consequence, Edward was heading straight towards the open sea.

Thomas saw it all as if in in slow motion. He was conscious as never before that his debilitated body was struggling to be where his son needed him in that moment.

'Edward,' he shouted. 'Someone catch him, *please!*'

Edward was almost over the side when the ship lurched the other way. One of the lifebuoys hanging on the outside of the ship was thrown into the air. As Edward was heading down and towards the open sea, he managed to grab it and rode its journey back over the side of the ship.

As the ship lurched the other way, the buoy smashed into its hard and roughened timbers, almost dislodging Edward who managed somehow to hang on. He and the buoy were dangling over the sea, swinging and being buffeted with every movement of a ship at the mercy of the merciless ocean.

Charlie was the first to steady himself, screaming to Edward to hang on. He reached over to grab the rope but his arms were not long enough. Thomas leant over, also screaming to his son to hang on.

Charlie was clambering over the side.

'Charlie,' Thomas shouted, grabbing the boy and hauling him back to safety. 'Ye'll only make it worse.'

Two burly sailors arrived at the scene.

'We could hold the lad over the side while he tries to haul the buoy back in,' one of them shouted.

'He won't be strong enough to haul it up,' Thomas said. 'Can ye hold *me* over the side?'

'*You*, sir?'

Thomas had kept fairly much to himself throughout the voyage, mainly because he was unwell. It had given the crew the impression he was a military toff of the sort they had dealt with all their lives. This type normally stood back and let the ranks do the hard work and take all the risks.

'Aye, he's my lad and I've the strength young Charlie dinna.'

The two sailors agreed. The burlier of them lifted Thomas as though to cradle him, placing him over the side while holding his legs just above the knees. The other one reached over and grabbed Thomas's belt.

'I'm here, lad. Hang on.'

'Da. I canna.'

Thomas reached down as far as he could, grabbed the sodden, slippery rope and began pulling. It was hopeless. The combined weight of the buoy and the boy was too much. He tried several times to no avail.

Thomas turned his head and called to the sailors to lower him further. They did as instructed but this made it even harder for Thomas to pull on the load beneath him.

Seeing the plight, Charlie took it on himself to clamber over the side and slip down the rope, making the weight on Thomas even heavier.

'Dinna lad, ye'll both fall!' Thomas shouted.

Charlie secured a foothold on the top of the buoy. Even in the sea spray, he could see that Edward's hands were blue. He held the rope with one hand and reached down with the other to grab one of Edward's wrists.

'Hoist yourself up, mate!'

Edward let the clenched hand go, grabbing onto Charlie's wrist. He used the other hand to hoist himself upwards. He began to get some purchase for his feet on the slippery buoy.

'That's it, mate. Keep going,' Charlie called.

'Keep going, lad. We're here for ye,' Thomas shouted.

After several unsuccessful attempts, Edward made his way up to join Charlie on the top of the buoy. Their combined weight was steadying it against the earlier buffeting but the ship was still lurching from side to side.

'Can ye reach up and grab me, lad?' Thomas called.

With Charlie holding him steady, Edward reached up and Thomas reached down as far as they could stretch. They linked hands. Thomas then reached one hand down to grab one of Edward's wrists, then the other one. He shouted to the sailors to hoist him up. They dragged first Thomas and then Edward back over the side of the ship.

There was no time for even the quickest hug. Charlie was still down there, clinging to the buoy. The loss of Edward's weight and Thomas's steadying grip had left the buoy even more susceptible to the elements. As Thomas was about to be lowered over the side once again, a larger than normal wave hit the ship, flinging the buoy further away than ever. As the ship lurched back the opposite way, Thomas and the sailors fell back on the deck. At the same time, the buoy, with Charlie still clinging to it, smashed with full force onto the unforgiving timbers of the ship's port side.

Edward, hanging onto the railing on the deck, was the only one to see Charlie fall. He took the full force of the impact, with the weight of the buoy acting as a hammer. It drove his weakened body into the timbers, flinging him off.

Charlie was probably dead before he hit the water. Edward saw his expressionless face for only a fleeting second before he disappeared beneath the waves.

'NO, NO, NO, NOOOOO!'

Edward was stepping over the railing as though to join Charlie in his fate. Thomas, by now on his feet, pulled him back and held him. The sailors peered over the side.

'He's gone, lad. No hope.'

'Lemme go, Da; *lemme* go!'

Edward fought to be free of his father's grip. To do what precisely, he did not know. He just knew he had to expend every possibility of saving the friend who had saved him. Thomas clung to him.

'I canna let ye go, lad. I'm sorry; I'm so sorry; I'm so sorry about yer *caraid*.'

Exhausted and resigned, Edward settled and sobbed. Thomas replaced his manhold with one of gentle care.

'He saved my life, Da. Charlie saved my *gorach* life.'

'Aye, he did, lad. He saved it for something special; so he'd nay want ye calling it *gorach*.'

Thomas knew that in time he would have to save his son from falling into despair. He had seen pointless, tragic death many times over but this was a new experience for his young boy.

And Thomas knew what these experiences could do to a man.

—⁂—

There were still thirty-six hours or so to go before arrival in Alexandria. The storm had blown out and the wind calmed. They were looking out over a sun-filled Mediterranean. It was hard to believe it was the same body of water.

Edward could not understand that everyone was going about their business as if nothing had happened. Other than for himself, and perhaps his father, his friend Charlie was going quite unmourned for. It was as though he had never existed.

'Canna we do something, Da? We canna just forget him.'

The first response from the captain, Master Rolandson, was to suggest they speak to a priest in Alexandria about a service of some kind.

'I'd truly appreciate it if we could do something while we're at sea. My lad's feeling *dona*, really bad, about his friend and the sea's his resting place.'

Thomas recounted a little of his own experience of burying a wife and child at sea. It was enough to gain the captain's attention.

'I see, Colonel. I'm sorry; I didn't know the boy had lost his mother and brother in such tragic circumstances.'

Thomas knew Rolandson had the details wrong but now was not the time to correct him.

'I can't spare any men. We're running badly behind schedule and the ship has taken some damage. And I don't have a parson of any sort on board so the best I could offer is a short service and I will read a few prayers. Will that do?'

'Aye, sir, thank ye. That'd be braw.'

Thomas hurried as fast as his battered body could manage to tell Edward.

'*Tapadh leat*, Da,' Edward blubbered. 'Thank ye.'

—ɷ—

Rolandson, a man given to functionality and little else, found a Bible somewhere in his cabin and began the small ceremony by demonstrating it was probably the first time he had ever opened its pages. He stumbled through the passage from the Gospel of John where Jesus raises Lazarus from the dead, going faster as he read.

'...I am the resurrection and the life. Amen.'

The ceremony had taken all of two minutes, including a period of silence. Apart from the disinterested captain, only Thomas, Edward and one of the burly sailors who had held Thomas over the ship's side were present.

Rolandson shook hands with Thomas and Edward and then ordered the sailor back to his post. As the sailor turned, he raised his hand in a friendly gesture and smiled at the father and son.

Edward was dumbstruck by the perfunctory nature of what he had hoped might be a meaningful farewell to his *caraid*, his friend who was now a hero for life.

'Come, lad, let's say our own *mar sin leats* to yer friend,' Thomas said, leading his son to the ship's rail.

'Remember I told ye about burying Mahdiya and our bairn at sea?'

'Aye, Da.'

'Well, I've probably nay told ye about the prayers I read at the time.'

'Nay, Da.'

'Remember I've told ye how my life was saved by Mahdiya's book being in my shirt pocket? How the bullet that would've killed me hit it?'

'Aye, Da.'

'Well this is the book,' Thomas said, pulling the bullet-pocked Qur'an from his pocket.

Edward ran his hand over the small, dark brown, leather-bound and now quite tattered object. He placed his first finger on the hole the bullet had made and ran it around the rim of the hole. He was silent as he considered that this fragile book was all that had stood between him and a completely parentless world.

'It's so small. Are all their beliefs in here?'

Thomas had not talked much about his experience of Islam. He had found early on that most people either did not understand or even frowned on the idea that he, reared in one of Catholicism's finest academies, could have anything but disdain for a heathen religion, as they saw it. His quiet admiration of Islam therefore became something of a sacred secret, and Mahdiya's Qur'an an especially important symbol of it. He had thought at times that he would like to share something of the symbol with his son but the occasion had never presented itself.

Here it was.

'My Mahdiya was a Shiite Muslim, lad, and this was her special book, a holy book, a wee bit like the Bible. They call it the Qur'an. It has some beautiful words in it but none as special as its first chapter that Mahdiya would have said at least once every day of her life.'

Edward was now fully attentive. He needed to find some sense in Charlie's senseless loss.

'So, this is what I read when I buried Mahdiya and our bairn.'

He opened the Qur'an at the first chapter and showed it to Edward. It was in Arabic.

'Ye read that, Da? How d'ye ken what it says?'

'I ken. Would ye like me to read it now for Charlie?'

'Aye, Da.'

Thomas read the chapter in Arabic. He knew it by heart now and he reflected on how much better his Arabic diction was than when he stumbled through it at Mahdiya's burial. He had even learned how to chant it in the way he had heard many years before in the mosque. So, his recitation gradually broke into a quiet and melodious song, one only he and Edward could hear. He noted how enchanted Edward steadily became, as if his mind had momentarily gone to another place.

When he finished, they stood silently, tears in their eyes but a calm resignation in Edward's that had not been there since the awful events of the previous day.

'Would ye like to ken what it says, lad?

'Aye, Da.'

'*In the name of Allah, the merciful, the compassionate. Praise belongs to Allah, the creator of all that is; the all-powerful, the all-compassionate, the master of all destiny. Thee only we serve; to thee only do we pray for help. Guide us in the straight path, the path of those whom thou hast blessed; not of those who deserve thy wrath or who have gone astray. May Allah reward you as he rewarded the Prophet.*'

'Could ye sing it again, Da?'

X

Sir Timothy Larkins, British High Commissioner in Alexandria, was at the dock to greet them. Larkins and Thomas had met over twenty years before, when Thomas was on the way to and from Persia the first time. Larkins was then a junior diplomat. Since that time, he had pursued a diplomatic career around the Middle East, including as Adjutant-Consul under Archibald in Algiers.

'Anything for Lord Lovat's cousin,' Larkins replied to Thomas's gratitude.

'Lord Lovat? I assume ye're speaking of Archibald. Is there something I'm nay aware of?'

'Oh no, Colonel. Not officially at least, but we all know it's merely a matter of time. Mr Lovat is so well thought of in all the right circles. He really did save our bacon in Algeria, you know?'

'Aye, so I keep hearing. Ye were with him there, were ye nay?'

'I was indeed. I learned more from him than from anyone, especially from Sir Robert, as you might remember.'

Larkins laughed at his own joke and Thomas raised an eyebrow.

'Aye, he seemed singularly disengaged, if I might be so rude as to say.'

'Too kindly, Colonel. Far too kindly.'

Sir Robert Dalrymple had been the loquacious, bumbling High Commissioner that Thomas and Mahdiya had to deal with on their flight from Shiraz. Thomas recalled how infuriated he had been with him, especially for his insensitive slurring of Islam in Mahdiya's presence. He recalled also how gracious Mahdiya was in the face of it all.

—ⴥ—

Thomas and Edward both slept until late the following day. They were exhausted, Thomas physically, Edward more mentally. Thomas knew first-hand what trauma like Edward's can do to one's mind. They arrived late for breakfast. Thomas was hoping to avoid Larkins until he felt more rested.

'Oh, jolly good. I'm pleased to see you. I was starting to think you might have died in your sleep,' Larkins said, laughing again at his own wit.

Thomas had never taken to Larkins and liked him less now. Nonetheless, he was the key to them getting any further on this venture.

'Good morning, Sir Timothy.'

'Oh, please do call me Timothy, Colonel. You know I'm not one to abide these conventions.'

'Certainly, Timothy. Thank ye but only if ye'll call me Thomas.'

'Indeed I will, sir,' Larkins replied and then turned to Edward. 'And how are you young man? Did you sleep well?'

'Aye, thank ye, sir,' Edward replied, his raw red eyes barely able to focus.

'Good, good, jolly good. I do hope you're both over your beastly experience. My heavens, it must have been frightening. I remember once having a rough trip across the Mediterranean. Mind you, nothing like yours, I gather, but I really thought I was going to meet my Maker, if you know what I mean.'

Larkins laughed again and sat down to join them, clicking his fingers at the young servant girl in the corner.

'You know how I like it,' he barked. 'Not lukewarm like last time.'

Thomas and Edward noted the look on the young girl's face.

'I imagine you'll never want to go on a boat again, young man. I remember it took me simply ages to be able to face the sea after my experience.'

'Nay, I love the sea. I wanna go back as soon as I can.'

Thomas was pleased to hear this.

'I dare say your mother will be relieved to know you've survived,' Larkins continued.

'Aye, sir. She will.'

'I believe I met your mother many years ago.'

'Nay, I dinna think so,' Thomas said. 'Ye met my first wife, Mahdiya, when I was on the way back from Shiraz.'

'Indeed, Mahdiya, the Muslim lady?'

'Aye, that's correct.'

'So did you divorce, if I might ask?'

Thomas was surprised that Larkins would not have known about Mahdiya's fate but then remembered that the sea battle between *HMS Hood* and the French Man o' War had been kept secret for political reasons.

'Nay, she was killed on the way home.'

'Oh, dear me. I'm so very sorry to hear that.'

There was a moment's silence while they ate.

'I dare say it might have been for the best though.'

'For the best?'

'Well, yes. I dare say it would have been difficult for the poor lady trying to establish herself in England. I mean people can be so intolerant in their ways, can't they?'

'Nay doubt,' Thomas said. 'But Mahdiya was an extraordinary woman and anyone who bothered to get to know her soon discovered that.'

'Oh, of course, old chap. I'm sure she was. Indeed, I'm sure she was.'

Thomas took a deep breath, assured this conversation was over.

'But you know how difficult it is when people don't stay where they belong. And especially the Muslims. Why, we have enough trouble just training them to do their duties here in the Commission. But the idea of them ever being able to integrate into a British way of life; well, it's just not worth the trouble, you know?'

Thomas was almost out of his chair when the servant girl returned with Larkins' cup of tea on a tray.

'*He's nay worth it,*' he resolved.

'Timothy, I was wondering what plans ye have for the next part of our journey. Archibald had said ye'd have something worked out for us.'

'Oh, did he indeed? I must say I wasn't sure just what you intended to do from here. I knew you were coming but I don't believe I was ever apprised of the whole plan.'

Thomas was sure that Archibald would have instructed Larkins on the plan but he went through it again. When he said he had assumed they would travel to Shiraz as he had before, across land to Sharm el Sheikh and then by sea around to Bandar Busheyr and then by land to Shiraz, Larkins scowled before filling them in on the latest developments.

'Well, for a start that ferry, as you call it, hasn't run down the Red Sea for years. Preposterous idea, if you ask me. Steam rather than sail. It was doomed to fail. If God had wanted us to get around by steam, he'd have given us kettles rather than wind. Kettles instead of wind. Can you imagine?'

Larkins convulsed with laughter, spilling tea from his cup all over the starched tablecloth. The young servant girl stood expressionless except, Edward noticed, for a fleeting glance his way that said as much as, *save me from this fool of a man.* They smiled at each other. How his father could have loved a Persian had always been a bit of a mystery to him. Now, he had his first insight.

'Besides, travel through the Arabian Sea and the Persian Gulf is just too dangerous these days,' Larkins carried on. 'If the pirates don't get you, the Arabs or the Persians will kidnap you and hold you to ransom. Things are not as settled as they once were. You do know about all the trouble that Wahhab fellow has been causing, I suppose?'

The mention of Wahhab had Thomas again pondering on Mahdiya and those remarkable conversations she had with the Admiral and the Corsican President on *HMS Hood*. How much he learned from her.

'Aye, I believe I ken something about that. So how do ye propose we get there then?'

'Well, if you're certain you want to keep going. I mean things are quite unsettled in many of those parts and after your recent experience, I thought you might perhaps prefer to go home.'

'I wanna keep going, Da,' Edward said.

'Aye, we wanna keep going.'

'Well it's your funeral, if you don't mind me saying,' Larkins chuckled. 'I must say you wouldn't catch me dead in those God-awful places. However, I'll certainly look into it and see what I can do.'

—m—

Edward was unusually keen to stay indoors for the first few days. Thomas initially put it down to the traumatic event at sea. He did not question it because he himself needed rest.

Edward would slip out of their bedroom with the promise that he would not take himself off into the streets as he had in Gibraltar.

'I just love the gardens, Da.'

Thomas had carried memories of the resplendent English gardens that surrounded the Georgian building, the entire establishment replanted from the home of the Empire. He could understand why Edward would feel at home there.

Some days into their stay, Thomas was walking along the upstairs corridor with a view to the gardens. He saw Edward speaking with a young servant girl. He recognised her as the one from the first breakfast.

He could see how animated they both were in their conversation but worried that they were also so exposed. He remembered how he had fallen for Aisha in the Tripoli Consulate and how that romance had been snuffed out owing to his lack of discretion. He did not want Edward to suffer in the same way – or the young girl to get into trouble.

—⁘—

'But we're just talking, Da.'

'I ken but ye need to be careful, especially for her sake. I'm sure she's a bonnie lass but she's here to work and she's nay meant to be spending her time chatting, especially with a white lad like ye. D'ye ken, lad? She could end up on the street and it'd be yer fault.'

Edward burst into tears.

'What am I supposed to do? Everything I do lately's wrong – and people get hurt.'

'I ken, lad. It's hard, nay?'

Thomas then told him the story of Aisha in more detail than he had divulged to anyone. He told how much she had meant to him and how she had counselled him against spending so much time with her. How unwisely he had pressed her into entering a coffee house and how they were seen and she was whisked away in the middle of the night, never to be seen again. He told how he carried the burden of not knowing whether she was alright or perhaps had been scarred for life. How he did not want the same fate for his son, or for Rania.

'Aye, Da, I ken. She's said things like that to me – but it's so braw talking to her.'

—⁘—

'It would be best if you went overland this time,' Larkins said.

It had been almost a week and Thomas was keen to keep moving eastward before he lost the incentive and before Edward's paltry attempts at discretion in his relationship with Rania were uncovered.

'Really? I dinna ken that was possible,' Thomas replied.

'Well, I didn't either but my military advisors tell me it is and that it would be best, granted the current dangers of sea travel in that part of the world. And it is shorter to go by land, did you know?'

'Aye, as the crow flies but we're nay crows.'

Larkins giggled like a child. He then commanded one of the servants to bring the Adjutant-General in from the parlour.

A few moments later, a dapper-looking chap walked in. Thomas's and Edward's eyes landed on his waxed moustache poking out like small swords on either side of his upper lip. He tucked his baton under his left arm-pit and removed his cap.

'Colonel Lovat, might I introduce our Chief Administrative Officer, General Caulfield. General, this is Colonel Lovat, the rather famous cousin of the even more famous Consul-General of Algiers. I'm sure you've heard of him.'

'Indeed, I have. It's my honour to meet you, sir,' Caulfield said as he moved his cap from his right to his left hand and saluted.

Thomas was not expecting to be treated as an army officer, much less saluted by one who outranked him. He saluted back and extended his hand.

'I'm very pleased to meet ye, General.'

'Jolly good,' Larkins said, a look of delight on his face. 'General, could you explain to the Colonel how you intend to oversee his travel to Shiraz?'

'Very good, sir.'

He reached for a brief case under the table, opened it, then pulled out and unfurled a map.

'If you could step around here, Colonel, I can show you the planned route. Commissioner Larkins has generously offered the army some assistance in this matter.'

Caulfield looked over his shoulder at Larkins as if his approval mattered.

'Indeed!' Larkins replied.

'The Commission can provide a carriage to take you as far as the city of Eilat, on the border with Arabia. Do you see it right here, sir?'

Thomas nodded.

'Any questions so far, Thomas?' Larkins asked.

'Nay, that's most generous, Sir Timothy.'

The exercise seemed to be as much about preening Larkins' ego as planning a journey.

'Jolly good, sir. You will then be escorted on horseback through Palestine, Jordan and Iraq, all the way to Baghdad.' Caulfield said as he beat the map with his baton, pointing progressively at each of the main ports. 'Finally, a carriage organised by the Consulate in Shiraz will take you all the way to that city. We estimate the whole journey will take approximately seven weeks. Any questions, sir?'

'Just a wee number. Sir Timothy's already mentioned troubles in these parts. How safe will we be in all this?'

'You can be assured of British protection at all times, sir. Iraq is the only area we don't control directly but we have much influence there because we helped the Mamluks take control from the Ottomans. They can't do enough for us. A Mamluk platoon will meet you in Ramadi and escort you to Baghdad and will then see the Consul carriage to the Persian border. There, you'll be met by a British patrol.'

'I'm a wee bit overwhelmed,' Thomas said. 'I'd hoped nay to cause ye any trouble.'

'I assure you, Colonel, this is no trouble whatsoever,' Larkins said. 'Your cousin asked that we take good care of you and that's what we're doing.'

—⁕—

'I still wish we were going by boat,' Edward said as they headed out to the Commission's carriage.

'Aye, so do I,' Thomas replied.

He was wondering how he would cope with such a long journey across rugged terrain and much of it on horseback.

As Edward reached down and helped Thomas into the carriage, a distinctive smell wafted from the boy to his father.

'Where were ye this morning when I was calling ye?'

'Nay anywhere, Da. I was just getting ready.'

The distinctive odour was of perfume.

XI

The journey was as arduous as Thomas had feared. By the time the carriage pulled into the Consulate grounds in Shiraz, he could barely walk. Edward helped him step down and one of the British soldiers took him by the arm.

The years fell away for Thomas. Nothing much had changed in the two decades since he had been there. Unlike the Commission in Alexandria, the Shiraz Consulate was all Middle Eastern in its architecture and gardens. A magnificent white, three storey building cloistered an elegant Persian garden with its centrepiece a large, rectangular pool containing fish of many varieties and colours. They swam freely through water lilies and assorted plants. He remembered Mahdiya naming each of the flowers and plants.

He also remembered her explaining how the architecture was a blend of ancient Persian and Islamic styles. The doorways and windows were tall, vaulted and rounded across the top.

He saw her in the shadows in the garden; he could even smell the distinctive blend of perfume and spices that exuded from her.

'What's the matter, Da?' Edward asked.

'Nay anything, lad.'

Edward knew it had something to do with Mahdiya.

The Consul-General rushed out the door.

'Oh, good show, I'm so delighted – and relieved I might say. I wasn't sure you'd make it.'

Thomas, bent over, strained to his full height and reached out his hand.

'Thomas Lovat, sir. And this is my lad, Edward. We're so very grateful to ye for all yer help.'

'Not at all, Colonel, Edward. I'm so pleased to meet you. I'm Malcolm Reynolds and I'm happy to say I share some of your heritage. My mother was a Murray from Fort Augustus.'

'Aye, well it's braw indeed to meet a Highlander – well, almost a Highlander – so far to the East.' Thomas said.

'No Highlander like yourself, sir. I'm afraid to say I've never even been to Scotland, much less the Highlands.'

'Well, the best awaits ye then, sir,' Edward said. 'If it's nay being rude, I wonder could we be shown to our room.'

'Why certainly, young man. Spoken like a true Scot; one is never left wondering, is one?' Reynolds said. 'Now, sir, I'm told on good authority that you once inhabited our master guest suite on the top floor so I have set that aside for you and I hope it'll be to your satisfaction.'

'Thank ye so much, Mr Reynolds. That's very gracious of ye.'

'Not at all, Colonel, and please call me Malcolm.'

'And me Thomas, then.'

—w—

Thomas took the opportunity of the next few days to fill Edward in on more of the story of his relationship with Mahdiya. Unlike in the past, Edward was all ears. He wanted to know every detail, especially about what it was that had attracted his father to this woman from a different world. Thomas happily shared everything – almost everything.

'Careful, Da. This's the one ye almost tripped on yes'day,' Edward said as he calculated Thomas was moving too quickly down the long, marble staircase.

'Thank ye, lad. Ye're good to yer *bodach*,' Thomas replied as he approached the well-worn step.

'Aye, well I wanna hear more of yer stories, dinna I? And ye're nay *that* auld!'

Something about the last few weeks had brought them to a newfound interdependence. Edward would cling to Thomas in the middle of the night when he woke from a nightmare reliving Charlie's death.

'D'ye ken Ma'll look after him up there?' Edward asked one night.

'Aye, I've nay doubt she will. And so will Mahdiya and yer wee brother or sister.'

'I hope so. Poor Charlie; d'ye ken he had no-one to care for him? Da, should nay everyone have someone to look after them?'

'Aye, they should but it's nay the way it always is, lad. Mahdiya used to say that God has a special love for those who've nay anyone to care for them.'

'D'ye believe that, Da?'

'I dinna ken, lad, but Mahdiya ken a lot more about God than I did. So, I trust she was *ceart*.'

'What is it about Muslim women, Da? They all seem to ken more than we do.'

Thomas had noticed Edward being friendly with the staff, but especially the female staff. They had only been there three days when he caught him lingering after lunch to chat with a young girl around about the same age. Then, he had woken from his siesta one afternoon to find Edward gone, wondering what he was doing and hoping he had not ventured outside the Consulate. He had questioned him when he returned, only to receive a vague answer about some "new friends".

'I dinna ken what it is,' Edward continued. 'But they seem to understand things better than we do, and it's nay just the women. There's something about their religion, is it nay?'

They chatted about Islam, its basic beliefs and differences. Thomas took the opportunity to tell him again why it was that he never went far without Mahdiya'a bullet-ridden Qur'an. Edward was now interested in a way that had evaded him beforehand.

'Anyway, time for ye to tell me why ye're so interested in these women all of a sudden. It's Rania, is it nay?'

'Aye.'

'Ye did see her on that last morning in Alexandria, dinna ye?'

'Aye, how d'ye ken?'

'I could smell it on ye, lad. Ye must've been mighty close.'

They smiled at each other.

'Aye, we were close.'

'How close?'

'Close, that's all.'

'D'ye like her then?'

'Aye, of course. We *are* going back there, are we nay, Da?'

'Aye, but we'll nay be staying long, ye ken?'

'I ken; but I can always go back later, canna I?'

'Aye, someday, I suppose. Anyway, tell me more. Who's the wee lass I've seen ye with here?'

'Aisha.'

'Aisha?'

'Aye, I ken ye had that bonnie lass in Tripoli called the same. But this's nay her.'

'Obviously nay. So what's her story?'

'She's supposed to be getting married soon to some *coigreach*. Imagine having to marry someone ye've nay even met. She's really scared.'

'So, how d'ye ken all this then?'

'She just likes to talk to me.'

'Well, be careful, lad. Like I said about Rania, the staff are nay really meant to mix with consular officials – *or guests.*'

'Aye, I ken, just like ye dinna mix with Mahdiya.'

'That was different,' Thomas said, showing surprise at his son's retort.

'How so? Was she nay staff? Were ye nay a guest?'

'Well, for a start, we were aulder than ye are. Mahdiya was twenty-five and she'd been married. How auld is Aisha?'

'About fourteen, she ken.'

'She ken?'

'Aye, her Ma and Da were killed when she was just a wee one, so she's nay sure about her birthday. Or that's what she says. An uncle's been bringing her up. He works in some other consulate and got her the job here. But only until she's fifteen. Then she has to marry and the uncle has a cousin who wants her for one of his wives. I ken that might be why she's vague about her birthday.'

'How auld's the cousin?'

'She dinna ken. But he has a few wives already so he must be really auld.'

'Aye, well just dinna get involved, lad. It's nay any of yer business.'

'I ken, Da. I ken.'

Thomas thought he would find the right moment to tell his boy about his experience with Sanjee, the young Indian girl in the Bombay Embassy, when he was on his way to Persia the first time. He was taken in by her story of being in a cruel marriage and wanting him to take her with him when he left. Then, when things did not turn out her way, she turned on him, accusing him of attacking her.

But that could wait for now.

—◊◊◊—

On the sixth day, Mahdiya's parents were allowed an appointment at the Consulate to see Thomas and Edward.

'*Salam*,' they both said, joining hands as they bowed.

'*Salam*,' Thomas and Edward replied.

Consul Reynolds invited them all to take a seat in the parlour and he served as translator, having learned sufficient Farsi to get by.

Thomas watched them seating themselves, both smaller than he was expecting because Mahdiya had been quite tall. Perhaps they had shrunken with age. The little lady had kindly deep brown eyes, like Mahdiya's. She was dressed as he remembered Mahdiya on their flight from Shiraz. A simple brown, flowing robe with a matching veil. The little man was squinting through reddened eyes. He looked unwell. He was dressed in a brown suit that was too big for him. Perhaps it fitted him once.

'We're so very pleased to meet ye,' Thomas began. 'This is my lad, Edward, as ye ken.'

Mahdiya's parents looked at each other. They had received a little tuition in English but Thomas's Highland brogue rendered it a waste of time. They waited for Reynolds' translation.

Once they knew what Thomas had said, they responded likewise, telling him what he already knew, that they were indeed Mahdiya's parents. He could see the tears welling in the mother's eyes as her daughter's name was mentioned.

Thomas remembered some of the things Mahdiya had shared about the family that was then estranged. He knew there were some brothers who were older, one of them quite a bit older, and that she was the youngest and the only girl. He remembered her saying that she came late in life for her parents, so they must now be well in their seventies, if not eighties. They looked it, the hardships of life etched on their faces.

The conversation was stilted initially. Thomas found himself distracted from it, more interested to see if he could see anything of Mahdiya in these old people. It was something that caused the old woman to smile that gave him the first glimpse. He could feel Mahdiya's presence in the room.

'*What would she want of this moment? To be gracious and forgiving.*'

'Mahdiya spoke often about ye. She loved ye very much, d'ye ken?'

The two parents looked to each other and then to Reynolds. His Farsi was not good but, to their ears, perfect compared to the incomprehensible Highlander talk.

As Reynolds translated, the parents began to weep. The mother started shouting at her husband, at one stage hitting him so hard it caused the other three in the room to jump. They feared the woman would hurt her clearly frail partner and were ready to intervene. The woman stopped hitting, descending into a grieving from the heart that bespoke many years of heartache and regret. The old man did nothing to protect himself. It was as though he would happily have been beaten to death.

'She's blaming her husband for throwing Mahdiya out of the family,' Reynolds said.

'*Chera? Chera? Chera?*' the old lady shouted at her husband.

'She's asking him why.'

'Why what?' Edward spoke for the first time.

'I don't know,' Reynolds replied.

Edward rose and went to the woman, offering her his kerchief.

'I'm so sorry for yer sadness, Ma,' he said as he handed her the cloth, turning and placing his arm on the old man's. 'And for yers too.'

'*Mamnoon,*' the old man said, placing his hand over Edward's.

Edward looked back to the woman and placed his other hand on her arm. Thomas wondered how she would react because, in traditional Persian custom, strange men do not touch women in any way. There was however no sense of unease, the gesture seeming to quieten her. She used the kerchief to wipe her eyes and nose.

'*Merci, pesaer jaevan. Merci.*'

The parents moved apart and made room for Edward to sit between them. He did so and took a hand each in his two hands.

'How proud would his mother be of her bairn,' Thomas thought. *'How happy would Mahdiya be as well.'*

The parents relayed, through the Consul, the story of the family break-up. How they had tried to counsel a young Mahdiya that the boy she loved was not right for her but they had relented and given their blessing. Then, of their sadness that their instincts had been correct as her husband turned against her and beat her, amidst drinking and prostitution. How his mysterious death had been blamed on Mahdiya and of the threats that the family of Mahdiya's husband had waged against her and the whole family.

Mahdiya's father had been an elder in the village and had worked for a relative of the husband's family. So did the elder son. They risked losing everything if they took Mahdiya's side, so the father and her brothers had insisted they must disown her. Her mother had never wanted that but the others used to say, *do you want to ruin us?* Once, the mother had tried to go and find Mahdiya but her sons tracked her down and forced her to come home.

Then, they heard she had run away with an "Englishman" and a "Christian" and had a baby and died. The mother was heartbroken. Finally, the father had softened to realise his mistake but it was too late.

Thomas felt a pang of guilt for having been a small part of their pain.

'Mahdiya so wanted to see ye before we left for Bandar Abbas.'

This news caused a new round of weeping. By now, Edward was not only holding their hands but providing a shoulder for each to cry on.

They knew that Mahdiya had died but did not have much detail. They seemed confused about the baby whom they had assumed had made it to England. Thomas filled them in on the sea battle that had caused both Mahdiya's and the baby's deaths. He spoke of their burial at sea and the fact that he had so often passed by the spot and prayed for them each time. The parents seemed comforted by the thought that their daughter was not forgotten.

Thomas also told them about his time in the Americas and the shooting that had almost killed him but for Mahdiya's small Qur'an. He showed them the bullet-ridden holy book. They asked if they could hold it. The father recounted how it had been given to her as a birthday gift by her grandmother. It seemed to give them so much comfort that, just for a moment, Thomas thought they might ask to keep it. They handed it back.

Mahdiya's Qur'an had become part of the family story, the artefact of hers that consoled him most.

After an exhausting couple of hours, the parents left but only after securing a promise from Thomas that he and Edward would come to their place before they left. They must do as Persians always do and treat honoured guests to a feast. Reynolds translated their invitation and Thomas's grateful acceptance, though Thomas could see from his glances that he was not happy with the idea.

'*Merci, pesaer jaevan. Merci*', the old lady said again to Edward as she reached up and kissed him on the cheek.

Even her husband seemed surprised by this gesture.

'*Mamnoon, pesaer jaevan. Merci,*' the old man said, shaking Edward's hand and patting him on the shoulder.

'*My lad has a gift,*' Thomas thought to himself.

—⁂—

'I don't think it's a good idea to go to their home,' Reynolds suggested the next morning at breakfast.

'Why on earth nay?' Thomas replied.

'They seem like braw people. I feel sorry for them,' Edward said.

'Well, there's been trouble around Sadra. It's become a hot spot for disgruntled folk, especially young ones, and most especially anti-British folk.'

'D'ye have a Scottish flag?' Edward said. 'If they ken we're Scots, they'll ken we're nay really British.'

Reynolds could share the wry humour, especially coming from a thirteen year-old.

'What do *you* think Thomas? Seriously, is it necessary?'

'I do Malcolm. I ken I'd like to see the home where my first wife was a bairn. And it'd mean so much to them. I ken Persian hospitality.'

'Alright, but we'll need to find you an escort.'

'Are ye sure that's necessary?'

'As the one responsible for your welfare while you're here, *yes*, it *is* necessary.'

'I'll take yer advice, Malcolm, but please make it discreet. The last thing we'd want is to ride up with the whole British Cavalry.'

'I'll ensure that doesn't happen, Thomas. I'll speak with the Adjutant General.'

'I canna wait,' Edward said.

—∞—

Three days later, Thomas and Edward set out on horseback to the home in Sadra. They were accompanied by two soldiers in the redcoated uniform of the British Army.

'Is that what ye looked like, Da?' Edward asked.

'Aye, except I wore an officer's hat.'

It had now been a week and a half since Thomas had been in the saddle. He wondered how he had managed those many days on horseback through Palestine and Iraq. He doubted he would make it back to this part of the world.

Pushing through the pain was the excitement of seeing Mahdiya's birth and rearing place.

'*Salam, Salam,*' the parents greeted them like long lost friends.

Thomas and Edward replied with the Persian greeting. They knew "*Salam*" meant "hello", "*Merci*" meant "thank you" and "*Bye*

Bye" would do for "goodbye". That would have to suffice for the occasion. The Adjutant-General had insisted that Reynolds should not expose himself to any potential danger. There was no other translator available.

The old lady greeted Edward in the same way she had said goodbye at the Consulate, hugging and kissing him on both cheeks. The old man greeted Thomas with a firm handshake and followed with a handshake and hug for Edward. The old lady extended her hand to Thomas and clasped his hand with her other one. In a Persian context, it was exceptional.

They stepped inside the tiny, single-storeyed mud house. Even Edward had to duck his head to fit in the doorway that led directly into the sitting room.

Unbeknown to the parents, the two soldiers kept a close eye on the movements, as instructed. They were out of sight behind some trees not far down the road.

'*Kernl, man pesar, Ahmed,*' the old man said, gesturing towards a large man whom Thomas assumed was his son, Ahmed.

Thomas stepped forward and extended his hand. The hand was taken with a limp grip, accompanied by an expressionless face.

'*Eh man pesar, Qasim,*' the old man repeated, pointing to an even more shadowy character who stepped from behind Ahmed and the gestures were repeated. This time, the face was mean.

'*Eh man pesar, Edward,*' the old lady said, laughing.

The old man laughed at the idea of Edward as their son. The two brothers did not react. Edward felt uncomfortable.

Thomas was on full military alert.

'*Your pesar, mether, yay,*' Ahmed shouted as he produced a pistol, rushing to grab Edward around the throat and levelling it at his temple.

In the same instant, Qasim grabbed Thomas from behind, pinning his arms.

'*No, Ahmed, no,*' the old lady shouted.

The old man repeated the words.

Thomas's training came to him in an instant. He sensed it was a situation unlikely to resolve itself except through force. He knew he had to act quickly, aching body notwithstanding.

While Ahmed was distracted shouting back at his parents, Thomas broke free of Qasim's grip and rushed towards Ahmed. As he hoped, Ahmed moved the pistol from Edward's head and took aim at himself.

Before he could fire, Thomas leapt on him, throwing him to the ground with one arm and pushing Edward away with the other. Ahmed fell back and the pistol fired aimlessly.

Thomas knew he had to immobilise this fitter man quickly. He laid three quick punches to Ahmed's temple, knocking him unconscious. As the last one was delivered, Qasim grabbed Thomas around the neck with one arm, attempting to pull him away from his brother. The fist on his free hand was clenched ready to do damage to Thomas's head.

Before he could land the punch, there was a shattering sound and Qasim fell to the floor.

Thomas got to his feet to see Edward standing over Qasim. He was holding the handle of what had been a large, two-handled pottery jug, now in pieces around Qasim's body.

'Stand aside everyone,' the first soldier through the door shouted, his rifle raised.

Thomas and Edward were holding each other. The two brothers were immobile on the floor. Mahdiya's mother was wailing. Her husband was trying to stem the bleeding from her arm where the bullet had hit.

—⚒—

'I won't tell you I told you so, Thomas,' Reynolds said, helping him dismount at the Consulate. 'Are you both unhurt?'

'Aye, we've just had a braw time,' Thomas replied.

'And you, Edward, boy, are you alright?'

'Aye,' Edward replied.

Reynolds noted Edward's pale face.

'Please report to your superior,' Reynolds barked at the soldiers. 'Tell him I want a full report of this incident on my desk by tomorrow morning.'

'Ye nay should blame them, Malcolm. They came as quickly as they ken there was trouble.'

'What do you mean "came quickly"? Why weren't they there all the time?'

'Because I told them to wait down the road. I dinna want to upset the auld couple.'

'You didn't want to upset the old couple? *You didn't want to upset the old couple*? Seriously, Colonel, did you learn nothing from your time in the army? And putting your child's life at risk like that. Truly!'

'I'm sorry sir. Ye're right. I should've ken better.'

As Reynolds dismissed the soldiers, they signalled their gratitude to Thomas for his taking the blame. They both knew what it might have meant had they been left with it.

Edward took note of his father's largesse.

—∞—

'Can we go and see Mrs Ahmadi?' Edward asked at dinner the following evening.

'Over my dead body, young man,' Reynolds replied. 'Over my dead body.'

'But she was so lovely and she might die.'

'I'm assured she won't die from that flesh wound. Although she might well die before her sons are out of prison.'

'About that, Malcolm,' Thomas said. 'Is there any way we can have them pardoned? They're all their parents have and I'd hate to think what might happen to them if their sons are nay there to look after them.'

'Well, I'm afraid they should have thought of that before they tried to kidnap young Edward – if that's what they were trying to do.'

'But Mr and Mrs Ahmadi dinna ken anything about that,' Edward shouted.

'I wouldn't be so sure of that, young man. I know it might be hard to accept but I've learned that these people cannot be trusted.'

'I ken they're nay those sorts of people, Malcolm. I truly do,' Thomas said.

'Perhaps, or perhaps not. From all I've heard from you, it seems to me they were *all* intent on kidnapping Edward. You did say the old lady referred to him as her son, did you not?'

'Aye, but I'm certain she was joshing. She and the auld man were laughing as they said it.'

'Perhaps, or perhaps not. They're different, these people. I thought you'd know that, Thomas. They have very different beliefs about all sorts of things, including vengeance. It can actually be a religious thing, you know? You took their child so their God requires they take your child. That sort of thing. I've seen it before.'

Edward asked to leave the room.

'I'm sorry to be so blunt, Thomas, but I think it's more than likely that this was all planned. I doubt those men would have done something like this without their parents being in on it.'

'But ye dinna hear the way they shouted at their sons. I ken there are differences but I ken these people's daughter and she was the finest human being to ever walk the Earth. She'd have been horrified at what her brothers did. I ken that for sure.'

'And *they're* fine people too. I ken that for sure,' Edward shouted, poking his head back through the door. 'And I *wanna* see them before we go.'

They heard his voice trailing off as he raced away.

'I can't let you do it, Thomas. I absolutely forbid it. Surely you understand.'

'Aye, I ken why ye're saying it but I feel terrible leaving them like this. Is there nay anything ye can do to help?'

They hatched a plan that would see the brothers given light sentences and returned to their parents. Reynolds promised to do what he could to effect this while Thomas would convince Edward that a letter to the old couple was the best they could do. Reynolds would translate it into Persian.

When Thomas got back to his room, Edward was asleep. He would tell him in the morning.

—⁓—

Thomas slept until late. He had not recovered from the travel much less the effects of the attack.

He looked across to Edward's bed and, as expected, it was empty. Edward liked to be up early and, no doubt, he had gone down to breakfast, perhaps for a stroll around the Consulate grounds and, heaven forbid, making trouble with Aisha. He thought he had better hurry and find out what his son was doing, especially knowing how upset he had been.

Thomas washed, dressed and struggled downstairs. His legs were working even less well than before and his right hand was throbbing. He reached the breakfast room and went to the table where cereal and milk routinely sat, normally not cleaned up until all had breakfasted. It seemed that no-one had breakfasted this morning. Alarmed, he rushed to find Reynolds who was in a meeting.

'I'm sorry to disturb you, sir, but I'm wondering if ye've seen Edward this morning.'

'No, I haven't. I assumed he was with you upstairs. Are you sure he's not in the grounds?'

'I apologise, sir. I'll let ye ken if he's nay there.'

Thomas moved as quickly as he could to the door that led to the internal gardens. He called Edward's name several times.

Nothing.

He thought then of Aisha. She was cleaning on the first floor. Somehow, he was able to communicate with her and receive the response that she did not know where Edward was.

He went to the stable to ask the stable hand if he had seen his son. Through gestures and the odd word, the young boy was able to tell him that the horse Edward had ridden to Sadra had been missing since early morning.

'I reckon he's gone to see the auld couple,' Thomas said as he burst into Reynolds' meeting for the second time.

'Are you sure?'

'Aye, I apologise for my rudeness but I think ye ken why.'

'Indeed.'

Reynolds apologised to his visitors and raced out the door, calling for his secretary who was ordered to summon the Adjutant-General.

—※—

'That's the house down there – and there's his horse,' Thomas called as the party of seven came over the hill.

Four soldiers were accompanying them this time. Reynolds had thrown caution to the wind and decided to accompany Thomas. This meant the Adjutant-General had to come as well.

Reynolds was first off his horse and first to beat on the door. Thomas was close behind. A moment before one of the soldiers was about to put his shoulder to the door, it opened.

'*Salam*,' Mahdiya's father said.

'Is my lad in there with ye?' Thomas asked, struggling for breath.

There was no need for translation. The old man knew what was being asked and invited them in. He looked frightened at the sight of the soldiers.

'General, tell your men to stay outside,' Reynolds said. 'We'll call them if necessary.'

Thomas, Reynolds and the general followed the old man through the front room. It was a small house so it took only a few steps to reach the bedroom. Edward was sitting next to the bedridden old lady, holding her hand.

'There's nay need to worry, Da. I was about to leave.'

'Laddie, ye better never do this to me again, d'ye hear?'

'I told ye, Da. I needed to see them. It would've haunted me if I dinna.'

Thomas pondered again on how like him his son was in these matters.

For Edward, it was as satisfying a closure as possible. He pressed the case for leniency for the two sons. Reynolds gained a guarantee from local authorities that the sons would be released as soon as Thomas and Edward had left the area.

—␣␣—

In the few days left to them in Shiraz, Thomas made sure Edward took in as much of the city as possible. As he had done decades earlier, he would don Middle Eastern garb and, with Edward dressed similarly, they would wander the streets, the markets and the mosques. Thomas wanted to make sure his son made the most of his time in this four thousand year-old site that could boast elements of civilization while the Britons of their day were still hunters and gatherers.

They took in the view, the smell and the feel of a place that had become an intimate part of Thomas's own folklore. The odour was a mix of live animals, coffee and roasted meats. The vista was of endless market carts of vegetables, dates and nuts, with mosques and their minarets rarely out of sight. People bustled in all directions, men and boys in plain soutanes, women and girls frocked and veiled in all colours of the rainbow. The sounds were of the bustling and marketeering with the calls to prayer from the minarets interspersed at the set times of day.

Edward expressed what Thomas had sensed all those years before. Of all Muslim cities, Shiraz was unique for its beauty and cultural cohesion.

Thomas especially wanted to show Edward the Vakil Mosque and the Eram Gardens where he had often retreated to gather his thoughts and restore his spirits.

'Aisha's asked if she can come with us, Da,' Edward said in a moment of silence in the Vakil Mosque.

He had noticed Edward was spending more time with Aisha than was wise. Reynolds had even mentioned it.

'Ye ken that's nay possible, dinna ye, lad?'

'Aye, but I just thought I'd tell ye anyway. She's very unhappy, ye ken? It's nay fair that she nay has a choice in who she marries.

'I ken, lad, but it's the way it is and that's that.'

Thomas then told Edward about Sanjee in Bombay and the trouble he had almost caused for everyone, including the girl herself, because he let his heart rule his head.

'Aye, I'm nay daft, Da. I ken I canna marry her myself.'

'Ye're a bonnie lad and I'm so proud of ye. I ken ye have more sense than I did at yer age; and that's as well.'

Their chatter was causing some of the prayers to notice them. They were under strict instructions from Reynolds to take care as he did not wish to send the British Army to save them again. They exited the mosque and walked down to the river, standing under a tree and allowing themselves to become mesmerised by the gentle flow and trickle of the *Rudkhaneye Khoshk*.

'I ken the way ye handled Mahdiya's parents was braw, by the way.'

'Did ye, Da? Ye're nay angry anymore?'

'I was nay angry, lad; just worried for ye.'

'Aye, I understand. It was a wee *gorach* to do what I did but I nay could've lived with myself if I'd left without seeing them. I had to ken they were alright.'

'Aye, and I should've heard ye when ye said that to me. I'm sorry, lad.'

'There's nay anything to be sorry for, Da.'

They clasped each other's arms and walked on.

XII

Five days after Edward had been found at Mahdiya's parents' place, he and his father set out on horseback for Bandar Busheyr on Persia's west coast. It was the port where Thomas had landed all those many years before, wanting then to go back home as quickly as possible. He had only pressed on to Shiraz because there was no vessel heading towards home for several weeks. Little did he know then what fate awaited him in Shiraz!

Reynolds had been concerned about Thomas's wellness ever since he arrived at the Consulate. Since the scuffle with Mahdiya's brothers, he could see even more signs of wear and tear. The idea of him travelling overland to Alexandria struck Reynolds as undesirable. He made enquiries of the military and found that a Royal Navy vessel was leaving Bandar Busheyr, heading to Port Sudan, in ten days' time. If Thomas and Edward could be there by then, they could secure a passage at least that far. There was a British fort in Port Sudan so they should be able to find a way back to Alexandria.

Reynolds was taking no chances so he had negotiated with the army for an escort of six horse soldiers, heavily armed. The army provided military rifles for Thomas and Edward as well.

'D'ye think I'll get a chance to use it, Da?'

'I hope nay, lad.'

'But *ye* did when ye were on this road, dinna ye?'

'Aye, but I dinna have six of the British Army's best sharpshooters with me that time.'

'So ye'll show me the spot where all that happened, will ye nay?'

'Aye, of course.'

The road was much improved from what Thomas could remember but the spot where he had marked his name in the history of the district by killing three bandits was easy to pick out. The road was still narrow at that point because of the steep cuttings on both sides. Thomas had asked Sergeant-Major Pennydale, the leader of the troop, if they could stop there so he could show his son how it had all happened.

'Of course, sir,' Pennydale replied. 'I'd love to hear about it too. I'm sure you know it's a story that goes around in these parts. In fact, the way I've heard it, you killed more like thirty-three that day, some of them with your bare hands.'

'Nay, three is all; and that was plenty enough too.'

As they approached the spot, Thomas sensed his muscles tensing. Unlikely as it was, could it be that bandits were waiting for them? Those rocks where they had hidden last time were still in place on the cliff top. It remained the perfect place for an ambush.

Thomas called a halt to the troop just before it would have been within range. Pennydale wheeled around. He was about to remind Thomas who was in charge but something on Thomas's face stopped him.

'Are you alright, Colonel?'

'Aye, I'm sorry. My mind might be playing tricks on me but that's the very spot where we were ambushed,' Thomas said, pointing at the rocks above.

'Did ye see something, Da?'

'Nay, I canna say but I have a *neonach* feeling.'

Pennydale was not used to responding to feelings so was inclined to carry on and take his chances.

'I'd nay do that, sir, if I were ye,' Edward said. 'When my Da says he feels something, it often turns out to be right.'

'Alright, boy, I'll take your word for it. Kennedy, Wishaw, dismount and take a look behind those rocks up there.'

The two soldiers did as they were commanded. Pennydale, making it clear he was not taking the situation seriously, began to chat and joke with the remaining soldiers.

Edward, meantime, had dismounted and was moving slowly in the direction that Privates Kennedy and Wishaw had taken. He had slipped around behind Thomas without his father knowing, rifle at the ready.

For his part, Thomas was still mounted with a steely eye glued in the direction of the rocks.

In a flash, he saw it. The shooter appeared and was firing at something. The two soldiers were still making their way up the back of the hill and so were out of his sight. Pennydale and the remaining soldiers took cover against the rock wall.

'*What is he firing at?*' Thomas wondered.

He turned and saw that Edward was missing. Then he saw that he was the one target within range of the shooter.

'Take cover, lad, quickly,' he shouted.

Edward took aim and fired. The shooter ducked and the bullet whistled off into the distance.

Thomas stayed on his horse, squeezing the stirrups into its side as he took careful aim at the shooter. He gently squeezed the trigger on his Pattern 1776 Infantry issue, a rifle with maximum range. It hit the shooter just left of the sternum that he had exposed as he lifted his own rifle to fire again at Edward. The shooter fell backwards, his rifle tumbling down on the rocks below.

'Braw shooting, Da,' Edward shouted.

'Get back down here, lad,' Thomas screamed.

Kennedy and Wishaw arrived at the shooter's spot from the rear. They called out that he was dead and it seemed he was alone. Pennydale and his colleagues moved away from the cliff face. Edward returned to his father who was still on his horse, re-loading.

'Laddie, ye're gonna be the death of both of us unless ye start to obey me. D'ye hear?'

'Sorry, Da. I ken I could help.'

'Well, I take it all back, Colonel,' Pennydale said. 'I thought you were imagining things.'

'Highlanders dinna imagine. We ken,' Edward replied. 'My Da always ken.'

Pennydale ignored the comment, suggesting they move on fast.

'Nay until we've buried the lad,' Thomas said.

'Buried?' Pennydale snapped back.

'Aye, he'll be a Muslim and it's important to them.'

Years before, Mahdiya had scolded him for not burying the young bandits he had killed on their escape from Shiraz.

Four of the soldiers dug a shallow grave at the rear of the hill where there was some soft soil. They placed the young bandit in it, buried him and placed some rocks over the grave. The whole procedure took a little over fifteen minutes.

'Let's go quickly now,' Pennydale ordered.

'Just a wee moment more,' Thomas said.

He lifted Mahdiya's Qur'an from his pocket, opened it at the first Sura and read it quietly in Arabic. Edward was the only one to bow his head.

'Are you ready *now*, sir?' Pennydale snapped.

'Aye, we've done the right thing.'

They struck out again along the narrow trail, this time rifles drawn and looking atop every craggy knoll.

Within a few minutes, they were passing the spot where Thomas had cut the throat of the first man he had ever killed, one of the three bandit kills by which he had come to be known all those years before. He noticed what looked like a primitive headstone and asked again if they could stop.

'What is it this time, Colonel? Another heathen ritual?' Pennydale asked.

'Aye, perhaps!'

Thomas moved to the headstone, Edward in pursuit. The stone had etchings written in what seemed a variant of Farsi. He could tell it was not Arabic or the Farsi he could recognise. There was also a faded drawing of a human face, a young angelic-looking man. It sent a shiver down Thomas's spine.

'What does it mean, Da?'

'Well, I'm guessing this is where the first one I killed is buried. And this'd be some braw words about him and a prayer for Allah to take care of him. I'm guessing that's a drawing of him.'

'How does it make ye feel, Da?'

'*Dona*, lad. Very bad.'

'But he would've killed ye, would he nay?'

'Aye, but it still hurts to kill. It's nay ever a braw thing to do.'

Thomas thought again of Mahdiya and her caution that he should never kill but, if he had to, he should always ask for God's forgiveness.

He reached again for the Qur'an and repeated the first Sura over the headstone. Edward joined in where he could. They prayed for the dead bandit and for those who loved him enough to have built the memorial.

'*Better late than never,*' Thomas pondered.

—◊◊◊—

Three days later, they arrived in Bandar Busheyr. They made their way to the docks where *HMS Repulse* was being prepared for sail. As he had been instructed to, Sergeant-Major Pennydale handed Thomas and Edward into the care of the ship's commander, Commodore George Mitchell. Pennydale gave the impression that the handover could not be done quickly enough.

'Thank you, Sergeant,' Mitchell said. 'Welcome Colonel Lovat. I'm delighted to have you aboard. I have of course heard about you and I know well of your cousin, the Consul-General. And welcome, Master Lovat.'

Pennydale walked off the boat with no acknowledgement of anyone, including the barely pubescent sailor who attempted to salute him at the top of the gangplank.

'I'm not an officer, you fool.'

'My, my. He seems happy in the service,' Mitchell said.

'Aye, well I'm sure he's happy to be rid of us,' Thomas replied.

'He's just a very unhappy *dhuine*,' Edward said.

'Well, let me show you to your cabin. I believe you're more than familiar with the British Man o' War, Colonel. Is that correct?'

'Aye, indeed, I am, sir.'

'And so am I,' Edward said.

'Are you indeed, young man? And tell me why.'

Edward filled Mitchell in on their journey from Portsmouth to Gibraltar aboard *HMS Stirling*, a smaller but otherwise identical sister ship to the *Repulse*. At 5100 tons, the *Repulse* was over a thousand tons larger and boasted 106 cannons, against the *Stirling*'s 84. Edward's eyes were bulging with excitement.

'Well, then, you'll know your way around, where you can go and where not, including when you can come on deck and when not, won't you young man?'

'Aye, sir, I ken what I can and canna do. I wanna be a sailor when I grow up so I wanna do the *rud* thing.'

'A sailor, do you? Well perhaps I can find a few things for you to do. Would you like that?'

'Aye, sir. Anything at all.'

'As long as that's alright with your father, mind you?'

Thomas nodded.

'Very well then. I'll see you both at my dinner table at 7.30 this evening, if that's suitable to you.'

'Aye, it's very suitable, thank ye, sir,' Edward said while Thomas was still forming the words.

'Excellent. Meanwhile, please feel free to settle in.'

Two mornings later, they set sail.

XIII

There was no cabin boy on the *Repulse* so Mitchell was able to assign similar duties to Edward. Edward relished the opportunity.

'Anything else I can do for ye, sir?' Edward asked, handing Mitchell a note from the boatswain.

'No, boatswain's mate,' Mitchell replied with a salute and a grin.

Edward was delighted with the title that he had acquired thanks to Clive Birmingham, the ship's boatswain. Birmingham was a swarthy seaman who had begun sailing as a cabin boy when fourteen years of age. He was now in his fifties and reputed to know more about ships than almost anyone in the Royal Navy. Mitchell might be the commander but it was to Birmingham that everyone turned, including Mitchell, if there was trouble with the ship.

Birmingham was delighted to have a ready-made helper on board. Normally, his status as boatswain meant he could order a sailor to do his bidding. But sailors were a tough bunch, not always compliant. Which meant Birmingham would often have to do the job himself. After forty years of rocking around on unsteady ships and a few too many toddies of rum, he was starting to feel his age. Having a young and agile Edward who would happily run around the ship all day doing whatever Birmingham desired was a godsend.

'See that sail up there, boy,' Birmingham said, coughing into his tobacco-stained hand.

'Aye, the one that's nay fully unfurled?'

'The same one, boy. Now, someone 'as to climb up and unfurl it. 'o do ye think that might be now?'

'The boatswain's mate, I reckon.'

Birmingham laughed, setting off another round of coughing and spitting.

'Off ye go, then.'

'Aye, aye, sir,' Edward said, saluting.

'Go off with ye now. We don't 'ave time for all that salutin' piffle, boy.'

As if brought up by monkeys, Edward scaled the excuse-for-a-ladder, reaching the sail at the top of the mast in a matter of seconds.

'That's the one, boy. See 'ow the edge's caught under that rope. Just pull it free.'

In one movement, Edward freed the sail and began the climb down, seeming to slide, so at home was he with such monkey-like routines.

Of an evening, Edward had stopped going to dinner at the Captain's Table, preferring to eat with the crew, as any boatswain's mate would.

'Are ye sure, lad?' Thomas asked when Edward first suggested it. 'Ye do ken it's considered an honour to eat with the Captain?'

'Aye, I ken, Da, but I wanna be one of the sailors. I canna be a boatswain's mate and be eating with the captain, can I?'

'I see yer point but I think ye'd better ask Commodore Mitchell. We dinna want to offend him, do we?'

Mitchell did not mind at all. He was enjoying seeing how Edward had taken to life as a sailor. He was also pleased to see the effect on Birmingham. He relied on him enormously but Birmingham could be moody, making life difficult for everyone on board. Since he had taken Edward under his wing, Birmingham had been at his happiest.

—∞—

'D'ye ken we'll see any pirates, Mr Birmingham?' Edward asked.

One of the reasons the *Repulse* was sailing this route was to discourage the increasing amount of piracy in the waters around the Persian Gulf.

'Well, if we do, I'll send ye out to deal with 'em. That's what boatswain's mates are there for, ye know?' Birmingham laughed amid coughs.

'As long as I can take my Da with me. He'll take care of 'em, for sure.'

'Ye love yer old man, don't ye boy?'

'Aye.'

'Ye're lucky. I never knew mine but from what I 'eard, I wasn't missin' much.'

—∞—

As they rounded the Gulf of Oman, the easterly wind picked up. The multiple sails of the *Repulse* were suddenly filled, seeming to pick the boat up and hurl it forward, accelerated further by the waves breaking in the same direction. As everyone on board was steadying themselves after the sudden movement, they heard the cry from the watch in the crow's nest. The pirate ship was heading diagonally away from them, chasing down a clipper with smaller sail.

'Man the guns,' Mitchell shouted from the bridge. 'Fifteen degrees to port.'

The *Repulse* began to turn.

In an action of this kind, the boatswain became central to all movements, be they of sails, sailors or liaising with those preparing the cannons. And Edward was there with him, ready to do his boss's bidding.

'Come inside, lad,' Thomas shouted. 'We need to take cover.'

With the noisy movements on the deck, Edward had plenty of excuses for not hearing, or pretending not to hear. Thomas began to move towards him but Edward ran quickly in the opposite direction, apparently to convey a message to one or other of Birmingham's charges.

Thomas was in no state to be chasing a thirteen-year-old around so he settled for keeping an eye on him – and praying for his safety. He moved to the bridge and stood next to Mitchell. The memories of the awful battle with the French ship, over twenty years before, came flooding back.

The pirate ship was catching up with the clipper but the *Repulse*, now under full sail, was larger than either of them and closing on its target.

'D'ye ken he's seen us?' Thomas asked.

'He's a bold one if he has,' Mitchell replied. 'His best chance of getting away'd be to turn and flee but he seems intent on overtaking the clipper. Even if he does, does he really think we're going to just stand by and watch while he loots it?'

'What of their gun power?' Thomas asked.

'Looks like half a dozen or so six or eight pounders,' Mitchell replied.

'So, well outgunned by us, then?'

'Five dozen thirty-six pounders, fourteen eighteen pounders and thirty long nines? I should think so.'

The pirate ship was only ten minutes or so from overtaking the clipper. There was no sign from the pirate ship that the *Repulse* had been sighted but it seemed unlikely that could be the case.

'So why's he nay firing on the clipper?' Thomas asked. 'Does he nay have any guns to the fore?'

Mitchell slapped himself on the forehead.

'The blighter's going to use the other ship as a shield. That's why he's not firing on it. He wants to hold it hostage while he keeps us at bay.'

Edward was by now standing next to the commander, having just conveyed a message from the boatswain.

'Boy, run to the boatswain and tell him to ask the head gunner to ascertain our range. Do you have that?'

'Aye, aye, sir,' Edward said, saluting.

Within no time, Edward was back with advice that the *Repulse* was well within range.

'Good, run back and tell the boatswain to trim the sail. We're about to turn to engage. Tell him to tell the head gunner to await my signal. Got that?'

'Aye, aye, sir.'

'And make sure to tell him to shoot straight; we don't want to hit the clipper.'

'Aye, aye, sir,' Edward called back as he turned around, saluting one way and running the other, stumbling over a coiled rope on the deck.

Thomas winced at the sight.

The sails were trimmed and the ship began to slow.

'Turn seventy-five degrees to port,' Mitchell commanded.

The pirate ship was closing on the clipper. By the time the *Repulse* was in place for action, there were barely two minutes left to fire on it and so avoid a game of cat and mouse, with the clipper caught in the middle.

The head gunner was watching for Mitchell's signal to engage.

'Now!' Mitchell shouted as he lowered his outstretched arm. 'Fire at will.'

The first twelve thirty-six pounders boomed in unison, shaking the deck and everyone on it. The sailor manning the tiller fell backwards, leaving the uncontrolled wheel spinning. The ship turned sharply to the portside.

'Quick, grab the tiller,' Mitchell shouted.

Officers and sailors alike ran to grab the wheel and steady the ship so firing could recommence.

Edward had left Birmingham's side to get a better look at the action. He was agog with the efficiency of the gunners, each cannon manned by five gunners working as a team. Two of them pulled the massive cannon in after each shot, while a third had a long stick with a sponge on the end, ready to clean out the leftover gunpowder and a fourth the new pouch of gunpowder. Once the sponge had done its job, the fresh gunpowder was inserted. Meantime, the sponger had grabbed a rammer to ensure the gunpowder was firmly in place. As he was doing this, the one who had placed the gunpowder in the barrel had reached down and grabbed the new cannon ball, inserting it in the barrel while the rammer came back to ensure it was firmly in place in front of the gunpowder. The fifth, the gunner in charge, then inserted a wick at the rear of the cannon, reaching down to the gunpowder. The two who had pulled the cannon in then pushed it back in place through the hole in the side of the ship, positioning it according to the instructions of the gunner in charge who would light the wick and wait for the boom.

Edward was so fascinated by this precision military action, he forgot for a moment that there was a target of all this activity.

'Good shooting, boys,' the gunner in charge shouted.

Edward was reminded about the target and raced to the side of the ship to get a better look. He arrived in time to see the next cannon ball hit the already damaged pirate ship's main mast, snapping it in two and bringing down its last sail. It slowed to a crawl and was now an even better target. Meantime, the clipper sailed on to safety.

Distracted by the excitement, Edward had moved too close to one of the cannons. Thomas had shouted to him to stand back but he could not be heard.

'You'd better get the boy away from there, Colonel,' one of the junior officers on the bridge yelled.

Thomas moved as quickly as his broken body would carry him, down from the bridge and towards Edward. He noticed that his son's right foot was positioned in the loop of one of the ropes attached to the cannon. This was one of the ropes the gunners used to slide the cannon in and out of position. If the cannon went off now, Edward would be flung back onto the deck and possibly break a leg, or even his neck.

Thomas was shouting as he shuffled towards him, but no-one could hear. The gunners were fully focussed on their task and Edward was oblivious to the danger. Thomas reached him as the cannon was firing, lifting his son up and away. The cannon fire was deafening and the rocking of the deck threw them both backwards, Edward cushioned in the fall by Thomas's body.

There was no cushioning for Thomas who lay flat on his back, unconscious.

—⚉—

'Da, Da, are ye alright?' were the first words Thomas heard as he awoke in his bunk.

'Colonel, can you see me?' the ship's doctor, Lieutenant Covill, was saying.

It was sixteen hours after the incident.

'Da, Da, I'm so sorry, Da.'

'Aye, I ken I'm alright, lad,' Thomas said, pressing Edward's hand. 'And aye, I can see ye, Lieutenant.'

Thomas closed his eyes to rest them but pressed Edward's hand more tightly.

'Are *ye* alright, lad? That's more to the point.'

'Aye, thanks to ye, I'm told. Ye make a bonnie cushion, Da.'

'That's what a Da's for, ye ken?'

Covill moved to examine Thomas.

'Your boy's right, sir. You were the cushion that saved him from any damage but it's done you no good, I'm afraid. You have a frightful lump on the back of your head. It must be very sore, isn't it?'

'Nay, I actually canna feel a thing.'

Edward noticed the look of concern on Covill's face. Covill then moved his fingers around Thomas's head and neck, pressing here and there and asking with each press whether his patient could feel anything. When he reached the back of his neck, Thomas winced.

'What's wrong, Da?'

'Well, I surely felt that. I'm guessing that's good news, is it nay, Lieutenant?'

'Yes, I suppose but it seems you've done some damage to your neck and I'd be happier if you were able to feel the back of your head. Anyway, you're seeing, hearing and talking and clearly your mind is working.'

'Aye, as braw as ever, at least,' Thomas said.

'Oh, Da. I ken I'd lost ye,' Edward began to cry. 'I'd nay abide it.'

'And I ken I'd lost *ye*, lad. If that cannon had gone off with yer foot in its rope, ye'd have been thrown all the way back to Shiraz.'

'I ken, Da. And ye saved me from being kidnapped in Sadra and ye saved me from drowning in the Mediterranean. Let's face it, Da, without ye, I'd be *marbh* a thousand times. So ye canna ever leave me, ye hear?'

'I hear, lad. I dinna ever wanna leave ye; though one day, ye ken…?'

'Aye, I ken; but nay just now, or for a very long time.'

'I'll see what I can do.'

'You'd better rest up, Colonel,' Covill said. 'Especially if you're going to live forever, as your boy's demanding.'

'Aye, I will; thank ye, Lieutenant. But first, I wanna hear what happened while I was sleeping. Did we put those pirates where they belong?'

'Indeed, we did but I'll let your son fill you in on all that as he saw far more than me. You know what they say if you want to know about anything that happens on a ship?'

'Ask the boatswain's mate,' the three of them choroused.

The doctor left them alone with instructions that Thomas must rest soon.

'Well, Da. How much did ye miss?'

Somewhere around the time that Edward started telling about how the pirate ship had sunk and a few pirates were taken prisoner, Thomas fell asleep. Edward placed his head on the edge of his bed and fell asleep as well.

—∞—

Sixteen days later, the *Repulse* sailed into Port Sudan. The three pirates were handed over to the authorities. Edward was struck by how young and innocent they looked. He reflected on how easily he might have been in their place had he been a victim of the poverty that seemed to have been their fate.

Thomas had managed to get out of bed but not much further than a chair. He was finding it difficult to walk at all. The feeling in his head had come back but was replaced by a persistent headache. He was also having dizzy spells, especially when he tried to stand and walk.

'I'm worried how you'll cope with the rest of your travels, Colonel,' Mitchell said shortly after their arrival. 'Lieutenant Covill says you really should be resting and recuperating for months. Are you sure you don't want me to arrange something with the base hospital here in Port Sudan?'

'Aye, I'm sure, thank ye, sir. I've a lad to get back to his home, ye ken?'

'Yes, I do, Colonel. Not that I think he'll be home for long anyway. I've never seen a young man take more easily to life at sea. I know my boatswain's going to miss him. Why he might even have to do some of his own work on the next trip.'

Mitchell looked at the other officers. They chuckled.

'Anyway, Colonel, I insist, and indeed Lieutenant Covill insists, that you submit yourself to examination at the hospital. There are some fine British-trained doctors there.'

'Aye, I will Commodore, and thank ye so much for all ye've done for me and my lad.'

'It's been my pleasure, indeed my honour, Colonel.'

'Speaking of my lad, where is he now?' Thomas asked.

'Saying his goodbyes, I dare say. He'll be genuinely missed, especially by Birmingham.'

Mitchell was right. Edward was doing the rounds, saying goodbye to the many sailors with whom he had bonded, feeling he was more one of them than a guest on board.

'When ye do go to sea, boy, just make sure ye're on my ship, won't ye?' Birmingham said.

'Aye, I surely will, sir,' Edward replied, saluting.

'I've told ye, boy, ye only salute officers and I'm never likely to be one o' them. On the other 'and, ye might well be. P'raps ye'll be my commanding officer one day.'

XIV

There were caravans moving between Port Sudan and various ports all the time. That had been the first plan for getting Thomas and Edward back to Alexandria. The army doctor was adamant, however, that such a trip was beyond Thomas and would likely kill him. Another plan was therefore hatched. They would be given berths on a boat sailing up the Red Sea to al-Adabiya and from there would be transported by land to Alexandria.

'I'm sorry, Colonel, but we think this is the safer option,' Major-General Brunswick, commander of the British fort in Port Sudan, announced. 'The only drawback is that it could be a few weeks before we can find the right boat but it will give you the opportunity to recuperate – hopefully.'

'Da, we could be in Alexandria in three weeks if we leave now.'

'Young man, we believe your father might not make it at all if he leaves now,' Brunswick snorted.

Thomas noticed Edward blanching, head down.

'Oh I'm sure I would, General, thank ye all the same but I ken ye're doing the best for us and I appreciate that – we both appreciate that, dinna we lad?' he said, looking at Edward. 'We'll do as ye recommend.'

—◇—

It was almost three weeks before the two set out on a small boat that carried goods up the Red Sea, stopping at various small ports along the way. The crew was Arabic and unused to Europeans so Thomas and Edward were largely ignored. They were accommodated on a few square feet on the upper deck.

Edward tried to help out where he could but it was made plain early on that his assistance was not wanted. He began by telling of his credentials as a former boatswain's mate with the Royal Navy. When this failed to impress, he reverted to his cabin boy persona. When this did not work, he made it known that he was happy to do whatever was needed, including carrying goods ashore when the boat moored. Even this was rejected.

'It's best ye just stay here with me, lad,' Thomas said. 'They clearly have their ways and, heaven ken, they might well ken we come from the devil.'

'The devil? What on earth d'ye mean, Da?'

Thomas filled Edward in on another of his adventures in the Middle East. He and Mahdiya had almost been thrown off a boat because the crew believed they were possessed by the devil. Why? They were Sunni and she a Shiite married to a Christian, the ultimate object of suspicion. It gave Thomas a chance to talk about some of the differences in Islam.

Edward yearned for the acceptance he had enjoyed on the *Repulse*. There is sea life and then there is sea life, he concluded. He determined yet again that, were he to go to sea in the future, it would be on a British ship and preferably in the Royal Navy.

Edward thought much about Rania. On those long, restless nights, he came to realise how much he missed her. He hoped they would get to spend a long time together in Alexandria.

—✺—

Fifteen days after leaving Port Sudan, they berthed in al-Adabiya in the middle of the afternoon, a particularly hot one. Edward could not wait to leave the boat.

'Come on, Da, I'll help ye,' he said, grabbing Thomas's arm and dragging him down the gangplank.

'It's alright, lad. I can do it,' Thomas replied, grabbing hold of the grimy rope.

No-one came to their aid. It was as if they had never been there.

—✺—

There was a small British garrison in the town. Thomas had been given a map to show its location. Brunswick had also written the garrison commander a letter, telling of the situation and asking that Thomas and Edward be transported to Alexandria by whatever means considered best.

They arrived at the garrison and asked if they could see the commanding officer.

'Certainly, sir, I'll go and find Major Sutherland for you,' the dishevelled-looking soldier replied.

The sound of the name shot through Thomas's head like a bullet out of a gun. Surely not.

The soldier returned.

'Major Sutherland is busy now but says to make yourselves comfortable and he'll see you presently.'

'Thank ye. Would it be possible to come inside then?' Thomas asked.

'I'm afraid not, sir, Major Sutherland doesn't allow anyone inside unless they're specifically under his watch.'

'Could ye tell him, please, that my Da's nay well?' Edward asked.

'I did tell him that neither of you looked hale and hearty but I'm afraid Major Sutherland is not one to be moved by such things.'

Thomas knew then that this Sutherland must indeed be his nemesis from Tralee. If he ever was to be moved to some compassion, it would not be through mention of the name, "Lovat".

The only "comfortable" option was a step outside the main gate, sitting at that time of day in the full glare of the setting sun. They sat and occasionally walked a little way down the path and stood in a sliver of shade. It was over two hours before another of the garrison soldiers called from the gate.

'Major Sutherland will see you now, Colonel.'

'Thank ye so much,' Thomas replied.

'Nay thanks from me,' Edward said.

They were led to an office towards the back of the barracks, past soldiers looking more disarrayed than Thomas could ever remember of British soldiers. They saw into some of their sleeping quarters, beds unmade and clothing strewn on the floor, then past the kitchen and eating quarters looking similarly uncared for. It was as though the place was abandoned, other than for the fact that its inhabitants were still there, in body if not in spirit.

They arrived at the door of the commanding officer. The soldier knocked and, after the distinctive sound of glass on glass, a voice emitted a gruff "come". The door opened and there sat Sutherland, clearly just awake from slumber, hair uncombed and the buttons on his grubby coat undone. A stench of alcohol mixed with body odour hung in the room. The bunk in the corner of the room was unmade, like all the other beds they had seen. The office was as lacking in resplendence as the Tralee office had been the opposite.

'Lieutenant Lovat, well I never,' he said.

'*Colonel* Lovat, actually, sir,' Edward corrected him.

'My, my, so this must be your son, I take it. I see he's inherited his father's respect for authority.'

'Aye, he respects what's there to be respected,' Thomas replied.

Sutherland blanched but rather than hit back, as he would once have done, the sting seemed to find its mark. Thomas noted a look of defeat on his face. Sutherland put his head in his hands. Thomas and Edward stood silently.

'So what can I do for you, *Colonel?*' he said, looking up and wiping his eyes. 'Surely a man of your fame and influence doesn't need a lowly garrison commander to help you.'

'All we need from ye is a means of transport to Alexandria. We've been told there are regular movements of goods between here and there.'

'And my Da needs a doctor to go with us,' Edward said.

'A doctor, did you say? Why, of course, I'll arrange for al-Adabiya's finest surgeon to accompany you. Would that be sufficient?'

'Aye,' Edward replied. 'That'd be much appreciated, thank ye.'

'If *only* they had one,' Sutherland said, raising his voice. 'Do you understand where you are, young man, or has your father taught you nothing except bad manners? If one of my men stubs his toe and gets an infection, I have to send him to Alexandria because there's no-one in this god-forsaken place who seems even to know what a toe is, much less what an infection is, and even less how to fix it. You've heard of the end of the earth, I presume, but you've never been there before you came here.'

With that, his voice receded. He slumped back in his chair and reached for the glass and bottle he had quickly placed in the drawer when they had knocked. He poured himself a tumbler-sized whisky and proceeded to gulp it down.

Edward was shocked. His only experience of British military to this point was of precision, discipline and control. Thomas had only rarely seen military at this low ebb and it was always ill-foreboding. For the first time on this long, rugged trip, he felt vulnerable. The establishment could no longer be relied on, least of all to protect his son.

Thomas's head began to whirl, running through the small range of options available to them.

'Dinna concern yerself with the doctor, Major. My lad gets a wee bit carried away at times.'

'Cantwell, in here,' Sutherland shouted, taking another gulp.

A young adjutant appeared at the open door. Thomas noted he was dressed as one would expect of a British officer.

'Yes, sir,' the young man said, saluting.

'Take the *Colonel* and his *bad-mannered son* to the cell block. They can bunk there tonight and tomorrow we'll work out what to do with them.'

'Yes, sir.'

'To the cell block?' Thomas asked. 'Are we to be locked up then?'

'Not unless you cause trouble – or I start to think your boy could do with a good lesson. We don't have any other beds available at present, do you understand? Now, if there's nothing else, I'm a busy man.'

Edward gave him a scornful look that seemed to say, *busy drinking*. Sutherland turned away.

Sub-Lieutenant Cantwell led them to the small cell block that, at the time, was holding no prisoners. It brought to Thomas's mind an ominous reminder of the cell block in Tralee where Sutherland had imprisoned and brutalised Liam Prendiville. Sick and tired as he was, he knew he could not place Edward's welfare at risk by staying in this place. For all he knew, Sutherland, clearly out of control, would be just as likely to imprison them there.

'I must say I'm most pleased to meet you, Colonel,' Cantwell said. 'I grew up on stories of your heroism in the American War.'

'Thank ye, Lieutenant. I'm afraid it's a long time ago and I'm nay longer feeling especially heroic.'

'I'm sure you're being too modest, sir.'

'Da, I dinna like this,' Edward said as they came to the filthy cell block.

'Lieutenant, my lad's saying what I'm thinking. Being asked to sleep in a cell block is insulting, to say the least, and especially one in this condition. What on earth is going on here? The whole garrison's a disgrace. With the exception of yerself, I might say, I've nay ever seen soldiers looking so unruly.'

'Colonel, it's difficult for me,' Cantwell said in lowered voice, glancing over his shoulder. 'I've only been here a few weeks and I'm just an intern. From what I'm told, things were normal here before Major Sutherland took over. He came in strange circumstances from Tralee. He was apparently promoted but sent here against his will. In some deal, he was allowed to bring a couple of his pick soldiers with him. No-one seems to know why this happened. I was as shocked as you when I arrived. It's not what I was expecting.'

'Pick soldiers? Like who, Lieutenant?'

'Well, Sergeant Pilgrim's the main one. He fairly much runs the place. He has the Major's ear so even the officers aren't prepared to challenge him.'

Thomas remembered Pilgrim as the one whose nose Liam had broken in Tralee and who was subsequently brought in by Sutherland to rough up Liam in the cell.

'Pilgrim, eh? Aye, that makes sense.'

'Do you know him, do you sir?'

'Aye, I ken who he is – and what he's like.'

Thomas filled Cantwell in on some of the history between them all.

'So ye see, Lieutenant, why I'm nay at all comfortable staying here with my lad. It was bad enough when I ken Sutherland was here, but Sutherland and Pilgrim between them. I just canna trust them.'

'Colonel, I have an idea.'

—◊◊◊—

'Come on, Da,' Edward said. 'Ye can make it.'

Edward had caught the first sight of Alexandria in the distance. The Citadel of Qaitbay, the large fifteenth century fortress of creamed stone that sat on the northern tip of the harbour mouth, was the unmistakeable signal that they had arrived.

'I'll make it, lad. Fear nay.'

They had been travelling for three days, the trip being slowed by staying off some of the main roads. They were technically horse thieves because they had taken two horses, along with some basic equipment, from the garrison without permission. Hence, they could not take the chance of being pursued by a patrol that Sutherland might send after them, quite likely with Pilgrim in charge.

'If you leave now, you'll be twelve hours on the way by the time anyone knows you're gone,' Cantwell had said after leading them to the stables. 'In fact, knowing the routine, the Major and Sergeant Pilgrim will be drinking until midnight and then not be seen until late morning, so you might be eighteen hours on the way.'

'D'ye ken they'd want to follow us anyway,' Thomas had asked.

'They just might,' Cantwell had said. 'They'd be frightened you might blow their cover when you get to Alexandria. You see, sir, no-one comes here. Adabiya truly is the end of the earth when it comes to British outposts. I'm sure that's why the Major was sent here. You're the first British visitors I've seen since arriving.'

Cantwell's only request had been that the situation there be reported and that it be made clear that he had nothing to do with it. He feared for his future career if he was associated with a garrison in that state. In the meantime, it had to look as though Thomas and Edward had escaped and stolen the horses and goods, or else Cantwell could be implicated.

Thomas and Edward had left the garrison by a back gate that was deliberately left unlocked from the inside. They followed the trail that Cantwell had drawn roughly on a piece of paper. He asked them to destroy it should they be captured. They had slept rough at night. It was now December so the cold of winter was setting in. Together with the long days of moving through off-road trails, these rough nights had further weakened Thomas.

He felt the stamina eking out of him, much as he had when so badly wounded in Boston fifteen years earlier.

XV

'Colonel and Master Lovat for Sir Timothy,' Edward said as the servant opened the Commission door. 'Quick, man, and please get a doctor.'

Edward helped Thomas stagger inside. The cool in the foyer felt good. By the time Edward had helped him into a chair, Larkins had appeared.

'My goodness, what's happened to you? I'm so relieved to see you, Thomas. I had no idea where you were or when you might be returning. I was expecting you'd be with an escort.'

Larkins finally took a breath. Edward filled him in on the main events of the past few weeks.

'And so we ended up in Adabiya,' he said.

'*Adabiya*? How on earth did you end up there and why did the garrison not provide you with an escort?'

'We've much to tell ye, Timothy,' Thomas said. 'But, first, can I possibly have a bath?'

—⁂—

When Thomas was safely ensconced in the bathroom, Edward hastened downstairs. Knowing Thomas's many cautions to him about the relationship with Rania, he had kept to himself just how excited he was at the thought of seeing her again. Especially on that long, dreaded boat ride up the Red Sea, he had spent many hours thinking of her and hoping they could pick up where they had left off. He had begun to daydream about coming back to Alexandria at some point in the future to court her, perhaps marry her. She was, after all, the only woman in his life at the time.

'Can I help you, sir?' the head servant asked of Edward as he moved through the corridors.

'Nay, I'm just looking for something I dropped, thank ye.'

'What is it, sir? I'm sure we can find it.'

'It's alright, thank ye. It's just a wee personal thing.'

'Very good, sir,' the servant replied, standing his ground.

It was clear there were boundaries to be respected, even for a guest. Edward took the hint and retreated.

He had seen enough of the kitchen area to know Rania was not there, so he made for the door to the garden. She often had duties that took her to the outside area. In fact, the garden had been a favourite place for them to meet. In his daydreaming, he had imagined them meeting up there. He would share his experiences since their last meeting. She in turn would listen attentively, offer her sympathies for the tragedy and her admiration for his bravery.

He searched every corner of the manicured, floral grounds but Rania was nowhere to be found, not even in that secret place where they had met in the hollow of a large cedar tree. Disappointment was now verging on despair. He could not bear the thought of not seeing her but he had no more energy left to search further.

He went inside and climbed the stairs.

'Ah, there ye are, lad. I was wondering where ye'd got to. Where've ye been then?'

'Nowhere, Da. I just needed a wee bit of fresh air.'

'So is yer friend here then?'

Edward said nothing. Thomas saw the sullen look, threw his towel on the bed and moved to give him a hug.

'What is it lad?'

'I canna find her.'

Thomas knew who he was talking about but could not remember her name.

'Have ye asked anyone where she is?'

'Nay, but I ken I'd find her if she was here. I ken she'd be waiting for me.'

'Well, why dinna we both go down and ask someone?'

'Really Da? Would ye do that? I ken ye disapproved.'

'Nay lad. I dinna disapprove. I ken I've been a wee bit overprotective of ye, and I'm sorry for that. So why dinna ye have a quick clean up and then we'll go and say, *d'ye ken where the young lass …?*'

'Rania.'

'Aye, exactly. D'ye ken where the young lass, Rania, is because my lad here wishes to speak with her?'

Edward threw some water over his face and hands and rubbed some through his hair. Cleaning up was of the least importance. They made their way down the stairs, Edward having to slow down to help his father.

They entered the corridor that led to the servants' quarters. The head servant, hearing them coming, stepped out from the kitchen area.

'Good evening, Colonel, can I assist you?'

'Aye, pardon our intrusion but I wonder if it'd be possible to speak with the young lass, Rania.'

'Rania Asfour?'

Thomas looked to Edward. He nodded.

'Aye, Rania Asfour. Would it be possible to see her?'

'I'm sorry, Colonel, but Miss Asfour has left the Commission. She's in preparation for her marriage.'

—ᴍ—

Edward moped around the Commission for the next three weeks. His first reaction had been to find Rania and try and talk her out of something he was certain she did not want. Then he found out she was hundreds of miles away, with an aunt and uncle who were the matchmakers. Desperation led to despair.

'Why'd she nay tell me?'

'Perhaps she dinna ken herself, lad.'

'But she must've ken. How could she nay?'

'It's another world, lad. It took me *uine mhor* to realise there are many differences. Things can happen quickly, unexpectedly, here, and women in particular dinna have that much say over what happens to them.'

'Aye, but from what people were saying, this dinna happen overnight. She must've ken but she kept it from me. Why would she do that? We talked about so many things and I ken we were really *sonraichte*.'

The conversation went around and around and there was no consoling a young man who felt betrayed.

—ᨊᨊ—

As time neared for going back on the Mediterranean, Edward began having nightmares.

'Careful Charlie; Charlie, Charlie,' he would call in the middle of the night.

'Laddie, laddie, wake up; it's alright. What was it this time?'

'The same one, Da. Charlie's standing on the edge of a huge, black hole. He starts to fall backwards and I try to save him but I canna. He's staring at me as though it's my fault but it's nay my fault. I'm trying to save him.'

'Of course it's nay yer fault and ye ken that Charlie'd nay want ye feeling that way. He cared for ye and he'd nay want ye to be making yerself miserable. Ye just have to do the best with yer own life now, d'ye ken? So ye can honour his memory. D'ye ken what I mean?'

The only good that was coming from Edward's traumas was that Thomas was given no space for worrying about his own debilitation. He knew his son would eventually get over his hurt about Rania but he was not sure how he would cope with the guilt over Charlie's death.

—⚉—

Once they were at sea, Edward made himself available for cabin boy duties. He let the captain know that he had served in His Majesty's Navy as a boatswain's mate so working as a cabin boy on a clipper was a demotion he would gladly suffer. He worked hard through the day and sometimes at night and would come to the cabin exhausted to sleep soundly until his next round of duty. As he fell asleep, he would remember Charlie and thank him for all he had taught him. He took some comfort in feeling Charlie was with him, perhaps living on through him.

Christmas came and went while they were at sea, as did New Year, 1790.

Thomas's health regressed as the sea journey wore on. All the recuperative effects of the weeks in Alexandria were lost on a rough journey on a ship with fewer comforts than normal.

'Are ye awake, Da?' Edward whispered as he stepped into the cabin.

'Aye lad. Can ye see the Rock yet?'

'Nay, but they tell me it canna be long now. Are ye alright?'

'Aye, of course.'

—⚉—

'Da, ye can see it now. D'ye wanna come up on deck?'

The clipper sailed into Gibraltar Harbour and in no time they were disembarking.

Thomas was exhausted as he walked along the wharf heading

to the guesthouse he had stayed in before. He was looking forward to resting up for a few days.

'Da, look, it's the *Stirling*,' Edward shouted.

HMS Stirling was a few boats along, clearly preparing to sail. Edward ran ahead.

'Hold yer horses, laddie. We dinna ken that's our ship.'

'I just wanna see it again, Da,' Edward called back, running further ahead.

Thomas hobbled after him, fearful of losing sight of his son on the busy thoroughfare.

Edward reached the bottom of the gangplank and halted, remembering there was a protocol to boarding a Royal Navy ship. Thomas finally caught up and they stood looking up.

'D'ye wish to come aboard, Colonel?' a voice with a memorable Scottish brogue boomed out.

Commodore MacGregor was standing on the edge of the bridge looking over towards them. They could not see him clearly because the sun was behind him.

'Aye, aye, sir,' Edward shouted before Thomas could reply.

'Speaking for yer Da still, I see.'

'Is it alright if we come aboard?' Thomas shouted.

'Indeed it is; welcome aboard,' MacGregor replied, stepping down from the bridge and heading for the gangplank.

'So tell me now what ye've been up to.'

—⚓—

HMS Stirling was setting sail the next day and MacGregor made it clear he would be happy if they could join him for the trip to Portsmouth. Thomas expressed some doubt, sensing his weakened body needed some time ashore.

'But I could be back for my birthday if we go now,' Edward said.

'How can ye say nay to that, Colonel? And I want to see just how *math* this boatswain's mate really is.'

'Can I really be yer boatswain's mate, sir?'

'Well, we'll have to see; perhaps ye can show me how well ye do as a cabin boy first.'

'I'll do anything ye want, sir, as long as I dinna have to sit around nay doing anything.'

'Well, I can guarantee that'll nay be allowed. But first we have to get yer Da's permission. What d'ye say, Colonel?'

'Do I have any choice? I must say it's *coibhneil* of ye, Commodore, to invite us and I canna ken a better way to get home. I suppose I was just hoping to have a few days to rest up.'

'Colonel, I'll make sure ye have the maximum comfort the *Stirling* can provide. As it happens, the guest quarters that were taken by Doctor Prewett on the way over are vacant. They'll be a wee bit more comfortable than the galley quarters ye had on the way over. And I promise not to press ye into service as a second cabin boy – unless ye really want to, of course.'

Edward broke into gales of laughter.

'What can I say?' Thomas said. 'It's a *fialaidh* offer and we accept.'

'Yay, Da. I love ye Da,' Edward shouted, grabbing his father around the neck.

'Steady lad. Ye almost knocked me out – again.'

—∿—

HMS Stirling sailed into Portsmouth on the 21st day of January, 1790. The father and son had been away from England for the best part of eight months.

'*Taing do dhia* – thank the Laird to be home,' Thomas muttered as the gangplank was being attached.

Edward had a few more cabin boy duties to dispense before they could disembark. MacGregor had explained along the way that he could not technically be a boatswain's mate because he was not enlisted in the navy. To compensate, MacGregor endowed him with the title "Senior Cabin Boy".

'Thank ye again, Angus, for all yer consideration,' Thomas said, extending his hand.

'It's been a pleasure, Colonel. If there's ever anything else I can do for ye and yer lad, just let me ken.'

After a brief pause, as if wondering if he should say it, he spoke so Edward could not hear.

'And if I might be so *dana*, Thomas, please do take care of yerself. I'm nay sure sailing is the best thing for ye these days.'

'Thank ye, Angus. I ken ye might be *ceart*.'

The two men shook hands again.

'And as for ye, lad,' MacGregor raised his voice and turned to Edward. 'I hope to see ye back here as an enlisted sailor one day. How does that sound?'

'I canna wait, sir,' Edward replied, saluting.

XVI

he two travellers arrived in Pemberton on the evening of the 25th
of January, the day before Edward's birthday.

'How are you, my darling boy?' Sarah said as Edward bounded from the carriage.

'Bonnie, Ma,' he replied, racing to her and giving her a hug.

'How's my laddie?' Emma shouted as Edward turned and raced to her. 'Oh my heavens, how ye've grown since ye've been away.'

Edward hugged Emma and then shook Will's hand.

'My, my, that's a man's handshake if ever I've had one,' Will said, wringing his hand.

Sarah had hastened to the carriage, expecting Thomas would have already stepped out. Emma was in hot pursuit.

'How are you, my love? It's so good to see you,' Sarah said, stepping up on the running board.

'Aye, and it's more than bonnie to see ye, my darling.'

'Well, I hope ye're nay going to sit there all evening,' Emma said.

'Nay, Ma. Just give me a wee moment.'

Will had reached the carriage and realised Thomas needed help to get down. He reached past the two women and offered his arm. Thomas took it gratefully and heaved himself out of the seat. With Will on one side and Sarah and Emma on the other, he was able to step down.

'Thank ye, thank ye. It's nay as bad as it looks. Which paddock did ye say needs ploughing?'

'Oh my heavens, lad, why dinna ye tell us ye were in such a *dona* way?' Emma said. 'I'm sorry. I nay should treat ye like ye're a bairn but I'm yer *mathair*, so ye'll have to forgive me.'

'I forgive ye, Ma.'

They managed to help Thomas inside and into a chair. There was no way he was climbing the stairs that night so they brought a tub down for him to wash, then helped him to the table for supper. They spent an hour or two recounting all that had happened. Edward did most of the talking.

'Well, ye'd better to bed, laddie, or there'll nay be any birthday for ye tomorrow,' Emma said.

Edward went to his room while Will and Emma set up a bed in the lounge room, pulling two couches together and laying a number of quilts on them.

'There, that'll have to do for tonight, lad,' Emma said. 'Hopefully ye'll be able to get to yer bedroom tomorrow night. I'm *ceart* Sarah'll be happy when ye can be together.'

Thomas and Sarah looked at each other and smiled. Will grinned.

'Alright, my darling,' Will said, taking Emma by the arm. 'We need to go and leave these young people to themselves.'

They left the room.

'So, are ye going to leave me here on my own all night?' Thomas asked Sarah.

'Well, I just might if you don't kiss me right now. And for at least as long as you've been away.'

'That's a right *fada* kiss,' Thomas said, pulling her down on top of him.

'Careful. I don't want to hurt you.'

'Ye can hurt me all ye want. All ye want.'

Thomas would rarely climb the stairs again. The first time he tried it, he had a fall and lay at the bottom of the stairwell for some time until discovered.

Doctors could never pinpoint the clinical problem. They offered diagnoses like "wear and tear", "body decay", "old injuries" and a range of explanations that left the listener wondering what medical doctors actually do during their training. Even when told there was a bullet still in him, somewhere near the kidneys, they could not say for sure whether it was part of the problem or not.

He was advised to exercise as much as possible but not to attempt to ride a horse, run or do anything too strenuous.

'I'm sure a short ride'd be fine,' he said on one occasion.

'Please, Thomas, don't do it,' Sarah said.

'Aye, lad, dinna be more of a fool than ye already are,' Emma added.

'I canna stand being locked up all the time.'

Will intervened and convinced the women that it might do Thomas some good to have a short ride. He knew he was in strife as they watched Thomas toppling from the horse and crashing into the ground before he was even past the gate way.

As far as Sarah and Emma were concerned, that settled it. There would be no more riding or even pretending he might get back to his upstairs bedroom. One of the sitting rooms was converted into a bedroom and that was where Thomas and Sarah slept at night.

—␣—

Sarah had handed over her teaching duties in Eskadale during the time that Thomas and Edward were away. She had anticipated that Thomas might not be able to resume his duties at the Inverness Military College.

General Eastley came to see him several times throughout 1790, hoping his star teacher would eventually come back to the College.

'Of course, I'll be back. Just a few more weeks is all I need,' Thomas said on the first occasion.

'I'll be back; ye just wait and see,' he said on the last occasion.

Eventually, at the behest of Sarah, Emma and even Will, Thomas wrote to Eastley.

Dear General Eastley, I regret to say that my recovery has not been as swift and complete as I had originally hoped. I must therefore submit my resignation from my post at the College. I will forever be grateful for the opportunity you provided me. Yours sincerely, Thomas Lovat.

Eastley, still hopeful that Thomas might make a recovery someday, convinced the army to deem him to be on extended sick leave, rather than de-commissioned. Hence, he remained a colonel but would never make it back to his post nor to Highlands living.

—⁓—

Thomas managed to do some teaching at Will's small school in Pemberton. Reverend Harry Thurlow, Thomas's former headmaster at St Bartholomew's Academy for Boys in Preston, was retired but now chair of the school council. He would call on Thomas from time to time to speak with parents and the wider community.

Be it about the advances of science, the role of the Crown versus liberal democracy or, especially, Christianity as just one of any number of world religions, Thomas's talks often caused some consternation among the listeners. Occasionally, a complaint was made to someone in authority. Still, Thurlow persisted, confident that Thomas's Jacobite heritage and life experiences deemed him a better representative of the world that was coming than were his critics.

Fortunately, there were always enough parents with connections and a strong voice to support Thurlow's view.

'Gentlemen, I'm not sure we are giving either Colonel Lovat or the Reverend Council Chair credit for the breadth of learning available at our Academy,' Mr Herbert Gibbs said at an open meeting of the school council.

Gibbs was the local member of the House of Commons. He belonged to the Whig Party, a liberal by disposition. He was speaking against a move to have Thomas banned from the school, deemed to be a "corrupter of sound Christian and British morality", and Thurlow censured for having supported him.

The move had come after a talk Thomas gave proffering the view that the most recent discoveries of new lands and cultures offered an opportunity for Britons to broaden their understanding of the world in all its differences. While the idea excited some in his audience, others surmised he was just another among the increasing number who failed to grasp the superiority of the British world into which he had been born.

'With respect, Colonel,' one of his critics began, 'I'm quite satisfied that if God had wanted us to know about the artefacts of these places, he would have made sure they were here in England.'

There was a small applause that Thomas ignored. His tired body was robbing him of tolerance for fools. Now it just served to fire him up to say candidly what he might have thought twice about in earlier times. He had nothing to lose.

Most of his audience did not mind and conveyed their interest in his openness to new thought.

Things changed a little, however, when he extended the logic to suggest that the further recent discovery of ancient peoples called into question the idea of God working exclusively in a Christian civilisation, as the church would have it. When he spoke of the importance of Christians coming to know and understand the beliefs of these peoples so they could know better the mind of God, things became heated.

'Are you seriously suggesting that these primitive savages have anything to teach us at all about anything, least of all about God?' one of his erstwhile supporters blurted out.

'I am, sir,' Thomas replied. 'I myself have learned much about the Laird through Islam. I would say, sir, without a doubt, that it was through a Muslim woman that I truly came to understand who the Laird is, both your Laird and mine.'

Thurlow listened as the murmuring grew louder.

'Sir,' one critic began. 'I have to say I find your attitude to be not only seditious but, in this case, blasphemous as well. There is obviously no room for you in God's good church but how you managed to stay in the army and command our forces without being thrown out is beyond me. No wonder our noble forces took such a beating in the Americas, with leaders like you.'

This time, the applause was loud and from what seemed to be a majority. When Thomas attempted to respond, he was silenced by booing.

Hence, the special council meeting was arranged. In light of its purpose, Thurlow had stood aside from his chairmanship and handed it to the headmaster, Mr Mead. Mead was inclined to keep the peace by siding with the majority, regardless of the facts or evidence. Thurlow felt resigned to being sacked as council chair as events were unfolding.

But then came the intervention of Mr Gibbs, who continued his defence.

'I believe we are most fortunate to have had the Reverend Thurlow leading us as both headmaster and council chair over these many years. I also have to offer my personal thanks to Colonel Lovat who was my teacher at this school over twenty years ago. He taught me more in the year or so he was here than any teacher at school or university. He taught me about the world beyond our shores, about ideas of rights and justice I had never pondered, and about the emerging world of science. It was because of him that I entered politics and have fought for the rights of our fellow man.

It was because of him that I sought out Sir Joseph Banks when he returned from Van Diemen's Land and have made sure that he continues to inform our Government about the implications of his findings for Britain's future security. And, gentlemen, I seem to recall how impressed and grateful you all were when Sir Joseph came to speak with our school community about things he had only shared with our Government and Monarch. I think you know this was a rare privilege and, in the end, one for which we were honoured because of one man, the very same one you now wish to ban from ever again stepping into the school gates. Is this truly what you want?'

'Thank you, Mr Gibbs,' Mead said. 'Does anyone else wish to speak?'

There was a moment of silence and then a single hand shot up.

'Headmaster, I wish to commend Mr Gibbs on his fine speech but our job as a council is to safeguard our children's morality and I am still not convinced that Colonel Lovat is a good influence on those children.'

Murmuring and then silence.

'Mr Gibbs, do you have anything more to say?' Mead asked.

'Yes, headmaster. Simply to say that if defending our children's morality has anything at all to do with defending our nation, then, I say with respect to all present that Colonel Lovat has likely done more than anyone here tonight. I think when any of us has gone to defend the Empire, been severely wounded in action, discharged with full honours and even gone back to help in training future officers to defend the Empire, then we might speak against him. But not before!'

Gibbs had spoken from the heart and without faltering. His parliamentary arts came to the fore when needed most. No-one was saying anything but there was much shuffling, stroking of beards, cleaning spectacles and shifting in chairs.

'Does anyone else wish to speak?' Mead asked.

'Mr Mead,' one of the less vocal critics spoke up. 'I propose that we suspend consideration of the ban on Colonel Lovat and the censure of the good Reverend. In proposing that, I further propose that Colonel Lovat be required to submit an outline of any further talks he might give to the parents or children of this school.'

The proposition was endorsed without dissent.

Nonetheless, Thomas never ventured onto the Academy grounds again.

—∞—

'Well, I dinna ever wanna go back there either,' Edward said.

Thomas had just received the verdict on the council's decision. He responded with an outburst about the petty English bourgeoisie he had spent too much of his life dealing with.

'We'll see about that, laddie,' Emma said.

'We'll *nay* see about it,' Edward replied.

'It's alright, Ma. Let the lad have his head,' Thomas said. 'He's nay a bairn any longer.'

Edward had been attending St Bartholomew's since returning from the Middle East. Attending but far from attentive. His mind was elsewhere.

'If you could give me your attention for just a moment,' one teacher said persistently.

'Where is that little brain of yours now, Mr Lovat?' another would say.

'Mr Lovat; calling Mr Lovat,' was the favourite refrain of yet another.

Then there were the more serious disciplinary moments, including one that required Thomas to travel to Preston to meet with Headmaster Mead.

'I'm so sorry, Da,' Edward said, knowing that no travel was easy for his father. 'I'm just nay made for schooling – nay at that posh school anyway!'

'It's alright, lad, ye remind me a wee bit of a young laddie I once ken.'

Edward's declared retirement from St Bartholomew's came as no surprise. The only part of school life he had enjoyed was when his father came to speak. He was as fascinated as any in the audience to hear his father's ideas, learn about his experiences and inevitably soak up the Jacobite spirit that he came to see was never far from the surface. He loved nothing better than when the odd rebellious comment would strike a hostile note in the audience. It was then he came to understand better than ever about the blood that flowed through him.

To see his father taken down by the pompous mob of "bourgeois English", as Thomas used to spit out the phrase, was the final nail in the coffin of Edward's career at St Bartholomew's Academy for Boys.

XVII

'*Thank ye so much for comin' to see me, sirs,*' *Emmaline Shorrock* said. 'Please come in.'

Thomas and Edward stepped over the worn parapet, through a broken door barely hanging on its hinges.

Edward had been pressuring Thomas to let him meet Charlie's next of kin from the time they arrived home. Miss Shorrock, Charlie's guardian, lived on the western-most point of the British Isles, a place called Porthcurno in Cornwall.

'Take a seat. Would ye's like a cuppa?'

'Nay, thank ye,' Thomas replied, noting the rat scurrying for cover.

Edward concurred. He had come back from his travels sensing he had seen "the way the other half live", including the half described widely as "the poor". Nevertheless, nothing he had seen in the barest of hovels or huts in the Middle East could compare with the destitution he was surveying. The floor consisted of a few beams of timber of various sorts scattered across the dirt, placed roughly where the inhabitants were most likely to walk. The only seats were unpolished stool-tops perched on ill-fitting legs. On one wall was a three-legged table, the fourth leg consisting of a stack of mud bricks. Against another wall was an unmade bed that looked as though it had been slept in for months without any attempt to clean it up. The stained mattress was decked with bed clothes piled on one side. On the table, a mouldy piece of bread sat surrounded by crumbs and a few cups, one with a handle, sitting upright or on their side.

The only barely comforting feature was the blazing fire in the hearth.

'Poor li'l mite,' Miss Shorrock said, reaching for a cloth and blowing her nose. 'Charlie was a good lad – ungrateful, I 'ave to say – but a good 'un all the same. I was so sad when I 'eard 'e'd gone to the Lord.'

'Aye, he was a braw lad,' Thomas replied. 'Edward and Charlie were bonnie friends.'

'Oh, I know. I got the few things Charlie left to this world. God bless 'im! 'e kept a li'l notebook; what do they call 'em when ye write somethin' in each day?'

'A diary?' Thomas and Edward echoed.

'That's it – and 'e said 'ow ye were the best mate 'e'd ever 'ad,' Miss Shorrock said, looking at Edward.

'Me? Really?' Edward said, his voice faltering. 'I miss him so much.'

'Charlie saved my lad's life. I'll be forever grateful to him.'

'Oh, ye're lovely people, aren't ye? Not like the toffs I was expectin'.'

'Why would ye be expecting toffs?' Thomas asked.

'It's just the way it is in this country, sir.'

'Well, we're nay really from this country, ye see?'

'I thought yer accent was different. Are ye from over the seas?'

'Nay, it's Scottish; Scottish Highlands in fact,' Thomas replied.

'That explains it then. I've never been; never likely to either. Now let me get somethin' for ye.'

She pulled an old trunk from under the bed, opened it and fossicked around until she found a toy bear. One eye was missing and its hairs were matted and discoloured from too much loving.

'It was Charlie's. It was about the only thing 'e brought with 'im when 'is Mum died and the only thing 'e insisted on takin' with 'im when the authorities took 'im from me. I'm sure 'e'd want ye to 'ave it, young lad.'

'Thank ye so much, Miss Shorrock,' Edward said. 'I'll cherish it – I mean him. What's his name?'

'Just "Bear". That's what 'e called it. So ye can call it anythin' ye like.'

'I'll call him Charlie Bear, then.'

'I think Charlie'd be 'appy with that. Now, it's late; can I offer ye's both a bed for the night?'

Thomas and Edward glanced at each other, mystified as to where they would be put for the night, even if inclined to stay.

'It'll be fine. Ye's two can share the bed and the baby and I'll just curl up next to the fire.'

'Ye have a bairn?' Thomas asked.

'Yeah, but only one at the moment. Sometimes, I 'ave four or five, dependin' on what their mothers are doin' and where their 'usbands are; if they 'ave 'usbands. We 'ave to stick together, we Porthcurnish, ye know?'

'I've heard that about the Cornish,' Thomas said.

'Oh, we're not Cornish; we're Porthcurnish, ye know?'

She moved to the bed and the bedclothes on one side of it, reached down and lifted a sleeping baby from the pile.

'There, ye see. There's plenty o' room for ye.'

XVIII

'So, how auld are ye now, lad?' *MacGregor asked.*

The commodore had arrived unexpectedly. He had diverted to Pemberton on the way from London to Scarborough for a naval conference.

'Almost fourteen and a half,' Edward replied.

'So why are ye nay at sea already, then?'

'I ken I was still too young.'

'Well ye're nay, be assured. The naval base at Scarborough, where I'm heading, is training young men yer age and younger for a naval career.'

The look on Edward's face told them all of his excitement at the idea.

'Angus, we'd be honoured if ye'd be our guest for the night,' Thomas said.

'Ye're far too kind. I ken being a day late to the conference'll nay hurt. I'll just tell them my carriage broke down.'

They all laughed, except Emma.

'But that would be a lie then, Commodore. Would it nay?'

'Aye, Madam, it would. Thank ye for seeing to my immortal welfare.'

Will wondered again at the change in Emma. For most of her life, she had exhibited the rebellious spirit of her heritage. It was one of the things that first attracted him to her. She was the great questioner of established ideas. She had been through the consternation caused by their stand against the church's strictures around their marriage. She had encouraged Sarah to hope for a future with Thomas, even while Sarah was still married – even advising divorce at one point. Yet, here she was quibbling about a small lie from someone she barely knew.

—ɷ—

Two months later, Edward went to Scarborough to train in the Royal Navy as a boatswain's mate, this time a proper one.

Thomas was insistent that he and Sarah accompany him on the journey.

'Are ye certain, lad, it won't be too much for ye?' Emma asked Thomas. 'It'll be the farthest ye've travelled since ye got home.'

'I'll be fine, Ma,' Thomas replied. 'I'll have Sarah with me to tend to my every need.'

'Are ye sure Will and I should nay come as well?'

'Nay, Ma. It'll all be fine.'

'No, Emma, thank you,' Sarah jumped in. 'All will be good!'

Thomas and Sarah had spoken about the excitement of returning to that place where they had first pledged their troth when she returned from France. It would be a chance to re-live some of those happy moments away from the household for a few days. They had booked the same guesthouse for a week, two nights with Edward and then five nights on their own.

'Well, d'ye remember this bed, my faithful wife?' Thomas whispered on their arrival.

Edward was in the next room, settling in.

'No, not at all,' Sarah replied in similar hushed tones. 'Have we been here before, have we?'

Edward spent two months in Scarborough, training as a boatswain's mate. After a short break at home, he was assigned as fourth mate (effectively standing in the shadows of the boatswain's mate) on his favourite Royal Navy vessel, *HMS Stirling*. MacGregor had pulled some strings and asked for Edward to join his ship for a routine voyage to Morocco and back.

'*I wonder if I should look for Rania*,' Edward thought to himself.

It was the night before the crew was to take a short shore leave in Morocco. As it was, he saw plenty of young girls who looked sufficiently like Rania to tear at his heart but, alas, no Rania.

By the time he returned to England, a now seasoned sailor, it was close to Christmas and he had been granted leave to celebrate with his family.

—⚏—

Because they had missed celebrating Christmas with Thomas and Edward the year before, the plan was for the extended family to come together. Owing to Thomas's poorly state, the celebration was to be held at Pemberton. It would be the first time the whole family had been together for many years.

Tommy and Margaret came over from Burnley, just thirty miles away, while Archibald and Jane took the four day journey from Castle Dounie. Tommy and Margaret were childless but Archibald and Jane had three children. Their youngest was William Henry who was just a year or so younger than Edward. They had often played together while Edward was living in the Highlands but had not seen each other for some time. Edward was pleased when he heard that William Henry would be joining his parents. They would have much to talk about.

'I wanna be a boatswain's mate as well,' William Henry said after listening to Edward's recounting his recent travels.

'Well, we'll see about that,' Jane replied.

Jane and Archibald had lost two of their children in infancy, a third, referred to warmly as young Archibald, was incapacitated in an institution in Edinburgh and their eldest son, John, was away with the British Army in Lisbon. Hence, Jane had become very protective of William Henry whom she often referred to as her "baby".

'I'm nay a bairn, Ma. I'm almost grown up.'

'Almost, but not quite.'

Thomas noted how Jane had changed from the fiercely independent woman he had first met and come to know so well in Tripoli all those years ago. He could not have imagined her then as a mother at all, much less the over-protective one he was witnessing.

'William Henry and I are going for a ride,' Edward said.

'Well, not too far now,' Jane cautioned. 'Make sure the horse is not one of those frisky ones. William Henry had a bad fall recently.'

'I'd nay call it *dona*, dear,' Archibald said.

'Aye, a wee stumble was all,' William Henry added.

'Well, just be careful all the same.'

Edward and William Henry rode away at speed, sensing the freedom that came with each mile. They found a grassy sward, tethered the horses to a small tree and sat on a rock looking out over the valley. The lake looked like glass, surrounded by rolling green hills.

'How d'ye stand it?' Edward said. 'Yer Ma, I mean.'

'Aye, I sometimes feel as though I canna relieve myself without her watching me.'

They laughed at the thought.

'So d'ye really want to go to sea?' Edward asked.

'Aye, well, ye make it sound so exciting – and it'd get me out of home. But I'm nay sure Ma would allow it.'

'How would yer Da feel about it? Surely it's up to him in the end.'

'Da will always agree with Ma – but he *can* be sneaky too.'

'What d'ye mean sneaky?'

'Well, he'll nay ever confront Ma but then he'll go and do things behind her back or he'll find some excuse to do something she'd nay want done – but then she does want it done because he's convinced her. He's clever. He's a diplomat, ye ken?'

'Oh, so like what?'

'Well, Ma wants me to stay in school in Inverness but Da talks with her about how he thinks the school's nay *math* enough for me and if I'm going to be a diplomat like him – which is what she wants desperately – then I should go to a different school. Then he talks about Stonyhurst as being so *gu math* and how so many important people have gone there. And so it goes on and, in the end, Ma wants me to go to Stonyhurst.'

'So, will ye?'

'Aye, I ken so, after the summer.'

'Are ye happy with that?'

'Aye, I canna wait. For one thing, I'll be out from under Ma's wings – and I'll be close to ye, at least when ye're home.'

'That'll be grand,' Edward said. 'My Da went to Stonyhurst, ye ken?'

'Oh, aye, I ken. Da tells me about that all the time. Yer Da's his hero, ye ken? Thomas this and Thomas that. Sometimes, Ma gets cross and says, *ye have yer own boys, did ye ken?* Then he gets sad.'

'Why sad?'

'I ken because he dinna ken his own bairns so well. Ma excuses him most of the time – she says he was too busy with his work – but I ken he feels bad, especially about my two dead brothers – and young Archibald. He and Ma have had some really *bronach* times about him.'

'Aye, that's *bronach*,' Edward said. 'But it's braw that yer Da and my Da are so close. I ken my Da thinks yer Da's a bit like *his* Da. My Da never ken his own Da.'

'Yer Da's *fortanach*. My Da's a noble gentleman. That's what everyone says about him. But he's found it *duilich* to be a normal father, ye ken? Ye and yer Da seem close. I wish I could say the same.'

William Henry's voice trailed off.

'Aye, I suppose we are now but it's taken a *fada* time. Our travels together helped. Maybe ye and yer Da should go to Persia.'

—✷—

A few days after Christmas, when the wider family had dispersed, Pemberton received two unexpected visitors, a few hours apart. In the late morning, Commodore MacGregor knocked on the door. A few hours later, Sir Joseph Banks did the same. Neither of the gentlemen knew each other, except that MacGregor knew Banks by reputation, as did most of the British Isles.

They were seated with the family for an afternoon tea.

'What a splendid opportunity,' MacGregor said.

'So, what do you say, young Edward?' Banks asked.

'I canna wait,' Edward replied.

Emma looked to Thomas, then to Sarah and Will, anyone who might stop this headlong surge into unspeakable danger. She had hardly slept during the eight months that Thomas and Edward had been away, and only fitfully while Edward was on his voyage to Morocco. The stress would pale to insignificance compared with the thought of Edward going to New South Wales. As far as she was concerned, it might as well be on the moon.

'How long would the lad be away?' she asked.

'Well, it would be six months there, six months back and several weeks, perhaps three months, in the colony,' Banks replied. 'What would you say, Commodore?'

'Aye, that would be the minimum time, I ken. It depends on the weather and other elements.'

'Aye, like shipwrecks, pirates and wild savages, d'ye mean, gentlemen?' Emma spat out.

'Oh Ma, the lad's in the navy, not in a knitting club,' Thomas said.

Those gathered were not surprised at Thomas's annoyance. They knew he was not well. That was partly why MacGregor and Banks had come to Pemberton this day. They wanted to satisfy themselves that he was not in as poorly a way as had been reported to them.

'Are ye certain there's been no skulduggery here, gentlemen?' Emma asked.

'What on earth do you mean, dear?' Will said.

'Well, I think it's awfully suspicious that Commodore MacGregor should be putting forward the idea of our wee lad going to the other side of the world and then, hot on his heels, Mr Banks comes along with the same idea.'

'Sir Joseph, dear,' Will whispered to his wife.

'*Sir Joseph*,' Emma said. 'My apologies, Mr Banks.'

'I assure ye, Mrs Hartshorne,' MacGregor said. 'I've never met Sir Joseph and I nay had any idea he'd be here today.'

'I concur, Madam,' Banks said. 'I hadn't even thought of the idea. Indeed, I didn't even know young Edward was in the navy until today. But, as I've put before you, I believe that travel on the *Gorgon* is a golden opportunity for a young man with ambition to see the world and broaden his horizons.'

'Aye, and I wanna go, Gran, I surely do,' Edward said.

There was a moment of silence as the players considered their next move.

'Well then, tell us a wee bit more about this Mr Solander, Mr Banks,' Emma said, side-stepping Edward's plea and ignoring Will's correction. 'Is he a reputable gentleman?'

'Oh, Madam, of the very best kind. Carl Solander is the son of Daniel Solander. You might remember that Daniel accompanied me to Preston in '79 when I gave a lecture organised by Thomas. You remember him, don't you, Thomas?'

'I certainly do, Sir Joseph,' Thomas replied, turning to his mother. 'Ma, I dinna believe ye were there but remember I used to organise lectures for the students and others at St Bartholomew's and Sir Joseph and Mr Solander came and presented on their travels to the South Seas with Captain James Cook. Ye remember, Will, dinna ye?'

'Indeed,' Will replied. 'It was one of the best attended of all the lectures; and no wonder. What fascinating discoveries of fauna and flora.'

'I've nay doubt it was,' Emma said. 'So why dinna ye just give young Edward a lecture and then he'll ken all about it without having to risk his *luachmhor* life on that *treubhach* journey?'

Another moment of silence.

'I well understand yer concern, Mrs Hartshorne, I truly do,' MacGregor said. 'But if it's any consolation to ye, I ken Commodore Parker extremely well. There'd nay be a finer commander in the Royal Navy and *HMS Gorgon* is an especially braw ship. It's almost brand new and built for speed. It weighs little more than a thousand tons but still carries an impressive forty-four cannons. I only wish I was commanding it, I must say, but only the very best are chosen for these new ships.'

'Forty-four cannons, did ye say?' Emma said. 'I'm afraid that nay means anything to me, Commodore. But do tell me more about Mr Solander, Mr Banks.'

'Carl is Daniel's son. I've known him from the time he was born. Daniel and I were friends even before we sailed with Cook but we became the closest of colleagues afterwards. Indeed, he was staying at my house in London the night he died. He was only forty-nine and had so much more to give. It was tragic.'

Banks took a gulp of ale and a moment to compose himself. Emma's eyes softened at the sight.

'Young Carl was staying with us as well, so he witnessed the gruesome spectre of his beloved father being carried out of the house with a sheet over his entirety. The poor boy. He adored his father and was so looking forward to going back to the Great Southern Lands to help him with his work. This trip on the *Gorgon*, as part of what's being called the Third Fleet to New South Wales, finally gives him the chance to carry on with that work. He truly is the most thoroughly honourable young man and I just wish my own commitments afforded me the time to go with him.'

'I fully appreciate how ye feel, Sir Joseph,' Thomas said. 'Were I a wee bit fitter, I'd be going as well.'

'Nay, lad. Ye'd nay be going, trust me,' Emma said.

'Well, ye'll nay need to, Thomas,' MacGregor said. 'If young Edward's there, so will be yer spirit.'

'Indeed, it will,' Thomas said, looking at his son.

'Aye, Da. Ye'll be with me. Ye always are.'

XIX

O n the 15th day of March, 1791, the fifteen year-old Edward sailed out of Portsmouth, heading for New South Wales. He was thrilled to be on one of the Royal Navy's sleekest ships. The Adventure Class, *HMS Gorgon*, was far smaller than the likes of *HMS Stirling* and *Repulse*, consisting of a mere two-decks, forty-four cannons and a relatively small complement of three hundred, including just thirty convicts. The *Gorgon's* main charter was to deliver goods and a new marine corps to the colony. It was, as MacGregor had said, built for speed, rather than battle. As such, it should take only six months, rather than eight or nine, fair weather allowing.

Edward had hoped to receive a commission as boatswain's mate, also known as second mate. But, granted the length and complexity of the *Gorgon's* role as part of the Third Fleet, it required a third mate, a role he was more than happy to fill. Granted his excitement at going to the South Seas, he would have settled for being cabin boy.

Edward was also given a second responsibility. He was to serve as Carl Solander's assistant in his work in collecting the various flora that would be shipped back to England.

MacGregor and Banks had managed most of these arrangements between them.

—⁓—

'I think ye should get yer own meal, *sir*,' Edward replied to boatswain's mate, Bernard Grovely.

'D'ye wanna court martial for sedition, boy?' Grovely replied.

'If ye ken what I'm doing is seditious, by all means, *sir*.'

Grovely was a bare year older than Edward but his father and grandfather had been boatswains and so he thought he owned the trade. He was short but nuggety, with eyes that seemed too big for their sockets and ears too large for his small, misshapened head.

'I dinna ken I'm here to serve ye,' Edward said. 'I'm here to assist ye in assisting the boatswain but at this point I canna see that ye've been doing any assisting at all. I might as well be boatswain's mate because I'm the only one doing the job – sir.'

'Careful what ye say, Lovat. My Pa knows Commodore Parker and 'e could make life 'ell for ye.'

'Thank ye for the warning, sir. Now, I ken ye'd better go and get yer meal before ye miss out and starve – that *would* be a shame!'

'Ye're a cheeky toff. Ye think ye're better than the rest of us just 'cause your grandpa was a Scottish 'ero – more like a Scottish traitor, I'd say.'

Edward could sense a couple of sailors pressing against him from behind, edging him towards Grovely. It was the same move that Grovely had orchestrated on the first night out to sea, now five weeks ago. On that occasion, Grovely had confronted him with the fact that Edward's first duty would be to do everything Grovely commanded. According to him, that was what a third mate did – serve the second mate. When Edward questioned it, his two arms were pinned from behind while Grovely landed a solid punch to his midriff, leaving him decked and winded.

'Oh, and ye'll call me *sir*!' Grovely had said as he and his mates walked away, laughing.

Edward had been careful since then to attend to the boatswain, Mr Bush, taking orders directly from him and avoiding Grovely where possible.

'What are ye doin', Lovat? 'o ordered ye to do that?' Grovely would ask.

'The boatswain, *sir*!'

'Ye're not supposed to speak with Mr Bush. Ye speak with me. Understand?'

'I dinna speak with him, *sir*. He spoke with me.'

It did not take long for Edward to work out that he knew the boatswain's mate's job better than Grovely. It took Boatswain Bush even less time to work it out. He began treating Edward as though he was his second mate, fuelling Grovely's anger. The bullying increased.

'So ye're going to get yer mates to pin my arms again so their cowardly mate can hit me without his pretty face getting hurt. Is that the game, is it, Mr Grovely? Cowards unite?'

Grovely was on his feet and taking a swing before his mates could restrain Edward's arms. Edward saw the fist coming, ducked to the right and down and, as he had been taught by his father, used the ducking as the beginning of a circular movement upwards, right fist at the ready and accelerating with the motion towards Grovely's lower jaw. He hit him with the uppercut. Grovely was flat on his back and unconscious before he saw anything coming.

Edward turned and took a step back, both fists ready to engage Grovely's mates.

'So which of ye wants to join yer friend first?'

The two sailors bolted. Edward ordered a third sailor to help him lift Grovely back to his bunk. He made sure he was breathing and left him to sleep it off.

'So, where's Mr Grovely?' Boatswain Bush asked the next day. 'I heard there was a scuffle below deck. Would ye know anything about that, Mr Lovat?'

'I ken Mr Grovely might've stumbled and hit his head, sir.'

'Stumbled, did ye say? Onto an uppercut perhaps?'

'Perhaps, sir!'

'Just don't let him get under yer skin, d'ye hear?'

'Aye, sir.'

'Now, Mr Lovat, as Mr Grovely's indisposed, ye'll have to help me guide the ship into port. We arrive in Dakar today. The port's called *Plage des Amoureux* which, I gather, means "Lovers' Beach". Maybe ye'll be lucky on yer shore leave. But ye'll only have two days to be lucky and most of that time ye'll be with me overseeing re-supply.'

It was clear Edward's time to find a lover would be limited. Not that he minded. Short of seeing Rania at the foot of the gangplank, he really was not interested. Least of all was he taken with the idea of visiting a brothel, as many of the crew were loudly anticipating. He was fifteen and, by navy rules, allowed to spend his time in such pursuits, as well as drink. But his interests were elsewhere, especially since coming under the influence of Carl Solander.

—⁂—

'I wonder if Mr Lovat could be freed for a few hours to accompany me to the hills behind the beach,' Solander asked Commodore Parker.

'I'm sure Mr Bush could manage without him this afternoon. Would that be alright, Mr Bush?'

Parker glanced in the boatswain's direction.

'As long as he's back by sundown, sir.'

'Thank you both,' Solander said as he hurried off to tell Edward the news.

Carl Solander had never been to Africa but had been intrigued by some of the notes left by his father and Sir Joseph Banks about their earlier discoveries of African plant life.

'I'm sure this is what my father called "the Persian Shield",' Solander shouted to Edward as he rushed towards the most starkly purple object either of them had ever seen. 'My father describes it here in his notebook: *a richly endowed purple leaf atop bottle green storks*. And here's the leaf he pasted into his book. See, it's faded but one can see the same patterns.'

'Aye, it's beautiful. So did yer father and Sir Joseph come to Dakar then?'

'No, I don't believe they landed here at all. I'm not sure what their first stop was but I know most of his African findings were further south.'

'So we're the first botanists to discover these plants here?'

Solander looked amused.

'Yes, I believe we might be the first two botanists to have discovered these. Other than the millions of Africans before us, mind you.'

'Oh, I'm sorry, Mr Solander. Of course.'

'That's alright, Mr Lovat. I do believe I'm the first Swedish botanist and you the first English botanist to discover them here.'

'I dinna consider myself a botanist, Mr Solander, nor indeed English.'

'Is that so? But I'm sure you'd like to be both.'

'Well, a botanist, aye, but nay English. I'm a Highlander and proud of it.'

Amidst their banter, they moved as quickly as they could through the foliage, taking samples and Edward making the notes that Solander was directing.

'I can see why my father was so fascinated with African flora. I've never seen anything so beautiful.'

'Aye, it's another world, is it nay? Ye ken, my Da and I saw similar colours in Persia but I dinna take much notice. It's only because I'm with ye that I'm noticing now.'

'So, I suppose you saw Persian Shield in Persia, surely?' Solander asked.

'Aye, I must've, but I dinna remember.'

'I was the same as a boy. I only began to notice what was around me because of my father's work. Sadly, my interest only peaked after he was gone.'

'Aye, I suppose nay any of us appreciates our parents until it's a wee bit too late.'

In the following weeks, the two spent much of their spare time together. Solander was fascinated with Edward's stories about the Jacobites, the plight of the Highlands and his adventures with his father to Persia. On Edward's side, the fascination was mainly with Solander's stories of his father's travels with Banks and Cook and, especially, with anything to do with the plant life of the world.

Solander became something of a stand-in father figure *cum* older brother for Edward, while Edward for him was a protector. There was less than a decade between them in age but a world of difference in their temperament and worldly-wise ways. Like his father, Solander was the academic type, focussed almost solely on his plant life. He was pale and slight, his ruffled fair hair always in his eyes, strands of it invariably between his pupils and the rimless, ever-grimy spectacles that looked as though they had been given to him at birth. As such, he was the butt of many jokes and could have been bullied had Edward not taken it on himself to protect him.

'Leave him be,' he would say if he caught any of the sailors teasing.

'And that goes for ye as well, *sir*,' he said once to Grovely, now with too much time on his hands.

'I don't want to be a bother to you, Edward,' Solander said.

'Ye're nay bother to me at all, Carl. Ye're helping me work out what I wanna do with my life.'

'I thought you wanted to be a sailor. You're obviously good at it. I've heard Mrs Parker say the commodore thinks you're the best young sailor on board.'

'Truly? Mrs Parker said that?'

'Yes, she did, and I'm sure she's the most reliable source about her husband's opinions. Indeed, I'm fairly certain she *provides* him with his opinions.'

Mary Beth Parker, the Commodore's wife, came from a well-to-do London family. She was in her early twenties, almost two decades younger than her husband. She stood out on the ship, being the only female aboard who was not a convict. Much to the commodore's chagrin, she moved freely across the social classes aboard. Her lean and shapely figure, invariably dressed as one would in high society, and her light brown hair pulled back neatly under an amply shading hat, made for quite a talking point among the sailors.

It was not always seemly talk.

It quickly became known that anything that was said to her would find its way back to her husband. If she liked what she heard, it would come out in an act of benevolence from him. If she did not like it, the result might be a retribution. Either way, everyone became cautious about the advice they gave her.

Solander had a particular way with Mary Beth and this served Edward's interests as well. Bush had made a passing comment to Solander about Edward's proficiency, one that Solander mentioned to Mary Beth who, in turn, told the commodore. He, in turn, had confirmed it with Bush and so Edward's status was assured.

In time, Mary Beth became a confidant of both Solander and Edward and spent whatever spare time the three of them could find talking about their journey and how they could make the most of it. Like Edward, she became fascinated with Solander's work and wished to join them on their botanical work when next in port.

—⟋⟍—

It was several weeks later that the ship berthed at Kapstadt on Africa's southernmost point.

'This is so exciting for me,' Solander said to Mary Beth. 'My father was here on his way back from the South Seas. I have copious notes of his time here with Sir Joseph.'

The ship was in port for five days and on two of those days, Edward, Solander and Mary Beth spent many hours exploring the flora lying not far from the shore. On one of the days, they borrowed horses and rode into the mountains to see a different variety of plant life. Solander had negotiated with Commodore Parker to have one of the convicts join them. He had noticed something about him in the manifest that was of interest. Parker had agreed but only on the basis that a soldier, Private Bushell, would accompany them.

'Mrs Parker, Mr Lovat, this is Angus Fraser,' Solander said. 'He and his father worked on an estate in Ireland where certain species of African plant life have been grown. I thought it would be useful to have him along.'

'I know about Mr Fraser, Mr Solander,' Mary Beth replied. 'I have received strict instructions from my husband to have nothing to do with him.'

For a moment, they were left thinking this was all a bad idea.

'But, as I'm not accustomed to obeying my husband, I'm delighted to meet you, Mr Fraser,' Mary Beth said, extending her hand.

Mary Beth and Fraser gazed at each other, just long enough for each to make a judgement about the other. She was struck by the deep blue of his eyes circled by reddening from too many tears. His long, scorched auburn hair and muscular frame spoke of long days of hard outside work. She could not see the criminal in him.

Fraser noted the warmth in her eyes. Since being caught stealing food from the estate kitchen some months before, he had experienced little human kindness. He had been brutalised and tormented by a show trial. No amount of explaining, pleading or positive testimonies could impede a magistrate out to make an example of him.

'Thank ye, Ma'am,' Fraser replied, casting his eyes down and extending his hand only as far as Mary Beth's fingertips.

'And I'm Edward Lovat, Mr Fraser,' Edward said, grabbing Fraser's hand to ensure a firmer greeting. 'I have to say Angus Fraser dinna sound like an Irish name.'

'Nay, sir, my Da's Scottish. From the Highlands. He and Ma came to Ireland for work during the Clearances, and that's where my sister and I were born.'

'Aye, I thought that might be the case. I'm a Scot too, only I was born in Lancashire, for much the same reason.'

'Oh, aye, sir, I ken about yer family. My Da always talked about Edward Lovat, the *sgoinneil* Jacobite. He always thought we were somehow related.'

'Well, that's not me, of course. My Grand Da was Edward. He died at Culloden, the same day my Da was born.'

'Oh, my,' exclaimed Mary Beth. 'What a tragedy. I had no idea.'

'It's alright. I dinna have many opportunities to talk about it. In England, anyone with Jacobite blood's called a traitor, even if he was nay born at the time, so I learned to keep things to myself.'

'I ken what ye mean, sir, if I might be so bold,' Fraser said. 'Even in Ireland, it's a bit the same. My Da used to say, *just remember, lad, ye have nay friends here. The English will hate ye for one reason and the Irish for another. Just ken who ye are on the inside and cling to that.*'

'Good advice, Mr Fraser,' Edward replied. 'I ken yer Da and mine'd get on well. Where did ye grow up, then?'

'In Listellick, sir. That's where the estate is my Da works on – and where I worked until ...'

There was an awkward silence while he regained his composure.

'That's alright, Mr Fraser,' Edward said. 'Ye're among friends here.'

'I don't think that's altogether correct, sir,' Private Bushell butted in. 'With the greatest respect, this man's a felon and ain't to be trusted. I'm under strict instructions ...'

'Yes that will be fine, Private,' Mary Beth said. 'I'm sure between us we can manage Mr Fraser.'

Mary Beth looked in Fraser's direction and he noted again the warmth in her eyes, this time matched with the kindliest smile he had seen in months. Fraser was only a little older than Edward, perhaps sixteen. He had never been out of his mother's care before falling foul of the law. The smile of a caring woman was a tonic.

'Aye,' Edward agreed, placing his hand on Fraser's shoulder. 'And he is after all a relative of mine. Any Fraser from the Highlands has to be.'

—⁓—

'This is what he called the King Protea,' Solander called out, some distance away from the others. 'And there is the Funchal. I recognise them from my father's descriptions. Edward, bring the notebook here quickly.'

'Aye, we grew the Funchal in a glasshouse in Listellick,' Fraser said. 'But they were never as rich in colour as this.'

'Oh, I know,' Mary Beth said. 'I could not have believed such colours existed. I know now what I've always called yellow or red or orange were but some paltry shadow of them.'

'Aye,' Fraser replied. 'My Da was always disappointed with the colours he'd get in the glasshouse. We always thought they were beautiful but he ken somehow they were nay like the real thing. I'm nay sure how he ken that but he was surely *deas*.'

They stopped every few hundred yards to take in an even more eye-catching vista. Fraser directed their movements while Solander filled in bits and pieces of knowledge from his father's log. Edward continued making notes while Mary Beth kept up a running commentary on the beauty of it all. Fraser's practical and Solander's scientific insights combined well in explaining why one species needed certain soil and much water to thrive while others grew in rock that meant the water that could damage them would run off.

—⟶—

'So, where did ye learn all these things?' Edward asked Solander one evening on the deck. 'Just from yer Da?'

'Oh, much from my father but I also studied agronomy at Uppsala.'

Edward and Mary Beth looked at each other.

'Agro what?' Mary Beth asked.

'What's Uppsala?' Edward added.

'Well, let me answer the easy one first,' Solander laughed. 'Uppsala is in Sweden. I studied at the university there. My father was keen for me to go there even though he was in England at the time.'

'Well, I admit I did know where Uppsala was,' Mary Beth said. 'It was the other word I didn't understand.'

'Agronomy,' Solander said. 'It's a new science – in a way. Or at least the name is. It's the study of plant production, soil conservation, how to grow the best kinds of crops and plants in the soils and other surfaces – like waterbeds – that you have for growing. Of course, it's not really new because people have been doing this for a long time – including native peoples. But now we know a lot more and it's become its own science.'

'So, is that what your father studied too?' Mary Beth asked.

'No, he was what's called a natural historian. He understood a lot about the science of agronomy but he also knew about the history of the people who sowed the crops and how the plant life became part of their culture. He had an amazing knowledge not only of the science but of the people. When he came back from the South Seas, I was only a small boy but I remember being transfixed with his stories of the very different kinds of people and how they would bedeck themselves with the flora and speak of a plant as sacred. I think I decided then that I had to come on a trip like this and see it all for myself.'

'So, why didn't you study natural history then?' Mary Beth asked.

'Well, it was my father. Uppsala was the first university to have a specialised study in agronomy and he wanted me to be among the first to really understand the science of it all because that's the knowledge the world will need as we expand our horizons. *It's not all just about beautiful flowers*, he used to say. *As Europeans go to strange places and settle there, they'll have to learn how to grow crops in very different environments.* I hear him saying it now. Almost all European colonies have suffered from starvation at some point because the settlers didn't know how to grow what they needed.'

'Well, how true that is,' Mary Beth said. 'From what my husband tells me, the latest reports from New South Wales are of near famine and disease. Not only are the convicts not being properly fed but even some of the authorities are struggling to feed themselves. That's why we're carrying all this stock and feed.'

'I feel for poor Angus then,' Edward said. 'Why are we taking more prisoners to a place that canna provide for those already there? How many are we carrying altogether?'

'Thirty,' Mary Beth said. 'But that's only the beginning. We're not really a convict ship. We're mainly taking goods and reinforcements for a new New South Wales Corps. The other ships of the Fleet are carrying hundreds of prisoners.'

'That seems inhuman,' Edward said.

'Between you and me,' Mary Beth continued, 'I'm not certain anyone back in England really cares. Out of sight, out of mind, you know?'

—◊—

On the last day ashore, Private Bushell was indisposed with a mild tropical fever. Mary Beth took it on herself to tend to him, though he had done nothing to endear himself to the group. Not for the first time did they wonder that the more decent human beings aboard might well be among the convicts, whereas many of those going to the penal colony to oversee them for the sake of "civilised society" seemed to be lowlife. While Mary Beth was helping this particular lowlife under the shade of a tree and Carl Solander was gathering the last of the samples he needed, Edward took the opportunity to have a few words with Fraser as they stood under the shade of a tree.

'So, ye stole some stuff, did ye? Is that why ye're here?'

'Aye, I stole some food and a blanket.'

'Were ye hungry then, or cold?'

'Nay, it was nay for me.'

'Who then?'

'Oh, I've been over this so many times in my head. Please dinna tell anyone because I have to protect my sister. Amy's the bravest lass but she sometimes does senseless things. There was this man who was on the run and she was hiding him in the fowl yard and stealing food for him. When I found out, I roused at her. I said, *ye'll get the whole family into trouble.* I told her to stop; she'd have to tell him to leave. She dinna like that and we quarrelled. In the end, she could see what I was saying but she said, *I have to get him some food and a blanket.* So, I said I'd get it if that'd be the end of it. And, of course, I got caught. The only time I tried anything like that, I got caught.'

'So did ye explain what'd happened?'

'Aye, at least as much as I could without getting Amy into trouble. She wanted to tell the magistrate it was her all along but the thought of her being thrown in prison or, worse still, being on one of these boats ... I could nay bear it. I might survive; she'd nay have.'

'That's so brave of ye.'

'Nay. She's family and she'd do the same for me. My Ma and Da were heartbroken when I was sentenced to the colony but they both thanked me for protecting Amy.'

'So, how long will ye be there?'

'Seven years. Maybe I can get some time off for good behaviour.'

'Oh my Laird. For a bit of food and a blanket. What would ye get for murder?'

'Aye, I might as well have murdered a few of the Redcoats while I was at it. I canna say I've nay been tempted.'

'Aye, perhaps ye could start with Bushell. I might give ye a hand.'

They laughed.

'So where's that estate, did ye say? Liste...?' Edward asked.

'Listellick. It's nay far from Tralee.'

'Tralee? That's the one part of Ireland I ken well. My Da has friends there and I've gone there often over the years.'

'Well, would ye do me a favour, sir? If ye're ever there again, would ye look up my family and make sure they're alright and tell them ye met me on the boat? They'd be *air biorhan*. It's so hard on them, my Ma and Da. I dinna ken I'll ever see them again. And Amy feels so *dona* about what happened.'

Edward rested his hand on his back.

'Consider it done. I'll make a point to get there as soon as I'm home.'

'Thank ye, sir.'

'Ye can call me Edward, though nay in earshot of Bushell.'

'What do ye think ye're doin' there, Fraser?' Bushell was shouting as he raced towards them. 'Ye get yer 'ands off that fine gentleman.'

Bushell had the butt of his rifle raised as if to strike Fraser. Edward wrestled the weapon from him.

'He dinna have his hands on me, Private. I had my hands on him.'

'Yes, sir,' Bushell said, snatching the rifle back.

'Time for ye to go back where ye belong,' Bushell shouted at Fraser, pointing the rifle in the direction of the ship. 'If *that's alright* with *Mr Lovat*.'

'Aye, time for us all to go back to the ship anyway,' Edward said, beckoning to Mary Beth and Solander.

—〰—

Edward made several attempts to speak with Fraser on the next leg of the journey but the sergeant-at-arms was insistent that no-one on board should speak with the convicts. Even Mary Beth's cajoling of her husband to change the sergeant's mind did not work this time.

'I think my husband thinks we've been a little too familiar with him,' she said to Edward. 'British officers stick to each other like glue, you know.'

—〰—

The next port of call was the Dutch East Indies town of Batavia. The ship berthed there for four days. Edward could be spared for only a few hours on the third day.

'I dinna ken I've ever been so resentful,' he said when his friends asked if he had missed them on their first two ventures ashore.

'Well, maybe you're more of an agronomist than a sailor,' Mary Beth said. 'I don't think my husband or any sailor would prefer roaming through flower beds than being at sea.'

'Perhaps I am,' Edward said. 'Perhaps I am.'

XX

The *Gorgon* sailed into Port Jackson, New South Wales, on the 21st of September, 1791. It was six months and two days since it had left Portsmouth.

Except for the convicts and their guards, almost everyone was up on deck to take in the view. Those freed of immediate duties scurried from one side to the other to note the tall craggy cliff faces on either side of the Heads. The rocky entry on a chilly spring morning gave way to a warm calm they had not experienced in six months. It was as though they had entered upon a giant, enclosed pool, one whose sides expanded with each few yards of the ship's passage.

'My word, this has to be the finest harbour anywhere,' Parker said to his first officer.

'And well done to you, sir.'

Parker knew what the comment meant. Unlike many ships in the first fleets, the *Gorgon* did not have to spend time in quarantine. This was a feather in the cap of its commander who, unusually for the time, delivered his crew, passengers and thirty convicts in the same number that had left Portsmouth six months before, each of them disease-free.

As the ship approached Sydney Cove, the picturesque scenes gave way to a look of squalor. The fresh air of sea mist and gum tree was gradually replaced with the stench of acrid smoke, human and animal odour and more than a hint of cheap alcohol. The closer they came, the more obvious the plight of the place became.

'One wonders what British settlement has done for this place,' Mary Beth said to Solander.

'I dare say you'll be keeping those views to yourself,' he replied.

'Except at night in bed,' she said, smiling.

As the ship berthed, preparations were underway to disgorge the passengers and convicts to their proper place of abode. For the convicts, this meant more chains until such time as they could be assigned to a work gang. For Mary Beth, it meant accommodation in the Governor's residence, with her husband when he was not required on the ship. She had arranged with him that he should see if Carl Solander could stay with them in the residence. She was after all intent on accompanying him whenever possible on his forays into the bush.

'You must come with us anytime we go,' Mary Beth said to Edward.

'Aye, I'd love to but I'm nay sure yet just what my duties are.'

'Well, do come around to Government House when you know.'

'I'm nay sure I can just roll up to the Governor's House.'

'I'll make sure you get an invitation as soon as possible,' Mary Beth said, reaching forward and giving him a gentle kiss on the cheek. 'I've so enjoyed our times together. I'd love to meet your father sometime when we're home.'

'Thank ye Mary Beth,' Edward replied, blushing from her familiarity in front of the crew. 'It's been a braw highlight for me too.'

'And that means it was good, I hope?' Mary Beth laughed.

'It was good.'

Edward reflected how fortunate Parker was to have a wife like Mary Beth.

It was several days before Edward could leave the ship. Mr Bush had been happy to see Grovely off the boat altogether. Edward was his boatswain's mate and the one he wanted beside him in his duties of standing the ship down.

Edward was about to disembark when he was called to Commodore Parker's cabin.

'Mr Lovat, I need you to form a small party and row out to the *Active*,' Parker said.

'Ah, certainly, sir. The *Active*, did ye say?'

'Yes, the *Active* is part of our fleet though we've never sighted her. She left almost a fortnight after us but has arrived only a few days later. Being a convict ship mainly, she didn't make the stops we did.'

'So what would ye have me do, sir?'

'I'm sorry to ask this of you, and I must insist you do not tell my wife who I know is fond of you, almost as a younger brother.'

Parker took a deep breath and looked down at his desk. Edward stood silently, waiting.

'The *Active* is being held in quarantine out in the harbour. They've had heavy losses of life apparently and fear they'll lose more unless they can get the sickest men off the ship. There's a special facility being prepared for them in one of the bays.'

'Heavy losses, sir? How many and what's the disease?'

'Over twenty, and most of it's happened in the last few days so whatever the disease is, it's spreading fast. That's why they want to get the worst cases off the ship quickly.'

Parker noted the look on Edward's face.

'I understand this is a big thing to ask of you but I have few others I can call on and John Mitchinson, the Master of the *Active*, tells me he has no-one he can spare. I've selected Barnes and Gleeson to accompany you. They're able men but frankly I can't rely on their good sense to carry out this mission alone.'

'Of course, sir. Whatever ye command,' Edward said, saluting.

'Good man; good man.'

—ᴡ—

The lifeboat left the dock in the early morning, with Barnes and Gleeson rowing. Edward had been given the directions for locating the *Active* and for the destination of the three men they were to pick up.

'So why doesn't Parker go 'n' pick up these wretches?' Gleeson asked.

'Oh, 'cause 'e's a gentleman,' Barnes replied. 'An' gentlemen don't risk their lives, matey. That's for ones 'o don't matter, like you 'n' me.'

'I'm sure Commodore Parker's often put his life at risk,' Edward said.

'Oh, you mean when 'e's started a row with 'is missus?' Barnes laughed.

'I wouldn' mind startin' a row with that piece o' pie,' Gleeson said, joining in the laughter.

'Yeah, I could take a small bite out o' 'er,' Barnes said. 'That's for sure.'

Edward stared ahead in the mist, trying to ignore these men not much older than himself.

'Don't ye agree, Mr Lovat?' Barnes asked. 'Or maybe ye've 'ad a piece o' pie already. What with all the shore time ye spent with 'er.'

'There's the *Active*,' Edward said. 'Ahoy!'

'Ahoy,' came the response through the mist.

'Permission to come aboard?' Edward called.

'Permission granted but please don't come aboard. I'm Commander Mitchinson. We'll bring the men down to you.'

No time was spared in getting the sick down into the lifeboat. They kept coming.

'I was told there were only three,' Edward shouted to Mitchinson, standing above him on the deck.

'There were,' Mitchinson shouted back. 'There's now seven, I'm afraid. Four more overnight. I'm sure you can fit them in. Please know you won't have to handle them when you get them to shore. There'll be a doctor and some convicts at the other end. Please keep as far away from them as you can.'

'Aye, aye, sir,' Edward replied, surveying the tiny space left in the lifeboat.

'And please thank Commodore Parker for this. Tell him I owe him a stiff drink when we meet onshore.'

'And what about a stiff drink for us?' Barnes grumbled when the lifeboat was out of earshot.

'Oh, that's just for gentlemen,' Gleeson replied.

As they neared the shore of the assigned landing, one of the sick men at the rear of the boat launched himself into the sea.

'Grab him,' Edward called. 'Dinna lose sight of him.'

'Let 'im go,' Gleeson said. 'The wretch'll be dead soon anyway by the looks of 'im.'

'Yeah, let's not spoil 'is last bit o' fun,' Barnes agreed.

Edward sprang to his feet and dived into the water as close as he could to the spot where the man was last seen. The cold almost sucked what breath he had stored in his lungs. He came up for air before diving again into the inky blackness. Each time he came up, Barnes and Gleeson shouted for him to come back to the boat. He knew he was running out of time. He dived one last time, stumbling onto as much as seeing the floating body. He grabbed it and forced the man to the surface.

By this time, a couple of the convicts had been sent into the water to assist in getting the man to shore, along with the others.

'Did the master nay say ye canna touch these creatures?' the doctor shouted at Edward in a familiar Highland brogue.

'Aye, sir, he did.'

'Then what d'ye ken ye're doing, ye *amadan*?' Doctor Brown, ruddy face reddened further with anger, shouted even louder.

'He was goin' to drown, sir.'

'Well, he's gonna die anyway – but now *ye* will as well.'

—⁂—

'Perhaps ye're nay gonna die,' Brown said several days later as he examined Edward.

Because of the physical contact, Edward had been forced to stay at the makeshift hospital along with the sick he had helped off the *Active*.

'How are the others?' he asked.

'There's only one still alive. And would ye guess who that might be?'

'Surely nay.'

'Aye, the one ye almost killed yerself for,' Brown laughed. 'And he's asked to see ye before ye leave. Ye dinna need to though; he's English riff-raff, ye ken? Worst of the lot; worse even than the Irish – and he'll be dead soon anyway.'

Two days later, Edward was told a boat was coming to pick him up to take him back to Sydney Cove.

'Is that man still alive?' he asked Brown.

'Aye, they obviously breed 'em tough in Jordie land.'

'Then I'd like to see him.'

'Suit yerself. See that stretcher down on the beach. He asked if he could soak up some sun. Dying man's wish and all.'

Edward walked up to the man. He was not much older than himself. The thin, sickly pale body looked no better than the corpses he had seen too many of in the past few days.

'*Halo*,' Edward said, leaning over the stretcher. 'My name's Edward Lovat. I was told ye wanted to see me.'

The man clenched Edward's hand. Tears rolled down his cheeks.

'Thank ye, Mr Lovat. Not so much for me but for my Ma and Pa.'

'I nay did anything anyone'd nay do.'

'With respect, sir, I think ye know that's not true. I'm just one of life's leftovers now. No hope, no future. Anyone else would've let me drown.'

Edward recalled the consensus in the lifeboat.

'Well, ye were under my watch, so I could nay let that happen. What's yer name, man?'

'Bellamy, sir. William Bellamy from Gateshead.'

'What did ye do to end up here, Bellamy?'

'Stole some shoes.'

'Why?'

'Mainly so my Ma and Pa and my brothers wouldn't have to walk around bare-foot.'

'Did ye plead yer case?'

'Much good it did me. I stole them from the magistrate's brother. How smart was that?'

'Aye, very smart. Ye chose well.'

They shared a smile.

'Yer boat's here, Mr Lovat,' Doctor Brown called from down the beach.

'Well, good luck with it all, Mr Bellamy. Please look after yerself. Dinna let my efforts to save ye go to waste.'

'Thank ye again, sir. For saving me but for being kind as well. I haven't seen much of that since I left my Ma and Pa's house.'

—⚹—

Before Edward finally went ashore from the *Gorgon*, a note had arrived from Mary Beth inviting him to attend tea at Government House, "at his pleasure". He wondered if anyone at the Governor's House had ever spent time in a makeshift hospital with dying men around. The two worlds seemed a million miles apart and, at this point, the idea of dining with the toffs had no appeal. He just needed a place to lay his head.

He was told he could find something at what was described as the "Army Barracks".

'Put yer gear over there and find yerself a bunk,' the corporal ordered.

Corporal Endicott was in charge of the barracks for the New South Wales Marine Corps, a group of non-professional soldiers, virtually mercenaries, who had been paid to guard the convicts on the First Fleet some three years earlier. Edward pondered again on the lowlife that too often donned the red coat of the British Army. He had seen a hint of it in al-Adabiya and heard his father talk of similar things he had seen in the Americas. All the same, he felt he was seeing the worst of it here in New South Wales. He lamented for Angus Fraser and William Bellamy being overseen by such an army.

There was no bunk in this rough dwelling, half-timber, half-tent, and no-one who cared to find one for him. Edward pulled together some spare bedding and laid it out on the floor. His tiny hole in the wall on the *Gorgon* looked better by the moment but going back was not an option as the ship was being fumigated.

'What ye doin', young fella?' the raucous voice peeled out. 'Too early for bed; come and share a toddy with us.'

Edward looked up to see another unbecoming Redcoat, but at least a friendly one.

'Dargan's my name, what's yers?'

'Lovat. I'm the boatswain's mate from the *Gorgon*.'

'Lovat, did ye say? I'll bet ye love it then.'

Dargan's laughter was quickly accompanied by that of his friends.

'Well, come on then, ye're lucky ye're in with us. This is good rum, better than ye'll find anywhere else in this god forsaken 'ole.'

'Well, just a small one then. I dinna drink much.'

'Yeah, that's what I always say, don' I boys?' Dargan laughed. 'Just make mine *a small one*.'

Edward was true to his word. He had been turned off drink from an early age. His Gran had cautioned him that drink could turn a man into a monster. He knew his father had a drinking problem at some point.

All the same, this was good rum.

'So, who sells this then?' Edward asked after his fourth or fifth mug.

'Let's just say it's 'ome brew,' Tyndale said, placing his first finger on his nose.

Edward would come to know all about the rum trade that had overtaken normal trading in the colony. It was the most valued currency as well as the prime means of all corruption and torpor in Sydney Cove.

But, Edward had found a new pastime and was, for a time, happy enough to be corrupted by his friends. They had heard all about his confrontation with Grovely and committed to *knock his bleedin' 'ead off* should he come around to do any mischief. Edward figured he needed some friends in this place at the end of the Earth, especially ones who could provide some quality rum and half decent food where anything edible was so scarce. The odd strand of tasteless pork and even the rotted potato could be rendered acceptable if washed down by rum.

There were occasions nonetheless when he dreamed of the Captain's Table on the *Stirling*.

—◊◊—

After a week of long drinking nights and sleeping it off during the day, Edward was in no shape to receive visitors.

'There's a lady to see Mr Lovat,' Corporal Endicott shouted at the raggedy curtain they called the door.

'A *lady* to see Mr Lovat,' Dargan parroted. 'Now, I bet ye *love that*.'

Edward lay still, guessing who it was and hoping she would go away.

'Up ye get, Lovat,' Endicott said, shaking him awake. 'Mrs Parker's not one to be waiting too long for yer likes.'

'Please tell her I'm unwell and I'll come to see her later.'

Mary Beth entered the bunkroom, to the horror of its inhabitants. She walked straight over to Edward's pile of bedclothes.

'Edward, get out of that bed. Gather up your things and come with me. I mean this instant.'

'Ye 'eard Mrs Parker, ye drunken sod,' Endicott shouted. 'Get out o' that bed now before I throw ye out.'

'Thank you, Corporal, but I'm sure that won't be necessary. Come now, Edward.'

Edward struggled out of bed, apologising for his state. Mary Beth helped him gather his few possessions and they walked out.

—◊—

'Thank ye, Mary Beth. I'm sorry to have caused ye such *bron*.'

'You haven't caused *me* grief so much as yourself. You need to take this as a lesson how even a decent young man can be brought low by alcohol and the wrong company. Do you hear me?'

It was a drubbing worthy of his grandmother.

'And where have you been anyway? I went to the ship and was told you were on special assignment. I asked my husband but he wouldn't tell me.'

'Oh, it was nay anything important. Just some navy business. I'm very grateful to ye, Mary Beth, but I must nay impose on ye. I'll just go back to the ship.'

'No you won't. I've spoken with my husband who has spoken with the Governor and there's a place for you at his residence. Carl has a spare bed in his room and he'll be delighted if you take it while ever you're on shore. My husband has also spoken with Mr Bush about releasing you to accompany Carl and me when we "go bush", so to speak.'

'But Mr Bush'll need me on board.'

'Yes, but not right now. Mr Grovely is being requisitioned to the *Gorgon*. He'll fill in for you until you're ready to resume your duties. Is that clear?'

'Aye, Ma'am.'

They laughed. It was the first time for many months that Edward had referred to her so formally.

'Well, that's that, then. Now go clean yourself up. You'll be expected at dinner tonight.'

'Me? At the Governor's table?' Edward asked, eyes popping in disbelief.

'You! At the Governor's table. And don't drink too much.'

'Aye, *Ma'am*!'

—w—

'I believe your father served in the American War, Mr Lovat?' Governor Arthur Philip asked as the meal began.

Mary Beth had warned Edward that no-one spoke at dinner until the Governor began proceedings. Furthermore, that he should not speak to the whole table unless invited by the Governor.

'Aye, sir, he was in Boston and Philadelphia mainly.'

'I envy him, I must say. It was one of the regrets of my career that I was not assigned there. Though, as things turned out, it might have been as well. Is your father quite well?'

'Nay, sir. He was badly wounded and he's nay ever fully recovered.'

'I'm so very sorry to hear that. Does he speak about his time there?'

'Nay a great deal, sir. But I ken he had some sympathy for the American cause. I've heard him say things could have been handled differently.'

The tinkling of cutlery on crockery ceased, as did the talk. All eyes were on the Governor.

'In precisely what way, Mr Lovat?' Major Ross asked.

Major Robert Ross had been introduced before the meal. He was the deputy governor, considerably younger and less genial looking than Arthur Philip.

'I'm really nay sure, sir.'

'Oh, come now, young man. That's a fairly extraordinary thing for a British officer to suggest, is it not? The only different handling might have been the appointment of Cornwallis some years before. He would *not* have allowed the treachery of the colonists to get out of hand as his predecessors did. By the time he got there, it was too late.'

'Well, we don't know that, Mr Ross, do we?' the Governor said. 'Wisdom after the event is a wonderful thing.'

'Yes, sir, it is but, with respect, there are lessons to be learned from the American situation. Lessons that should not go astray here in this place.'

Mary Beth regretted she had not had time to fill Edward in on some of the politics around the table. Arthur Philip and his deputy were of differing views about many things, including how to handle the convicts, the Indigenous population and the New South Wales Marine Corps.

The Governor had a view that the convicts should be freed as soon as possible to become the workforce needed to build the productive country he foresaw for the colony. He believed the Aboriginal people must be treated with respect and their beliefs and way of life honoured. On the Corps, he had a view that it was entirely unsuitable as a policing force and was more of a problem than a benefit.

Major Ross held polar opposite views on almost all counts.

'And what lesson would that be, Major?' Reverend Johnson asked.

Richard Johnson was the chaplain who had accompanied the First Fleet. He had been recommended for the job by the politician and abolitionist, William Wilberforce, and the prominent clergyman and abolitionist, John Newton. Wilberforce and Newton were members of the Eclectic Society, fighting for abolition of slavery and concerned that the worldwide slave-traders had their eyes on the new colony of New South Wales. Johnson held similar views to those of Wilberforce and Newton, as did the Governor. Johnson was a regular confidant of the Governor, a matter of constant irritation to Deputy Governor Ross.

Edward had warmed to Johnson during their brief pre-dinner chat. His pastoral engagement had helped to ease Edward out of his discomfort. Ross, on the other hand, had studiously ignored him, as though he was a convict intruder.

'What lesson, Reverend?' Ross replied. 'Well, for a start, not to be too friendly with the enemy.'

'And who's the enemy in this instance, sir?' Johnson asked.

'We're surrounded by the enemy, Reverend. Here we are, halfway around the world with no support, inadequate food, surrounded by felons and savages. *Surely* that's sufficient for an enemy.'

'Well, I don't know about you, gentlemen,' Mary Beth cut in. 'But I think the food is more than adequate; quite delicious in fact.'

'Indeed it is,' the Governor said. 'And let's enjoy it. We can leave these heavy matters until after dinner.'

There was little in the way of general table conversation after that, each person merely chatting to those on either side. It was a large table, allowing for some private conversations unlikely to be heard by others.

Edward was seated to the left of Mary Beth and spent most time speaking with her. He asked her about the three women who were serving the table and the gentleman directing their movements.

'I dare say all three are convicts or former convicts at least,' Mary Beth said. 'If indeed, that makes any difference for these poor souls. The gentleman is an attache, but out of uniform for tonight. It will be his job to make sure the women don't take the opportunity to run away. It happens, you know?'

'But where would they go?'

'I don't know. It's a vast country. Perhaps they'd prefer to take their chances in the bush than live as slaves. For that's effectively what they are. But let's not stare at the poor things.'

Edward did not stare but he stole a few glances at the three young girls, muted by their circumstances. The frightened but resigned looks on their faces; the shapeless dresses and drab headwear. The stark contrast with the portraits on the walls of a king, a governor, a cleric of some kind, all resplendent in their fine clothes, power and control written all over their faces. During one of the glances, the eyes of one girl met his. The tiniest of smiles told Edward she understood what he was thinking. That he would gladly have carried her away and cared for her. She looked away.

Commodore Parker was on Mary Beth's other side and he was engaged mainly with the Reverend Johnson. Opposite were the Governor and Ross, together with Solander and Johnson's wife, Mary. On Edward's other side was a man who had been on the *Gorgon* but whom he had not met formally until tonight. Captain Philip Gidley King was an unusually quiet man who had spent almost all his time on the voyage in his cabin. Edward was awestruck by his self-composure and uncertain what he might speak with him about if ever there was an opportunity. It was a relief when he spoke first.

'I agree with your father, young man,' he said in a moment when Mary Beth had turned briefly to speak with her husband.

'Thank ye, sir. I'm afraid I might have put my foot in it though.'

'Oh don't be put off by Major Ross. He's just an angry young man who thinks everything can be put right with the lash.'

'Oh, so ye ken Major Ross then?'

'Well, yes, one could say that. We came out together in '88 but I went quickly to Norfolk Island as Governor. He's been Acting Governor there while I've been in England. Now, I have to go back to Norfolk and clean up the mess.'

Edward was surprised at the candour. Gidley King had said nothing to him for six months on the ship but was now sharing his deepest grievances. Perhaps it was the ale. He had noticed him filling up his cup quite regularly.

'I'm sorry young man, I shouldn't burden you. I do know of your father's exploits, by the way. I've always thought we were of one mind about how to handle colonial situations.'

'Aye, well, my Da's Da fought at Culloden. I ken he always saw the "American loyalists", as he called them, as being a bit like the Scots. All they wanted was their own freedom.'

'Only too true. That's all anyone wants. Fortunately, Governor Philip sees things that way but I dread to think what will become of this place if someone like Ross ever gets hold of it. Sorry, again, I'm being far too frank.'

'Nay at all, sir, I'm enjoying talking with ye.'

'Me too. Would you care for an ale? I notice you haven't been drinking at all.'

Edward turned to see if Mary Beth had heard the invitation.

'I believe Mr Lovat might enjoy one of Mr Squire's ales, Captain,' she said.

Gidley King took a spare cup and poured from the tumbler as Mary Beth whispered in Edward's ear.

'If you're going to drink, drink something that will leave your innards intact.'

'This is the finest ale you'll find anywhere,' Gidley King said, handing Edward a cup now filled to the brim and frothing over. 'And I mean anywhere, including in all of England.'

'Ah, I see you're introducing the young man to Mr Squire's delights,' the Governor said from across the table.

Edward had only drunk a few ales in his life, the most memorable when his father had taken him to an inn at Portsmouth on their return from their travels. He had found it quite bitter in taste. The few subsequent ales had not changed his mind. Tonight was different. There was a sweet taste as delightful as the Governor had suggested.

'So, who's Mr Squire?' he asked.

'Some would say the most important convict on the island,' Gidley King replied.

They laughed as the Governor toasted James Squire's continued good health. Squire had arrived in chains on the First Fleet but just three years later had found a position that straddled the two ends of society in the colony. He was still doing his time but had discovered how to grow the one product that counted most, barley, and how to turn it into an ale that was ultimately too good, therefore too expensive, for the poor. On the other hand, the establishment would pay well for it.

'Well, ladies and gentlemen, shall we retire to the lounge?' the Governor commanded, rather than asked.

—⧖—

In their room afterwards, Edward and Carl reflected on the fine meal they had just taken when the rest of the colony was apparently starving. The soup seemed to have been made from fresh vegetables, the meat was salty but delicious, bread freshly baked and the ale was better than in London. After the week that Edward had spent with his Corps friends, eating slops and drinking home-made rum that felt like it was ripping at one's gut with each swill, he could not help but ponder on the gap between the haves and have-nots in this place.

He was happy to be among the haves for a while.

XXI

A t breakfast several days later, Governor Philip announced he had secured the assistance of a local person to accompany Mary Beth, Carl and Edward on their first exploration of the surrounding flora.

'His name is Bennelong,' the Governor said. 'He is a most gracious gentleman and a good friend. I've personally learned much from him and his dear wife, I might say, including about matters of humility and civility. If they are typical of the natives of this land, then they are far from savages.'

'Indeed,' Gidley King said. 'I think most of the savages around here wear red coats.'

Edward blurted out in laughter before realising that the rest of the table sat in silence. They knew that the remark was a barb directed at Major Ross, sitting opposite. Edward had missed a huge row from the night before, one that saw no less than the Governor himself, aided by Parker, having to stand between the two men lest they hit each other. It had begun as a fact-finding and planning session for how Gidley King was to attempt restoring order on Norfolk Island, a premise that Ross found highly offensive. A scuffle ensued. Governor Philip had ordered the two men to stand down, go to bed and sleep off their anger. The strategy had worked up until Gidley King's remark.

'Mr King,' Ross said, pushing his chair away and standing. 'I challenge you to a duel.'

'There'll be no duels while I'm in command,' the Governor said. 'For heaven's sake, Mr Ross. It was a joke. Not a particularly funny one, I concede, but a joke nonetheless, hardly duelling territory – and besides, we're not French.'

'Then, I demand an apology.'

'Mr King,' the Governor said. 'Apologise to Mr Ross.'

There was a moment's silence. No-one was eating, half expecting one or other of the men might leap across the table at the other.

'I apologise, *sir*,' Gidley King eventually said.

All went about finishing their breakfast.

'Now, as I was saying,' the Governor continued. 'This Bennelong gent, and his wife, Barangaroo, are the most delightful and helpful people. Bennelong has spent quite some time here in the settlement, giving me the opportunity to get to know him and his fascinating beliefs. We see less of Barangaroo but whenever she does come here, she seems to have a remarkably civilising effect on the men, Corps and convicts alike. A truly beautiful woman who complements him splendidly.'

The Governor went silent for a moment, looking deeply into his food. Some at the table knew that he and his wife were estranged.

'Anyway, I've spoken with Mr Bennelong about your work, Mr Solander, and he would be delighted to escort you to some rich flora not so far from here and to explain their spiritual significance.'

'*Spiritual* significance?' Mary Beth asked.

'Yes, not that he uses that word but it's how I've come to understand these people's beliefs. They identify so strongly with the natural world around them that they see themselves as part of it. They don't distinguish between human life and other life, animal or plant, or indeed geological life, in the way we do. I don't know what you think, Mr Johnson, but spiritual is the best word I can use to describe their beliefs.'

'How about primitive and godless?' Ross blurted out.

Gidley King flinched as if he was about to say something but the Reverend Johnson beat him to it.

'I think spiritual is a good way to see it, sir. I'm sure we all believe that our religion is the true one but I do believe our God is a patient God. He doesn't mind if people take their time to find their way to him. And in the meantime, these heathen beliefs are part of what's allowed these people to survive in this harsh environment.'

Edward liked what he heard from Johnson, except for the word "heathen". He recalled the word being used often by the British in the Middle East to characterise Muslim beliefs. But he had come to see, through Rania and Mahdiya's parents and others, how those beliefs influenced such positive demeanour and behaviour. He also remembered hearing his father speak about Mahdiya's deeply held beliefs and how he had come to respect them. Yet, how they too were often referred to as "heathen".

'Precisely,' the Governor said. 'I think you'll find Mr Bennelong very helpful. For one thing, he'll be able to guide you quickly to what you want to see.'

'Does he speak English?' Mary Beth asked.

'Better than some of the Corps, I dare say,' Gidley King replied.

There was restrained laughter as they looked to Major Ross.

—⚬—

Carl, Mary Beth and Edward, accompanied by the now uniformed attache and two other soldiers, left early the next day. The sky on the horizon was red with the sun's first light signalling that a hot day awaited. The attache and one soldier were on horseback, while the other soldier drove the carriage. They arrived at the appointed meeting place some miles inland. Bennelong met them and led them off the beaten track. The smell of gum tree hung in the air. It became heavier as the crispness of dawn gave way to a breathless heat.

'Here the wallabi,' Bennelong said, pointing to an ochre and green flower atop a sharp, spindly stork.

'Wallabi?' Carl asked.

'Mmm, kangaroo paw.'

Having already encountered several kangaroos, they could see that the flower did resemble a kangaroo paw.

'Wonderful,' Carl said, slipping his knife out of its scabbard and moving towards the plant.

'Wait,' Bennelong said, cautioning him to step back.

Bennelong then moved over to the plant, held one of its storks, seeming to speak with it. He pulled the stork out and handed it to Carl as if the action was a ceremony rather than merely a function. He went on to instruct them in the importance of the plant as part of Baiame's (the Sky God's) overall plan, for its spiritual significance but also for its healing power.

'So what power does it have?' Edward asked.

'Women; they need,' Bennelong said, pointing to Mary Beth's stomach.

This became the pattern through the day, a slower procedure than Carl Solander had been hoping for.

What became obvious was that, for the Aboriginal people, a plant was far more than an adornment. It was an integral part of their world. Bennelong treated the plants with at least as much respect as he treated fellow human beings, more so in some cases. He spoke with them as if they were family which, in his belief system, they were.

Hence, it took several more days than they had planned to gather the number of specimens that Carl had wanted. Nonetheless, he managed to add to his store with samples of distinctive flora from the Great Southern Land, many more than his father had managed in his short time in these parts. There was bottlebrush, gum, a rich red blossom that would come to be known as the waratah and a daisy that Carl named the "poached egg daisy" after Edward described it as such. Some of the stark colours of Africa were not here but they were beautiful in their own way, suited to a climate that seemed dry in a way none of them had experienced before, not even in Africa.

For Edward, the spiritual and medicinal significance added to his growing fascination with what the ground produces.

'So what's this one for?' he would persistently ask of Bennelong.

Bennelong was always generous with his time, sensing in the young man an interest in and respect for his ways that he found only rarely among the invaders. Edward learned some invaluable lessons not only about the spiritual aspects of plant life but about any number of practicalities. Such as how to protect plant life through deluges and droughts, and how to manage the wider environment through the way one managed the plants, including against floods and bushfires.

—w—

'Why don't you join me on the voyage to Norfolk Island?' Gidley King asked the three young friends over drinks one evening.

'Oh I'd love to,' Carl replied.

'Aye, if Commodore Parker can spare me,' Edward said.

'Well, I think I'm going anyway,' Mary Beth added. 'And I don't think my husband needs to spare you, Edward, because he's coming too.'

There had been some problem with the ship that was supposed to be taking Gidley King back to Norfolk so the decision had been made to use the *Gorgon*.

'I'm most grateful for this, Mr Parker,' Governor Philip said. 'From all reports, the sooner Mr King gets there and restores some order, the better.'

Major Ross was absent that night.

'Will we be safe, though?' Carl asked.

'I believe so,' the Governor replied. 'I'm sure once everyone sees that Mr King is back in command, things will settle down. Nonetheless, I'm sending a dozen of the Marine Corps and another dozen of the new New South Wales Corps with you just to make sure. Their job will be mainly to protect the ship and passengers but, if necessary, some of them will stay with Mr King until order is restored.'

'Splendid,' Gidley King said. 'So, we sail in three days' time, Mr Parker?'

'Three days it is. And might I say I would not be allowing my wife to accompany us if I didn't consider it perfectly safe to do so.'

Mary Beth smiled at Carl and Edward.

The ship was delayed by a day, owing to a damaged gangplank. They left at dawn on the fourth day. It was early October and chilly but Mary Beth and Carl chose to take in the harbour view. They saw more this time, being better rested than when they arrived. By the time they were mid-harbour, the stench of Sydney had given way to the freshness of a sea breeze blowing a combination of saltiness and gum.

Two weeks later, they were nestled in Kingston on Norfolk Island's south coast.

'I do wish Bennelong was here,' Edward said as the party of five moved through the bushland.

'What, that black fella?' Dargan replied, sniggering with his friend, Quirk.

Dargan and Quirk had been assigned as part of the Marine Corps on the *Gorgon*. It had given Edward an opportunity to renew acquaintance with them, though this time under the steely eye of Mary Beth. Commodore Parker had insisted on the party having some military accompaniment if they were to go into the bush.

'Aye,' Edward replied. 'He had so many stories to tell about the plants – everything in fact – the animals, the hills and rocks, the ponds – billabongs, I mean – and how to manage it all in whatever weather conditions. *Inntinneach* beliefs. Ye two've been here for three years; ye must have picked up on some of these things.'

Dargan and Quirk looked at each other.

'Listen to a black fella? Ye gotta be joshin',' Dargan said.

'Yeah,' Quirk added. 'I 'eard that Johnson vicar fella sayin' somethin' about 'ow their beliefs were interestin' but I asked the corporal and 'e said to take no notice of 'im. Somethin' about 'im bein' a bit mad.'

Edward could sense a difference between him and his friends that he had not noticed when imbibing with them. He felt grateful that Mary Beth had saved him from their worst effects. Still, he sensed they were not bad men, just products of their upbringing.

Carl was not altogether sorry at Bennelong's absence. While he had enjoyed listening to the old man and observing his rituals, he was also impatient to make the most of what would likely be his only trip to these parts. He busied himself gathering samples.

'Pink is the word that comes most to mind,' Mary Beth said.

'Indeed, it's the dominant colour for sure,' Carl replied.

Norfolk's flora were different again. Neither the stunning colours of Africa nor the rich but rank colours of New South Wales. Instead, a paradise of pink.

'It's like the Garden of Eden,' Mary Beth said.

'Aye, it's magnificent,' Edward replied, struggling to maintain the notetaking against Carl's speedy descriptions.

'Where's Eden?' Dargan asked.

—◠◠◠—

When Edward was not in the bush, he was back on the ship, preparing it to sail again. He and Grovely were sharing duties as boatswain's mate. Edward was becoming less enthusiastic about seamanship and would happily have handed all responsibilities to Grovely so he could be with his friends exploring the landscape. The bush bug had bitten.

Grovely's resentment peaked when Gidley King invited Edward, along with Commodore Parker, Mary Beth and Carl to dine at his house. This happened twice in the two weeks they were on Norfolk.

'I frankly don't know what to do about this situation,' Gidley King said at the first dinner, three days into the stay. 'I've never seen a population fracture as quickly and completely as this one. I don't wish to blame it all on Ross. There've been some unfortunate setbacks that no-one could have predicted, including the shipwreck of the *Sirius* and all its goods. But I have to say most of the complaints I'm hearing concern Major Ross and his harsh, un-Christian ways of dealing with people.'

'It's a mammoth challenge you have here, sir,' Parker said. 'But I have great faith in Governor Philip's judgement and he has great faith in yours. I say you must trust your own. I'm sure most of the people here know your intentions will be for the best so take them into your confidence – the ones you know you can trust – and gradually you'll weed out the others, the troublemakers.'

'I believe my husband is right, Mr King,' Mary Beth said. 'People know you're an honourable man. If you draw on the good will of those you know you can trust, they'll help you restore order here.'

'Thank you, Mrs Parker, Commodore, your counsel is well taken.'

The second dinner, nine days later, was a far larger event. There were fourteen guests, the additional ones being some of those trusted parties that Gidley King had been working tirelessly to bring into his confidence in the interim. It was a working dinner, with Gidley King displaying the gifts of leadership that would come to be his legacy. Edward took notes in his head for future reference.

On the day before Edward and the others set sail for New South Wales, Gidley King held a public meeting. There were five men in chains, representing the five prime troublemakers, the rotten apples to be excised from the bowl. They would be going back to Sydney Cove to spend some time at His Majesty's pleasure. Gidley King spoke frankly of the trouble the island had been enduring but also of its positive future now that he was back. His optimistic view was endorsed by the additional guests at the second dinner.

Edward sensed that Gidley King was destined to be Governor of New South Wales at some point. If so, he knew the colony would be in good hands under his leadership. He also knew that whoever was Governor of New South Wales or Norfolk would need all their leadership to manage the New South Wales Corps that was to supplant the Dargans and Quirks of this world.

Mary Beth had been right to doubt the new Corps would be any better than the old one.

—⁓—

Back in Sydney, Parker received a message that Bennelong's wife, Barangaroo, had died. While Bennelong had liaised with the colonists, Barangaroo had stayed close to her Cammeraygal people and their ways. When she was due to give birth to their first child, Governor Philip had encouraged Bennelong to make use of the colony's doctors and the hospital. Reluctantly, Barangaroo acceded but there she died, fuelling the belief that the white settlers could only bring disease and death to the aboriginal population.

Governor Philip was devastated, ordering that, after the traditional ceremony and burning of the body, her ashes were to be spread on the garden of his own residence. Many of the settlers thought a traditional aboriginal ceremony in the grounds of Government House was sacrilegious. Most of the aboriginal population thought that spreading her ashes in the garden of the invaders was disrespectful towards their ways. The Governor, Bennelong and the Reverend Johnson, between them, tried their best to bridge cultures but history would record it as a bad day for aboriginal and settler relations.

—⁓—

A few days before the ship sailed, Edward tried to make contact with Angus Fraser and William Bellamy to see how they were. Mary-Beth had cautioned him against it but had nonetheless secured a note from the Governor providing Edward with access to the convict settlements. He had no luck locating Fraser who was on a road gang some miles away but he did find Bellamy who thanked him again. He gave him a note for his parents, asking that he post it when back in England.

'Would ye like me to see them if I can?' Edward asked.

'There's no need for that, sir. Just post it if ye can. Thank ye. I won't forget ye.'

XXII

On the 18th of December, 1791, the Gorgon sailed out of Port Jackson headed for home. It had the full complement of the old Marine Corps on board. Major Ross's main responsibility was to keep the Corps under better control than he had done in Sydney or on Norfolk. The journey would prove a major test for Commodore Parker and the crew. Disease was rife, causing many unscheduled stops.

In Kapstadt, they picked up more potential trouble in the form of escaped prisoners, including Mary Bryant and her daughter, Charlotte. They had absconded from New South Wales almost a year earlier. Along the way, the ship also took on board ten of the mutineers from Captain Bligh's *HMS Bounty*.

Between the rabble that was the Marine Corps, Ross's brutal oversight of them and the influence of unexpected passengers, along with disease and bad weather, it was an almost unmanageable trip. Even Commodore Parker's proven commanding skills were tested beyond endurance.

—◊◊◊—

'I want him out of there,' Mary Beth said to her husband. 'The boy will be dead before we hit Portsmouth if you *don't* get him out of there.'

'Alright, my dear. I'll think of something.'

Unlike Carl Solander, who stayed in his cabin as much as possible, Edward was required to be on duty in his boatswain's mate duties, shared with Grovely. Grovely and his friends targeted Edward constantly, roughing him up just enough to intimidate him but not to draw too much attention to themselves. The fact that Edward had some friends among the Marine Corps, like Dargan and Quirk, simply made matters worse. Ross had secured the support of some of the crew, like Grovely and his friends, to help in trying to keep the old Corps under control. Edward found himself smack in the middle of these rivalries and was paying for it.

'What is it this time?' Mary Beth asked.

'It's nay anything to concern yerself with, Mary Beth. I'm braw.'

'Come here and let me look at you.'

She pressed her hand against his ribs where she could see some discolouring on his shirt. Edward winced.

'Braw, you say? I presume that means you're in pain. Who did this to you?'

'Please, Mary Beth, dinna concern yerself.'

'How can I not concern myself? I can't sit by and watch you being brutalised.'

After Kapstadt and the intervention of Commodore Parker, Edward was relieved of his duties as boatswain's mate. He was given responsibility to oversee the newly installed prisoners on board, the escapees from Sydney and the *Bounty* mutineers. To match these new duties, he was given the title of Acting Warrant Officer.

'We were not expecting to have these people on board, Mr Lovat,' Parker said. 'On top of all our other trouble, they could be quite a handful. I'll be relying on your good sense and way with people of no rank to manage them for the good order of the ship; is that clear?'

'Aye, aye, sir, I hope I can live up to yer trust.'

'Well, my wife's trust is more to the point.'

Edward's sixteenth birthday came and went without ceremony, bar a hand-written note and small kiss on the cheek from Mary Beth. Carl made a point of coming out of his cabin to congratulate him.

'When you can, come and see me,' Carl said. 'We've much to talk about.'

—◊◊◊—

'Ye're very kind to me, sir,' Mary Bryant said as Edward handed her a blanket.

'Ye can thank Mrs Parker when ye see her. We're all grateful for her influence, especially over the commodore.'

'Well, I doubt I'll get to see 'er. The likes of 'er and me don't mix in case ye 'adn't noticed.'

'Ye might be surprised. Mrs Parker has some sympathy for ye, and canna believe what ye've achieved.'

'What I've achieved?' Bryant blurted out. 'What 'ave I achieved? I'm a convict, a widow, a grievin' Ma. And I've achieved all this by twenty-six years of age. What an achievement! And I'll be a grievin' Ma twice over if Charlotte doesn't …'

Her voice broke.

Mary Bryant had escaped from Sydney some months earlier with her husband, William, and two children, Charlotte and Emanuel. They had both been transported there for seven years for crimes back in England. With other escapees, they had made it to Kupang on the island of Timor in an open boat, a trip that took sixty-six days. No-one thought the trip possible.

In Kupang, they were re-captured and sent on a Dutch boat to Batavia, where William and Emanuel died of fever. Mary and her infant had then been transported to Kapstadt to rendezvous with the *Gorgon* for transport back to England. There, she would be placed on trial as an escaped prisoner. Hanging was the normal punishment.

—⟋⟍—

'No, dear, I'm sorry but I forbid you to mix with the prisoners,' Parker said.

Mary Beth recognised the abnormal strain her husband was suffering so she desisted from the argumentation that normally rendered her whatever she wanted.

'Well, then, please get her away from the other prisoners so she can look after the baby properly.'

'I don't have any spare quarters, my dear.'

'I believe Edward would give up his. Indeed I'm certain of it.'

'If you ask him, my dear, I'm certain of it too.'

Bryant and her daughter, Charlotte, were moved into their own tiny cabin where she could tend to her unwell child. Edward moved in with Carl, an equally tiny cabin but they were both happy with the move.

—⟋⟍—

In spite of their best efforts, Charlotte died, still short by a month of her first birthday. The brief burial at sea happened within hours, urged by the surgeon against Bryant's protests and even Mary Beth's intervention.

'The poor woman just wants a little longer to mourn,' Mary Beth said to her husband. 'Holding her dead child and saying a proper goodbye is part of that. Surely you understand.'

'What I understand, my dear, is that my responsibilities rest with the surgeon's advice. And his advice is that any delay in disposing of the child's body poses a risk to everyone else on board.'

Bryant was allowed on deck. She had asked if Edward could serve as the presiding officer and Parker had reluctantly agreed. As ever, the request came through Mary Beth.

'We commend Charlotte Bryant to yer care, O Laird, and we pray as yer Son taught us. Our Father ...'

Edward had taken a moment to recall the words he had heard too often in his short life.

The ship rocked and rolled in the fierce wind. Edward clung to Bryant, fearful she would fall. As the sailor assigned to lift the board holding the baby was about to do his duty, she cried out.

'No, please let me.'

Edward nodded to the sailor. He moved closer with Bryant as she took hold of the board. She rested her hand one last time on the infant's chest, then raised the board with both hands. The baby slid into the sea. She shrieked and crumbled to the deck. Edward lent down to comfort her and Mary Beth rushed forward and put her arms around her.

'I'm so sorry for your loss,' Mary Beth said, tears welling in her eyes.

In her cabin, later in the day, Bryant shared the story of her desperate upbringing. Edward and Mary Beth listened in silence. She spoke of the poverty and starvation, the helplessness and despair she saw overtake her parents and all those around her.

'What are we supposed to do? If we don't take from them that's got too much, we starve.'

'Those of us who have too much should never judge,' Mary Beth said. 'We've no idea, do we? It's not that we're bad people, Mary. It's just that we don't understand.'

'I know. I'm sorry, Ma'am. I didn' mean to say ye was bad. Ye're very kind, Ma'am. If only I'd 'ad a little more of it, things might be different. I might 'ave a life instead of nothin'. All I ever 'ad, gone.'

She wept. Edward and Mary Beth said nothing because nothing could be said. They pondered on the uneven chances that life presents and whether, in her circumstances, they would have done anything differently.

'No. you will not,' Mary Beth said later to her husband when he suggested Mary Bryant could go back to the chains below. 'She is staying right where she is until we hit land in England.'

Parker relented, knowing this was one battle he would not win, except at a price he was not prepared to pay.

—ᴍ—

Among the marines aboard, there was a young lieutenant who had kept strictly to himself ever since leaving Sydney. Edward had seen him board quietly almost as the ship was about to sail. He was still in uniform but was not saluted nor even seeming to be acknowledged. He had gone straight to his cabin and been barely seen in weeks.

'You had best bunk in with Mr Dawes,' Parker said when told Carl was suffering from a fever.

'Mr Dawes?' Edward asked.

'Lieutenant Dawes, if you will. He's in the cabin three along from yours. Be about your business now.'

Edward stole down the narrow, creaking corridor and knocked gingerly on the door.

'*Halo*, sir,' he said as the door opened, revealing a sad-looking, dishevelled figure. 'Commodore Parker's suggested I might bunk in with ye while my roommate is ill.'

He stood aside and gestured for Edward to enter the tiny cabin.

'I'm sorry that I can't offer you anything better,' he said in the finest English accent. 'And I've no idea just where you can fit. *But*, I've learned from experience that when an order is given, no matter how unwise, it's best to abide by it.'

'Thank ye, sir. My name's Edward, Edward Lovat.'

'Yes, I know. Warrant Officer Lovat, is it not? I'm William Dawes.'

'*Lieutenant* Dawes, is it nay?'

'Perhaps, but not for long.'

Edward was about to meet one of the people who would impress him most throughout his entire life. William Dawes was an astronomer and linguist, the latter explaining the fineness of his diction. He combined the best of scientific and cultural minds. Dawes had arrived on the First Fleet on board *HMS Sirius*, the same ship as Governor Philip. He had been one of the Governor's main supporters, especially in his reaching out to the aboriginal population. Dawes himself became very close to members of the Eora people, especially the teenage girl, Patyegarang, who taught him her language.

'I thought the Governor and I were of the same mind. But, in the end, he sided with those who just wanted to bring the local people to heel.'

Edward told of his own experiences with Bennelong, how warmly the Governor had spoken about him and how he had allowed Barangaroo's ashes to be buried in his garden.

'Oh, I know, the old man's a bundle of contradictions, except about one thing. Power.'

He told Edward about his falling out with the Governor over an order he received to execute some aboriginal people for a crime allegedly committed. When he refused, he was decommissioned and sent home in spite of his desire to stay in the colony and the fact that he had made more inroads into liaising with the aboriginal population than any of the British.

'I'm surprised the Governor would've behaved like that,' Edward said.

'I was surprised too. I thought we were of the same mind about dealing with the native population. But, in the end, it's all about power for these people.'

Dawes told Edward about his relationship with "Patye", as he referred to Patyegarang. How they had become "soul-mates" who were able to reach out beyond the cultural barriers that divided almost everyone else in the country. How he had been berated by some for treating the girl as if an equal and spurned by others for taking advantage of her.

'We were not lovers though we might have been,' he said, a sadness in his voice. 'Perhaps if I'd been allowed to stay, I'd have married her for I truly did love her but I never took advantage of her, I swear.'

Edward was reminded of the love between his father and Mahdiya, of the difficulties of cross-cultural love and the criticism his father had suffered for the relationship. Yet, how much he always said he had learned because of it. For Dawes, it was the same with his Patye.

'I'll never forget her and I'll do all I can to preserve her story and the story of her people. I dare say I'm the only non-aboriginal who knows one of their languages.'

'How will ye do that?' Edward asked.

'Through my writing. I have my writing and I'll command my own audience. I'm not letting these imperious brutes crush the innocence and beauty of those people. And I'll do everything I can to get back here someday.'

'So, perhaps ye will get to marry yer Patye?'

'Perhaps I will.'

During the week or so that he shared Dawes' cabin, Edward told him of his own interest in and discovery of native flora. They had much in common.

'You're another soul-mate, Edward Lovat,' Dawes said as Edward packed up his bed and few possessions to go back to the cabin he shared with Carl.

'It's been an honour knowing ye, William. Ye remind me so much of my cousin and best friend, who also happens to be William. William Henry, in fact.'

—⚹—

'But how would I get in?' Edward asked.

Carl, now fully recovered, had told Edward that his former university, Uppsala, offered a shortened agronomy course for those looking to have practical knowledge, such as farmers, gardeners and estate managers.

'It's just six months and all you need is some senior school science.'

'It sounds *math* but I'm committed to the navy for a while yet.'

'My friend, if I might be so bold. I've been with you now for many months, long enough to gain impressions. To me, you seem like a very good sailor, better than most on board, I might say. And perhaps you could be a senior officer at some time in the future, a commodore even. But I've never seen you once show the excitement about sailing that I've seen when you're around nature.'

Carl paused to give time for his words to settle in.

'And, like my father always said, as the world expands, it will need more people who understand its differences and how to transplant some of them for everyone's sake.'

Again, he paused in order to reel in his prey.

'And, haven't we just been given a lesson in that in Sydney? Without imported goods, they'd all be starving.'

'Aye, but Mr Squire's ale'd keep them happy,' Edward said, grinning.

'True, but isn't that another lesson in how important this knowledge is? Mr Squire learned how to produce the best barley in such a totally different environment from what he was used to at home.'

'Aye, and then there's the sheer beauty of it all.'

'Ah, yes, the sheer beauty of it all,' Carl agreed.

'So, tell me more about this course then.'

XXIII

'*And they call this summer,*' Mary Beth said as the *Gorgon* berthed in Portsmouth Harbour. It was a chilly morning on the 18th of June, 1792.

None of them had forgotten the heat of a Sydney Cove summer.

'I never thought England could look so good,' Edward said.

'Well-spoken for a Scotsman,' Carl replied.

'Edward, are you well?' Mary Beth asked, feeling his forehead. 'You look awfully pale and, oh my heavens, you're burning up.'

'Aye, I ken I might have a rest after I've finished duties.'

'What more duties do you have? All your charges will be in the hands of the constabulary from hereon. You can rest now. I mean immediately. That's an order.'

'I need to make sure Mary Bryant is alright.'

'I'll make sure she's alright. And I'll let her know you said goodbye.'

Mary Beth had noticed how Edward's attentions had turned to Mary Bryant in the past few weeks.

'I'll have the surgeon attend to you at once.'

As Edward was heading to his cabin, Mary Bryant was being led down the same passageway, in chains for the first time in weeks.

'Please, just a moment,' Edward said to the constable who was pulling her along like a tethered animal. 'Do ye have to treat her like that?'

'Don' worry, my friend. I'm used to this and I'll be fine – come 'n' see me if ye're able, won' ye?'

'Aye, I'll be there, come what may,' he replied, squeezing her arm.

—✷—

Edward was sicker than anyone realised. He had succumbed to the fever that had taken so many of them on the trip home. He was fortunate it happened when it did so he could be transported immediately to a naval hospital practised in shipboard diseases. He was there for some weeks before being released into the care of his father and step grandfather who had travelled down from Pemberton. Thomas had wanted to come alone but Will insisted he accompany him.

The reason was soon obvious to Edward.

'Da, is that ye?' Edward asked in the half light of the hospital ward.

He had recognised the voice but could not reconcile the stooped, shadowy image with the father he remembered.

'Aye, lad, it's me. Who were ye expecting? King George? Well, sorry to say he's a wee bit busy today.'

The young man and his father hugged while Will rested his hand on Edward's shoulder.

'It's so good to see you, Edward,' Will said.

'Aye, and ye, Grand Da.'

—✷—

'Please can ye nay tell her about Mrs Bryant?' Edward asked Thomas and Will as the carriage drew up to Commodore and Mary Beth Parker's house in Highgate, London.

'Whatever ye like, lad,' Thomas replied.

He and Will looked at each other, agreeing there was a story here. They had spent ninety minutes early that morning waiting outside the dockyard prison while Edward enquired about Mary Bryant. Finally, he had been told she was in Newgate Prison in London seeing out her sentence and awaiting a possible second trial. It would not be possible to see her there. Edward was disappointed.

'Welcome, gentlemen,' Mary Beth said as she greeted them at the foot of the long steps leading from her front door down to the roadway. 'It's so lovely to meet you.'

She turned to Edward and gave him a long hug followed by a kiss on both cheeks. Thomas and Will stole another quick glance at each other.

'Mary Beth, this is my Da, Thomas, and my Grand Da, William Hartshorne; we call him Will. This is Mary Beth Parker, Commodore Parker's wife.'

Thomas apologised as he declined the invitation to tour the grounds of the magnificent home. He insisted he would be happy to sit in the carriage while Mary Beth showed Edward and Will around. Once they were finished, Thomas was helped up the steps and they entered the grand foyer. They were ushered to their rooms and then served cocktails. Commodore Parker and Carl Solander joined them for a dinner of turkey and vegetables, along with fine French wine.

'*What would Mary Bryant think of this?*' Edward pondered. '*Mary Beth Parker and Mary Bryant, about the same age yet at two ends of the uneven spectrum that is life's circumstances. Both good women in their very different ways.*'

'So, did you manage to see Mary, Edward?' Mary Beth asked.

Thomas and Will looked to their food.

'Well, seeing as you ask, I did try but she's been taken to Newgate and I'm told it'll be impossible to see her there.'

'I dare say it will but you shouldn't concern yourself. She'll be cared for.'

'Oh, so ye've been in contact?'

'No, my wife will not be having anything to do with her,' Commodore Parker interrupted before Mary Beth could speak. 'But she has urged me to be in contact with Lord Boswell who has a reputation for looking after people in her circumstance.'

'Oh, in what way, if I might ask, sir?' Edward asked.

'Certainly. James Boswell is what we might call a philanthropist who looks for good causes, especially among the poor. He is also a lawyer who uses his skills to help people who cannot afford legal representation.'

'And he's a Scot,' Thomas interjected.

'D'ye ken him, Da?'

'Aye, I've had some wee dealings with him, mainly through Tommy Harding.'

'So, why does he do these things?' Edward asked.

'Well you might ask,' Mary Beth entered the conversation before her husband could silence her again. 'Let's just say he is especially generous with young *women* in desperate circumstances.'

'Now, now, my dear,' Parker said. 'We don't indulge in baseless rumours, do we?'

'Of course not, dear. Let's just say Lord Boswell would not have been my first choice to be brought to bear in poor Mary Bryant's situation.'

'You did ask me to assist, dear. And people with his skills and resources don't grow on trees.'

'I'm grateful for anything that can be done for Mrs Bryant,' Edward said. 'So thank ye, sir.'

'And so you should be, young man. But it's to my wife that you owe the thanks.'

'I don't need any thanks, Edward,' Mary Beth said. 'I'm happy to help the poor lady in any way. I simply want you to abandon any sense of duty you might have to her. Do you understand?'

'I'm nay sure I do.'

'All I'm saying is you shouldn't burden yourself any longer with concern for Mary Bryant. She'll be taken care of and you should just get on with your life. There is *no* place for her in your life. *Is that understood?*'

The table went silent.

'Well, that sounds like braw advice to me,' Thomas said. 'My lad does have a tendency to take his responsibilities very seriously. When we were in Persia, they almost got us both killed.'

'Oh, my heavens, yes,' Will said. 'Tell them about that incident, Thomas.'

'Yes, please do,' Carl said.

'Indeed, I want to hear *all* about this,' Mary Beth said, her deep bluey-green eyes softening as she looked at Edward.

—∿—

The next day, Commodore Parker had to leave for an unknown voyage. The rest of the party stayed on for another night. Dinner on the second evening was a less formal affair, something for which they all seemed grateful.

'Well, it's none of my business, *of course*,' Mary Beth said. 'But I think it's a splendid idea. Frankly, Edward, you're too lovely a man to be caught up in the ridiculous pomposity of the Royal Navy.'

Even before the dinner had begun, Mary Beth had consumed more wine than for the entire previous evening.

'If it's what ye want, lad,' Thomas said. 'I ken yer Grand Ma'd be delighted if ye dinna go back to sea.'

'I can vouch for that,' Will agreed. 'She's been a bundle of nerves ever since you went the first time.'

With Mary Beth's urging and Edward's agreement, Carl had laid out his plan for Edward to do the short course at Uppsala, preceded by gaining the necessary senior science credentials.

'Could I do the science at St Bartholomew's?' Edward asked, looking in Will's direction.

'Well, much as I hate to admit it, I think Stonyhurst would be the place,' he replied.

'I agree with that,' Carl said. 'Uppsala would look at the quality of the school and Stonyhurst is known as one of the best.'

'Aye,' said Thomas. 'They do produce some outstanding gentlemen.'

'Yes, even out of the odd Highlander,' Will replied.

'So, I suppose I could start in the middle of next year?' Edward asked.

'Why so late?' Mary Beth said. 'Why not at the *start* of the year?'

'Well, I'm still committed to the navy until mid-year.'

'My boy. You're not going back to sea, believe me. The surgeon said any return to sea would be bad for your health.'

'I dinna ken that,' Edward said.

'Well, believe me, he did.'

'If that's the case,' Thomas said. 'We'll need the surgeon to put it in writing.'

'Leave that to me,' Mary Beth said.

—⚬—

The next morning, they left for their respective homes, Carl to Oxford and Edward, Thomas and Will to Pemberton.

'So, I'll let you know when I'm presenting to the Naturalist Society,' Carl said to Edward. 'And I definitely want you there, remember?'

'And don't forget me,' Mary Beth said. 'We're a team, aren't we?'

'And you too, Mary Beth.'

Carl said his goodbyes and mounted his horse for the ride home. Thomas and Will thanked Mary Beth before climbing into the carriage, leaving Edward to his farewells.

'Thank ye so much, Mary Beth, for all ye've done for me.'

'There's no need. No need at all. It's been a pleasure and a privilege.'

'Ye've been like the mother I've nay ever had.'

'And just a little more than that, I hope.'

Mary Beth embraced him. They held each other for sufficient time for Thomas and Will to peer out the window of the carriage.

'Aye, a lot more,' Edward said, his arms tight around her.

'Let's just say a very special friend,' Mary Beth said.

She kissed him firmly on both cheeks, then stood back and looked at him with tears in her eyes.

'Very, very special,' Edward said, returning the kisses.

— ∽ —

Edward had posted William Bellamy's letter to his parents. He added a note to say he would be happy to visit them in Gateshead if they wished. He quickly received a reply thanking him for saving their son but making no mention of a visit.

This left Edward with one more duty to despatch before beginning his studies at Stonyhurst. He needed to see Angus Fraser's family in Listellick.

'Da, ye have to come with me. Imagine if I turn up at the Prendivilles without ye.'

'Yer Da's nay going anywhere,' Emma said. 'He almost killed himself coming to get ye in Portsmouth.'

Edward had noticed how irritable his grandmother was these days. She was also increasingly absent-minded. He heard her once calling out for him, only to find her staring blankly and talking to the wall.

'Wait for me, Edward, my darling. Wait for me, will ye nay?'

It was as if she was asleep and dreaming but her eyes were open.

'I'm nay going anywhere, Gran,' he said, moving closer and holding her hand. 'I'm just here.'

'Oh, laddie, go get yer Da's slippers. His feet are cold.'

Emma was having increasing periods where her mind would slip. At other times, she was razor sharp, knowing exactly what was going on around her and of what she approved and disapproved.

Edward went on his own to stay a while with the Prendivilles in Tralee and to try and connect with Angus's family.

XXIV

'*Tha e marbh; tha e marbh,*' the young, fair, auburn-haired girl shouted at him at the door. '*A dhuine aingidh; fhalbh's tarraing, a dhuine aingidh.*'

Edward's familiarity with Scottish Gaelic failed him and the more he tried to placate her, the more she shouted. She moved back into the house, so he stepped inside, only to see her returning with a kitchen knife, raised and ready for action.

'*Amy, cuir sin sios,*' an older man called out.

The girl raced back into the kitchen. Edward could hear the knife bouncing on the floor. He saw her flee out the back door.

'I apologise for my daughter,' the man said, extending his hand. 'I'm Robert Fraser; how can I help ye, lad?'

'My name's Edward Lovat. I've come to pass on some news about Angus.'

'If it's to tell us he's dead, I'm afraid ye're too late.'

'Oh, my Laird, nay. I'd nay idea. What happened?'

'We dinna ken. Only that he died while he was working as part of a gang. Heaven ken if we'll ever find out more than that.'

'I'm so sorry,' Edward said, shaking his head. 'He was a fine *dhuine.* We got on well.'

There was a moment's silence as the two men composed themselves.

'So, how did ye ken Angus?' Fraser asked.

'We were on the *Gorgon* together to New South Wales.'

'Were ye released early, then?'

'Oh, nay, sorry. I was an officer. That's what I was trying to explain to yer daughter.'

'Well, I'm nay surprised at my daughter's reaction then,' Fraser said, his face hardening. 'What business d'ye have here, then?'

'Angus and I became friends, of a sort. I ken that sounds strange but he was assigned to help me and my friend in Africa. My friend's an agronomist and he saw that Angus had worked on an estate where African flora had been transplanted. He asked the ship's captain if Angus could accompany us on some of our land explorations. We got to talking and he told me what happened and why he was being transported. He wanted me to come and make sure ye were all alright. He was especially worried about his sister. He ken she felt bad because she blamed herself.'

'*Chan e mise as coireach; chan e mise as coireach,*' came the shouting voice once again.

Amy Fraser ran past her father, fist in the air, landing several punches on Edward before he could avoid it. Her father pulled her from him and held her arms.

'*Amy, stad sin. Tha e an oifigear british,*' the father said.

Edward's Gaelic was good enough this time.

'I'm *nay* a British officer any longer; I'm a friend of yer brother. He asked me to come and see ye because he was worried about ye.'

Amy went quiet. Her father let her go.

'Why would Angus take up with an officer?' she said, speaking in English for the first time.

Edward explained again.

'Well, it still sounds to me as though ye're an *oifigear british.*'

She spat the words out, staring at him with her deep blue eyes. She turned and hurried away.

'I'm sorry, lad,' Fraser said. 'Ye've obviously come a long way to see us and I'm sure my lad'd want us to treat ye well. Can I make ye a cup of tea?'

Edward spent an hour or so with Robert Fraser learning about how his father had come to these parts during the Highland Clearances. The family had come from a place called Achanalt on Loch Achanalt, not far from Inverness. Robert's father had been the head gardener on an estate that was devastated by the English and so had come to Tralee where he picked up bits and pieces of agricultural work. He had taught Robert his trade and Robert now worked for a wealthy Englishman who lived in London but owned the estate in Listellick. Robert had done his job so well that the Englishman had negotiated for him to own the management title, a rare status in those times.

In spite of the Englishman's benevolence, Amy despised the fact they were dependent on anything English. Since Angus had been deported, she had rejected all English ways, including their language.

'So, what was she saying to me at the door?' Edward asked.

'Oh, ye'd nay want to ken all of it, but the gist was ye're a *duine aingidh* and ye should go to Hell.'

'Aye, I thought it might've been something about me being evil.'

'Amy and my wife are taking this all very badly. Amy's thrashing out, as ye've seen; my wife has just gone into herself. I apologise for her, but I ken she'd nay want to see ye.'

Edward left the house. He scanned the horizon to see if Amy was anywhere in sight.

—⚒—

'So, 'asn't the Lord been good to us to 'ave kept our li'l Redcoat safe?' Mrs Prendiville said. 'Let's say three 'ail Marys to thank God and ask Our Lady to keep 'im safe. 'ail Mary, full o' grace …'

Liam Prendiville, the eldest son, was there with his wife and three children and Mary with her husband, Michael O'Rourke, and two small children. Louise was still living in the old home helping her mother look after Mr Prendiville who did little these days but sit and stare at the fire. He had never said much; now, he said nothing at all. Paddy was stationed at a parish in Limerick so could not make the dinner.

Mary and Louise insisted Edward sit between them, as in the past. Nothing much had changed. All just a little older, perhaps wiser and, in the case of the old man, decaying. Not so Mrs Prendiville.

'Ye've nay changed a bit, Mrs P.'

'So, what were ye expectin'?' she said, rollicking. 'That I'd turned into a princess?'

'Nay, it's just that ye're still so sharp in yer mind. My Gran's nay so these days.'

'She's been through too much in 'er life, the poor dear.'

'Unlike ye, eh Ma?' Liam said.

'Oh I've been fortunate, thank the Lord. So many are worse off, and anyone 'o lost loved ones in the Rebellion, like yer Gran, Edward, well these things tear at the soul – and the mind, ye know?'

'Aye, I suppose, but she's always been so sharp. All of a sudden, it's gone.'

'Well, what did she lose? 'er 'usband, father, brothers, and then 'er poor mother? Glory be! 'er 'ome, 'er land, everythin' she'd known? These things eventually show. Ye need to be very sweet to 'er, my li'l Redcoat. She'll be sufferin' more than ye know.'

'Thanks, Mrs P. Ye've always been a pillar of wisdom.'

'Oh, go on with ye, boy. Now, just eat up. Ye'll need yer strength for tomorrow and that god forsaken Irish Sea. Thank the Lord I've never 'ad to go on it.'

'I'm sure it's like a stroll next door compared with a trip to the bottom of the world,' Liam said.

'Yeah, ye're so brave, Eddie,' Mary said, brushing his arm.

'Our 'ero, Teddy,' Louise said, throwing her arm around his back and kissing him on the cheek.

Edward loved the attention of the Prendiville girls as much as ever.

'Speaking of suffering, I need to tell ye about the Frasers.'

'Yeah, ye went to see 'em today, didn't ye?' Liam asked.

'Aye, and it's very sad.'

Edward recounted the story from his meeting with Angus through to the day's encounter with his father and daughter. He spared most of the details about the daughter.

'We'll make sure Paddy visits 'em when 'e's back in town,' Mrs Prendiville said. 'Poor souls. Robert was the father, did ye say? And the mother?'

'I dinna ken her name?'

'And ye said there's a daughter?'

'Amy.'

XXV

'I'm so excited ye're here,' William Henry said, helping Edward with his bags.

William Henry had been at Stonyhurst for two years. He was almost two years younger but they would be in many of the same classes.

'Ye'll love the science classes. Especially the ones with Father Pritchard.'

Father Anthony Pritchard had been a scientist and medical doctor before joining the Jesuit Order of Catholic priests. Will had been a Jesuit, also teaching at Stonyhurst, before leaving the Order to marry Emma.

Pritchard had a way of seeming to obey his superiors even when flagrantly disobeying. The headmaster, Father Cassidy, had been appointed directly from Rome twenty years beforehand. The appointing Pope was Clement XIV, Will's nemesis and main cause of departure from the Jesuits. Father Cassidy had been appointed to get the Stonyhurst Jesuits under Rome's control.

Clement's successor, Pope Pius VI, took a more kindly view of the Jesuits but was too caught up in his own survival to be worried about who was headmaster of a far-flung English school. Hence, the arch-conservative old man, Cassidy, was still there supposedly holding the fort for Pope Clement, dead by then for a decade and a half.

'Of course, Father,' was Pritchard's standard response to inane instructions.

Cassidy would subject protestors to unannounced classroom visits. Pritchard's ruse would ensure he could do exactly as he wanted without ever being visited.

'How is it you get away with it?' his colleagues would ask.

'Because I do what I'm told,' he would reply, the smirk almost inconspicuous.

Father Pritchard gave Edward one of the most far-reaching science tuitions available in England at the time. He would begin classes with a round of provocations:

'How do you think the world began?'

'God made it.'

'And what if there was no God?'

'But we know there's a God.'

'But just imagine there wasn't; how could it all begin then? That's when you're thinking like a scientist!'

Another line of questioning might be along the lines:

'What if I said your long lost relative was a fish?'

'Then, why don't fish have arms and legs?'

'Arms and legs and outer appearance don't matter but the basics of life on the inside do.'

Or, he might ask other questions:

'Ancient people believed they were related to all life, even the rocks and especially the plants and animals. Why do you think that was?'

'Because they didn't have the church to guide them.'

'Or it's because they were closer to the truth than we are.'

William Henry was shocked at some of it. Edward relished it. Pritchard's views reminded him of his father's. He tolerated other classes but saved his best for science. He asked Pritchard if he could attend all his classes, even ones not on his syllabus.

From time to time, some parents became concerned about Pritchard's views and brought the matter to the headmaster. Cassidy tended to shield Pritchard but if complaints built up, a meeting would be called. At these times, Pritchard handled himself with a combination of charm and appeal to parents' deepest concerns for their children. He would listen patiently and only when parents were convinced they were being heard, would he begin the appeal.

'I only ask the questions for that's what science is about. Your children have religious instruction to provide the church's answers. Important as those are, the world around us is changing so we need a generation that won't be overwhelmed by change, such as has happened in France, for instance. Your children can control changes rather than be overwhelmed by them. I'm sure that's what you want for them.'

The reference to France always worked with the English clientele. There was lingering concern among establishment folk that England might follow the French into revolution.

Edward attended two of these meetings, ready to defend his teacher. Thomas attended once, as a parent, also ready to defend what Pritchard was doing but only after vowing to Will that he would not lose his temper.

'I'm sure Father Pritchard can acquit himself without your kindly assistance,' Will said.

—◊◊◊—

Edward was given privileged access to Pritchard's visionary mind, even to ideas he was not prepared to parade before the class. These were precious moments, normally in Pritchard's study of an evening. Edward loved visiting him there, normally under the pretext of needing to go to confession. Pritchard had a well-tattered leather chair for visitors. Anyone willing to negotiate the obstacle course of books and papers that littered the floor was welcome to sit in it. Edward was more than willing.

'Doctor Newton said he thought there were likely many worlds beyond the one we know,' Pritchard said one night.

'Ye mean Isaac Newton, do ye, Father?'

'Yes, arguably the most brilliant man born to this time – apart from Jesus, of course.'

'So, if there are other worlds, does God ken about them?'

'Presumably, God *created* them.'

'That's a very different idea of God from what we hear in church, is it nay?'

'Indeed. Another of Doctor Newton's gems is that the bigger the world becomes, the bigger our ideas about God will need to be.'

'Or else God gets left behind?'

'No. Just the church's *idea* of God.'

—ɯ—

There were times when Edward could not wait to get home to Pemberton to talk these things through with his father and Will, and his grandmother if she was well.

'Ye need to be careful, lad,' Emma said one night after a long conversation about such things. 'Sometimes, ye just need to accept what is and be thankful. Anyway, it's past my bedtime. Sarah, darling, would ye help me to bed? I'm sure my dear husband wants to stay and talk about these godless things.'

Will looked at his wife. The Jacobite daughter urging caution.

'Yer Father Pritchard sounds like one in a million, lad,' Thomas said. 'Ye're very fortunate to have found someone like that to take ye through yer science tuition.'

'Indeed,' Will concurred. 'Perhaps there's hope for the Jesuits yet.'

'Ye dinna ever regret that ye're nay still there?' Thomas asked.

'Not a bit,' Will said. 'Imagine a life without your mother. I can't contemplate the emptiness.'

XXVI

'Charles, this is my friend, Edward Lovat,' Carl said. 'Edward, this is Mr Charles Towneley.'

'So nice to meet ye, Mr Towneley,' Edward said, shaking the old man's hand.

Towneley was the owner of the Towneley Estate in Burnley, Lancashire, a large tract of land with a grand manor house, including a chapel, some workers' cottages and surrounded by one of the most impressive gardens in the British Isles. They were filled with a mix of agriculture for produce and ornate flora, including some from Africa, Asia and from around Sydney Cove, thanks to the Solanders. The estate had remained in Towneley hands since the Norman Conquest in the eleventh century.

'Mr Solander tells me you have an interest in agricultural matters,' Towneley asked.

'I do, sir. I hope to go to Uppsala University to study agronomy when I'm finished at school.'

'Well, might I encourage you to do so, young man? The world's in desperate need of people who understand these things.

I fear we're heading into a time that could well destroy land productivity just as our burgeoning populations will need it more than ever.'

'I agree, sir.'

'Good, well, if you have any time, I'd be pleased for you to accompany Mr Solander as he surveys the estate. I'm sure you could only benefit from his postulations about the future of the place and, indeed, you might even have a few suggestions yourself. Would that be alright?'

'I'd be honoured, sir. Thank ye so much, Mr Towneley.'

Carl was in Burnley at Towneley's request to provide advice on future directions for the estate. In turn, Carl was keen to introduce Edward to Towneley. Edward was staying at Tommy and Margaret Harding's place for the weekend. Thomas and Sarah were there as well.

'Good, well I'll no doubt see you in church tomorrow,'Towneley said. 'I know Mr and Mrs Harding will want to bring you along. They're among our most faithful parishioners.'

There was no Catholic Church in Burnley. Any attempts to establish one in this very Protestant town had been resisted. The chapel in the Towneley Estate, named St Mary of the Assumption, served the purpose for local Catholics. The Towneleys had remained staunchly Catholic throughout all the religious wars, getting away with it largely because of their vast wealth. The estate was therefore a kind of haven for Catholics in the district. Its nickname was "Little Rome".

'Ah, aye, I'm certain I will then, sir,' Edward said with less enthusiasm than he would have wished.

'Aye, of course we'll come,' Thomas said when Edward mentioned about going to church the next day. 'It's the chapel where yer Ma and I were married and she's buried in the grounds. D'ye nay remember?'

Edward had childhood memories of going to visit his mother's grave but had forgotten where it was. Because these visits had affected Edward, Thomas had considered it better not to take him with him on his regular visits to tend to the grave.

'Sorry, Da. Of course. I'd forgotten Ma's there.'

—✺—

The next day, a Sunday, they all attended the 9.30am Mass. Tommy and Margaret went straight to the front row where Tommy could position himself for his church warden duties. Sarah and Edward helped Thomas down the aisle and into the same row. Edward hoped he would remember when to stand, sit and kneel without a Jesuit to direct him.

'*On this Feast of Saints Peter and Paul, we rejoice with all those who've given their lives for their faith,*' Father Philip Cocklin began his sermon. '*The many martyrs who have died at the hands of pagans, Jews and Muslims.*'

Thomas and Edward flinched. Edward had been settling back to daydream as was his wont through the sermons at Stonyhurst – unless Father Pritchard was preaching. Now, he was fully attentive. He wanted to be awake should his father want to take to the priest with the increasingly ample cane he carried these days.

'*Would we be prepared to die for our faith should the call come?*' Cocklin rambled on. '*Would we be ready to follow the lead of the Holy Pope, Urban II, when he commanded the brave Crusaders to go to the Holy Land to rescue Christianity's most sacred sites from the evil Muslim invaders?*'

Thomas began a series of loud sneezes, intermittent with coughing, clearing his throat and blowing his nose. In the small, high-ceilinged chapel in which the slightest noise echoed, it made it difficult for the congregation to hear the priest.

'*Know you … the Lord's work … kill the enemy ….fall to their sword … to Heaven … eternal reward.*'

The congregation was by now more concerned with Thomas than what the priest was saying. Charles Towneley crossed the aisle to escort Thomas out of the church. Just then, the priest finished.

'*In the name of the Father, the Son and the Holy Ghost.*'

'*Amen,*' the congregation said as one.

Thomas recovered immediately. Edward looked past Sarah to reassure himself his father was out of trouble. Thomas caught his eye and winked. The Mass proceeded without further incident.

After Mass, Thomas and Edward avoided meeting Cocklin while others, including Tommy and Margaret, milled around him.

'Lovely sermon, Father.'

'Thank you so much, Father.'

Thomas and Edward wandered over to the graveyard. Thomas bent over as best he could to clear some twigs and leaves from the headstone that stood in the shadow of an old oak. Edward went down on hands and knees to help.

Sacred to the Memory
Eliza Catherine Lovat
Beloved wife of Thomas
And mother of Edward
29th day of January, 1776
Aged 26 years
Requiescat in Pace

'I only wish I'd ken her, even for a day,' Edward said.

'Ye probably have, even if ye've nay realised it. She and Sarah are so much alike.'

'That's comforting. D'ye still miss her, even though ye have Sarah?'

'Oh, aye. She still has a very special place in my heart.'

'Along with Mahdiya?'

'Along with Mahdiya.'

'Ye have a big heart, Da.'

'I hope so, lad. Life's so much richer if ye do.'

'So, were ye sad being in there where ye were married and Ma was buried from?'

'Aye, until the sermon began,' Thomas replied, grinning.

'That was quite a performance, Da.'

'Well, it was either that or I'd throw this stick at him,' Thomas said, waving his cane above his head.

'If ye had, Da, I'd've jumped up and stuck it ...'

'Thomas, Edward,' Tommy was calling. 'Could I introduce you to my friends, Charles and Elizabeth Braithwaite? Charles, Elizabeth, this is my lifelong friend, Thomas Lovat and his son, Edward.'

'I'm so pleased to meet you, Colonel,' Charles Braithwaite said. 'Of course, we know all about you. And we're delighted to meet you too, young man.'

'Are you alright, Colonel?' Elizabeth Braithwaite asked. 'You had us all quite concerned in there.'

'Aye, I'm fine now. These coughing fits come on me now and again. I do hope I dinna disturb ye too much.'

'No, not at all. I've heard that sermon from Father Cocklin before – a few times in fact.'

'Yes, well, he does give it on this Sunday each year – and a version of it every other Sunday,' Charles Braithwaite said, smiling. 'Mind you, I think it's quite relevant to being a Catholic in this very Protestant environment. One needs to be reminded just how important our faith is to us. Don't you agree, Tommy?'

'Indeed I do, Charles,' Tommy said while Margaret nodded.

Thomas and Edward said nothing. Sarah smiled.

The Braithwaites had converted to Catholicism some time before. Like most converts, they were more Catholic than the lifetime Catholics.

'Jane, Henry, come over here and meet the Hardings' friends,' Charles Braithwaite called out.

'These are our children, Jane and Henry.'

Edward shook hands with Henry, who was perhaps twelve years of age. He was more taken by the shy brunette, Jane, fifteen years of age or so. Jane did not extend her hand. Instead, she made a small curtsey as if Edward was royalty. She was wearing a large summer hat that almost hid her deep brown eyes but, as she arose from the curtsey, he saw them flutter a little.

'Please, would you join us for lunch?' Braithwaite asked. 'It would be our pleasure to entertain you.'

'Aye, that'd be braw,' Edward said with more enthusiasm than intended.

He glanced quickly in Jane's direction. She smiled.

'If everyone else is happy with that, I mean.'

'Splendid,' said Braithwaite. 'I'll just go and see if Father Cocklin can join us.'

Edward caught his father's eye.

'I may have use for that cane yet,' Thomas whispered.

—◊—

The Crusader priest could not join them, so Thomas's cane remained intact. It was as well because the conversation between the enclaved Catholic Braithwaites and the ever gullible Hardings reminded Thomas how much clearer the air was outside denominational religious settings.

Every so often, he would wriggle in a way that told Sarah he might be about to say something that would spoil the otherwise pleasant Sunday lunch. At that point, she would rest her hand on his knee or, on one occasion when she almost moved too late, kicked him under the table.

Edward had noticed these things as well. Even at the tender age of seventeen, he had seen more of the world in all its differences than these people locked in their entrenched dogmas.

'Jane, why don't you show young Edward around the grounds while we adults retire to the lounge room for tea?' Charles said. 'Unless, of course, you'd prefer to join us for tea as well, young man.'

'Nay, I'd love to see the grounds,' Edward replied.

'And you go with them, Henry,' Elizabeth said.

'Mummy, Henry hates walking around the grounds. You know that.'

Edward had wondered at one point if Jane was mute. She had sat through the meal saying nothing, merely looking up from time to time and offering a shy smile in his direction.

'All the same,' Elizabeth said. 'I think it only proper that Henry goes with you. And that's that. Do you hear me?'

'Yes, Mummy, I hear you.'

Henry was a very young twelve-year-old, uninterested in socialising. He merely wanted to run ahead and find a stick, a nest of ants, or generally let out some energy. This left Edward and Jane fairly much to themselves.

'Henry, leave it alone; you'll get stung,' Jane called out to her brother who was worrying a bee that just wanted to suck on a bright yellow flower.

'Aaaahh,' Henry shrieked as the bee took to hovering around his head.

His antics had been a useful distraction for two young people who wanted to connect but had little idea how to do it.

'So, you like flowers, do you?' Jane asked.

'Aye, I love all sorts of things about nature. What about ye?'

'No, not really. Some flowers are pretty but I prefer being inside.'

'What d'ye like doing most, then?'

'Oh, I read and sew and my mother's teaching me how to cook. Just a few basic things I'll probably never need anyway because we have a cook – and a maid as well, you know?'

Henry came running back and began to encircle them, laughing as though it was the funniest thing ever.

'Henry, don't be a pest!' Jane said.

'Are you going to marry him?' Henry asked.

'Don't be ridiculous, you silly boy.'

'Why don't you marry my sister and take her away so I never see her again?' Henry shouted as he ran away to do some more mischief.

'Please forgive my brother. He's very impolite.'

'It's alright. I dinna mind.'

'Do you mind if I ask you something?'

'Nay at all.'

'Why is it you speak like a Scotsman when you're really English?'

'Well, I was born in England, it's true, but my Da's a Highlander and my Gran also. So, I suppose I've just copied them.'

'Doesn't it bother you?'

'What? Sounding like a Highlander? Nay. Why should it?'

'Well, Scots are not particularly welcome around here, especially Highlanders. Many people refer to them as traitors. Did you not know that?'

'Aye, my Da tells of when he was at school and how he was often called "traitor" or "traitor's son" or something like that.'

'What would he do about it?'

'As I ken my Da, he'd have pummelled them.'

'Pummelled? What does that mean?'

'He'd have punched them so hard, they'd never say it again,' Edward laughed.

'How vulgar.'

Henry came running back, this time holding something behind his back. Jane tensed up as though this had happened before. She reached for Edward's arm.

'Do you want a present, Jane?'

'What is it, you silly boy? Not another beetle!'

'No, it's not a beetle,' he said as he placed a small spider on her sleeve and ran away before she could hit him.

'Ooohh, get it off me,' Jane shrieked, flaying her arm up and down trying to shake the beast off.

'Hold still,' Edward said, grabbing her arm.

'Get it off me; get it off,' Jane shouted, trembling.

'There ye go,' Edward said as he picked the spider up in a pincer grip and placed it on the ground.

'Kill it; kill it,' Jane shouted, huddling under Edward's arm.

'It's alright. The wee thing's nay doubt more frightened than ye're.'

Jane went quiet but continued to shake. Edward threw his other arm around her. The top of her head was close to his nose, the odd hair fluttering in the breeze and tickling it. He could smell soap and perfume, just as he had when hugging Mary Beth. Her cotton and silk dress felt clean and smooth and he could feel her body underneath it. They were like this for barely ten seconds but the moment would stay with Edward for some time.

'What on earth is going on?' Elizabeth was calling as she stepped into the backyard. 'Young man, unhand my daughter.'

Elizabeth wrenched Jane from Edward's arms and stood between them.

'What are you doing to my daughter? Are you alright, darling?'

'Mummy, please. It was Henry's fault. He put a spider on my dress and Edward was being a perfect gentleman in helping get rid of it.'

'Well, thank you, young man, but my daughter will be fine now. Jane, I want you inside and where's that brother of yours? Henry, come here this instant.'

With Henry banished to his bedroom and Elizabeth tending to her daughter, Edward recounted what had happened. The men were amused, Sarah less so.

'Poor Jane,' she said. 'I can remember you doing things like that to me, Tommy. So scary!'

'Did you?' Margaret asked her husband.

'Possibly!' Tommy replied.

'Probably!' Thomas added.

They laughed.

'My wife's very protective of our children,' Charles said. 'I apologise if she overreacted, young man.'

'That's quite alright, sir. I understand why she'd wanna protect such *boidheach* bairns.'

'Edward means your children are beautiful,' Sarah explained. 'Children are so precious.'

Thomas and Sarah glanced at each other. It had not been their fate to have their own child.

As the guests were stepping into the carriage, Elizabeth and Jane came out of the house.

'Jane insisted on saying goodbye,' Elizabeth said.

Amidst the farewells, Jane made her way to Edward who was standing slightly apart.

'Thank you, Edward. You were my gallant hero.'

'It was nay anything. I enjoyed our talk.'

'So did I.'

She reached up and gave him a delicate kiss on the cheek. At the same time, she pressed something into his vest pocket.

—⁊⁊—

That night, in his room at the Hardings, he pulled out the tiniest of blue envelopes, smelled its perfume and opened the contents. It was an equally small piece of blue paper with the words, *you can write if you wish*, followed by the Harding address.

XXVII

'I*'m so excited,' William Henry said, alighting from the carriage.* 'This is gonna be the *as fhearr* holiday.'

William Henry's parents had arranged for him to stay at Pemberton over Christmas while they were in Edinburgh caring for their other son, still unwell.

'Aye, it'll be grand,' Edward replied.

Edward had worried how he would cope with the long break without his studies and his frequent conversations with Father Pritchard. Part of him was impatient to move onto Uppsala and the rest of his life. But another part was enjoying the secure environment of the school, and especially the two ends of friendship with Pritchard and William Henry.

Having William Henry staying over would help to distract him. It would also provide some young company in a household that was coming to seem decrepit. Thomas was increasingly disabled and Emma frail and vague.

'So, are ye still going into the army?' Edward asked.

'Aye, I expect so. What d'ye ken about that?'

'It's up to ye.'

'Ye dinna sound enthusiastic. Remember when the only thing ye wanted was to be in the navy?'

'Aye, and it was a *math* thing to do then but nay anymore.'

'Why's that?'

'There's just other things. I love the science and there's the course in Uppsala – and I'll probably wanna get married someday and I dinna ken a naval career and being a husband and father go well together. So many of the sailors said things like that to me...'

'Whoa, horsie,' William Henry said, laughing. 'Ye wanna get married all of a sudden? Where's all that coming from? Have ye met a girl, have ye? Who is it? Tell me all about it – now!'

Edward had kept the relationship with Jane to himself. After all, there had only been a few letters between them. So, even William Henry, favourite cousin and best friend, did not know about her.

'Possibly,' Edward replied. 'But ye have to keep this strictly to yerself.'

Edward filled him in on the basic details. The meeting after church and the letters.

'What about that girl in Ireland, though?' William Henry asked.

'Oh, that was nay serious. I'd forgotten I even mentioned it. She'd be a nightmare anyway. But with Jane, it seems real. She's lovely and I miss her, even though I've only met her twice.'

'Twice? I thought ye said ye'd only met her that once.'

'Nay, twice. That first time and then one morning at Stonyhurst.'

'She was at Stonyhurst? When? Why did ye nay tell me?'

'Ah, it was the worst morning of my life. I'd slept in so I went straight to chapel without washing or even doing my hair. Father Bingham stopped me at the chapel door and said, *what are you doing coming to chapel like that?* I said I was sorry and I'd go back and wash; but he said, *no, you're not getting out of chapel that easily. Go in there and smell the place out. It'll serve you right.*'

'Sewer-pit Lovat,' William Henry laughed.

'Sewer-pit's right. I could smell myself as I walked up the aisle; thankfully, I was late so no-one was next to me. Then, just as I was genuflecting and about to step into the pew, who do I see staring at me from the side chapel?'

'Dinna tell me. Queen Charlotte?'

'Oh, how I wish! Jane Braithwaite – looking as clean and nay doubt smelling like a rose – and there's me looking like I'd just risen from the dead.'

'So what did ye do?'

'I could nay believe it. I'd been so wanting to see her, imagining us meeting up in some beautiful field, rose petals everywhere, and here am I smelling like poo. The more I panicked, the more I could feel the sweat piling up inside my clothes. I wanted to die.'

'So what *did* ye do?'

'I had to see it out. When I went to communion, I moved over to the farthest row and hoped she'd nay smell me from where she was. Then, at the end of Mass, we all processed out together and were supposed to go straight to class. But Bingham was haranguing some of the students at the head of the row, so we were slow getting away. Before I ken, I felt this tug on my sleeve. I turned and there she was, smiling sweetly. *I thought maybe you hadn't seen me, Edward*, she said. It was *dorainneach*. I felt like – what's that saying? – pearls before swine. She was the pearl and I was the stinking hog!'

'So what happened?'

'I just said how I was really happy to see her but I had to go straight to class. I was holding my breath most of the time, thinking if I could nay smell myself, maybe she'd nay either. Then, Bingham called out and told me I was nay meant to be talking. I tell ye, I nay ever felt so kindly to Bully Bingham. But then he noticed it was Jane I was talking to and said, *I'm sorry Miss Braithwaite, of course you can talk with Edward if you wish*, and then went and marched the rest of the class away. I was stuck there, torn between wanting to be there and wanting to be in my grave.'

'So, did she say anything? I mean about yer appearance and – how shall I put it *finealta* like – piggish odour?'

'Very *finealta*, Billy Boy, very delicate! Nay she dinna say a word. It was as though I'd just bathed and had a haircut. She just kept saying, *I'm so looking forward to our next time together*. And then when I finally had to go, she said, *I love your letters*.'

'Oh, that lassie is *ann an gaol* with ye, Eddie. There's nay doubt. Her eyes and especially her nostrils were deceiving her because she's totally in love with ye. Poor, poor lassie!'

Edward picked up a pebble and threw it at William Henry who ducked and let it sail by.

'Sorry if I'm being too *maol*,' Wiliam Henry said, 'but when *are* ye two getting married?'

Edward picked up a stone and threw it. William Henry caught and made to throw it back harder but let it fall.

'Now, seriously, when are ye going to see her again?'

'I dinna ken. I dinna ken.'

'Well what about yer birthday? Ye could invite her to yer birthday. Let's face it, ye're in desperate need of some guests.'

—⁂—

The seed was sown and, when Sarah asked who he would like to celebrate his birthday with, Edward rattled off a few names, with Jane and Henry Braithwaite inserted in the middle.

'Jane and Henry …?' Sarah asked.

'Aye, I ken Henry's only young but we got on well that day at their place.'

'Well, how about we just invite Henry then?' Thomas laughed.

'Don't be cruel, Thomas. It's obvious the boy has some feelings for Jane.'

'Yes, and I seem to remember another birthday event that brought some special people together,' Will said.

'Who are these people?' Emma asked. 'I dinna want too many *srainnsearan* here.'

'It's alright, Ma,' Thomas said. 'They're friends of ours; especially Edward's, aren't they lad?'

'Aye, Da. They are!'

—⟞⟝—

Elizabeth Braithwaite insisted on accompanying her children to Pemberton on the 26th of January for Edward's eighteenth birthday celebration. Sarah had intervened to convince her it would be alright and that her daughter would be in safe hands the whole time. On the day, Elizabeth hovered over her daughter, hardly letting her out of her sight. Emma caught onto what was happening and, in one of her sharper moments, invited Elizabeth to come inside and look at some of her embroidery.

'Mummy's gone inside,' Jane said. 'I can't believe it.'

'Can we go for a walk then? Just over there in the garden. And there'll nay be any spiders at this time of year, I promise.'

'Happy birthday. I was really pleased to be asked.'

'Thank ye. I dinna ken when I'd get to see ye again. And *of course* I wanted to catch up with yer brother.'

'Oh, my brother. He drives me crazy – and on top of Mummy's protectiveness!'

'I was worried yer Ma'd nay let ye come.'

'You had every reason to be worried. We have my father and your stepmother to thank. They corralled her like a stubborn mare and coaxed the bridle into place. Where she drew the line was in allowing me to come without her.'

'Oh, well,' Edward said. 'I'm sure she must be enjoying an eighteenth birthday celebration.'

It was a fine afternoon but chilly away from the fire and, by now, they had wandered further than intended. Jane shivered at one point and Edward took off his coat and laid it over her shoulders.

'You'll freeze, Edward.'

'Nay. I feel perfectly warm.'

'So do I,' Jane said, squeezing his hand. 'So do I.'

—◊—

A week later, Edward and William Henry were back within the damp walls of Stonyhurst. Final exams were due by June. Science classes were now taken by Father Docherty. He was introduced to the students as one of the best biologists and geologists in the whole Jesuit Order. Edward's excitement was short-lived as Docherty proved to be as boring a teacher as Father Pritchard was stimulating.

'He might ken a lot about it but he has nay idea how to teach.' Edward told his father on the first visit home. 'I suppose it's because he's so auld.'

'Docherty?' Will said. 'He was old when he was born. He's supposed to be a specialist in natural science but, by reputation, the dullest of teachers.'

'Well, ye ken what they say, lad,' Thomas said. 'A good teacher makes for dependent students but a bad one for independent learners. So, ye just have to do the learning yerself. It's braw ye've had the experience of Father Pritchard but I'm afraid to say there are more Dochertys than Pritchards in the teaching world – and ye might even find that in Uppsala.'

Edward took his father's advice to heart and he and William Henry spent night after night reading up on all the learning they were missing in Docherty's classes. When they found themselves in a quagmire, Edward would take the matter to Father Pritchard who always seemed to know the answer.

'So, why do ye nay teach Biology and Geology, Father?' Edward asked on one occasion.

'Because Father Docherty is the expert,' Pritchard said, winking.

—◊—

In the final exams, Edward passed English and European History with moderate results. On the other hand, he scored top marks in all science subjects, including Botany. In Cosmology, he scored 99%, the highest result the Jesuits could remember.

'I've Father Pritchard to thank for that.'

Edward applied for the short course in Uppsala with Pritchard and Carl Solander as his two referees. He was accepted and invited to take his place on the 1st of September, 1794. William Henry was heading to the Military College in Manchester.

'Do write, Edward; ye ken ye're my best friend by far,' William Henry said.

They were sitting looking over the lights of Preston, having drunk too much ale.

'Of course I will,' Edward slurred. 'But ye must do the same. And we'll meet up at the end of the year. Will ye be coming to stay at Pemberton for Christmas?'

'Aye, I ken so. My brother's still very *tinn*. It's tearing Ma and Da apart.'

XXVIII

Edward had never seen the colours that abounded in Uppsala. Even on a very warm September day, signs of autumn were apparent. Leaves of various hue were everywhere, many still on the trees but at least as many on the ground. The blood orange and egg yellow were the most striking.

'You must come to the main cemetery then,' Anna Karlsson said after Edward had commented on the colours.

Anna had been assigned to show the "Scottish boy" around the town. She was in her third year of a History major, with a special strand in Medieval Swedish Rune Stones.

'The cemetery, did ye say?'

'Yes. It's important to Swedes to die well and rest in pleasant surroundings. We try to create a Heaven on Earth.'

Edward was thinking of the cemeteries he had seen. The one in Eskadale was pleasant enough but the one in Sydney Cove, without a blade of grass, was in his mind. Nothing could have prepared him for what he saw as they turned into the cemetery gates.

'Where are the graves?'

'They're here. You just have to look for them.'

As if an afterthought, the gravestones were wedged in between the array of trees, shrubs and flower beds. It was as though the foliage mattered more.

'I've nay seen anything like it.'

Edward began naming genus and species of the varieties of flora before them. It was as much to impress Anna as to do justice to the botanical science.

As they moved outside the gates at the other end, Edward spotted what initially looked like other gravestones but, in this case, outside the cemetery and free of floral adornment.

'What are these then?'

'Ah, how long do you have? These are rune stones, my speciality. I warn you I can talk for hours about these.'

'Please do, then.'

'Alright, let's have a quick look at these and then I'll take you to the inn for an ale or two. You're looking as hot as I feel. You do take an ale, do you? I must admit I've never known a Scotsman. Perhaps you don't drink?'

'An ale sounds braw.'

'Braw?' Anna laughed. 'Is that good or bad?'

'Good. It means it's a very braw idea.'

They moved among the rune stones and Anna explained that they were partly like medieval newspapers. They carried messages about all sorts of things, day to day humdrum all the way to the most profound beliefs about life, death and afterlife. Normally, there was writing of some sort to convey the message but at other times an image carved into the stone and, still at other times, nothing. Just the stone that would symbolise something important to those who understood what it meant.

'So, who were these people?' Edward asked, taking the first gulp from a very good Swedish beer.

'Not as good as James Squire would make,' he thought to himself. *'But good enough.'*

What the ale lacked, the company made up for. He looked at Anna's abundant blonde hair hanging loosely across her cheeks and down over her shoulders. The most piercing bluey-green eyes looked out from blemish-free olive skin. Since sitting in the inn, she had pushed her loose-fitting sleeves up so her arms were bare, as were her lower legs as she pulled the dress above her knees.

Edward had been taken by surprise when he first met Anna that morning. He was certain a girl would not be assigned to show a new boy around in an English school. Then, she appeared in a striking summer dress of orange hue that matched some of the autumn leaves they saw that day. It hung loosely over her body. Added to a level of confidence he was unused to finding in a woman, Anna Karlsson presented as someone not to be taken for granted.

As the day unfolded, he managed to distract himself with the beauty of the surroundings and the genuine interest of cemeteries and rune stones. But here, now, sitting across from such a knowledgeable woman, displaying more flesh than he'd seen before in female form, he felt quite defenceless.

'Who were these people?' Anne replied. 'Well, you'd call them Vikings, I believe. They're our Swedish ancestors. They hailed from here and the other Scandinavian parts and then moved to the British Isles, especially Scotland.'

'Oh, aye, they had a fearsome reputation.'

'Ha. Fearsome? I think all you English find Scandinavians fearsome. You are so correct!'

Edward took the final swig of an ale he could feel going straight to his head.

'Well, for a start, I'm *nay* English. I'm a Highlander, grandson of a Jacobite warrior and probably have more Viking in me than ye.'

'Oh, is that so, Edward Lovat?' Anna said, raising two fingers in the direction of the waiter. 'So, you don't find me fearsome, is that what you're saying?'

'Nay at all. I've been to the wildest parts of the world and seen *far* more fearsome creatures than ye.'

'Well, why is it you keep staring at me the way you do then?'

'Staring? I dinna ken I've been staring at ye.'

'You've been staring at me since we met this morning. Every time I looked at you, you turned away, but I knew you were staring at me. Is there something about me you don't like?'

'Oh, my God, no,' Edward blurted out.

The two ales arrived at that point and Edward quickly reached for his and drank half the tumbler. When he put it down, he looked at Anna who was smiling.

'Well, you were saying?'

'You're perfect!'

'Thank you. I agree. Finish your drink and let's go.'

It was only later that Edward would learn about the strength of Swedish ale. He felt as if he was floating as he walked alongside Anna, fearful of where she was taking him. At one point, he stumbled and she grabbed him to stop him falling.

'There, there, Jacobite warrior. We can't have you breaking anything on your first day in Uppsala.'

Anna wrapped her arm around Edward's arm and led him back to the dormitory.

'What number is your flat?' she asked.

'102.'

She led him to the door, helped him find his key and watched him open the door and begin to move inside.

'Aren't you forgetting something, Jacobite?'

'Oh, I'm so sorry. Thank ye so much for showing me around today.'

'It was my pleasure. Now, would you like me to teach you about some Swedish courtesies?'

'Ah, aye, of course.'

'Well, this is how the Vikings used to say farewell,' she said, holding his two cheeks in her hands and kissing him on one cheek, then the other.

'Thank ye. That's a bonnie custom.'

'Bonnie? Not so fearsome then?'

'Nay at all.'

Then, without saying a word and continuing to hold his two cheeks, she placed her lips on his lips and kissed him, first lips on lips and then slowly placed the tip of her tongue in his mouth. He felt it flitting across his teeth and then touching the tip of his own tongue.

'I'm in 313, two floors above,' she said as she pulled away.

'In the same building? Lads and lassies in the same building?'

'Of course. This is Sweden; we are the real Vikings, Jacobite.'

—⁂—

There were four beds in Edward's room but the other three occupants had not arrived. He slept fitfully that night, torn between excitement and guilt each time he thought of Jane.

'Now, don't you even look at those Swedish girls, will you?' were all but her last words to him.

'I'll be far too busy – except when I'm thinking of ye.'

Yet, here he was, barely in the place twenty-four hours and dreaming of a girl he had met only today.

The next morning, Edward ate breakfast alone in the refectory. He came in late, hoping to avoid Anna. The refectory was half empty and most seemed to be finishing. He took a plate from the pile and filled it with an egg, slice of bacon and a buttered roll. As he turned to his table, Anna and three of her friends walked in.

'Good morning, Jacobite. These are my friends, Elsa, Lilly and Ebba. Girls, this is my good friend, Edward Lovat. He's a Jacobite warrior so be careful of him.'

'Good morning; I'm pleased to make yer acquaintance,' Edward said, gripping the plate with both hands.

'Pleased to make *yer* acquaintance too,' Lilly parroted, while the others laughed as if all secrets had been revealed.

'Now, don't make fun of my friend, girls,' Anna said, placing her hand gently on his arm. 'It's nice to see you, Edward.'

She gave him a small kiss on the cheek and walked away with her friends.

Edward felt the moisture lingering on his cheek as he hurried to finish his breakfast. The feeling brought to mind some of those troubling thoughts through the night. He left the refectory without looking around at the girls. He raced out of the dormitory building and headed for the town, found a church and entered.

There was a service happening but not one with which he was familiar. He simply sat in the back, hoping to regain a measure of the tranquillity and clear purpose of twenty-four hours beforehand.

—⚬⚬⚬—

Two days later, Edward was attending his first class. While focussed on the practical side of agronomy, there was enough science to explain why he had needed at least a high school level of it in order to enrol. The format was for a formal lecture to be given to all the students, in this case just seventeen hand-picked from five countries. Five tutorials would follow, one for each language group, Swedish, French, German, Spanish and English.

The first lecture, *Introduction to Agronomic Science*, sounded sufficiently non-intimidatory. It was to be given by Professor Andersson who was Swedish but said to be multilingual. Edward could not testify to his skill across the other languages but concluded his English was almost non-existent. Fortunately, the word "agronomy" was sufficiently new to be universal, so, whenever he heard *agronomi*, he knew exactly what was being spoken about. Not so, however, basic words like "soil" (*jord*), "plant" (*vaxt*) and flower (*blomma*), though he quickly caught onto the latter and the rest would eventually become recognisable.

The first hour of the two-hour tutorial was a virtual repeat of the lecture in the native tongue of the language group in question.

Edward's tutor was Lars Bengtsson who was completing his Masters degree in agronomy. He was working at the same time on an agricultural estate near the university, so he understood the practical side in a way that seemed as distant to Professor Andersson as was his English.

In the first lecture, Edward learned about the evolution of agronomy from its related sciences. He learned how the genetics and physiology of plant life and the science of soil types had been known for some time, as had a great deal of practical knowledge about what works and does not work in different soils and environments. Agronomy developed as a distinctive blend of scientific and practical knowledge.

Over the first five weeks, he learned how his new science was especially timely, granted the age of discovery that was upon the world, seeing European populations moving into new environments where they would have to survive or perish. In week Six, he was asked to share with the tutorial group his experiences of the challenges that New South Wales was confronting in this regard. He also spoke about the flora he had seen on his travels. In week Eight, he gave the same talk to the entire group during lecture time, with Lars helping in the translation.

—∞—

'You *are* coming to the party in 313, are you not, *Edouard*?' Louis Gasquet asked.

'Nay, I've too much work to do.'

'Oh, but Anna *will* be disappointed. She expressly asked that you be there,'

Louis was the French student who shared lodgings with Edward. The other two were German twins, Ulrich and Heinrich Oser. The Germans were as serious about their studies as Louis was not.

'That's alright. Tell her I'll come to the next one.'

'Oh, but you don't want them to think you're a *German*, do you?' Louis persisted.

The German boys looked up from their deskwork and over their shoulders in that coordinated way they did everything. Even the disapproving look was identical. Only their dominant hand separated them, Ulrich being right-handed and Heinrich a "southpaw".

'I am only joking,' the French boy said with a poor imitation of a German accent. 'Go back to your books now. I will not disturb you again.'

Edward was ready to step in and prevent an affray, as he had done several times since the foursome had come together.

'*I'm beginning to see why the French and Germans have had so many wars,*' he wrote to his father.

Edward liked Louis in spite of his disregard for study. He also liked the German boys notwithstanding their abject seriousness. They made it easier to resist the many invitations that came to party away these precious few months. If it had not been for that first encounter with Anna, he might have been less guarded about social opportunities.

'Well, *c'est la vie*, as we say in Paris,' Louis said as he hastened out the door. 'Don't wait up for me.'

The German boys went back to their study in the undistracted way they always did. Meanwhile, Edward read over his notes for the test coming the next day, trying not to think of what he might have been missing in Room 313. Apart from the study, it was the constant letters from Jane that kept him focussed.

'*I hear those Swedish girls are rather libertarian in their ways,*' she had written just recently.

He had looked up the word "libertarian", finding the definition, "seeking individual pleasure", especially distracting. Tonight, he had to focus on his notes.

There was a knock on the door. Edward thought nothing of it.

'You're coming with us, Edward Lovat,' Anna said as she and two of her friends grabbed his arms and yanked him out the door, marching him along the corridor and upstairs.

In the flurry of activity, he noted that the three girls were clad in a way he had not seen girls before. Bare arms, legs and cleavages seemed to envelope him. He could feel Anna's soft hand in his, her other hand pressing him forward. The other girls were helping in a propulsion that almost had him falling flat on his face. They reached the stairs and he hesitated.

'Nay, nay, please, I have work to do.'

'Work later, play now,' Anna said.

The girls pushed him up the stairs and along the third floor corridor.

'Success,' Anna shouted, pushing him through the door of 313.

'*Hourra*, welcome *Edouard*,' Louis called out.

Several other voices joined in.

'Now, what would you like to drink?' Anna said. 'We have beer, wine and vodka. Sorry, no Scotch Whisky!'

'Just a quick ale then, thank you.'

'Beer it is,' Anna called to a boy standing in the corner, the keeper of the drinks. 'I like this boy when he drinks beer.'

The drink-keeper brought over a large tumbler, contents frothing over the sides.

'Edward, this is Hugo,' Anna said. 'He is my boyfriend.'

Edward felt a mix of relief and envy.

'And Hugo, this is Edward. He's my boyfriend too.'

The envy evaporated, replaced by fear.

'So, where have you been hiding? I've missed you, Edward Lovat.'

Anna was slurring her words. Edward had a small sip, remembering his overindulgence at their last meeting.

'Oh, I've been busy studying.'

'Well, you shouldn't lead a girl on, Edward. Didn't your mother teach you that?'

'I dinna ken what ye mean.'

'Well, kissing me the way you did that first night. I was expecting we'd be seeing lots of each other. I've been very sad.'

'I'm sorry, Anna, if I gave ye the wrong impression.'

'What wrong impression? Did you not like kissing me?'

He took a large gulp of ale.

'Nay, I liked it very much.'

'Well so did I,' Anna said, moving next to him.

Before he could manoeuvre away, she drew his face towards her and kissed him just as she had that first night. This time, the kiss lingered, the tongue reached further.

Edward was aware of bodily responses that seemed beyond control. They were doused when he felt a rising tide of damp around his crotch. He pulled away to see his ale pouring steadily over his trousers from a leaning tumbler.

'Oh my,' Anna laughed. 'I didn't realise I was exciting you *that* much. Look everyone. I knew he liked me.'

The guests looked over and joined in the laughter.

'See, *Edouard*,' Louis called out. 'I told you this was better than study.'

'I really must go,' Edward said, trying to stand.

'Oh, no, you don't,' Anna said, dragging him back down. 'It's alright. I'll help you clean up.'

She grabbed a nearby cloth and began to rub his trousers where the damp was most obvious.

'Oh, please nay. Please, I canna!'

He managed to stand. Lilly pushed him down again.

'No, Edward, you can't go. Poor Anna's been so sad because you've been ignoring her. Look at her now.'

Anna had her head in her hands.

'I'm sorry, Anna. It's nay that I dinna like ye. I really like ye. I mean *really*. But I have a girl waiting for me at home.'

'What? In room 102? I'm going to report you.'

'Nay, In England.'

'In England? So, will you be kissing her tonight?'

'Nay. I suppose nay.'

'You *suppose*? Edward, my love, all I want is to be your girl tonight. I don't want to steal you. I don't want to marry you. Tomorrow, you can go home to your girl if you want but, tonight, I want you to be mine.'

'But I canna.'

'Oh, but from what I felt just before, you *can*,' she laughed, looking at his crotch.

'Nay, I canna, I'm sorry.'

'Edward,' Anna said, moving closer and taking him in her arms. 'Think of it this way. I'm doing your girl a favour because there are many girls here who would lead you astray and they *might* want to steal you. You are such a beautiful man. They might want you forever but I only want you tonight – and maybe tomorrow night and the night after that.'

Edward could feel every curve and protusion of her body pressing into him and her arms caressing his back and moving over the upper reaches of his bottom.

He pulled her arms away and looked her in the eyes.

'Anna, ye're a beautiful lass and I'm honoured ye'd want me but *I have a girl waiting for me.* I'm sorry.'

He turned and headed out the door. He raced down the stairs and was breathless by the time he reached his room. He had left without his key so he hoped the German boys were still inside.

They were.

'What happened?' Ulrich asked.

'Oh, nay anything. The lassies were just being a wee bit playful.'

'Well, you are a stronger man than either of us,' Heinrich said. 'Ulrich and I agreed that if those girls had dragged us out like that, we wouldn't be back until morning.'

Edward was surprised to hear the Germans speaking like that.

'But, I suppose you had too much work to do?' Ulrich said.

'Aye, perhaps, but I ken I'll go to bed anyway.'

Edward lay thinking about all that had occurred, including feelings he barely knew he possessed. He pondered on the words of the Germans and wondered if he had made the right decision.

He lay for a long time, trying to keep the image of Anna out of his mind.

Jane seemed a long way away that night.

—◊—

'Good morning,' Edward said to Anna and her friends one morning at breakfast.

He had avoided the refectory as much as possible after the 313 incident. Now, some weeks later, he felt it might be safe.

The girls continued eating their breakfast and chatting as though he was not there.

—◊—

The last few weeks of his short time in Uppsala went quickly. The fact of being drawn into sharing his rare experiences of the exotic worlds of Africa, Asia and the Antipodes had offered a sense of self-confidence he was not expecting. He could see clearly the importance of the opportunity he had been given and, for the first time, knew for sure that he had made the right choice about his future.

Amidst distractions and temptations, he had managed to attain a Distinction in Practical Agronomy.

—◊—

In early November, he received a letter from Mary Beth.

Dear Edward, I am sorry to be the bearer of sad news. My beloved John (Commodore Parker) procured a deadly fever on his last voyage. He died and was buried at sea. I am devastated, as you can imagine …

Also, I received word that Mary Bryant is very ill and has asked to see you ... I believe you will be home soon. Please come and see me at your earliest convenience and I will accompany you to see her. I do hope your last weeks in Uppsala are happy and beneficent ones. Your loving friend always, Mary Beth.

Between Jane, Mary Bryant, Mary Beth and Anna, Edward felt full of conflicting emotions, all of them to do with women.

He would be glad to leave Uppsala so he could re-connect with Jane.

—⁓—

'Surely you're coming, *Edouard*,' Louis urged. 'It's our last night here and our last chance to "kick up our heels", as you English say.'

'Nay, I have to pack and I'm leaving in the wee hours.'

'*Cieux au-dessus, Edouard*, even the Germans are coming to the party.'

'Yes, we are, Edward,' said Ulrich. '*Even the Germans*. What will people think of the Scots if you don't come?'

'Let them ken what they like. Please say goodbye to everyone for me.'

'Well, *mon cher ami*,' Louis said. 'If you're leaving early in the morning, I doubt I'll see you again because I don't plan to be back here tonight. *Adieu, que ton Dieu t'accompagne.*'

'From us too,' Heinrich said. 'We've enjoyed getting to know you.'

'Aye. Me too. I wish ye all well in yer future.'

When he woke at four in the morning, the room was empty. Not even the Germans had returned. With one last thought of what he might have missed that evening, he headed for the docks and sailed out of the harbour a little after dawn.

XXIX

Two weeks before Christmas, 1794, the boat sailed into Edinburgh Harbour.

'Where's Da?' Edward asked as Will and Sarah greeted him.

'He just couldn't make the trip in the end, darling,' Sarah replied, holding him tightly. 'He's so looking forward to seeing you.'

'Indeed he is,' Will said. 'We almost had to tie him down to stop him from coming.'

—✕—

'Lovely to see ye, lad,' Thomas said, hobbling out to the carriage.

They embraced. Edward could feel how feeble his father was. He held him for a second longer to regain some composure.

'So braw to see ye, Da.'

'I'm sorry I was nay there to greet ye off the ship but ye'll have to blame my doctor and nurse here,' Thomas said, motioning to Will and Sarah. 'And, of course, my chief surgeon who's inside waiting to see ye.'

Edward and Sarah took one arm each of Thomas and helped him inside. Will took care of the luggage.

'*Halo*, Gran.'

'*Halo*,' Emma said, a distant look in her eyes.

'*I'm losing both of them*,' he thought.

At dinner that night, they wanted a detailed rundown on all the events in Uppsala.

'It was mainly studying. But I had some braw walks around the town and countryside. It's a bonnie place.'

He told them about his room-mates, Louis the libertarian and the studious German twins.

'And what about those Swedish girls?' Will asked, smirking.

'Aye, I met some bonnie lassies.'

'So, do you have anything to tell us?'

'Of course he doesn't, Will,' Sarah said. 'He has his girl here in England, don't you, Edward?'

'Aye, I surely do. Speaking of which, I'd like to go and see her soon, and I need to get to London too.'

'London?' Emma said out of nowhere. 'Devilish place. Devilish. Dinna go to London.'

'Thanks for yer advice, Ma,' Thomas said. 'Why d'ye have to go to London, lad?'

Edward told them about Mary Beth's loss and Mary Bryant's illness.

'Poor Mrs Parker,' Thomas said. 'She must be devastated.'

'Well, I don't think you should go alone,' Sarah said.

'Ye should nay be mixing with bad folk,' Emma said.

'He's nay a bairn,' Thomas said.

Will remained silent, Sarah rolled her eyes and Emma returned to her private world.

—⁓—

'So, how did you find the people in Sweden?' Elizabeth Braithwaite asked as the family sat for tea.

'Most accommodating,' Edward replied.

'I hear they're quite liberal in their approach to things. Did you find that?'

'I was too busy studying, Ma'am.'

'So, you didn't meet any female students then? I've heard they cohabit with the boys. Surely that's not true!'

'Aye, they do. I met them at meals.'

'Really, Mummy,' Jane said. 'You're treating Edward as though he's on trial.'

After tea, Jane and Edward were given time to themselves in an outer closed veranda. Elizabeth sat within earshot and Henry raced around them, playing a game only he understood.

'It's cold away from the fire,' Jane said.

'Aye, but I doubt we'll be staying too long here,' Edward laughed.

'Yes, I'm certain that's the idea. So, tell me all about your time away.'

'There's really nay more to tell.'

'Even about the girls? You can tell me, you know?'

'Even about the lassies. To be truthful, perhaps if I hadn't had the most bonnie lassie here waiting for me…'

'Oh, you do know all the right things to say, Edward Lovat,' Jane said more loudly than intended.

Her mother coughed.

'So, when can we see each other to really talk?' Edward asked.

'Well, are you able to stay at the Hardings for a few days now?'

'Nay, I have to go to London before Christmas but I could come sometime in January – or you could come to my birthday again.'

'Oh, I wish I could. But I'm not sure Mummy will let me. So, why do you have to go to London?'

Edward told Jane more about Mary Bryant and Mary Beth.

'Truly, Edward? You're going to visit a criminal? Someone who stole from hardworking people and still didn't get what she deserved, by the sounds of it.'

'It's different when ye ken these people, Jane. She's just a poor lass who nay had a chance – and she's paid a terrible price.'

'Well, I think everyone has their chances. Some of us take them and others don't. Anyway, if you really want to see this wretched woman before she goes to Hell, then that's your choice.'

Edward was silent.

'And who's this widow you're going to visit?'

'Mary Beth Parker was the wife of the commander of my ship to Sydney and back. She was like a second mother to me. And now she's lost her husband in tragic circumstances.'

'Well, I still can't see why you have to go and see her. How old is she?'

'I dinna ken exactly. Maybe mid-twenties.'

'Then a very young mother one might say,' Elizabeth said, appearing out of nowhere and walking towards them.

Edward felt like he had on the ship when Grovely and his mates had him pinned in a corner.

'I'd prefer that you not go,' Jane said.

'I agree. If you wish the hand of my daughter – *in time*, mind you – then you need to desist from any other liaisons with women. Truly, I can't help but wonder now what really happened in Sweden.'

Edward's mind turned fleetingly to Anna.

—⚮—

'So, how's your girl?' Will asked on Edward's return to Pemberton.

Edward told of Jane's reaction – and the mother's.

'Mmm, well you know what they say, look at the mother and there's the daughter in a few years.'

'Aye, but I'd nay seen that before. Jane seemed so braw and, if anything, quite critical of her mother's mother-hen ways.'

'Oh, well, it's good to find these things out early on. But she's only young, isn't she?'

'Not that young. She's nearly seventeen.'

'Oh, quite ancient then. So, will you see her again?'

'Aye, I'm sure I will. She was upset in the end but we agreed to write after Christmas.'

—ന—

'Thank you so much for coming, Edward, dear,' Mary Beth said, greeting him off the coach.

Edward noted her bluey-green eyes shining through dark circles. There was a vulnerability he had not seen before.

She gave him the kind of hug she had given on their last meeting, only longer. It felt good and uncomplicated.

They spoke at length over dinner, just the two of them, one at either end of a table made for eight or so. Mary Beth still had two servants, one a cook and the other a butler of sorts. They were served a pleasant meal of fowl and vegetables, followed by apple pie and cream. The wine was as good as last time.

They retired to the lounge room.

Over dinner, they had spoken about all manner of things, from Mary Beth's loss of her husband, the fact that the house was secure because it belonged to her brother and then about Edward's time at Stonyhurst and in Uppsala.

It had been some time since they had seen each other but sitting in front of the fire, facing one another and talking freely, it felt as though they had never been separated

'And what of poor Mary,' Edward asked. 'When can we see her?'

'I'm sorry to break it to you like this, Edward, but Mary died; almost three weeks ago now.'

'Oh, my Laird, nay,' Edward said, putting his glass down. 'I really wanted to see her.'

'I know, darling Edward, and she knew too. Lord Boswell delivered a letter from Mary for you to read. She knew you were overseas and couldn't be here.'

'Oh, I'm so sad. Poor Mary; such a good person in her own way.'

'Yes, she was. Perhaps it's best that it's happened this way. Mary was very needy, you know?'

'Why did ye nay let me ken before this?'

Mary Beth hesitated.

'Well, if I can be totally honest, dear one, because I feared you might not come.'

'But I'd have come anyway.'

'Would you, my darling? Truly, would you have come to me?'

'Of course I would've.'

'Why?'

'Because we're auld friends.'

Mary Beth took a deep breath and stared into the fire. She remained silent but Edward could see her eyes were glistening.

'Are ye alright, Mary Beth?'

She wiped her eyes and stood up.

'I think it's time for bed; I'm very tired. You know where your room is. Please feel free to sleep in as long as you want. You must be exhausted.'

Edward stood up to see her out. She took a few steps towards the door and then turned and walked back to him. She held him by both arms and then drew her arms in around his body, pressing her head into his chest. Edward placed his arms around her. They stood silent.

Edward could feel her breathing heavily. The glistening brown hair he had been admiring all night was now tickling his cheek. He buried his nose deeply into its strands, taking in the sweet smell.

'I'm just so pleased you're here,' she said. 'Is that alright? Do you mind?'

'Of course I dinna mind. I'd nay be here if I did.'

'Thank you for saying that. Thank you; you're my best friend, you know?'

She pulled away and looked into his eyes. Edward noted her tears, almost hiding the hue of her eyes that he remembered from their first meeting. He drew her to him and they embraced again.

He slept well that night. The fine food, alcohol and soft bed helped. So did the feeling of contentment.

—⁂—

The next day, they went to Mary Beth's favourite teahouse for tea, scones and cake. They had a table in the corner of the small room, table cloth and starched serviettes immaculately pressed. The handle on the delicately etched teacup was smaller than Edward had ever had to manage before. It caused some amusement.

'And I never ken whether the jam should go first or the cream,' Edward said, his knife hovering over both.

'Oh, I know. It all depends on whom you ask; the Devons say one thing and the Cornish the opposite. I can never remember which is which.'

'Why dinna we do both then? And we'll vote on which is *nas fhearr*.'

'Wonderful idea.'

Whatever had been weighing on Mary Beth's mind the night before seemed to have eased.

'I have two things I want to ask you about for our dinner conversation tonight,' Mary Beth said.

'What are they then?'

'Well, I want to hear all about what you learned, especially at Uppsala, and how that might change what you did on our trip to the South Seas.'

'Aye, I ken I can talk about that. So what's the second question?'

'I'll leave that until tonight. And is there anything you want to ask me?'

'Nay, but I must get that letter from Mary from ye.'

'Of course,' Mary Beth said, a look of disappointment flashing across her face. 'Of course.'

—๗๗—

The roast that night was lamb and the pie was pumpkin. The wine was the same but Edward drank more than the previous night. Over dinner, they had talked at length about Father Pritchard's science classes at Stonyhurst and all he had learned, especially in cosmology lessons. Then, over pumpkin pie, it was all about agronomy at Uppsala and how he wanted to use his new knowledge.

Mary Beth was the perfect listener.

By the time they reached the lounge, Edward was light-headed.

'Now, remember I have a second question.'

'Oh, aye, I'd forgotten,' he slurred. 'Fire away, as we'd say in the navy.'

He noticed the look of hurt on Mary Beth's face.

'Oh, Mary Beth, I'm so sorry, so very sorry. How *neo-mhothochail* of me.'

'Neo what?' Mary Beth laughed.

'Insensitive. Stupid.'

'That's alright, my darling. I know you didn't mean anything by it.'

'Please, then, ask me anything ye want, anything at all and I'll tell ye. I owe it to ye.'

'Well, that's too good an invitation to ignore.'

Mary Beth hesitated for a moment.

'I want you to tell me about your romances. And especially in Uppsala. I don't doubt you maintained your virginity in Stonyhurst with a lot of priests looking over your shoulder. But I've been to

Sweden. I know what those girls look like and how they dress and how liberated they are. I cannot believe you were there for months and didn't want to ravage them.'

Edward was shocked. He had never heard his grandmother or Sarah as much as breathe about relations between men and women, much less about ravaging.

'Well, seeing as ye ask, there was one particular lass.'

'I wouldn't have believed you if you'd said otherwise. Tell me all about her. What was her name?'

'Anna; oh my Laird, Mary Beth. I'd better have another drink.'

Apart from the few snippets he had shared with William Henry, Edward had kept his emotional struggle in Uppsala to himself. Tonight, he shed the lot. Mary Beth listened, saying nothing until he had finished.

'You're such a beautiful man, Edward Lovat. I love you so much for who you are.'

'Thank ye. I'm thankful to share it all. It's been worrying me.'

'Why, in heaven's name? Everything you've described is perfectly normal, don't you know?'

'Aye, but not if I had a lass waiting for me.'

'And *do* you?'

'Well, I ken I did at the time.'

'And now?'

'I'm nay so sure.'

'Tell me about it.'

Again, Mary Beth listened without interrupting.

'Well, my dear, I can't tell you what to do. But what I can tell you is I'm here for you whenever you need me. I think you're a very special man.'

She stood, this time going straight to him and helping him to his feet. They hugged again.

'I'll see you at breakfast,' Mary Beth said, peeling herself away.

The time with Mary Beth had been the tonic he needed. He felt there was more she had wanted to say but had chosen not to.

He left reading the letter from Mary Bryant until well on the way to Pemberton. He dozed in the carriage and then woke and opened the envelope.

Dear Ed, I think ye know Im dyin. And it fels ok. I dont think Im goin to last to see ye. I wooda likd to. Yu wer kind to me. Not many hav bin. So thanks for bein such a nice men. I wish Id meet sum one lik yu wen I was yung. I luv yu. Mary xxx

The little boy sitting opposite stared at the grown man with tears in his eyes. Edward smiled and he looked away.

Another thing to ponder. It felt good to have shown kindness, especially to someone like Mary Bryant who seemed to have had too little of it in her life.

'*What was her life about?*' he wondered. '*Tragic and short – and she goes down in the history books as a criminal, even when she did no real harm to anyone. Then there are those who live long and well-endowed lives yet do endless harm. What is this about? Shouldn't there be a God who evens things out?*'

He dozed again but soon arrived in Manchester where Will was waiting.

'We have a guest,' Will said, reaching for Edward's hand.

'*Halo* Edward,' came the familiar voice.

'William Henry. What a great surprise!'

It was another quiet Christmas at Pemberton. The heavy snow kept them inside and close to the fire. Sarah did most of the cooking, with some help from Will. Emma was absent-minded and Thomas was struggling even more to get around.

Sarah, Will, Edward and William Henry went to St Bartholomew's in Preston on Christmas Eve where Reverend Harry Thurlow's funeral was held at noon. They stayed on for a carols service in the early evening.

'I canna nay be there,' Thomas had said when Sarah and Will forbade him from attending the funeral. 'He was always so braw to me.'

'He wouldn't expect you to be there, Thomas,' Will replied.

'Especially if it was to kill you,' Sarah added.

'We'll be there to represent ye, Da. Please dinna even ken ye should go. Anyway, someone needs to be here for Gran.'

After the funeral, they went around to Harry's place for a small wake held by his family.

'So, this is where your father stayed while your mother was in labour with you,' Sarah said to Edward.

'Truly? What a *draghail* time it must've been.'

'Your father was beside himself. He was in so much pain from his injuries; he could hardly move but he made it to the hospital every day and would stay there until they asked him to leave. Then, he'd have to ride back here in the snow, get a few hours of sleep if he was lucky and start the whole thing again the next day. It was mind over matter that got him through.'

'Aye, and then, of course, he had to make that *uamhasach* decision about whether to save me or Ma.'

'Yes, although my darling sister made sure he didn't have to go through with that. I think that would really have killed him.'

'My Ma was so brave, was she nay? She really gave her life for me.'

'She did. She was the dearest sister – and mother – anyone could have had. We were both very fortunate.'

They hugged.

—⁓—

The funeral, the grieving relatives and the cosy carols service had their combined effect on Edward's state of mind. As he pondered life's shortness, two things became clear. He had to find work and he wanted to give the relationship with Jane another chance.

'So, what d'ye ken then?' Edward asked William Henry.

'Aye, I ken ye should get the best job ye can, wherever it is, and knock on Jane's door at least once more.'

'Only once?'

'Aye, I'd nay be tearing yerself apart over her. There are other fish in the sea, ye ken?'

'Like who?'

'Well, there's Anna in Uppsala,' William Henry laughed. 'Tell me about her again, and dinna spare any detail this time.'

—⁂—

Dear Jane, I hope you and your family had a very happy and holy Christmas and I would like to wish you every blessing for the Year of Our Lord, 1795 …. I would very much like to see you. Please let me know if I would be welcome to come and visit you. Yours in friendship, Edward.

The letter was dated 27th of December, 1794. There was no reply by mid-January.

Dear Jane, I know we spoke about the possibility of you coming to celebrate my birthday with me at the end of the month. I am just writing to let you know that you would be most welcome, as would any or all of your family. Your friend, Edward.

The letter was dated 15th of January, 1795.

No reply.

Edward's birthday was even quieter than Christmas, mainly because William Henry had gone back to his military training. The most exciting part of the day came when Sarah handed him some letters that she had been storing over the past few days.

'Don't be disappointed if there's nothing from Jane.'

Among a handful of letters and greeting cards, there was a card from Mary Beth.

My dearest Edward, be assured of my earnest best wishes and fondest thoughts on your special day. You know you carry me in your heart always. All my love, Mary Beth.

Edward pondered on the ease with which he and Mary Beth had spent those days and evenings together.

—◊—

Dear Little Redcoat, Louise and I continue to visit Mr Fraser at Listellick. I don't know if you heard that Mrs Fraser died so there is now only Mr Fraser and his daughter to tend to the estate. Mr Fraser said there is a job there anytime you want it. Please think about it. You could stay here with us. Pa is no good these days but Louise looks after both of us so well and she would be so excited if her little Teddy came and stayed with us. We miss you and your dear father. Please give him all our love and tell him he is always welcome here too. Have the happiest birthday, dear boy. Love, Ma, Pa, Louise and the Prendivilles (especially Liam, who is writing this for us).

It was the sign Edward had been looking for. He had intended to write to Charles Towneley about work on the Towneley Estate but, knowing that the Towneleys and Braithwaites were friends, he had wanted to make sure things were aright with Jane.

It seemed they were not.

'What d'ye ken, Da?' Edward asked.

'I ken ye should go.'

'What about ye and Gran, though?'

'We've been coping without ye for long enough, lad. Besides, ye canna live yer life for yer Da and Grand Ma. Ye have to follow yer own dreams.'

'It sounds like a wonderful opportunity for you to practise your newfound skills,' Will said.

'Where are ye going, lad?' Emma called from her place in front of the fire.

'To Ireland, Gran.'

'I'd nay go there, laddie. They're *daoine neonach* over there.'

XXX

'Ye'll need to talk with Amy about that,' Robert Fraser replied when Edward had asked about a particular species of plant. 'She ken more than me or my Da. And she's learned it all by herself. Never had a day's training in her life.'

'Is that why she hates me? Because I've done training?'

'She dinna hate ye, lad. She's just an angry *og* lass.'

'Because of Angus?'

'Aye, and what it all did to her Ma. She blames herself for all of it and it dinna matter how often I tell her it's nay her fault, it dinna help.'

'I wish I could help. But I dinna ken how. She acts like she canna stand the sight of me.'

'Aye, but dinna take it too seriously. Amy's always been *feargach* – angry with the world – but especially with the English. And she's a fierce fighter. Those *Sassanachs* are lucky she was nay around at Culloden.'

They laughed.

'What was it she said to me when I arrived?' Edward asked.

'*Tha an t-oifigear british aig an doras,*' Robert replied.

'I recognise "British officer". What was the rest?'

'It's better ye dinna ken, lad.'

—⁓—

'Amy,' Robert said, spooning the soup. 'Edward was asking about the name of that wild flower, the rich blue one, on the far side of the glasshouse.'

'*Flur fiadhaich gorm.*'

'In English?' Robert asked.

'I dinna ken or care.'

'I love the colour,' Edward said.

'Aye, they're *bualadh*,' Amy replied, looking at him for the first time without evil intent.

'How do you know so much?' Edward said, smiling at her.

'*Oir cha do chaith mi mo chuid uine a oifigear british,*' Amy shouted.

She stood up and stormed out, leaving her soup unfinished.

'Amy, come back here,' Robert called after her.

The door slammed.

'I apologise again for my daughter, lad. Dinna take it to heart.'

'What did she say? I heard something about British officer again.'

'That she ken about the flowers because she didn't waste her time being one. Unlike ye, I ken is what she's saying.'

'Oh my. I need to be more careful, dinna I?'

'Aye, but dinna give up on her. If ye ever do make a *caraid* of her, ye'll have a friend for life, believe me.'

'I dinna doubt that, sir. I dinna doubt it.'

—⁓—

'So 'ow are ye gettin' on with the daughter, Teddy?' Louise asked at supper.

'Well, I ken we'll nay ever be married, put it that way.'

'Oh, yes, she's a bit of a 'andful, that one,' Mrs Prendiville said.

'Well, just remember ye can always marry me, Teddy,' Louise said, resting her hand on his back. 'Ye know I've been waitin' all these years for ye.'

'Thank ye, Louise, but ye ken ye're too holy for me.'

'I am *not*,' she replied, poking him in the side.

'Stop it ye two,' Mrs Prendiville said. 'Louise, ye can't be married because ye 'ave to look after yer Pa 'n' me.'

'Yeah, Ma. I know but it's not fair that Mary got to marry but I 'ave to stay at 'ome.'

'Well, it's just the way the good Lord's organised things, darlin'.'

With the treatment being meted out by Amy in Listellick, Edward needed respite with the Prendivilles from time to time.

—⚒—

'So, prove to me ye're nay a British officer then,' Amy said one day as they worked in the fields.

Edward had been working wth the Frasers for some months. Amy had heard him speaking with her father about their common Jacobite history and Thomas's views on the British Army.

'How would I do that then?'

'Come to a meeting with me.'

'A meeting? What meeting?'

'D'ye trust me?' Amy said, looking straight at him with her probing blue eyes.

'Aye, I do. I do, Amy Fraser.'

—⚒—

The meeting was late that night. Edward had taken to staying over in the loft when there was an early start the next day. They had all gone to bed but, by arrangement, Amy and Edward slipped out of the house late at night. It was a short walk to the meeting house.

'*Failte, Amy,*' the seven attendees said in unison.

'*Halo a h-uile duine,*' Amy said, pointing to Edward. '*Seo mo charaid, Eideard.*'

'*Failte, Eideard,*' they all said.

'*Halo,*' he replied.

'*An e do leannan a th 'ann?*' a rough, swarthy-looking man asked Amy as the others laughed.

'*Tha, tha sinn a 'posadh,*' she replied.

They stopped laughing. The swarthy man glanced at Edward, pierced eyes and curled lip.

'Now,' Amy said. 'We need to speak in the hated language because my friend here's nay too *math* with our *mathair* tongue.'

'So ye're nay a Highlander then?' the only other woman in the group asked.

'Aye, I was born in Preston but I'm a Highlander by heritage. My Grand Da was Edward Lovat, one of the leaders of the Lovat Scouts at Culloden.'

'Aye, I thought I ken the name,' she said. 'Well, ye're welcome then. Perhaps some of yer Grand Da's spirit'll help our cause.'

'What cause?' Edward asked.

'*Nach do dh 'innis thu dha?*' the swarthy man directed at Amy.

'*Is e sin as coireach gu bheil sinn an seo that thu gorach,*' Amy spat back.

'*An urrainn dhuinn earbsa a bhith aige?*' one of the other men asked.

'*Tha,*' Amy said.

Edward knew enough Scottish Gaelic to know she had just affirmed her trust in him.

'Well, that's *math* enough for me,' the woman said.

The men grumbled a form of agreement.

Edward was brought into the germination of a reprised Jacobite Rebellion to right the wrongs of the "Auld '45" and Culloden.

'But isn't Prince Charlie dead?' he asked. 'And his only male heir died as a bairn?'

'Well, what does "male" have to do with it?' Amy snapped back. 'In case ye dinna ken, there've been plenty of female kings, including our own Mary of Scots, and of course that English trollop who took her head off. Ye *dhuine* are all the same. Ye've no respect for women even though we're all smarter than ye.'

'Now, now, Amy, that's no way to talk to yer future husband,' the swarthy Scot, now known as Roy, said.

'*Oh dunadh suas, Roy,*' Amy said in a way needing no translation. 'For yer information, Highlander, Princess Charlotte was alive 'til recently. She's the one we hoped to put back on the throne. As ye nay doubt ken, she was Prince Charles's eldest daughter and she would've been a *math* Queen. I tell ye, she had all the sass of Mary of Scots and more. *Gu duilich*, she died but she's a son whose name's none other than Charles Edward Stuart, self-same as the Bonnie Prince himself. So, he's now the one we want to place on the throne – and ye're part of that now whether ye *mar* it or nay.'

Amy was the youngest by far but clearly a leader of this band of would be rebels. As Edward watched her, his mind turned to the Highland warrior princess of the Pictish myths. His grandmother used to tell him those stories as a child.

'Umm, so how auld is this Prince Charles then?' he asked.

'Eleven,' Amy replied. 'By the time we're ready, he'll be auld enough.'

It seemed the rebellion was not imminent.

—ɯ—

As they walked back to the house, Edward's head was spinning with questions.

'Why did Roy refer to me as yer future husband?'

'Because I said we were getting married,' Amy replied.

'Why did ye do that?'

'Dinna get any ideas. Roy Adair's been pressuring me to be his girl – as if I'm so desperate – so I just wanted to shut him up. That's all.'

'I dinna mind.'

'Well it'd be *ro dhona* if ye did.'

'Aye, but I still dinna mind – and I ken ye'd nay be desperate.'

In the pale moonlight, he saw Amy turn and smile.

They reached the door of the house and Amy stopped him, resting her hand on his forearm.

'Thank ye for coming tonight. Ye ken I trust ye?'

'I ken. And I trust ye's well.'

'Now, be quiet getting to bed, for the Laird's sake.'

—⁓—

Sometime in May of that year, 1795, Edward went to the Prendivilles for a family meal. He was spending more and more time with the Frasers but did enjoy the better meals at the old house. Amy made no pretence at being a cook and the old man seemed beyond caring.

'There's some letters there for ye,' Mrs Prendiville said. 'Dinner's still a way off so why not read 'em before everyone arrives?'

Edward found a quiet spot in the backyard and looked over the letters. He recognised a couple from Sarah, one from his father and another from William Henry. The writing on the last envelope took him by surprise.

He opened it first.

Dear Edward, I'm so very sorry for not writing earlier. We have been having a difficult time at home. My father was very unwell for a while and my mother was beside herself with worry. Also, my little brother, Henry, you would remember him, had a bad fall. I really wanted to come to your birthday but it was just not possible. Then, when I did not hear from you for my birthday, I felt sad and so decided to write. I do hope you are well and forgive me if I have not been the good friend you had hoped for. I hope we can meet again soon. My fond regards, Jane.

Edward had not even realised he had missed Jane's birthday in March. It occurred to him that he had not been thinking of her at all these past weeks. He decided he would do the courteous thing and reply to the letter – in time.

—⬝—

The next day, he returned to Listellick only to find a crowd standing around the house. People were chatting quietly; some were crying.

'What's happened?' he asked one of the neighbours.

'Old man Fraser died last night.'

'Oh my Laird, where's Amy?'

'In there with the priest.'

He hurried inside and went straight to Robert's bedroom. The priest and others were kneeling around his body, reciting the rosary. Amy was standing by the window, unengaged in the ritual. She spotted him as he entered the room.

'Where've ye been?' she said as she rushed to him. 'Where *were* ye when I *needed* ye?'

She made as if to hit him. He held her arms. She fell into his. He cradled the back of her head into his chest. She wept.

'I'm sorry I was nay here. If I'd ken ye needed me…'

'I ken. I ken,' she said. 'I'm *duilich*.'

'There's nay anything to be sorry for.'

—⬝—

The funeral was held two days later in the little church in Listellick. All the neighbours were there, along with a number of the Prendivilles. Some of the group from the secret Jacobite meeting were there, including Roy Adair.

'I want ye to sit with me in the church,' Amy said. 'I've nay anyone else.'

'Of course I will.'

Throughout the ceremony, Amy did not sit, stand or kneel at the appointed times. Nor did she take communion. Edward saw his main job as being there to support her, so he did the same.

'I need to talk with ye, lass – *privately*,' Roy said outside the church.

Amy stepped away with him. Edward could not hear what was being said but the body language told him that Amy was being harassed. She turned to him with a look of appeal. He moved closer.

'Ye can stay out of this, lad,' Roy said. 'Ye've caused enough trouble already.'

'*Faigh air falbh bhuam,*' Amy shouted at Roy, moving quickly to Edward and holding his hand. '*Bidh Eideard agus mise posta.*'

'*Cha bhith e beo cho fada,*' Roy shouted.

Amy and Edward hastened back to the crowd. Roy went off in the other direction.

'What was that all about, dear?' Mrs Prendiville asked Amy.

'Oh, nay anything. He's just a crazy auld man.'

'Well, ye let us know if ye need any 'elp,' Liam said. 'Anythin' at all.'

'Thank ye. Ye're very kind.'

'Well, now, my li'l Redcoat, we need to take ye 'ome,' Mrs Prendiville said to Edward.

'Redcoat?' Amy asked, frowning.

Edward spotted that raised eyebrow that signalled he was about to be flailed.

'My Da was in the British Army, ye ken?'

'So what's that got to do with ye?'

'It's just a wee joke. Da was nay ever a Redcoat in his heart. The Prendivilles ken that.'

'Indeed,' Liam said. 'Edward's Da's one of the finest men we've ever known. 'is Jacobite blood meant 'e could never've been a British officer at 'eart.'

'Like father like son, then,' Amy said, resting her hand on Edward's arm.

He noticed the telltale eyebrow was back where it belonged. They shared a smile.

'Well, now, let's go, li'l Redcoat,' Mrs Prendiville said again. 'Pa'll be expectin' 'is supper.'

Edward and Amy exchanged glances.

'Ah, I'm staying here, Mrs P. There's a wake at the house and we have a lot of sorting out to do with the estate.'

'But ye can't stay 'ere together under the same roof. It's not proper.'

'It's alright, Mrs Prendiville,' Amy said. 'I have some relatives staying tonight.'

'Well, if ye're sure then. Ye come 'ome to us when ye can, boy.'

—ᴡ—

Some of the other women were also concerned about leaving Amy alone in the house with a man. Edward left at one stage as if going away. Amy signalled with the kitchen curtain when it was safe for him to return. They ate some of the food people had brought around. There was also some liquor.

'I hope ye dinna mind staying here with me,' Amy said late in the night.

'I dinna mind at all. Nay at all.'

'I hope ye dinna ken I mean to sleep with ye.'

'I'd nay ever ken that.'

'Ye're a *bochd* liar, Redcoat. So dinna even try.'

'Aye, I'm a horrendous liar. Well, nay regularly, but...'

'So ye *would* like to sleep with me then?'

'Ah, aye, but only if ye wanted it too.'

'Well, I'm sorry but I dinna want to sleep with ye.'

'Oh, *du gearbh*. I understand.'

'I wanna *marry* ye.'

—◊—

This conversation came after lengthy, liquor-imbibed talk about all manner of things. Among them was Amy's despair at losing her father and her disbelief in any of the Catholic ritual and the beliefs behind it.

'He's gone; that's it. He's dust.'

'Dinna ye even contemplate there might be a heaven?' Edward asked.

'Nay, it's all a hoax. It's all a way of keeping us under control. Imagine the King of England without the church. How long do ye ken he'd last? All the talk about loving and caring and sharing and forgiveness. How much of that d'ye actually see in the King – or the Pope – or any religion? Hoax! It's all a hoax!'

Edward had liked Father Pritchard's liberal approach to religion but he had never questioned the fundamentals. There was a God of some sort and the church represented God on Earth. It gave some assurance that life did not end at death.

'My Da talks about his experiences with Islam and the Muslim woman he was married to.'

Amy thumped the table and attempted to stand, only to fall back into her chair.

'What? Yer Redcoat Da was married to a Muslim? I dinna even ken what a Muslim is but I wanna hear all about it.'

The alcohol was flowing even further by this time and so the thumb nail sketch Edward gave of his father's time with Mahdiya was confusing.

'Tell me more. I wanna meet yer Da and talk about it. So what did he say about Muslims? My Ma and Da, and Father Shanahan down the road there, I ken they'd all say they're heathens and going to Hell.'

'Well, ye need to talk with him but I ken it was a big part of his life. He talks about Mahdiya as though she was a saint. He still says he consults her about big decisions.'

'What? Is she still around? Is he married twice?'

'Nay, she was killed in a sea battle and buried at sea, along with my little brother or sister.'

'Oh, my heavens. Yer poor Da.'

'Aye, he's had lots of sadness and now he's fair crippled from his wounds in America.'

'I've meant to ask ye what he was doing in America. Dinna tell me he was fighting the Americans.'

'Aye, but I ken that's where his Jacobite blood started to come through. He dinna believe in what the British were fighting for. He tried to make peace with the Americans but then he was shot and almost died and ...'

'And what?'

'Well, that's when he says Mahdiya saved him.'

'Mahdiya who was buried at sea saved him?'

'Aye, because he was carrying her holy book in his shirt pocket and the bullet that would've killed him hit the book. The doctors told him that.'

'That's just *fortan* – luck. Nay anyone saved him. There's nay anyone to save any of us.'

'Well, perhaps, but I ken he hopes to see her again.'

'He'll be disappointed.'

'Anyway, I hope ye get the chance to meet my Da.'

'I do too, wee Redcoat. I do too.'

'So, what were ye and Roy talking about after the funeral?'

'Oh, he's a pig of a *dhuine*. He's been trying to get me into his bed for years, I mean literally from when I was only *og*.'

'That's horrid. How young? Did ye tell yer Da?'

'Nay, Roy always said if I did he'd cause more trouble than I could handle. I dinna ken what he meant exactly but I dinna want to find out.'

'So did he?'

'Did he what?'

'Get ye into his bed?'

'Of course nay, ye fool. What d'ye ken I am? I worked out how to avoid it, mainly by being strong, I mean like a *dhuine*. It was always worst when he was drunk but I learned how to handle him when he was like that. Once I even *reidh* him in front of his friends. One good crack on the back of the head with a pole and down he went. He left me alone after that for a while and when he tried again, I reminded him what I'd done and that I'd do it again. It's been *tireome* though and now that Da's gone, I'm nay sure what to do.'

'So, what was today's conversation about then?'

'About the estate and Da's stake in the management contract. Da made a will leaving the title to me. He sorted all that out with the English owner but Roy said the law'd nay honour it because it has to go to a *dhuine* and so I should marry him. He's probably right about the law, especially because he pisses in the pockets of the authorities, the army, the constable, the magistrate.'

'Roy, the Jacobite?'

'Aye, Roy plays it both ways; all ways. We all ken he canna be trusted so we dinna tell him all our plans.'

'So, what were ye shouting about after the funeral and why did he say I'd caused enough trouble already?'

'I said ye and I were getting married – *soon*.'

'Oh, my Laird, no wonder he wants to pummel me.'

'Dinna worry. I'll protect ye. And dinna ken ye have to marry me either. It was just a way of getting him off my back.'

Edward went silent. The alcohol was having its effect on both of them.

It was then that the conversation turned to Edward lying and Amy asking him to marry her.

—◊—

'So ye wanna marry me but only because it'll save the estate?' Edward asked.

'And because I like ye a lot more than Roy. Would it be so *dona*?'

'Nay, I dinna think it'd be bad at all. To be *onorach*, I've thought a lot about ye – ever since we met.'

'I ken. I could tell.'

'How?'

'Oh, *boireannaech* have their ways.'

'But ye treated me so *gu dona*. I ken ye hated me.'

'Nay, I only treat people like that when I love them.'

'Love?'

'Aye, do ye ken I'd marry ye if I dinna love ye?'

They laughed, her for the first time that Edward had seen.

'So, will ye then?'

'Will I what?'

'Marry me, *wee Redcoat*?'

'Of course.'

'Braw, that's settled then.'

'So, what do we do now?' Edward asked.

'We go to bed, me to my room and ye to the loft.'

'Can I at least kiss ye, then, seeing as we're going to be *dhuine* and wife?'

'Nay, there'll be time for that.'

XXXI

E dward woke late and heard voices downstairs. He recognised Amy's
but could not make out the other one, familiar as it was.

'Edward, are ye there?' Amy called.

He quickly sat up but fell back on the pillow as his head began
to spin.

'*Edward*, are ye there?'

'Aye, I'm coming.'

'Well, hurry then. Father Shanahan dinna have all day.'

'*Father Shanahan, the priest from yesterday's funeral?*'

He hastened downstairs to see Amy handing a cup of tea to
the priest.

'Edward, I dinna ken ye met Father Shanahan properly
yesterday. Father, this is my fiancé, Edward Lovat.'

'Well, congratulations, young man,' Shanahan said, extending
his hand. 'Amy tells me ye wish to marry as soon as possible.'

Edward shook his hand, saying nothing.

'Well, ye *do* want to marry, d'ye not? The one thing I *have* to
be sure of, according to the laws of the church, is that you're both
willing parties to this marriage.'

'Of course he does, Father', Amy said, wrapping her arm through Edward's. 'We talked about it *fada* last night; dinna we, darling?'

'Aye, we did.'

'Good, then I'll make arrangements for next Saturday. Will that give ye sufficient time to make arrangements?'

This was Wednesday morning.

'Ah, does it have to be so fast?' Edward said. 'My family's in England so it'll take a while to get a message to them.'

'Nay, it must be *this* Saturday,' Amy said, giving him a steely glare.

'I agree. It's always best to cut the devil off at the pass. I'm sure ye know what I mean,' Shanahan said, grinning. 'Saturday it is, then. Now, if you can come to the presbytery tomorrow afternoon, I can hear yer confessions and give ye the necessary instructions.'

'Thank ye, Father,' Amy said. 'We'll be there.'

The priest finished his cup of tea and left.

'So d'ye wanna marry me or nay, Redcoat?'

'Aye, but I ken we might take a wee bit more time.'

'Why do we need time? I love ye and I ken ye said ye love me. Why wait?'

'Well, I'd like my family here if it's possible.'

'I ken that. Of course, I ken. But Father Shanahan was telling me that Roy went straight to the magistrate after the funeral. He's already put in a claim to the management title. We have to move fast. And we have to keep it quiet. Nay even yer friends in Tralee should ken. Is that alright?'

'Aye,' Edward said, looking away.

'I'm sorry about yer family.'

'It's alright.'

'Thank ye, wee Redcoat,' she said, smiling. 'I do love ye, ye ken?'

'Aye, me too,' he replied, looking into her eyes.

—⚏—

They worked long and hard in the fields that day. They came in late.

Amy told Edward to wash while she prepared the meal. As he washed, he wondered again about the headlong rush into marriage he had not seen coming. If only he could talk to someone about it.

He came down from the loft. The table was filled with more of the leftovers from the wake, meats, cold vegetables and some sweets, along with a flagon of ale. It was arranged more neatly than he expected. He was looking at the table, hoping Amy would not be long.

'Ah, there ye are,' she said. 'There's nay anything like a wash at the end of a *fada* day.'

Edward turned around. Gone were the rough outside working clothes and galoshes, the hair pulled back and scarfed. He had thought how pretty she looked at the funeral when, for the first time, she had worn a dress and had her hair pulled back less than normal, with a black mantilla on her head.

That picture paled compared to what he was looking at now. The simple yellow frock was hanging over her neat breast, two nipples showing discreetly through the garment. Her hair was untied, stretching down to her shoulders. He saw her bare arms and legs for the first time, both with soft auburn body hair lightly covering them.

'So, what are ye staring at, then? Let's eat.'

They ate the meal in silence, washing down the food with strong ale.

'Ye're very quiet,' Amy said. 'Are ye sick?'

'Nay.'

'Well, what d'ye want to talk about then? Married people always have lots to talk about.'

'Speaking of that. What d'ye ken Roy'll do when he finds out we're married?'

'He'll be angry but that's why it has to happen quickly. He's a *salach cu* and he'd do anything to get his hands on that title.'

'And on ye, I bet.'

'That too. As I said, he's a *salach cu*.'

'Well, aye, but it's nay only dirty dogs that'd like to get their hands on ye.'

'Is that so?' she said, brushing away a strand of hair that had fallen over her eyes. 'Like who?'

'Oh, I'm sure there are braw *duilich* out there … I might even ken one or two of them.'

'Say what ye mean, Redcoat. Yer rambling ways infuriate me.'

Edward was silent. Amy sensed the change of mood.

'I'm sorry. What I mean to say is do ye want me or nay?'

Edward saw for the first time the extent of her vulnerability. He had seen grief in her eyes when her father died but this was a different sadness, one borne of unknown rejection, hurt, lack of self-belief, the things she hid from the world through her rough demeanour. For just a moment, he could see her fear that he might reject her.

'Aye, I want ye, Amy Fraser. I want ye like I've nay wanted anything before.'

She was now the silent one.

'Let's go to my bed,' she said.

'Are ye sure?'

'I'd nay say it if I dinna mean it, ye ken?'

She led him silently down the short hallway. He had spotted once the unmade bed and general untidiness of her room. It fitted with someone with more important things on her mind. Now, the bed was made and the external mess tidied. It struck him that she knew how this night was going to end.

There were no shoes to kick off so she lay fully dressed on the narrow bed and invited him to join her, lying side by side. She wrapped her arms around him, holding him tightly, and tucking her head in under his chin. It was as if he was holding a baby or a child who merely wanted a good cuddle.

'Thank ye, Edward Lovat. Thank ye for wanting me.'

'Are ye alright?'

'Aye, but I just feel so *aonar*. Since all the awful stuff with Angus, everything's gone *dona*.'

They lay in silence.

'Well, what do ye wanna do then?' she finally asked.

'Right now?'

'Nay, d'ye really wanna marry me?'

Edward took a moment. If he wanted an escape, this was his final chance.

'Well, how long d'ye need?' Amy asked.

'Nay time at all, Amy Fraser. I wanna marry ye. I wanna spend my life with ye. I wanna have bairns with ye. I wanna die beside ye. I adore ye and I'm yers – forever if ye'll have me.'

'Thank ye,' she said, tucking in even further. 'So, let me ask ye again, what do ye wanna do then?'

'Right now?'

'Right now!'

'I've had some impure thoughts, Father,' Edward said.

It had been some time since he had been to confession and he was struggling to remember the kinds of things he had said routinely as a child. "Impure thoughts" was a regular standby.

'How often, my son?' Shanahan asked.

'Now and then, Father.'

'Be more specific, my boy. How many times a day?'

'Perhaps three or four.'

'And did you ever give into these thoughts?'

'Nay really, Father.'

'What do ye mean "not really"? Did ye or didn't ye?'

Amy had been insistent that neither of them tell the truth of what happened the night before.

'He mightn't marry us, d'ye understand? Besides, it's all mumbo-jumbo. There's nay any God who cares. Just a lot of dirty auld scoundrels who like to hear all about ye touching yerself and all that. I ken they get together and talk about it. They're all *sgreamhail*.'

'Well, what're ye going to say in there then?'

'Just what I always say if I have to go. *I swore, Father. I was unkind, Father. I forgot to say my prayers, Father.* And when he says something like, *and do ye ever have any troubling urges?* then I say, *nay, Father, never.* I enjoy disappointing them.'

'I love ye, Amy Fraser; I truly do.'

They walked hand in hand towards their mock confessions.

—⁓—

Afterwards, Edward believed he detected a look of disappointment on the priest's face as he led them into the parlour for their instructions. He and Amy were seated on one side of the lacquered table with the priest on the other. Behind the priest was a chest of drawers with statues of Our Lady and various saints, with a crucifix attached to the wall behind it. There was a musty smell in the room, suggesting it needed airing more often.

'Now, ye do understand ye'll be making these vows before Almighty God?'

'Aye, Father,' they responded in unison.

'And will ye be coming here freely and without reservation to give yerselves to each other?'

'Aye, Father.'

'And any marital embracing ye do in marriage'll be open to God's plan for procreation?'

'Aye, Father.'

They glanced quickly at each other.

'And any children who come along as a result of yer marital embracing'll be brought up in the Holy Roman Catholic Church?'

'Aye, Father.'

Shanahan read from a manual of some sort about the sacrament of matrimony and how it was instituted by God to help men and women contain their natural urges.

Edward wondered how the celibate priest contained his.

'So, now, do either of ye have any questions?'

'Nay, Father.'

'Are ye sure now? Anything at all?'

'Aye, we're sure, Father.'

'So, ye do know what's involved on yer wedding night, do ye?'

'Aye, Father.'

'I only ask because, ye see, sometimes a priest has to become involved in these things. I had a young girl once come along most distressed the day after the wedding, saying her husband had tried to do all sorts of disgusting things with her. Well, it turned out she knew nothing about the way God, in his infinite wisdom, has arranged for procreation to take place.'

'So, I just want to make sure ye both know these things.'

'Thank ye, Father.'

—∞—

It was dark by the time they got home, so they sat straight down to finish off the last of the leftover food and poured themselves some more ale.

'See, they're all dirty auld *fhir*, I tell ye.'

'And what was all that about marital embracing?' Edward said, laughing. 'What on earth is that?'

'Ye ken, Redcoat; ye ken. But what about the lass who dinna ken anything about it and the priest had to get involved. What did he do? Show her how?'

They swapped yarns and laughed together as they had not before. Then the ale was gone.

'So, what do ye wanna do then?' Amy asked.

'Right now?'
'Right now!'

—◊—

On the Friday, they spent long hours in the field, coming late into the house. They washed and ate a few vegetables they had brought in from the field.

'Well, we'd best get a good sleep tonight, wee Redcoat. We have to be at church by 9am.'

'So, I should sleep in the loft then?'

'I dinna say that.'

—◊—

They were at the church a little before 9am. It was a small, mud brick church but filled on the inside with countless statues and surprisingly ornate "Stations of the Cross" around the walls. The altar was bedecked with flowers of all hue and tall candles of the sort one might better expect in a vast cathedral.

Amy went into one of the back rooms and changed into her mother's wedding dress and veil. The simple white dress was too big for her but it was the one she wanted to wear. The white lacy veil was perfect, sitting loosely across her shiny auburn hair hanging down over her shoulders. When she stepped into the church, Edward's breath was taken away, just as three nights before.

'*Halo*, Mrs Lovat,' he whispered.

'Nay yet, Redcoat. Just be patient.'

'It's hard when ye're looking like that.'

She smiled, blushing.

Father Shanahan introduced them to the two witnesses he had promised to organise. The organist's husband, a blacksmith, had fashioned a wedding ring out of some base metal. There were just eight people in the church, including two altar boys, but the hour long service included all the trappings of a cathedral full.

Apart from the ceremony itself, there was a Mass with communion, five hymns they struggled to join in and a twenty-five minute sermon. It was fairly much a repeat of what Shanahan had said to them during their instructions. Even "marital embracing" got a mention, several times over.

So, on the 6th day of June, 1795, the nineteen year old Edward and his eighteen year old bride walked out of the church as husband and wife. They were back in the home by 10.30 and in the field by 11am. They worked extra hard that day to make up for the morning's loss. They ate even more barely that night and there was no ale left. They washed and went to bed.

'We might have to get a bigger bed,' Edward said as they huddled together.

'Dinna ye like being close to me, Jacobite?'

'Let me show ye how I dinna like being close to ye.'

They made love for the first time that night – fully – and several times.

XXXII

'W ho?' Emma said.

'Edward, Ma,' Thomas replied. 'He's gone and got himself married.'

'Who to? Nay that Braithwaite girl?'

'Nay, someone we dinna even ken.'

'Thank the Laird. The Braithwaite girl's nay but *trioblaid*. Her mother's *seolta*.'

'Well, thanks for that, Ma, but at least we could put a face to her.'

The first they knew of Edward's marriage came through a letter from Mrs Prendiville.

Dear Thomas, I imagine this will come as a shock. When we had not heard from Edward for a week or so after Mr Fraser's funeral, we went to see how he was getting on. To our dismay, he told us he had been married the Saturday before to Miss Amy Fraser – now Mrs Amy Lovat, I suppose. Father Shanahan from Listellick did the ceremony so thankfully it's all proper in God's eyes but, between you and me, Paddy thinks Father Shanahan has done the wrong thing, letting them marry so quickly and so young. You can be sure we will keep an eye on them.

I've asked Paddy to go and see them when he is home and Liam will, of course, keep an eye on them too. Louise is heartbroken. I think she always hoped she and her Teddy might get married. But of course that was never going to happen. Let us know if there is anything more we can do. Love, Mrs P. PS. Personally, I don't like the girl (Amy, ie.). She seems a bit ungodly to me, but that's none of my business. PPS. Edward did say he was going to write to you but he had been busy.

'I'm sure he's been busy,' Will said.

'What do you think she means by "ungodly"?' Sarah asked.

'I've nay idea,' Thomas replied. 'But probably that she dinna spend too much time in church. I dinna worry about that. I'm just annoyed that he dinna tell us before he went and did something like that.'

'Well, let's meet his Miss Fraser, or Mrs Lovat or whatever her name is, before we jump to conclusions,' Emma said. 'I'm sure Edward'd nay rush into something unless he was sure.'

It was one of Emma's better days but her deep-seated bond with Edward was also showing.

Two days later, Edward's letter came.

Dear Da, Gran, Sarah and Will, You have probably heard through Mrs P that Amy Fraser and I were married a week ago at the Catholic Church at Listellick. I'm sure it has come as a surprise and I'm sorry there was no opportunity to inform you beforehand. There are reasons for that and I look forward to sharing them with you. For now, please be assured that I am so very happy. I love Amy deeply and I'm sure you will see why when you meet her. Your loving son and grandson, Edward.

'There ye are,' Emma said. 'I ken he'd nay do anything *amaideach*.'

Edward's letter had crossed with one Thomas had written to him.

Dear Edward, We heard of your marriage from Mrs P. Needless to say, it came as a surprise because we didn't even know you were engaged. All the same, we wish you the very best and we look forward to meeting your bride. All our love to you and your new wife, Da, Gran, Sarah and Will.

—⬥—

'See,' Amy said. 'I ken they'd be *ceart gu leor* about it.'

'Aye, I'm sure they're disappointed nay to have been invited but I ken they'll forget once we're there and part of the family.'

'What d'ye mean *when we're there*? We canna leave the estate.'

'Nay, I mean when we go to visit. Let's go as soon as we can.'

Some days later, there was another letter, this time from Mary Beth, responding to Edward's letter to her.

My dearest Edward, I'm so delighted to hear your news. Yes, I would have been there, of course, if it had been possible. I fully understand, however, that you needed to ensure that it was a private affair. I'm sure I'll hear all about it in time. Please extend my heartiest congratulations and best wishes to Miss Fraser (now Mrs Lovat), an extremely lucky girl, if I might say. Do know that you will both be welcome here anytime. My love, as always, Mary Beth.

'Ye have such braw friends, dinna ye?' Amy said. 'People who really love ye.'

'Aye, I suppose.'

'I wonder why,' she said, smiling.

'Aye, but I dinna wonder why *I love ye*.'

—⬥—

Plans for an early trip to Pemberton were put on hold when Amy became ill. What she was certain was food poisoning caused by uncured meat turned out to be morning sickness.

'Oh, my Laird, I canna believe it,' an excited Edward said, grabbing and whirling her around.

'Careful. Careful of the bairn.'

It was September and the first chill of autumn by the time Amy was well enough to travel.

—⁓—

'I've nay ever been here,' she said as the ship docked at Blackpool.

'Truly? Ye came straight from Scotland to Ireland then?'

'Nay, I was born in Tralee, remember. I've always pined to see Scotland but nay ever wanted to go to England.'

'Spoken like a true Jacobite,' Edward said louder than intended.

'Sshh. I dinna want to be arrested on the first day here.'

They stepped from the gangplank. Will was waiting.

'Will, this is my wife, Amy. Amy, this is Will, the Grand Da I never had.'

'Lovely to meet you, Amy,' Will said, holding her hand and kissing her on the cheek. 'You're most welcome to England and in this family.'

'Thank ye, sir. I'm pleased to meet ye too.'

Edward was surprised at Amy's nervousness. He sat up next to her in the carriage while Will was instructing the driver.

'Are ye alright?'

'Aye, he's so nice. Ye're all so nice.'

They arrived at Pemberton near nightfall. Sarah was quickly out to meet the carriage. After quick greetings in the chilly air, she hurried them inside.

'How did you cope with the trip, Amy?' she asked with the concern women reserve for pregnant women.

'Nay *dona*, thank ye, but I'll be pleased to get my feet up.'

'Well, come in and put your feet up wherever you can.'

'Dinna get up, Da,' Edward called out, watching Thomas struggling out of the chair.

'I wasn't standing for ye, lad. But I *was* standing for yer *boidheach* bride.'

'Da, this is Amy. Amy, this is my Da.'

Thomas put both walking sticks in one hand and reached out the spare one, drawing Amy in for a kiss on the cheek.

'I'm so *very* pleased to meet ye, Amy.'

'Ye too, sir.'

'Please call me Da, why dinna ye? And I must say it's music to my ears to hear yer Highland brogue. Where did yer family come from?'

'Achanalt, sir. I mean, Da.'

'Ah, yer a true Highlander, then, and a Fraser. Ye ken we're all Frasers originally?'

'Nay, I dinna ken that.'

'Aye, it was my Grand Da, another Thomas, who changed our name to Lovat because of some disagreement with other members of the Fraser Clan.'

'Ye mean we might have all been related sometime in the past?'

'Well, ye certainly are now, lassie,' Emma said, catching the end of the conversation.

'Amy, this is my Gran,' Edward said.

'Lovely to meet ye, dear. Oh, I see ye're showing already. Do come and rest yer weary legs next to me. Now, tell me how my *ogha* has been treating ye. He can be a wee bit forgetful at times.'

Emma commandeered Amy for most of the evening. The others were struck by her alertness. It was the old Emma. Will was the most excited about this.

—⚬⚬—

'They're all so lovely,' Amy said in bed that night. 'Yer whole family. Ye're all so welcoming. I've nay ever ken a family like this.'

'Well, they love ye, that's for sure. Especially my Gran. Ye're nay ever left guessing with Gran. If she likes ye, ye ken it, and if she dinna, ye ken that, nay doubt.'

—⚬⚬—

Three days later, they headed for the Highlands. This was at Amy's insistence in spite of her condition.

'I just wanna smell that air,' she said. 'They say there's nay anything like it.'

The plan had been for Will to accompany the couple while Sarah stayed at home to tend to Thomas and Emma.

'Ye're nay leaving me behind,' Thomas said when he heard the plan. 'I've been wanting to get back there for ages.'

'Me too,' Emma said. 'Besides, someone will need to look after Amy. Three men and a woman with a bairn on the way. Ha!'

'Well, I might as well come too then,' Sarah said.

Will arranged for a larger carriage and worked out a different plan, one more befitting a journey for the infirmed.

They made it to Castle Dounie where an aged Georgina greeted them. Georgina was still the matriarch of the Fraser Clan and effectively Lady Lovat. Archibald and Jane were in London and William Henry on duty with the army.

'So, this is the lassie who won our dear Edward's heart,' Georgina began. 'Ye must be a very special lass and I'm sure he's a *most* fortunate lad.'

It was a night they would all remember for years to come. It was in all of their minds that this might be the last time this particular group would be together in one place.

'Ye're all such bonnie people,' Amy said, her eyes watering. 'I canna get over yer kindness.'

'Have ye nay had enough of that in yer wee life?' Georgina asked.

'I suppose but I'd nay realised it until now. My Ma and Da were fine folk, dinna get me wrong. But they were stern and nay given to warmth, least of all Ma – and then so many horrid things came our way.'

'Aye, as it did to most people who lived through the Clearances,' Emma said.

Georgina and Emma spoke at length about past experiences

from the day of Culloden to the occupation by the English, the Clearances and then the move to Pemberton.

'I was nay even born so I dinna ken anything but I still feel as though my whole life has been marked by it,' Amy said.

Edward moved closer and placed his arm around her.

'Aye,' Thomas said. 'That's exactly how I feel. My Da was dead before I took my first breath but I dinna ken I could imagine my life without it all, the battle and everything that followed.'

There was much reflection and tears that night and it was as though Amy had always been part of this family. Edward was thrilled with the warmth they all displayed for her.

'So, Amy, my darling,' Georgina said late in the night. 'I've been wondering about yer family and our family. There are lots of Frasers, as ye ken, but I wonder if we're related.'

'Except through marriage, ye mean?' Edward said.

'Aye, except through marriage. I just recall my father, the Old Fox, God rest his soul, talking about part of the Clan in Achanalt and what fine fighters they were. I imagine ye must be part of that.'

'Aye, I hope so. My Da used to talk about his Da and how he fought in some of the earlier rebellions. I ken I've inherited that Highland spirit.'

'Ye have my darling,' Edward said, pulling her head towards him and planting a kiss on her cheek. 'I was terrified of ye the first time we met.'

'Ye were nay. I was the one who was terrified.'

'Ye? Why would ye've been terrified?'

'Because I ken I might fall in love with ye, *amaideach* lad.'

'Ye're so much in love, ye two,' Emma said. 'Ye remind me of my own first love.'

Emma wiped her eyes while the rest of them looked at Will. He signalled they should say nothing. He knew he had always lived in the shadow of the famous Jacobite.

—◠◠—

Edward and Amy could only stay another few days before having to get back to Listellick. During that time, they went to Culloden, Achanalt, Tarradale, the Wardlaw Mausoleum at Kirkhill and the cemetery at Eskadale. Thomas and Emma accompanied them to the latter.

'Oh, my Laird,' Emma shrieked. 'They've taken away his gravestone. The rotten English've stolen it. We'll never ken where his body lies.'

'It's alright, Ma,' Thomas said. 'Georgina warned us about this. What they've done is change his name from "Lovat" to "Fraser". See, they've done the same with his Da and Ma.'

Thomas pointed to where one name had been chiselled out and replaced with another.

'Why would they do that?'

'It's just another way of trying to eradicate everything to do with the Rebellion. There were so many "Frasers", some even on the English side. But "Lovat" meant just one thing. Like the Old Fox himself, it meant treachery – even one that could fuel another rebellion.'

'Well, I'm proud to be a Lovat then,' Amy said. 'I hope there *is* another rebellion.'

Edward had urged Amy not to tell them about their connection with the Jacobite group in Listellick.

'Aye,' said Emma. 'Well, if they keep on trying to suppress even our name, then ye can be sure of it. One day!'

XXXIII

'*Oh, my Dia,*' *Amy shrieked.*
It was early October and bitterly cold in the late
afternoon when they arrived home. Their estate cottage had
been trashed. Red paint was splattered on external walls,
making rough signage, including "Jacobite traitor" and "Go
home, Scottish Scum". Most telling was, "Off with your head,
Lovat".

'It's obviously directed at me,' Edward said.

'Are ye saying I'm nay a Lovat?' Amy shot back. 'And what
difference does it make, anyway? As if I'd walk away from ye even
if it was. D'ye ken so poorly of me?'

'Of course I dinna.'

They walked inside to find an even more devastating scene of
broken crockery and furniture. The beds were soiled with animal
waste. A decapitated dog hung by the legs from the back door
architrave.

'Who would do this?' Edward asked.

'I dinna ken but I can guess.'

'Roy?'

'Aye. Or some of his *cronies*. I've told ye he plays it both ways. He's always been a wee too friendly with the army, for my liking. And he really wants to control that title, and …'

'And he wants to control ye?'

'Aye, he's a *salach scoundrel*.'

'So, what do we do? Go to the authorities?'

'Nay, dinna be so foolish, *dhuine*. That'd only draw attention to us. Let's get out in the morning and wash everything away and hope nay many saw it. Then we'll put the place together and stay here and guard it. Nay more going away.'

'Are ye angry at me for taking ye away?'

'Of course nay. I loved every minute of it. But this shows what can happen quickly when ye turn yer head away for even a wee moment.'

They settled for the night, using what unsoiled pillows and blankets they could find and piling them onto the upturned kitchen table. They were exhausted and fell asleep quickly.

'I love ye, Amy Lovat.'

There was silence. Edward assumed she had fallen asleep.

'Thank ye,' came the tired voice a moment later. 'I *ghaoil* ye too.'

—ᴍ—

The next day, they went out to the field to find damage there as well, though not as bad as in the cottage. They worked night and day for the next week to restore things as best they could, keeping a close eye on passers-by. Edward carried Robert's old rifle with him wherever he went.

'Whoa boy, whoa,' Liam called out, holding his arms in the air. 'Ma'd never forgive ye if ye shot me. Or, then again, maybe she would, if it was 'er li'l Redcoat.'

Liam and Denis Prendiville, Liam's twelve year old son, had come to see how things were. Mrs Prendiville had woken distressed one morning, fearing things were not well.

'What 'appened 'ere?' Liam asked.

Edward recounted all they knew.

'Ma was right then. She 'ad a feelin' it might've been to do with the Jacobite thing.'

'Why would she think that?' Amy asked.

'Well, it's on the rise again and Ma wondered if ye might be involved.'

Amy blushed and looked away.

'Look, both o' ye. Ye know what I think o' the English but, just at the moment, things are not too bad around 'ere. The army's been tryin' to meet us 'alfway but it wouldn't take much to stir the pot and all 'ell to break loose. I'd say ye've 'ad a warnin' and, if I were ye, I'd take it seriously.'

Amy continued to say nothing.

'Anyway. Ma says ye're to come to 'er place if ye're in any kind o' trouble. D'ye 'ear me then?'

'Aye, thank ye Liam,' Edward replied. 'Thank ye for coming. Good to see ye, Denis. My heavens, ye're growing.'

Edward saw Liam and Denis out to their horses and then walked back inside. Amy was slumped in the corner, crying.

'What is it, my darling?' Edward asked, sitting next to her.

'I canna let them beat me.'

'Who?'

'I dinna ken who. The English, the toffs, the pathetic Irish, the turncoats like Roy. Whoever's against us! Getting our homeland back's what my Grand Da died for and my Da lived for. I have to keep fighting for that or I've nay anything left, d'ye ken?'

'Aye, I do. It's in my blood too. It's what my Grand Da died for – and my Gran lives for, as ye saw. But we dinna ken who the enemy is just now. Who would we be after if we were to start anything? As ye said yerself, is it the English, the Irish, the turncoats? And we have a bairn to be thinking of too.'

Amy began wailing.

'I ken that. I ken that. There's nay need to remind me. I'm so scared, Edward. I'm so scared something might happen to our bairn.'

'D'ye wanna go to the Prendivilles then?'

'How can we? We have to look after the estate.'

'I could come here every day. Perhaps I can get some help; Denis might be interested in some work. He's a strapping lad.'

'Nay, nay. I wanna stay.'

—⁓—

'What's that?' Amy called, sitting upright in bed.

It was as though a hundred cannon balls were being fired at the cottage. Edward jumped out of bed, grabbed the rifle and ran outside to see the last of a dozen or so figures running away.

'And dinna ye come back,' he shouted, firing into the air.

'What are ye doing?' Amy shouted. 'D'ye want every soldier in Tralee coming out here?'

'I'm sorry. I'm just so angry.'

The next day, two soldiers came by and questioned them.

'It was just some *amaideach* lads,' Amy said. 'There's nay anything to concern yerselves with, officers; now, can I get ye a cup of tea?'

Edward teased her afterwards for the good job she did at playing the housewife.

'Shut yer mouth, Jacobite,' she said, grabbing hold of the rolling pin. 'Come here and I'll show ye how *math* a housewife I am.'

—⁓—

Some weeks later, there was a repeat of the stone and rock throwing at the house in the middle of the night. Edward again grabbed the loaded rifle and ran outside. This time, the unidentified group was waiting as he came out of the door. He was cocking and aiming the rifle when he felt the pain in the back of his head as a hard object whacked into it, throwing him to the ground.

He lay there, stunned, feeling the rifle being wrenched from his grip.

Barely conscious, he heard a gasp from Amy. As she exited the cottage, she was dealt a blow to the stomach. She reeled, falling heavily on her back.

'I told ye to nay do anything to the lass. Let's get out o' here.'

The familiar voice was ringing in Edward's head as the pounding feet receded. He lifted and turned his head to see Amy lying on her back, immobile.

'Amy! Amy!'

He crawled on hands and knees to examine her in the dim moonlight.

She regained consciousness and Edward helped her back inside, laying her on the bed.

'Are ye alright?' he asked over and over.

'The bairn, the bairn,' she cried.

—⚊—

Edward would countenance no opposition to them going to stay with the Prendivilles. They would worry about the estate later. Amy and their child were all that mattered.

By Christmas, they were fully settled in there, Amy virtually bedridden in confinement. The doctor came every day to check on her.

'I believe there's some internal injury but I daren't investigate too far,' Dr Slattery said.

'Should we take her to a hospital?' Edward asked.

'The only hospital worth taking her to's in Dublin. And, frankly, I don't think either of them'd survive the trip.'

Edward put his head in his hands. Louise placed her arm around his neck.

'It'll be alright, Teddy. Ma won't let anythin' 'appen to 'em.'

Christmas Day was a sombre one. Edward spent the day lying next to Amy and comforting her. Paddy arrived on Boxing Day.

'I think ye should give 'er the last rites, Paddy,' Mrs Prendiville whispered.

'Oh, Ma,' Louise called out. 'She's not goin' to die today. And ye said she's not goin' to die at all – or the baby. That's what ye said.'

Louise's voice broke.

'Girl, 'ush up, will ye?' Mrs Prendiville said, grabbing Louise's arm. 'I pray to God she won't – but I've seen death before.'

'*Halo*, Father Paddy,' Edward said, stepping out of the bedroom. 'And thank ye for yer thoughtfulness, Mrs P, but Amy'd nay be wanting any last rites even if she *was* dying. Nay disrespect, Father.'

'None taken, Edward.'

'Oh, I just don't understand that,' Mrs Prendiville said, wiping her eyes. 'Ye's are riskin' the devil gettin' 'is way like that.'

'If she dinna believe in God, Mrs P, she dinna believe in the devil,' Edward said.

'Oh, my Lord, a godless child under my roof. Paddy, you 'ave to do somethin'.'

'It's alright, Ma. The Lord knows all and I'm sure he'll be looking after Amy and the child, whether she wants it or not.'

'Thank ye Paddy,' Edward said. 'I'm sure Amy'd be pleased to speak with ye.'

They stepped into the darkened bedroom and tip-toed over to the bed.

'It's alright. I'm nay asleep. Pleased to meet ye, Father. I've heard all about ye.'

'And me about ye, my dear.'

'I hope *some* of it was braw.'

'All of it, I believe.'

'*Now*, Father, priests are nay meant to lie. So, I'm dying, I hear?'

'Nay anyone's saying that, my darling,' Edward replied.

'Well, I must've been dreaming, then. I could've sworn I heard Louise and Mrs P talking about it and the need for Father here to perform some of his magic tricks over me.'

'My apologies, Paddy. Amy is nay herself.'

'Well, then, who am I, Jacobite? Who am I if I'm nay myself? I dinna want to die as someone else. Lairdie, imagine if I died as a braw Catholic. What would become of me?'

Edward sat on the bed, stroking her forehead.

'Father, I ken ye mean well,' Amy said, her voice beginning to break. 'But please ken I dinna want any of the church's mumbo-jumbo being performed on me or my bairn. Is that nay clear?'

'Indeed, it is. I wouldn't dream of forcing ye to do anything ye didn't want.'

'So, am I damned then, Father? Will I go to the Devil to burn in Hell for eternity?'

'I doubt it,' Paddy replied.

'Well, why nay? This is what riles me about the church. Saying one thing and then doing another. Either ye believe or ye dinna. Either I need the mumbo-jumbo to get to Heaven or I dinna. Which is it?'

'Darling, Paddy's only here to help,' Edward said. 'There's nay any need to be rude.'

'Am I being rude because I'm asking a straight question? I'm *so* sorry, Father. *Please* forgive me for being rude.'

'Edward, could I have a word with Amy alone, perhaps?' Paddy asked.

'Nay, Father. Anything ye wanna say ye can say in front of my husband. If I'm to be gone soon, I wanna spend every second with the *dhuine* I love.'

Edward broke down. Amy reached up and brought his head down on her chest.

'Then, it's a privilege to be here with ye,' Paddy said. 'All I wanted to say is what I believe is bigger than the mumbo-jumbo, as ye call it. The mumbo-jumbo's just an outward expression of something way more important.'

'And what's that, then?' Amy asked, still cradling Edward.

'That God loves ye. And I know ye don't believe it and I respect that. But ye have to respect that I *do* believe it and I believe that, whenever ye die, whether today or in fifty years, God will take ye to himself.'

'But why would he? If I dinna believe in him, why would he, even if he does exist?'

'Because ye're such a braw lass,' Edward said, raising his head and choking on the words. 'Because ye're straight as an arrow and ye have so much love in ye.'

'Aye, but only for ye and our bairn.'

'What I believe's even more profound than that, though,' Paddy continued. 'I believe God loves ye even when ye're not a braw lass. Even when ye're at yer worst. God loves ye because he created ye and he loves all his creatures regardless.'

'It's a bonnie idea, Father,' Amy said. 'But I have to say I'm surprised to hear a priest talking like that. I ken ye'd be trying to get me under the spell of yer mumbo-jumbo.'

'Surprised to hear a priest quoting God's own words?' Paddy laughed. 'It's a shame ye haven't heard lots of priests doing that.'

'So, where did God say we dinna need the mumbo-jumbo, then?'

'Well, have ye ever heard the story about the prodigal son?'

'Aye, it rings a bell.'

'Then ye'll know it's about a father who forgives his wayward son even when he'd let him down completely.'

'Aye, I ken the story and I have to say I always felt sorry for the aulder brother who'd done everything his Da asked.'

'Yes, he did, Amy, and the father acknowledges that but then he goes on to underline the real point of the story. He says, *son, everything I have is yours but let's rejoice together because yer brother who was lost has now been found*. It's a story of absolute love and forgiveness.'

'Well, Father, if that's the kind of God I'd seen the English following, perhaps I'd have believed – perhaps!'

'What do ye mean, Amy?'

'When the English threw my Grand Da off his land, they told him it was the King's land. And how did they ken? Because God had given it to the King. Sometimes, they'd even bring a priest or minister along to back them up. I was nay ever much of a one for this God idea but, after hearing that, I thought why would anyone want to believe in a God who threw poor people off their land and gave it to the rich?'

'I understand, Amy. The Lord's name's been taken in vain far too many times, including by the English. Remember, I'm an Irishman; I understand these things.'

—☽—

'I like yer priest friend,' Amy said to Edward in bed that night. 'If I do die, tell him he can do his mumbo-jumbo on me.'

'Ye canna die, my darling. *Please* dinna die. I'd be so lost without ye.'

'Well, I canna die until I give ye yer bairn, can I?'

'Ye canna die ever. Especially when ye give me my lad.'

'So ye ken it's a laddie then?'

'Nay really. It's just that we keep on talking about "him" whenever we talk about the bairn.'

'Well, I ken it is. It's a wee laddie I'll be giving ye.'

—☽—

'Oh, my darlin',' Mrs Prendiville said, greeting Thomas and Sarah at the door. 'Look at ye, dear boy. I 'ad no idea ye was so poorly.'

It was the 25th of January and Thomas and Sarah had made the trip to support Edward and Amy. They had sailed from Blackpool to Blennerville, near Tralee, to make the trip as easy as possible for Thomas. He had insisted on being there.

The next day was Edward's twentieth birthday.

'Ye nay should've come, Da,' Edward said. 'We're being well looked after by Mrs P and Louise.'

'I've nay doubt about that, lad, but we wanted to be here for ye.'

'Ye're so welcome, both o' ye's,' Mrs Prendiville said. 'It'll be like old times with everyone 'ere.'

During the evening meal, Dr Slattery came for his daily visit.

'Has she still been sleeping a lot?'

'Aye, she's hardly awake these days,' Edward replied.

'I'm concerned she's fading. Her pulse is very weak. If her heart fails, we'll lose them both. You might have a choice to make, young man, I'm sorry to say.'

'What are ye suggesting, Doctor?' Edward said, his face paling as he spoke.

Thomas and Sarah looked at each other. It was all too reminiscent of Edward's own birth and the decision Thomas was told he might have to make.

'But could the baby survive anyway?' Sarah asked.

'Well, I admit I was hoping we could get through a few more weeks but, yes, at thirty-three weeks or so, it's possible. Far from guaranteed, mind you.'

'What are ye saying?' Edward howled. 'There's nay any way I'm doing anything to harm my wife. *Nay any way*, so let's stop even talking about it.'

—m—

Everyone retired early. It was bitterly cold. Mary had arrived in the early evening with her newborn, her third child. Paddy came in very late and made up a bed for himself next to the fire, with his father. This is where Mr Prendiville slept every night now in his chair.

'I heard ye talking with the doctor,' Amy said as Edward slipped into bed.

'The *dhuine*'s an *amadan*; fool. I wish we were in Pemberton where there's braw doctors.'

'Edward, my *ghradhaich*, I dinna ken I'm going to make it.'

'What d'ye *mean*?' Edward sobbed.

'I feel so *dona*, so weak. I ken I'm dying, Edward.'

'Nay, nay. Ye have to make it; ye *have to*. I canna live without ye; I'd nay wanna live without ye.'

'I ken, my *darling*, but ye must – for our lad. Ye must.'

Edward was silent, weeping.

'And. If ye do have to make a choice, ye choose the bairn. Is that clear? *Ye choose the bairn.* I'd nay ever forgive ye otherwise.'

'I love ye, my *bana-phrionnsa ghaisgeach*,' Edward said.

'*Tha gaol agam ort, Seumasach.*'

—⚊—

The piercing scream woke them to a person. It was sometime after midnight.

'What is it, Amy?' Edward called out as he reached for a candle. 'Amy, Amy!'

Within no time, the entire household was there, with the exception of the old man who slept on in front of the fire. Thomas was the last one in the room, having struggled out of bed and hobbled with his sticks as fast as he could.

'Someone get the doctor quickly,' Edward shouted, barely audible over Amy's screaming.

'I'll go,' Paddy said.

'No, ye 'ave more important things to do,' Mrs Prendiville said. 'Louise, go get the doctor.'

'It's fine, Ma,' Paddy said. 'Ye can't send Louise out on her own. I'll be back as quickly as possible.'

Paddy moved to the side of the bed and rested his hand gently on Amy's forehead. He muttered something under his breath and quickly headed for the door.

'She needs the last rites,' Mrs Prendiville said, moving to the bed. 'But 'o am I to know? Mary, Louise, get 'ot water and lots o' towels quickly. Sarah, can ye get every pillow ye can find? Edward, ye need to 'elp me lift 'er into a sitting position. Then ye need to leave the room; and ye too, Thomas. This is no place for a man.'

'I wanna stay,' Edward said. 'She's my wife and it's my bairn.'

'Ye'll only make things worse, boy,' Mrs Prendiville replied. 'Yer Amy'll never forgive ye if ye see 'er like this.'

'Come on, lad,' Thomas said. 'Women ken these things best.'

Dr Slattery arrived presently with Paddy in tow. He went straight to the bedroom where the women had done all they could to prepare for a birth that might or might not happen.

'I see the head,' the men heard Slattery saying amidst Amy's wailing.

'Keep her awake; keep her awake. Come on dear, one more push; that's it. Now, again, again.'

The instructions from the doctor, mixed with the women's shouting and Amy's screaming went on for what seemed an interminable time.

Finally, the feeble sound of a baby's cry. The men would not have heard it except that the rest of the room had gone silent.

'I dinna care if it's women's business,' Edward said, leaping to his feet. 'I need to be in there.'

He opened the door and stepped into the room to see Louise holding a small parcel wrapped in a shawl. Mrs Prendiville, Sarah and Mary were standing back staring at Amy slumped on the bed in a sea of blood.

Slattery hovered over her, moving his hands frenetically over her body, opening her closed eyelids, feeling her neck and reaching for her wrist. Finally, he applied a long, horn-shaped implement to her chest and placed his ear on the other end.

He straightened and stepped away, the horn-like implement resting at his side. The women began to wail.

'Nay, nay, *nay*,' Edward screamed, flinging himself over Amy's body. 'Do something; for *the Laird's sake*, do something.'

'There's nought to be done, boy,' Slattery said. 'I'm so sorry.'

—⁂—

'Doctor, it's not breathing,' Louise called.

Slattery rushed to her side and took the baby in his arms. He took both feet in one hand, tipped the baby upside down and, as the shawl was making its way to the floor, gave the baby's bottom a mighty smack.

Nothing.

'Come on, little one,' Slattery commanded. 'Don't have yer mother be dying for nought.'

He raised the upside-down naked child higher so as to give it an even firmer crack on the bottom, instinctively shaking it as he did. Startled by the smack, the baby inhaled and let out a cry.

'That's it, little one; that's it,' Slattery said, turning to the others with the only satisfied look of the night.

Mrs Prendiville was on her knees praying. Mary and Louise were holding each other and the baby, crying. Edward was lying over Amy's upper body, while Thomas had a hand on his shoulder. Paddy was performing some of the Catholic "mumbo-jumbo" on Amy. He knew she would be content with that.

'Paddy, ye'd better baptise the child,' Mrs Prendiville said between Hail Marys.

Paddy moved to the baby, resting in Louise's arms. He took some water in his hand and prepared himself to pour it over the baby's forehead.

'Does the baby have a name?'

'Thomas, of course,' Mrs Prendiville said.

'It's a boy, is it?' Paddy asked, looking to Slattery who nodded.

In the circumstances, the first name mentioned would have

to suffice. Edward was still prostrate over Amy, detached from anything else happening in the room.

'Thomas Lovat, I baptise ye in the name of the Father, the Son and the Holy Ghost,' Paddy said as he poured the dribble of water with his left hand and made the sign of the cross with the other one.

'He'll need a nursing mother to feed him,' Slattery said. 'D'ye know of one nearby?'

'I can do it,' Mary replied. 'I'm still feedin' my own babe.'

'Glory be to God,' Slattery said. 'See if ye can attach him. It's the only thing that'll save him.'

———

'Come, lad,' Thomas said, trying to lift Edward off Amy's chest. 'Ye need to say yer goodbyes and let her go.'

'I'll never let her go. *Never!*'

'Oh, my darlin' li'l Redcoat,' Mrs Prendiville said. 'A loss like this is too cruel but ye 'ave to trust she's with the Lord now.'

'*Dinna* talk to me about *yer Laird*. Amy was right. There's nay God. There canna be a God so cruel to do this.'

He flung himself back over Amy, oblivious to the blood and mess that now covered most of her body.

'I love ye so much, my *darling*. I dinna wanna live without ye. If ye with God, then ask him to take me too.'

'It would be good if the young man could take some interest in his son,' Slattery said, looking to Thomas. 'This baby's going to need all the help ye can give if he's to survive. Without a mother, the father becomes so much more important.'

'Of course, Doctor. I ken he will. I ken he will.'

'Teddy, look at yer beautiful li'l boy,' Louise said as she stood next to Mary, helping her to get the baby to attach.

'I dinna care. I *dinna want a bairn* without Amy.'

———

The next day, Amy was buried in the graveyard of the Catholic Church in Tralee. Paddy was the celebrant of an unusually low-key Catholic service.

'Just dinna make it a Mass,' Edward pleaded. 'I swear she'll haunt ye forever if there's too much Catholic mumbo-jumbo.'

'But ye can't 'ave a funeral without a Mass,' Mrs Prendiville said. 'It's not fair to the poor girl.'

'It's fine, Ma,' Paddy said. 'We have to respect the wishes of the deceased; that's also a Catholic thing to do.'

'Oh, ye and all yer fancy new ideas. Seriously, Paddy, sometimes I think ye were more Catholic before ye went to that seminary and learned way too much.'

'Thank ye, Paddy,' Edward whispered.

After the short ceremony with barely more than the family present, Amy was laid to rest, a simple unnamed cross marking the place. In time, a proper headstone would be struck.

Sacred to the Memory
Amy Fraser Lovat
Born 7 May, 1777
Departed this Life 26 January, 1796
Dachaigh anns a 'Ghaidhealtachd aice

At the time, the unmarked grave was not only inevitable but necessary for the anonymity the situation required. Least of all would the Gaelic words, *home in her beloved Highlands*, have been judicious in the circumstances.

Amy and Edward's location had been a well-kept secret ever since they had left the Listellick estate. Paddy had heard through Father Shanahan that Roy Adair had taken it over with his wild gang and the support of the English authorities. The case they had made to the magistrate was that it had been abandoned by two of the leaders of the local Jacobite movement. They had hoped to persuade the magistrate to hand the title over to Roy, granted Edward and Amy were deemed to be criminals on the run. The magistrate was unconvinced and unable to be persuaded or bribed, so he merely granted interim possession to Adair until such time as Edward's and Amy's whereabouts could be established and their credentials tested. Father Shanahan had warned Paddy that, especially with Amy's death, Edward, as the sole claimant on the estate, was at risk of being hunted down and killed by Adair's gang. They had after all nearly killed him beforehand. Now, the baby's life could similarly be at risk.

—⚹—

'We ken ye need to come home with us, lad,' Thomas said.

'Well, the child'll 'ave to stay,' Mrs Prendiville replied. 'Ye can't possibly take 'im with ye. 'e wouldn't make it five minutes from the gate.'

'Yeah, Doctor Slattery said as much,' Louise said.

Louise's enthusiasm was not altogether about what was best for the child, though that was beyond dispute. Little Tom, as he came to be known for a time, lingered at death's door, sustained largely through the tender care of Louise and the breast-feeding skills of Mary. For Louise, it was like having the child she feared she might never have amidst the duties of parental care.

'How do you feel about that?' Sarah asked Edward.

'I dinna care. The bairn'll die anyway.'

There was silence as they took in the weight of Edward's despair.

In mid-February, 1796, Edward accompanied Thomas and Sarah back to Pemberton. Little Tom remained with the Prendivilles in the constant care of his two stand-in mothers. They competed at times for his attention.

—⚹—

'Where's yer Jacobite lassie?' Emma asked.

Edward had been home for only a few days, sleeping late into the morning and starting on the rum before lunch.

'She's nay here, Gran,' Edward replied with a patience he reserved for his grandmother.

'Where's yer Amy, then?' Emma would say.

It was a constant and, to others, annoying conversation. Edward did not seem to mind, perhaps because it made it seem that Amy was present, even if only in Emma's delusion.

'She's dead, Gran.'

'She'll be back, laddie. Ye just wait and see.'

'Thanks, Gran.'

'I love that lassie. She's just like I was when I was young.'

'I ken, Gran, and she loved ye too.'

'Where is she? Tell her to come and see me. I've something to tell her.'

—⚬—

'Ye'd better go easy on that, lad,' Thomas said, pointing to the glass.

'It dulls the pain, Da.'

'Aye, it does indeed. I ken that all too well. When yer Ma died, I did a lot of dulling like that. But it comes at a price. I almost lost ye and Sarah and everyone because I was drowning in it.'

Edward said nothing. He wiped away a tear and took another gulp.

'And now ye have yer own bairn, ye dinna want to miss out on the joy.'

'Joy? What joy?'

Emma walked into the room.

'Where's yer wee Highland lass? She's still nay come to see me.'

XXXIV

I n late April, Edward travelled south to stay with Mary Beth.
   'Edward, my poor boy. What you've been through since I last saw you.'

They held each other even before moving inside. The feel of her caring body reminded Edward of the warmth he had been missing since Amy's death.

He settled into the familiar guest room with the large, comfortable four-poster, washed, dressed in fresh clothes and went down for dinner. As ever at Mary Beth's place, the dinner wanted for nothing. They sat together on two corners of the long table and were served venison and vegetables, followed by home-baked apple pie. Good French wine was, as ever, in no short supply.

Edward poured his heart out, leaving no details to discretion.

'You truly loved her, didn't you?' Mary Beth asked, having to interrupt to get a word in.

'Oh, aye, I adored her. I ken I'll nay ever find another one like her.'

'I understand how you feel – but give it time.'

'I dinna want to give it time.' Edward spat back.

He saw her flinch.

'I'm sorry, Mary Beth. I'm just so sad, so lost.'

'That's alright, dear boy. I understand. Anyway, let's away to the lounge.'

As they walked down the hallway, Mary Beth took his hand and squeezed it. Something inside Edward melted with the feel of her smooth skin softening his calloused hand. They sat on the chaise in front of the fireplace.

'So, you haven't mentioned your boy,' Mary Beth said.

'D'ye ken I dinna care about that?' Edward replied, his eyes ablaze again.

'Not at all. I'm just saying you haven't even mentioned this fairly significant addition to your life.'

Edward fell to silence, then slowly welled up. Mary Beth drew his head to her shoulder.

'Just tell me what you want to tell me,' she said as she held him to her with one hand and, with the other, ran her fingers through his hair.

'I dinna ken what to do. I just ken the bairn'd die. By all accounts, he should've. But he dinna – and now I dinna ken what to do.'

'Will you try and visit, at least?'

'Nay, I canna until things settle down.'

'Would you like to?'

'I dinna ken.'

'Remember, darling boy, it's not only *your* child. It's Amy's as well. He's the one bit of her you still have.'

No-one had quite put it that way before. Edward broke down as he had not since the night of Amy's death.

'Oh, dear. I'm so sad for you,' Mary Beth whispered, cuddling him closer.

'But he killed her,' Edward blurted out. 'The *wee bairn killed her.*'

'Oh, darling, that's really not fair. The poor little thing had no say in it.'

'Perhaps – but it might as well have.'

They sat silent for some time. Mary Beth's warm body felt good. He remembered the perfume.

'Well, we'd best go to bed,' she said eventually. 'We still have much to talk about.'

They stood and held each other again. Edward's body was stirring with a mix of relief, comfort and the first hint of passion he had felt since Amy's death. Mary Beth took him by the hand and led him upstairs, past her room to his. She opened the door, ushered him inside and bade him good night.

—∞—

Edward spent several weeks there, tending to the garden by day, dining at night and talking in the lounge into the wee hours. Each night, it was the same tender hug and, normally, alighting the stairs together to their separate bedrooms.

'Can I come in with ye?' Edward asked one night outside Mary Beth's room.

There was a moment of silence and then a sweet smile came over her face.

'Let's talk about it tomorrow,' she said, kissing him lightly on the cheek.

She entered the room and closed the door behind her.

—∞—

They did not see much of each other the next day. Edward worked hard in the garden. Mary Beth had gone into town to deal with some business and was home quite late. She apologised for the rushed meal.

'I dinna care about the meal,' Edward said. 'I just wanna talk.'

Mary Beth ordered a few sandwiches to be made. They took them into the lounge room with a bottle of wine.

'So, ye said we'd talk the next day. And the next day's almost gone.'

'Impatient, as ever. There are still several hours left of "the next day".'

'Ye're laughing at me, Mary Beth, and that's cruel because ye ken how I feel.'

'No, I'm not laughing at you. I promise I'm not laughing at you. You mean far too much to me for that.'

'How much do I mean to ye, then?'

'Enough to be very careful, dear boy. I know what's between us, what's been between us for a long time now, even on the voyage and certainly when you came here after my husband died. For all the age difference, I still wondered if perhaps our stars were aligning. I knew I couldn't say anything then. I just had to let you go and see what happened. Then, you wrote and told me you were married and so I got on with my life. Now, here you are again, but clearly broken-hearted and denying you have a child who must need you.'

She paused.

'There's just too many broken pieces in your life right now.'

'So, ye do feel something for me, then?' Edward asked.

'Yes, I just said as much, didn't I?'

'Then why did ye reject me last night?'

'Reject you? I didn't reject you. I promise you the easiest thing last night would have been to invite you to my bed. It's something I've thought about – and I hope that's not being too honest. Edward, I needed you so much when John died. I truly did. But I don't want to be your second best. When everything else goes wrong in your life, you turn to me. And I don't want to spoil anything between us. You're far too precious to me.'

'So, what do we do then?'

'Take our time. You need to get your life a little more in order, especially working out what to do with young Thomas. You'll regret it forever if you cast him adrift. He's your flesh and blood and, as I say, he's the bit of Amy you still have.'

'So, should I leave then?

'No, you don't have to leave. I want you to stay as long as you want. I love having you here. But I just know you *will* leave at some point because you still have places to go, things to do, and I'd never want our friendship to stop you doing those things.'

'Friendship? Is that all it is?'

'True friendships are the hardest things in life to come by, believe me. People can be married for years and have no friendship between them. I know that.'

Edward sat, saying not a word.

'But, what we have is also more than that,' Mary Beth said, moving closer and holding his hand. 'Let's call it friendship plus.'

'Aye, but plus what?'

—∞—

Mary Beth was away a lot through the coming days. Edward spent his days gardening, reading and pondering on those places to go and things to do that Mary Beth had referred to.

'We've been invited to a dinner party,' she said one evening over supper.

'We?'

'Yes, of course, we.'

'As a couple?'

'Yes, is that alright with you?'

'I'm nay sure. I'm nay much of a one for dinner parties.'

'Well, it's time you became more of a one for dinner parties. They're part of life.'

'Nay in Listellick.'

'Well, you're not in Listellick now.'

'When is it anyway? I've been thinking about those places to go that you talked about.'

'This Saturday. I doubt you'll be going anywhere before then.'

—∞—

The next Saturday evening, they set out for East Finchley, a fifteen-minute ride to the home of the Ratcliffes. Ernest Ratcliffe and John Parker had gone to school together. Mary Beth was in a full-length black dress with puffed short sleeves and arm-length white gloves. Her hair had been curled with three white ribbons strategically placed. They sat opposite, catching sight of each other and occasionally smiling as the light allowed. Edward noted her radiance. Mary Beth noted his nervousness. Upon arriving, she stepped from the carriage, assisted by Ernest.

'Ernest, Gladys,' Mary Beth said, gesturing towards Edward alighting behind her in one of her husband's ill-fitting black dinner suits. 'I'd like you to meet Edward Lovat, a very good friend of mine.'

'Delighted to meet you, Mr Lovat,' they said in unison.

'Thank ye for inviting me,' Edward replied, shaking hands with Ernest and taking Gladys's hand by the fingertips.

'That's a fine Scottish brogue you have there,' Ernest said. 'What part are you from?'

'Well, my family is from the Highlands originally, around Inverness.'

'Ah, and that's a famous Highlands name, is it not? Are you related to the infamous Lovats of the Jacobite Rebellion?'

'Aye, sir, I surely am.'

'Oh, my. Not to that horrid old man who had his head chopped off in the Tower, I hope,' Gladys said, turning up her nose.

'Aye, him too. He was a cousin but my Grand Da died at Culloden. He was one of the leaders of the Lovat Scouts.'

'Oh dearie me,' Gladys said, nose still pointing north. 'I'm not sure I'd be admitting to all that if I were you, young man.'

It was the rocky start to an even rockier night. Edward endured an evening of the kind of London social life that probably explained why the Jacobite Rebellion started in the first place. The small and inane talk was the same wherever he went. His name, the brogue, the putdowns, a very English versus Highlander night.

'*There's not a decent one among them,*' he thought to himself, surveying the scene from a safe corner.

He had lost sight of Mary Beth soon after entering. Then he saw her, noting how well she seemed to fit into this scene.

Eventually, they were called to table, men on one side, women on the other. The two men either side of him showed no interest in him, leaving him stranded. His thoughts alternated between the unendurable time it was all taking and watching Mary Beth opposite, looking as much at home as he felt an alien. Occasionally, she looked across and smiled at him. He just wanted to be alone with her.

When the table broke, Edward quickly made his way around to her, only to be cut off by a queue of men seeking her attention. They milled around like flies to the honeypot, young men, old men, married men, single and divorced. It seemed to make no difference, including to her.

He sought a quiet corner again where he could sit this out.

—ᴍ—

'It's just the way it is,' Mary Beth said later when he asked her about the flirtatious men. 'They mean nothing.'

'So do *I* mean nothing too?'

'Of course not. It's different. These people mean nothing to me. *You* mean the world.'

'So, why do ye bother with them, then?'

'Because it's part of my life. Obviously not a part you would enjoy.'

'Nay at all. I dinna enjoy seeing ye behaving like that.'

'Are you jealous, Edward Lovat?'

'Perhaps.'

'You've nothing to be jealous of, believe me. There's no man there I'm the slightest bit interested in.'

'Well, they're certainly interested in ye. I canna believe ye'd waste yer time with them.'

Mary Beth smiled.

'Waste, is it? Well, listen to this, my jealous best friend. One of those men you think I was flirting with happens to be the head of a new agricultural college up near Oxford. I was telling him about you and he said he'd like to speak with you. They're starting a new one-year Master of Agronomy course, beginning in September, and he thought you sounded like an ideal candidate. I was looking around to introduce you but I couldn't see you.'

'Nay, I was probably out talking with the horses by then. They were the only braw company of the night.'

Mary Beth laughed and Edward joined in.

'Well, there's nothing to worry about because he gave me his details and said I should bring you up to speak with him. So, is that a waste of time?'

'Nay, thank ye. I'm sorry.'

'It's important that you believe in me, Edward. I know most of these people are not worth the time I give to them and I really don't care what they think of me. But, what *you* think of me *is* important. Very important. I couldn't bear to know you thought poorly of me.'

'I swear I never would,' Edward said, drawing her to him. 'I love ye, Mary Beth. I ken I love ye.'

They stood silently, holding each other and breathing deeply.

'And I love you, my darling Edward.'

They sat down and studied each other as though trying to work out where to go from there.

'And that's why you must go to those places and do those things. And then come back to me if you wish. And if you do, I'll be here, I promise.'

—⚬⚬⚬—

'I was most impressed with your background and experience, Mr Lovat, at least as outlined to me by Mrs Parker, your patron.'

'Thank ye, sir,' Edward replied as Sir Henry Beaumont lit up a cigar and offered one to him.

Edward and Mary Beth had travelled together to Cirencester in Gloucestershire to meet with Sir Henry. He had recently taken up the position as Director of the Royal Agricultural Institute.

'The combination of the Uppsala diploma and the vast practical experience of plant life across the world is a rare one indeed. I believe you would be an ideal starter for our new degree programme. But would you have the means?'

'I'm nay sure, sir, I'll have to speak with my family.'

'Well, speak with them first and if there's a problem, let me know. The Government is making noises about providing a number of scholarships to the most promising candidates and I believe you could well be one of them.'

—⁓—

Edward mentioned this conversation to Mary Beth on the way home.

'I'll pay for you, my dear. I thought you'd know that.'

'Ye most certainly will nay. I'd nay dream of it.'

'But I want to do this for you. That way I'll have just a piece of you, no matter what else happens.'

'And that's why ye must nay pay for me.'

—⁓—

'I'll miss you so much,' Mary Beth said, farewelling Edward after his seven-week stay.

He was heading for Pemberton, thence to Beauly to meet up with William Henry who was home on leave.

'I'll be back.'

'If only for the dinner parties,' Mary Beth said, tears in her eyes.

'If only for the dinner parties. Thank ye for everything – but especially for them.'

They held each other, sharing a chuckle amidst the tears.

'I do hope you come back but you must do those things and go to those places first. The ones on the ground and the ones in your head.'

Edward had been about to mount the carriage but, with her words, he ran back and gave her a final hug.

'The ones on the ground and the ones in my head.'

The carriage was moving away.

'And the one in Ireland too,' Mary Beth called after him.

XXXV

After a short time in Pemberton sorting out family financing of the agronomy programme, Edward headed north to the Highlands to stay with William Henry at Castle Dounie.

'I ken ye'd nay go so well in that circle,' William Henry said. 'It'd drive ye *cuthach* in time.'

'But I do love Mary Beth. I truly ken that.'

'Aye, but ye'd have to love everything that goes with her. That's the problem.'

William Henry offered the listening ear that Edward needed. He had said little to anyone in Pemberton, sensing they were not happy with the idea of his relationship with an older woman.

'But Da, wasn't Mahdiya aulder than ye?' he had said.

'Aye but that was different,' Thomas replied.

Only Will seemed as open as ever to whatever might be transpiring but, even there, Edward felt disinclined to be overly frank with "the auld man".

Edward shared all his confusions and misgivings with William Henry who had scant opportunity to reply or comment.

'And congratulations on yer bairn,' William Henry said out of the blue.

'What? Oh, aye, thank ye,' Edward replied, then carried on with the prior conversation.

'*Stad*, man, halt. Are ye nay at all interested in yer bairn? A bairn's very special, d'ye ken? I ken because my parents have lost two of them and ken they'll lose a third, and I've seen what that does to people. Believe me, if yer bairn has survived against all the odds, then it's for a reason. God wants him here and ye'd better start taking some responsibility for him.'

Edward fell to silence.

'And it's the one piece of yer Amy ye've left to ye. Surely that on its own's enough to want to be with him.'

'Aye, that's what Mary Beth always said.'

'Well she's a smart *Sassanach*, then. Maybe not the right one for ye but a smart one all the same.'

—⁘—

'Nay, ye canna go there yet,' Thomas said. 'The advice from Paddy is that it's still too dangerous.'

'I'll go if you like,' Sarah said. 'Your father and I have talked about it. We'd love to bring him back here if it's possible.'

'I dinna want to put ye to that trouble,' Edward said. 'But I'd be relieved if someone could tell me first-hand how the wee laddie is.'

'Thank heavens ye've finally come to that place, lad,' Thomas said. 'Who do we have to thank for that?'

'Willian Henry, Da. And Mary Beth.'

'I dinna like that woman,' Emma interrupted.

'You haven't even met her, darling,' Will said, giving her a hug.

'I dinna need to,' Emma replied, looking to Edward. 'Where's yer Amy, laddie?'

—⁘—

In late August, Edward headed south to Cirencester to begin studying for a Master of Agronomy degree at the Royal Agricultural Institute. He found the focus of study in an area he loved to be just the tonic needed to clear his mind.

He saw Mary Beth only once in the Michaelmas semester. She came to visit and they spent a day wandering through Oxford, chatting about this and that. They were on a bench in the grounds of Christ Church College, watching the swans and ducks on the Thames.

'So, you haven't come to visit me?' Mary Beth said.

'Nay, I'm sorry. I've been very busy with assignments. I've nay had a social life at all.'

'Is that all I am to you? Just another item on your social calendar?'

'Of course nay. What I'm saying is I've been busy.'

'Will you be as busy in the future or might I expect to see you sometime before Christmas?'

'I'm really nay so sure.'

'You're not so sure?' Mary Beth said, choking on the words.

They sat for a while in silence.

'Is that alright? I truly am so busy trying to do everything I need to do for this course.'

'Edward, I'm delighted you're so committed to the course. I truly am. Remember, I'm the one who set this up for you? Offered to pay for you?'

'Aye. And I'll be forever grateful.'

'But leave that aside for the moment. Only a few months ago, you declared your love for me, wanted us to commit to each other there and then. Have you forgotten all that?'

'Nay, how could I? But ye were the one who said I should go places, do things, to be sure. So, here I am going places and doing things.'

'To be sure?'

'To be sure!'

The day ended with a vague promise from Edward that he would try to get to Mary Beth's place before the Christmas break.

—⁂—

Sometime in November, a letter arrived from Sarah.

Dear Edward, I have been to Tralee to see your little boy. They call him Little Tom, which suits him so well. He is such a beautiful little chap, although the doctor says he still needs much in the way of constant care. Apparently his lungs have not developed as they should. The doctor believes this is a product of his premature birth. Nonetheless, he is starting to crawl; it is so cute watching him. The Prendivilles have, of course, been wonderful. Louise dotes on him day and night and Mary is like a second mother. Mrs Prendiville is of course his grandmother in all things. She is such a kind heart. Even Denis, Liam's eldest boy, has struck up a special relationship, almost fatherly. There are other things to tell you best left for when you are home. For now, I believe it is better that Thomas stay where he is but Paddy thinks you might be able to visit early in the New Year. Our sincere love, Sarah and your father xx.

The idea of Denis playing a fatherly role stung him. Though he had almost willed the baby's death initially, he was now feeling envious that others were benefitting from his own child's existence. And the words of William Henry and Mary Beth continued to haunt him.

He is the one bit of Amy you have left.

—⁂—

Hence, it was with some intent that Edward set out for Pemberton before Christmas, his promise to visit Mary Beth beforehand broken and unacknowledged. He would find out whatever else it was that Sarah had to tell him and then book the earliest possible passage to Tralee.

'They're only doing what they think best for the child,' Sarah said.

Edward had erupted when told that Little Tom's birth had not been registered. He was commonly known as Tom O'Rourke, the twin of Bernadette O'Rourke, Mary's third child born just eleven days before Tom's birth.

'How can that be for the best? The laddie'll grow up confused about who he really is.'

'It's just for now, while things settle down,' Sarah said. 'Remember, his life could be at risk if Adair and his gang knew your child was in the district.'

'Well, he'll nay be once I bring him home.'

'Lad, just settle down,' Thomas said. 'Sarah's told ye she ken it'd be a *dona* idea at the moment. The laddie's getting better care there than we could give here and ye can hardly take him to the Institute. Go and visit him, once Paddy gives the all clear, but for heaven's sake dinna go barging over there and dragging the wee bairn away from the only home he's ever ken. Ye can fix it in time once ye're a wee bit more settled.'

'And when will that ever be, I wonder?' Edward said.

They all wondered too.

—⚬—

A few days after a very quiet Christmas and even quieter New Year, Edward received a letter from Paddy. It flagged the all clear for a discreet visit to Tralee.

He was no more than a few steps ashore in Dingle when he felt Amy's presence. The feeling increased the closer he came to Tralee. As he approached the Prendiville house, he could picture her peering through that bedroom window to the left of the front door, the room where he had last seen her alive.

'My li'l Redcoat,' Mrs Prendiville said. 'Ye're so welcome, as always.'

'Teddy, 'ello Teddy,' Louise shouted, pushing her mother aside and hugging him.

'*Halo*, Mrs P. *Halo*, Louise. It's so braw to see ye.'

'Not as braw as it is for us,' Louise said, dragging Edward into the house.

'Quiet, Louise,' Mrs Prendiville said. 'Ye'll wake the li'l one.'

'Well, we don't want 'im sleepin' through 'is Pa's visit, do we?' Louise snapped back.

'Girl, 'ush girl. Don't speak to yer Ma like that.'

The cry of an infant came from the bedroom.

'See, Ma. Li'l Tom knew his Da was 'ere.'

'Come and 'ave a look at what ye've produced,' Mrs Prendiville said. 'Ye won't believe 'ow well ye've done.'

Edward was led into the bedroom and the small enclosed cot where his son lay. Mrs Prendiville raised the blind so the dying embers of the sun could stream through the window and light up the room.

'Will ye look at that?' Louise said as the three of them peered down at the glowing face of an almost twelve-month old boy.

Little Tom beamed the warmest grin as Louise reached down to pick him up.

'They're like two peas in a pod, these two,' Mrs Prendiville said.

'So d'ye know 'o this is?' Louise said, pointing with her spare hand at Edward. 'This is yer very own Pa.'

Little Tom smiled and cooed and jumped in Louise's arms.

'D'ye want yer Pa to 'old ye?'

'Nay, nay,' Edward said. 'It's too soon.'

'It *might* be too soon, darlin',' Mrs Prendiville said.

'I don't think so,' Louise replied, taking a couple of strides towards Edward. 'Why don't we let li'l Tom decide?'

'So this is yer Pa. Ain't 'e the loveliest Pa a boy could 'ave? Ain't 'e the most 'andsome Pa in all the world? Would ye like to touch yer Pa?'

Louise reached her spare hand out and touched Edward's cheek lightly. Little Tom copied her action. He then reached both arms out to Edward.

'Take 'im, boy,' Mrs Prendiville said. 'Don't miss the moment.'

Edward took his son's two hands in his own two hands and kissed them.

'Nay, I dinna want him to cry,' he said as he stepped back.

Little Tom fell to tears.

'Oh isn't yer Pa a silly man?' Louise said. 'Why doesn't 'e ever know 'ow much 'e's loved?'

—◊◊◊—

Over the next few days, Edward had the opportunity to speak with Dr Slattery, Paddy and others in the family.

'The boy should stay here,' Slattery said. 'I understand ye're his father and would want him with ye but he really needs to be stronger before ye take him on such a long trip, especially in the depths of winter.'

'I agree,' Louise said. 'Ye can't take 'im away; I mean for 'is own sake. But ye should come and stay more often. We ... I mean 'e ... loves it when ye're 'ere.'

'And, of course, Louise is only ever thinkin' of what's best for the boy,' Liam said. 'Aren't ye, sis?'

Louise blushed and quickly left the room, handing Tom over to Denis as she passed him.

'Oh, don't tease the poor girl,' Mrs Prendiville said. 'Li'l Tom really 'as been the best thing that's ever 'appened to 'er.'

'Teddy's little Tommy, she calls him,' Denis said, bouncing the boy up and down, causing gales of toddler laughter.

'Ye're so braw with him,' Edward said. 'Ye're all so braw with him.'

'Would ye like a cuddle?' Denis asked.

'Nay just now, thank ye.'

A little later, Louise stepped back into the room, red-eyed, and took Tom back from Denis. She came and sat on the lounge in the spare spot next to Edward.

'I canna believe how much ye love the laddie,' Edward said.

'We love 'im 'cause 'e's yers,' she whispered.

XXXVI

'Where's yer bonnie Jacobite lassie?' Emma asked for the umpteenth time since Edward's return.

'She'll be coming soon, Gran.'

Will smiled.

'So, ye decided to keep the lad there after all?' Thomas asked.

'Aye, I ken it's for the best for now. He could nay be in better hands.'

'I'm glad you came to see it that way,' Sarah said. 'Like you, I went over quite sure he should be brought back but, in the end, I decided I'd be doing it for me, not for him.'

'Aye, I agree but I'll get over there whenever I can and when the lad's a wee bit stronger, perhaps he can come and live with us – or at least come and stay a while.'

'I ken I'd like to see him again,' Thomas said. 'My only memory's of this wee ball of reddened, blotchy flesh. It's nay the best memory of my only grandson.'

'And the only one ye're likely to have,' Edward said.

'I'm not sure Louise thinks that,' Sarah replied. 'I think she'd give her Teddy another child as quickly as you asked.'

They all laughed, except Edward who looked pained and Emma confused.

'Who?' Emma said.

'Louise Prendiville has set her sights on our Edward, Ma,' Thomas said.

'I dinna like that lass.'

—⟋∿⟍—

Edward was about to step into the carriage for the trip to Cirencester when Sarah remembered the letter that had arrived that morning. She ran back into the house to retrieve it. She handed it to him as he sat in the carriage.

Edward recognised Jane's writing. He put the letter in his pocket for later reading.

He dozed all the way to Stoke-on-Trent where the carriage stopped for watering the horses and allowing the passengers to take tea.

Back in the carriage, he took the letter from his pocket.

Dear Edward, I'm so very sorry to hear about the beastly things that have happened to you since we last saw each other. I wonder sometimes why God does such awful things to his creatures. But, of course, we know he knows best … I wanted you to know that I think of you often and wish we could meet and re-kindle our friendship. You truly are and remain one of the most treasured people in my life. Please write and let me know how you are and if we might meet sometime. I understand you are in Pemberton currently, not so very far away. Assuring you of my continued affection, Jane.

Edward had not been expecting to hear from Jane, probably ever, and certainly not a letter of this kind. The steady clip-clop of the horses and the picturesque sight of Staffordshire's rolling hills, babbling brooks and endless spires passing by put him in a more pensive mood than normal.

By the time the carriage reached Cirencester, nothing had been resolved but certain things clarified.

Edward entered into the Hilary semester with the same relish as in Michaelmas. He distracted himself from his personal confusions by focussing on his studies. Much as he had in Uppsala, he eschewed most of the social life that others enjoyed and by which some were consumed. He ended up passing his exams with distinction and gaining a *Cum Laude* for his degree.

—ᴍ—

'Please, would you come and see me in my office tomorrow?' Sir Henry Beaumont asked him at the end of the graduation festivities.

Edward slept late the next day, as did all the graduates. Upon waking, he hastened to the director's office.

'Thank you for coming to see me,' Beaumont began. 'There's a matter I wish to discuss with you. Have you ever heard of the Towneley Estate in Burnley?'

'Aye, sir. In fact I've been there; I've met Mr Towneley.'

'Well, well, how interesting. Charles Towneley and I are old friends. When we started this degree programme, he wrote and asked if I would keep an eye out for an outstanding graduate he might employ on the estate. I think your grades and your overall diligence mark you out as that outstanding graduate. So, if it's alright with you, I'd like to recommend you to Mr Towneley and I'm sure he'll then invite you to go to Burnley to speak with him. How do you feel about that?'

Edward's head was spinning. It was as if all sorts of stars were aligning, beneficent and maleficent mixed together. Work on the Towneley Estate would be every young agronomist's dream come true. It was so often a source of reference in his coursework and cited constantly as one of the finest garden estates in all of Britain, if not Europe. It was also known as a bit of a Catholic enclave and sympathetic to the Jacobite cause, albeit entirely passively these days. This would mean that the kind of snubbing his Jacobite-related name had caused at Mary Beth's party, something still common in many parts of England, would be largely absent.

On the maleficent side was the nagging issue of the Braithwaite connection with the Towneleys. Mrs Braithwaite did not approve of him and then there was Jane herself whom he had largely snubbed but for a cursory reply to her letter. There had been no follow-up from her, which was as he expected.

—⁓—

Dear Mary Beth, I'm sorry that again I have to decline the kind invitation to visit. An unexpected opportunity has arisen to be interviewed for a position at the Towneley Estate... I'm confident you will understand how important this is to my career and that you will forgive me for once again breaking my promise. I will make every effort to visit as soon as possible. Kindly, Edward.

The only time he had seen Mary Beth throughout Hilary semester was, again, when she visited and they repeated the traversing of Oxford. This time, however, conversation was reserved for the "this and that".

'Just promise to come and see me as soon as you finish,' Mary Beth had said late in the day.

'I promise.'

Edward had tossed and turned that night, wondering anew about their relationship. It was always so comfortable with Mary Beth. By morning, he had resolved that he would make up his mind one way or the other by the end of term and then go and see her.

Now, it was the end of term and he was heading in the opposite direction.

XXXVII

'Of course, you remember the Braithwaites, don't you?' Charles Towneley said outside the chapel on the first Sunday morning after Edward had begun his new job.

It was expected that any employee of the estate would attend Sunday Mass.

'Aye, I do indeed,' Edward said, shaking Charles Braithwaite's hand and nodding at his wife, Elizabeth.

'And I think you know my daughter, Jane?'

'Indeed!' Elizabeth said.

'Don't be silly, Mummy and Daddy,' Jane said. 'You know we're good friends. How are you Edward? It's lovely to see you again.'

'And ye, Jane,' Edward replied, taking her hand and kissing it in gentlemanly fashion.

Edward had been dreading the first meeting with the Braithwaites and especially Jane. As it was, her friendliness reminded him of what had attracted him to her in the first place.

For some weeks, they met each Sunday after Mass, each time exchanging pleasantries.

On the seventh Sunday, Jane invited him to come to their place for lunch.

'Thank ye but does yer Ma approve?'

'Oh, don't worry about Mummy. It's my approval that matters.'

She turned and walked a few steps away, stopped and turned back, staring at him with no smile.

'And my approval you should be seeking.'

—⁂—

Charles Towneley and his wife met with the Braithwaites for Sunday lunch almost every week, normally taking it in turns to host the event. On this occasion, it was at the Braithwaites and Edward went with the Towneleys in their carriage.

'Welcome everyone,' Braithwaite greeted them. 'Charles, Marie, please join us in the lounge room. Edward, you might prefer to be with the children in the yard. I think you'll find Jane out there.'

Jane was sitting on a white wooden bench seat surrounded by deep amber maple leaves, some still falling. She had changed out of her dowdy church dress and into a stark white, tightly fitting one with short sleeves and open front that offered just a hint of cleavage. For a moment, and with the sun in his eyes, Edward could not distinguish her from the bench she was sitting on. Her pale skin blended into the whiteness around her. It was her dark brown hair, now hanging loosely over her shoulders that first distinguished her.

'Come and sit with me, Edward,' she said, pointing to the vacant spot next to her.

They sat silent for some time.

'Where's yer brother?'

'At a friend's place. Are you disappointed?'

'Nay at all.'

'Why not?'

'I prefer to have ye to myself.'

More silence.

'Really?' Jane eventually said. 'You'd prefer to have me to yourself but you can't even write me a decent letter when I put myself out to write to you. Are you truly the heartless philanderer Mummy says you are?'

Her anger took them both by surprise.

'I'm sorry,' Edward said. 'Perhaps we should go inside and join the others.'

'No!' Jane said, grabbing him firmly by the arm. 'You are *not* getting away so easily this time.'

More silence as Jane's grip tightened and she began to shake.

'Edward, I'm sorry for everything that's happened to you. I truly am. I said that in the letter and I meant it. Please believe me. It must have been heartbreaking and I want you to tell me all about it sometime.'

Jane had loosened the grip as she spoke but then went silent and tightened it again. Edward felt the pain in his arm as though there was a vice around it.

'*But*, you can't just dismiss the people who genuinely care for you. You have to take some responsibility for your friendships. Life is not all about you. It's about others too, people who love you and want to look after you. Do you know what I mean?'

'Aye, I ken so.'

'You *think* so? You *think* so? Truly, Edward Lovat, you're the *most* frustrating man.'

Edward had noted how Jane's pale skin was reddening as she spoke. He noticed how the hairs on her arm were standing to attention as if they were the subjects of her tirade. He found himself smiling involuntarily.

'And *what* are you smiling at?'

'Smiling? I was nay smiling.'

'Well, it looked like smiling to me. Or was it laughing? If you're laughing at me, Edward Lovat, I'm going to hit you right now.'

'I ken I'd enjoy that. And if I was smiling, it's because I just realised how much I've missed you.'

Jane said nothing. She released the grip and sat silent, looking down at the hand she was now wringing and shaking.

'That's nice but it's not enough,' she said, her voice choking. 'It's *not* enough. If you want my approval, there has to be more.'

There was another prolonged period of silence. It was broken by the call to lunch. Jane responded first by standing and moving towards the door.

'Wait,' Edward called. 'I *do* want yer approval.'

'Then prove it.'

—⟋⟍—

Over the next few months, they met now and again after Sunday Mass. Sometimes, it was for lunch at one or other of the Towneley or Braithwaite homes or sometimes during an extended parish event. Wherever they were, it was difficult to catch any time alone before the inevitable *come dear* from Jane's mother.

Work on the estate was busy, with twelve hour days normal. Sunday was the only day off so it was the only chance to prove whatever needed proving.

It therefore took some time before Edward and Jane found themselves alone. The occasion was a parish picnic and the paper-chase event. As the rules were being explained, a look passed between them. They deliberately took the wrong trail together.

'Well, have I proven myself yet?' Edward asked as they paused behind a huge oak tree.

'Hardly!'

'What more can I do?'

'Let your intentions be known, Edward.'

'How do I do that?'

'Truly, Edward Lovat, do you want to marry me or not?'

In twilight hours in bed, the only thinking time Edward had, he had fairly much decided that Jane's was the relationship he wanted to pursue. But there were nagging doubts.

'*Is it just convenience? Are my feelings strong enough? Can I ever replace Amy? Did I really miss Jane when I said I did? What about Mary Beth? Should I be thinking more about wee Tom?*'

The thoughts would go around and around. He would fall asleep and, as often as not, find himself dreaming about Jane. The image of her in that flattering white dress, amidst the maple leaves. The long dark hair falling loosely over her fair skin. The tiny hairs on her arm standing at attention.

'Oh forget it,' Jane said, hurrying away to join the other paper-chasers.

'Jane, wait.'

'Edward, Jane, over here,' two of the young parishioners were calling to them. 'We wondered where you were.'

'Sorry,' Jane said. 'We must have been following a false trail.'

She turned back to face Edward.

'Or I was at least.'

—◊◊—

On the following Sunday, Edward knew the two families were meeting for lunch at the Braithwaites. He hovered around after Mass, hoping to receive an invitation. It was not forthcoming. Jane and her mother went straight to the carriage. He headed after them.

'I'd leave them be, young man,' Charles Braithwaite said. 'Jane is unwell and it might be best to leave her be.'

'Please give her my fondest regards. I hope she's well soon.'

The Sunday afterwards, he went to Pemberton for Emma's birthday. She seemed not to understand what the occasion was about and retired to her bed mid-afternoon. Thomas was having a bad day, in severe pain, and excused himself soon afterwards.

Edward was left with Sarah and Will. He was desperate to talk about his confusion. When they asked how things were going, he opened up. The good whisky helped to loosen his tongue.

'Well, I think you've as much as given us the answer yourself,' Sarah said.

'I agree,' Will added.

'Have I though? I thought I was just sharing lots of confusion.'

'No, if any woman can replace Amy in your dreams, that's a good sign for me,' Sarah said.

'But what about her mother?'

'You're not marrying the mother,' Will said. 'I agree with Sarah the object of your dreaming offers a clue but I'm sure she'd agree there's more to it than that. The right one's the one you can imagine yourself with through the thick and thin of life. Somehow, you know you love enough to be there for them, regardless. Do you feel that way about this girl?'

'Like you do about Gran?'

'Like I do about your Gran.'

'About Amy, I nay ever doubted it. I'd have followed her into Hell. With Jane, it's different. It's more a matter of will. I ken it's what I want but the feelings are different.'

'Nothing can replace the first love, Edward,' Sarah said. 'I know all about that.'

'So do I,' Will said. 'But a second love can be good too – or so your Gran tells me.'

'Whatever you do, Edward,' Sarah said. 'Don't compare Jane – or anyone – with Amy. If you do, you'll always find them wanting. Just take whoever it is as they are. See the good and be happy with that.'

—∞—

The following Sunday, Edward missed Mass again because William Henry arrived in Burnley late on the Saturday night. It was unexpected and Edward was annoyed because he had made a firm intention to plead his case with Jane. Feigned illness or motherly interference would not stop him.

'Would ye come to Mass with me at least?' Edward asked.

'Nay, I dinna have the time. I have to be on the noon coach to the north.'

'Alright then, let's go for a ride.'

They rode out some distance and stopped by the side of the road.

'So, how's that crazy love life of yers?' William Henry asked.

'*Seolta* as ever. Perhaps crazier.'

Edward shared all that had happened, including his conversation with Sarah and Will.

'So what d'ye ken?'

'I dinna ken but it makes more sense than with that auld socialite in London,' William Henry replied.

'She's nay auld and she's nay a socialite.'

'Just tell me, cousin and best friend, did ye ever notice Mary Beth's skin changing colour before yer eyes? Did ye ever notice the hairs on Mary Beth's arm standing at attention?'

'Nay. It's different.'

'So, it says something, does it nay?'

—⚊—

When William Henry left, Edward went back to his room. He began to write a letter to Jane. Started, stopped, tore it up, and started again. He put the pen down. He needed to see her. It was now mid-afternoon. He rode to the Braithwaite home.

'Mister Lovat to see Miss Jane,' Edward said to the maid at the door.

'I'll take care of this, Emily,' Elizabeth could be heard calling from inside.

'Young man, if you should ever wish to see my daughter, you do not come unannounced and you ask for me first. Is that clear?'

'Aye, Ma'am. I sincerely apologise but it's urgent that I see yer daughter.'

'Well, I will let her know you were here and, if she wishes to see you, I'm sure she will let you know somehow. Now, good afternoon. It is rest time in this household.'

Edward was cantering away, frustrated and confused. He recalled some of the words he had heard recently.

'You're not marrying the mother.'

'Make your intentions clear.'

'Then prove it.'

He turned the horse around and rode quietly back to the house. He dismounted and made his way to the side that accommodated Jane's bedroom on the second floor. He knew that the parents' bedroom was on the other side.

He noticed that the blind was only half down and the window slightly ajar. He found a small pebble and threw it at the window. It fell short, as did the second one. On the third attempt, he threw something between a pebble and a small rock. The tinkle of broken glass told him he was in trouble.

Jane appeared at the window, inspected the damage and glared below.

'What do you think you're doing?' she called out louder than he would have hoped.

'I'm sorry but I need to see ye.'

'So badly you're prepared to break my window?'

'What's going on in there?' Elizabeth was calling.

She was quickly at the window.

'Young man, I will call the constable if you do not leave these premises immediately.'

'I'm very sorry Mrs Braithwaite but I'm nay leaving until I can speak with Jane. It is, as I said at the door, *urgent*.'

'I've made myself perfectly clear. You'll not be speaking with Jane but I *will* be informing the constable that you're an unwelcome intruder on this property.'

'Oh, Mummy, for heaven's sake. All he wants is to speak with me. What do you wish to say, Edward?'

'I'd prefer to speak with ye alone if I could.'

'Under no circumstances is my daughter coming down. Heaven knows what you're capable of.'

'Mummy, I can handle this. What is it? Tell me from here.'

'Alright, ye said to prove it and I'm proving it.'

He stood, hardly breathing.

'And what does that mean exactly?'

Edward took a deep breath and bent down on one knee.

'I'm asking ye to be my wife.'

—m—

On the following Sunday, the banns of marriage were announced between Edward Lovat and Jane Braithwaite. It was a busy week of gaining Charles Braithwaite's approval, smoothing over the ruffles with Mrs Braithwaite, as far as was possible, and making a late evening trip to Pemberton to let his own family know.

'I dinna like that girl,' Emma said.

'Which girl?' Will asked.

'The fancy London toff.'

'Whatever makes ye happy, lad,' Thomas said.

'I'll let the Prendivilles know if you wish,' Sarah said.

'Nay, let me do that.'

Dear Mr & Mrs Prendiville, & Louise, I am writing to let you know that I am engaged to be married to Jane Braithwaite from Burnley, an old friend. Jane and I were near to courting some time ago, before I came to Ireland and met Amy. Our friendship has rekindled and she has accepted my proposal for marriage. I will be over before Christmas to see you all, and especially my darling lad, Tom. Please give him a kiss for me and tell him how much I love him. All my love, Edward. PS. Louise, thank you for all the loving care you continue to give to my lad. You truly have been like a mother to him and I will always hold a special place in my heart for you.

Then, the other letter, the hardest of all.

Dear Mary Beth, You remain my dearest friend and I will be forever grateful for everything that has passed between us. This is a difficult letter for me to write and only you would know fully why that is the case. I have asked Jane Braithwaite to marry me and she has said yes. I know I have spoken with you about Jane in the past. She was a dear friend and, in some ways, my court before I moved to Ireland and met Amy. Since being here, our friendship has grown to be much more than that and so we will be marrying sometime during next year. I do hope and pray you are not angry with me for not telling you sooner but this has all happened very quickly. I hope this is not inappropriate but I would love for you to be at the wedding as you will always be the dearest of friends and confidants. I feel I could never repay you for all you have done for me. In all fondness, Edward.

The reply came more quickly than Edward expected.

Dear Edward, You mean more to me than I can say. You know that. So how could I be angry that you have found the woman of your dreams? If that be so, just know that I will be there for you, as I always will be however our paths might cross or not in future years. Of course I will be at your wedding should I be fortunate enough to receive your invitation. Your friend always, Mary Beth.

The letter was welcome but left Edward wondering again about his choices.

XXXVIII

Edward's and Jane's courtship was a formal one. The combination of English upper class and tribal Catholicism ensured it would be so. Those who clung to their tenure in the Towneley Estate were determined to show their Protestant neighbours that Catholics did everything the proper way. Hence, engagement meant that all encounters were chaperoned. The most ardent chaperone was Elizabeth Braithwaite. She kept the parish priest apprised of any near misses, such as when Edward and Jane had slipped behind a tree for a quick kiss. She had spotted them and swiftly intervened to prevent even a venial sin being committed.

Her proudest save was when Edward had come around in the evening and climbed the vine growing up the lattice to Jane's window.

'I just sensed there was some evil afoot, Father. Mothers have a sixth sense, you know.'

Jane seemed happy to conform to what was required. Edward noted how she and her mother seemed closer than ever before.

Edward's broader life experience had him railing against much of Towneley Estate's constrictions.

'It sounds as though you might as well join the Jesuits,' Will said to him once.

'I dinna like those people,' Emma murmured from her chair.

For Edward, marriage could not happen quickly enough. He figured it would be the key to release him from the prison he was in.

—⁓—

In late January of 1798, Edward travelled to Tralee for the double celebration of his birthday and that of his two year-old boy. Mr Prendiville had died just before Christmas, so it was also a chance to offer his personal condolences.

"Li'l Tom's comin' on so well,' Mrs Prendiville said.

'But the doctor still thinks 'e shouldn' travel far,' Louise added.

'Dinna worry, Louise. I've nay any intention of taking him with me just yet.'

'Just yet? Or never? Please say never.'

'Nay ever's a long time. But nay for now, at least.'

'Oh darlin',' Mrs Prendiville said to her daughter. 'The time'll come when our li'l Redcoat'll want 'is son with 'im. We've been blessed to 'ave 'ad 'im for so long. 'e's been such a wonderful distraction in our sorrows.'

'More than a distraction,' Louise said. 'I'll probably never 'ave my own child, let's face it. So 'e's all I got. And 'e's all I got o' ye, Teddy. The only piece ye left me.'

She burst into tears and hurried out of the room.

'Forgive 'er, dear. She took the news o' yer marriage very 'ard. I know ye was never gonna marry 'er but she's 'eld a candle for ye for so long.'

'I'm sorry. Should I go? Would it be better if I took Tom with me now?'

'Oh, no. Ye mustn' do that to the little one. When ye're nice and settled and 'e's a little older. For now, just get 'ere when ye can so 'e knows ye.'

Edward slept badly. He could barely remember the troubling dreams in the morning. Just Little Tom's face – in tears.

He recalled the one short conversation with Jane about him.

'I always wanted to give you your first child.'

He hoped she would feel differently in time. Once they had their own child, he hoped Tom would join them. There had been so little time to sort these things out.

—∞—

'Give a kiss to yer Pa then, Tom, darlin',' Mrs Prendiville said when Louise brought him into the breakfast room.

Edward stood to embrace the child. Little Tom pulled back and buried his head in Louise's chest.

'It's alright. Dinna force the lad.'

Louise put the boy down and he quickly ran to the chair at the farthest point from Edward.

'Oh, he's walking?'

'And runnin', as ye can see,' Louise said with the kind of delight that suggested, *see how well I'm doing with him.*

There were no kisses or hugs on this trip. The rejection Edward felt was one beyond the normal shyness children feel with strangers. To Edward, it felt more like a judgement from on high, one that howled parental failure.

Edward went to the church and visited Amy's still unmarked grave. He enquired of Paddy whether it was now timely to mark the grave. The rights to the management title had finally been given to Adair and his thugs. Paddy believed so, so Edward left the words he wanted inscribed in the hope they would be there on his next visit. It felt like the least he could do for his first love.

'Dinna compare,' he reminded himself.

The wedding took place on the 25th of June, 1798. As the guest list grew, almost entirely on Jane's side, it became obvious that the small chapel on the estate would not accommodate the number. Edward suggested the College chapel at Stonyhurst.

'I ken one of the priests there too.'

'Oh, a Jesuit?' Elizabeth said. 'That would look so good on the invitations.'

The location and securing the agreement of his old science teacher, Father Pritchard, were about the only things Edward contributed to an affair entirely coordinated by Elizabeth.

'Seriously,' Edward said one evening. 'A coronation'd be less work.'

'Don't be so ungrateful,' Jane snapped back. 'Weddings are always for the bride's mother. Surely you know that.'

Edward reflected on his first marriage, concluding that the difference was not merely owing to Amy not having a mother, but to the difference between his two brides. The contrast between the quietest wedding in Ireland's history and what was shaping up to be England's wedding of the year could not have been more profound.

'*Dinna compare.*'

—ⵡ—

Father Pritchard welcomed the congregation. It was sufficiently large that there was standing room only even in the ample Jesuit chapel.

As with the seat in the garden years before, Jane's pallid skin blended seamlessly with the full-flowing white dress and long crocheted veil. Only her dark hair and rouged cheeks made it clear there was a body inside the clothes. Edward was in a plain black suit, white shirt and black necktie, having resisted

Elizabeth's pleading to have him borrow a naval uniform for the event.

'Now, any two people who take this step deserve our support, so let's show it with a round of applause.'

Father Pritchard led the way. The congregation slowly followed until the clapping was deafening.

'In church? Really!' Elizabeth whispered to her husband as he slowed his own hand clap.

Some of the congregation clearly approved of the entertaining priest. Others, like Elizabeth, were wishing they could take the ceremony back to Towneley and the safety of Father Cocklin.

'*These are such interesting times to be alive,*' Pritchard began the sermon. '*Times when old divisions are failing us and we are coming to see the world in all its majestic grandeur and differences. Daily scientific discoveries are leading us to new visions of how the world holds together and indeed how we should organise ourselves. Old ideas of nationhood, of who is better than the other; of religions, which is the true and which the false; and even of man and woman and how we should regard their inherent equality. All these things are upon us and we rejoice that soon we will no longer see ourselves as English, Scottish, Irish, French, Russian, but as human beings sharing life on a fragile planet that needs us to serve and act as one, rather than divided. A time when we will no longer speak of Catholic, Protestant, Jew, Muslim and Buddhist but as human beings responding to their common creator. A time when women and men will share the burdens of work and family care far more closely than in the past, and with mutual respect and understanding of their inherent equality before God. I know it is in this spirit that this young couple comes before us, committed to a new kind of love, one that is not about mastery and subservience, with the woman as a domestic slave, but about a love of equals, different but equal in the eyes of God. To those who say man came first and then woman, let us remember that man was made from dust but woman from the rib of a human being ... We congratulate you on your love, Jane and Edward, and I now ask you to come forward to commit yourselves to each other for life.'*

By this time, Elizabeth was ready to stand and throw something at Pritchard. Her tut-tutting and gasping became so vocal, her husband had to enjoin her to be quiet; something he rarely did. She then turned around searching for any ally who might support her quiet revolt.

'I, Edward Thomas Fraser Lovat take you, Jane …'

'You may now kiss the bride,' Pritchard said at the end of the vows. 'And let's make it a worthwhile one – not one of those little pecks I see too often.'

Edward and Jane did as instructed. As the congregation murmured a mix of approval and disapproval, Elizabeth seemed as if she would bound over the front pew and tear them apart.

Edward reflected that the best kiss so far in this relationship had been here in front of a crowd too large to fit in the space.

—∞—

The festivities outshone anything the religious ceremony had to offer. It was held at a grand hotel with no cost spared. The food was of the highest quality and constituted of a seemingly endless number of serves. Alcohol was equally in plentiful supply and of all varieties. The speeches were long and by and large boring and self-serving. Jane was in her element, Edward reminding himself of the evils of comparison.

Father Pritchard was several seats up from Elizabeth. She made a bee line to him straight after the speeches. She was well inebriated. He had not taken a drop.

'Father, I just want to say I found that the most extraordinary sermon I have ever heard in a Catholic church.'

'Thank you so much, Ma'am.'

'Oh no, I didn't mean it that way, Father. With the greatest of respect, there were some non-Catholics there today who might have thought why would I bother being a Catholic if it's just the same as being a Protestant, a Jew or indeed a Muslim? A Muslim, of all things! Surely you didn't mean to say that, Father, and if that's so, please tell me so I can call everyone to attention and have you clarify what you meant.'

'I don't think that will be necessary but thank you all the same.'

'Why is it not necessary, Father? Surely you don't mean to say that being a Catholic is no better than being any of those other heathen things?'

'Well, it depends on the person, I suppose. Perhaps God loves a good Protestant or indeed Muslim more than a bad Catholic. I assume you've heard of the story of the Good Samaritan?'

'I really can't see what that has to do with anything, Father.'

Thomas, also seated nearby, saw the situation and hobbled over to them.

'Elizabeth, I wonder if I could steal Father Pritchard from ye for a moment. There are some matters important to the church's welfare that I need to discuss with him.'

'Well, if you insist, Colonel, by all means,' Elizabeth slurred. 'But I do wish to continue our conversation before the night's out, Father.'

'I look forward to it, Ma'am.'

Elizabeth walked away and Thomas sat in her place.

'So, what is it of ecclesiastical concern that you wish to discuss, Colonel?' Pritchard asked, grinning widely.

'I just wanted to say how much I enjoyed yer sermon, Father. I ken that might be important church business, dinna ye?'

'Indeed. As important as it gets.'

—⚹—

The best room in this lavish hotel had been booked for the newly married couple. They had spent most of the festive time apart.

Jane was with her extended family and friends who accounted for most of the guests. Edward divided his time between his small family gathering and Mary Beth and Carl Solander, the only friends there.

Edward noted late in the evening that Jane had been drinking more than he would have expected.

'I'm just so tired,' she said.

Jane threw her dress over the trunk at the foot of the bed. She fell into the bed in her undergarments and pulled up the blankets. Edward undressed, washed and stepped into new pyjamas Emma had given him for the occasion.

He slipped into the largest bed he had ever seen. He placed one arm around Jane's waist. She was facing away.

'So, here we are at last,' he whispered, moving his hand up and cupping her breast over the furls of undergarments.

Jane reached up and grabbed his hand, moving it down to her waist.

'Not tonight, Edward. I'm so tired.'

The next day they went to a small house in Nelson. It was a getaway cottage owned by the Towneleys who had set it aside for three days for the couple.

It was an idyllic spot and they spent most of the first day wandering through the fields. They came in and ate a dinner prepared by local farmers who worked for the Towneleys.

They went to bed quite early. On this occasion, the marriage was consummated in a short but successful encounter.

'I'm glad we've done that,' Jane said, turning away.

Edward had another restless night.

—⚬—

After three nights and one more successful encounter, they moved back to the married quarters on the estate.

'So, this is the larger flat?' Jane asked.

'Aye, is it nay to yer liking?'

'Well, I wouldn't want to see the smaller ones. Anyway, it will have to do for now but I'll need to get Mummy over to help me turn it into something more befitting a lady. Clearly, no woman has been in here for a while. Do you mind if I get her over tomorrow?'

'Not at all.'

—◊—

The next few months were busy for Edward. Work on the estate seemed endless. He was sure the staffing was inadequate and he seemed to be bearing the burden of running things without adequate recognition or financial reward.

'I'll get my husband to speak with Mr Towneley,' Elizabeth said after Jane had complained about Edward's wage.

'Oh, please, nay, Mrs Braithwaite. I'd rather ye nay do that.'

'Don't be silly, boy. Leave it to me.'

It was part of a daily ritual of maternal interference in their lives, as far as Edward was concerned. Jane seemed entirely happy with it.

—◊—

In late November, Jane, with Elizabeth by her side, announced that she thought she might be with child.

'I'm surprised ye told yer Ma first is all I'm saying.'

'Your problems with Mummy cannot be my concern. And I'm sorry if a woman consulting her mother about a very motherly thing bothers you.'

'I ken most women would tell their husband first.'

'Well, I've never been married before – *unlike you* – so I wouldn't know.'

And so it went on.

—⚬—

Early the following year, Edward and Jane received an invitation to attend the wedding of Carl Solander and Mary Beth Parker in Highgate. The formal invitation had an enclosed letter tucked within.

Dear Edward, I did not wish for you to receive this invitation without a personal note to let you know that our dear friend, Carl, asked me to marry him recently and I have agreed to be his wife. I know this is sudden but we decided, at our age, that there was no point in waiting so we are to be married at the local church next month. We both have you to thank for bringing us together again at your wedding. We have seen each other quite regularly since then. I had asked Carl if he would come to Highgate to advise on how best to manage the gardens. He kindly did so but then one thing led to another, as is often the case in life. I knew you would want to know that I am extremely happy but also that I will never forget the wonderful times that have passed between us. Your fondest friend always, Mary Beth. PS. I do hope that you and Jane will be free to attend the wedding.

The letter had arrived, addressed to Mr and Mrs E. Lovat, so Jane opened it. When Edward came home, she was crying and being comforted by her mother.

'What's the matter?'

'You tell me,' Jane replied, flinging the invitation and letter on the floor.

Edward sat at the table and read them.

'Well, this is quite a shock. I'd nay idea they were even seeing each other. But why the tears? I dinna ken what the problem is.'

'Oh, you men!' Elizabeth said. 'You're as shallow as I always expected. Don't you think it's enough that my daughter has to endure the knowledge that you went off and married that Scottish whore without having all your other women flung in her face?'

'Please, get out of my house,' Edward shouted as he stood. 'Get out and stay out.'

Elizabeth made for the door.

'No, Mummy, ignore him. Please stay.'

'No, darling. You've made this bed so you must now sleep in it.'

Elizabeth left, slamming the door behind her. Jane stood and approached the table as Edward sat back down.

'How could you?' Jane said through her tears. 'How could you speak to Mummy like that?'

'Did ye hear what she called my first wife?'

'The one you'd still rather be married to, you mean?'

'That's nay fair, Jane. I married ye and I was delighted to do so but I dinna ken I have to take that kind of thing from yer Ma. Calling my dead wife that *uamhas* name.'

'But *is* she dead, Edward?'

'What d'ye mean?'

'In your head? Is she still alive in your head? If she came back today, would you stay one minute with me?'

'That's daft thinking, Jane.'

Jane began to walk away. She turned back.

'So, you think I'm mad, do you?'

'I dinna say that.'

They were silent for a moment.

'I'm sorry. Mummy went too far, I admit. She's just concerned for me.'

'But why?'

'I don't know. She's always been protective and ...'

'And what?'

'She doesn't trust you. She's never trusted you. I'm not sure she's ever trusted anyone but then when you went off and married that other woman.'

'Amy was her name.'

'Amy, if you must – then she felt vindicated. I was the one who kept on saying I trusted you and all she could say was, *I told you so.*'

'I'm sorry. But why dinna ye tell *me* that ye trusted me instead of ignoring me. What was I to think?'

'I didn't ignore you. You ignored me.'

'Nay, that's nay the way it was. Anyway, let's nay start that again. What I wanna ken is what is it about Mary Beth's letter that upset ye? I canna see the problem, Jane.'

'Well, I know you've spent a lot of time with her in the past. You've stayed with her at her place. You can imagine what Mummy had to say about that.'

'Aye, but that's all in the past. Can we nay get past that?'

'But *is* it all in the past, Edward? I saw the way you were with her at the wedding.'

'How was I?'

'I can't explain it. You looked so happy to be with her and it was obvious she's in love with you. So, I suppose I just started to wonder if I'll spend my life competing with your other loves, the dead ones and the live ones.'

'Nay, Jane. I chose *ye* and I was happy to. Ye can believe that or nay believe it.'

Jane was silent. She wiped her eyes. She came back to the table and sat down opposite him.

'Thank you, Edward. I want to believe it.'

'And I want you to believe it too. Now, will ye please come to the wedding?'

'Oh, no, I couldn't, Edward. Even if I wanted to. Imagine trying to compete with a seven month old baby showing through my dress.'

'It's nay a competition, darling.'

—w—

Edward went alone to the wedding. He noted how happy Mary Beth and Carl seemed to be.

He slept badly that night.

—w—

On the 6th of July, 1799, their first son was born in the new Women's Hospital in Preston, one of the finest in England at the time.

'*No home births for a Braithwaite*,' Edward mused.

'I'd like to call him Charles after Papa,' Jane said.

'Aye, and I'll call him Charles after the dear friend who died to save me.'

'Well, at least we agree on one thing – even if for different reasons.'

Charles Joseph Edward Lovat was baptised in the hospital chapel two days later.

'And don't even suggest that horrid priest who did your wedding should do the christening,' Elizabeth said. 'I've asked Father Cocklin.

'Thanks Mummy. You think of everything.'

XXXIX

Turning into the nineteenth-century would bring major changes to the Pemberton household. Emma spent her days sitting and staring out the window. The only word she uttered, day or night, was *Edward.*

'D'ye ken she's calling for me?' Edward asked Will.

'No, I don't think so.'

In October of 1800, Thomas's health deteriorated. His regular uncomplaining demeanour gave way to constant groaning, sometimes wailing. The doctor put it down to major kidney failure. That unremoved bullet from a quarter of a century ago was having its way.

His spirits lifted in November when he heard of the election of Thomas Jefferson as fourth President of the United States. He wrote to him.

Dear Mr President, I dare say you will not remember me but I met and stayed with you one evening at the behest of a common friend, Mr Henry Coolidge. We spoke at length about matters of mutual import. I also attended a court session the following day in which you defended a young man seeking free status. I wrote down some of the fine words you used that day and have never forgotten them. I recognised the sentiments when your first Constitution was formed. My meeting with you was in the early 1770s from memory. Regardless, I did wish to congratulate you on your election. From all I learned from you, I believe the United States will be in excellent hands under your guidance. I remain, yours faithfully, Thomas Lovat (ex-Colonel, British Army).

Christmas and New Year came and went. In mid-January, Thomas received an unexpected reply.

Dear Colonel Lovat (Thomas), Indeed, I do remember you and the highly stimulating evening we spent with our dear departed Henry. Such a fine man and unrecognised hero of our noble cause. Even now, I recall Henry and I agreeing that if there had been more British officers of your ilk, things might have transpired differently between our two nations. In my experience, most differences can be ameliorated when men and women of good will and common sense address them. Unfortunately, this kind of person is too rarely present when needed most. You, however, were an exception and this is not forgotten. Thank you for your congratulations. I hope, with God's help, I can assist in forging a stronger nation amidst our ongoing challenges. Please pray for me. Yours sincerely, Thomas Jefferson (US President designate). PS. I did see you one other time, though you would not remember. I'm delighted to know you survived your wounds.

'So it *was* his voice I recognised that day I was wounded,' Thomas said to Edward.

'Ye must be so proud, Da. A man like that remembering ye from a quarter of a century ago. Ye obviously made an impression.'

'Your father always made an impression,' Sarah said. 'On me and so many others. We're all so proud of you, darling.'

'While I have ye both here,' Thomas said. 'Lad, Sarah and I have discussed this and there's a couple of things we ken ye should have in yer possession.'

Thomas handed him a small box which Edward opened in front of them. It contained the diary that Thomas had kept up until his wounding in America. He had intended to keep it going but upon the death of Eliza, he had slipped into what became known as his "dark period" and so never got back to it. The other item was his most precious possession, Mahdiya's bullet-torn Qur'an.

'I can only ken it was Allah who saved me that day. I took it from Mahdiya's dying hands and it's been with me ever since.'

'I'll treasure both of them. Sarah, are ye sure ye dinna mind me having them?'

'Not at all, dear boy. I know it's what your father wants.'

When Edward returned home, he placed the small box in a special place and sat Charlie Bear atop to guard it.

—◊◊◊—

Edward had wished to bring Charles, now twenty-one months, with him to Pemberton. It was partly for his birthday, the only celebration he was likely to get that year. He had initially suggested taking Charles to Tralee for a double birthday celebration with Little Tom.

'He's far too young to make that kind of trip,' Jane said.

'The very idea,' Elizabeth added.

So, taking him to Pemberton was a compromise but also timely as he knew things were not good there. In the end, he travelled alone because Charles was deemed to "have a cold".

The day of his birthday, 26th of January, was overtaken by Emma falling into a coma the night before. The doctor was called, saying nothing could be done. It was a matter of time.

'My goodness, what's that?' the doctor said as a wailing came from down the hallway.

'It's Thomas,' Sarah said. 'That's when he's really bad.'

'I'd no idea the pain was so great. Can I see him?'

The doctor walked in to find Thomas writhing in pain. He reached into his bag and handed Sarah a bottle of medicine.

'Give him just a small teaspoon of this every two hours. No more. It's very strong but it should ease the pain.'

It was late in the morning that Thomas, in one of his rare waking moments, asked to be helped into his mother's room. He was seated in a chair next to her bed but found it too uncomfortable. They moved him onto the bed to lie next to her. He held her hand.

Emma died mid-afternoon just after Thomas had been given another small dose of the medicine that seemed to anaesthetise him for most of the next hour.

The doctor was called and confirmed Emma's death. Will kissed her on the lips for one last time and then laid his head over her chest. Sarah and Edward wept at a distance.

'Does Thomas know about his mother?' the doctor asked.

'No,' Sarah replied. 'He's been unconscious all the time.'

The doctor examined him.

'His heart's very weak. The pain's taking its toll. Perhaps give him the medicine by the hour.'

'But, Doctor, you said this morning that it's too strong.'

'I'm sorry, Mrs Lovat, but your husband is failing so it's a case of whether to leave him in pain or not. I'm afraid the outcome will be the same either way. I'm truly very sorry.'

There are times in life when the world seems unbearably brutish.

'Happy birthday, by the way,' Will said to Edward. 'Not much of a celebration, is it?'

'Nay, indeed.'

He was on the other side of the bed to Will, sitting next to Sarah who was clinging to Thomas's spare hand. Thomas's other one was still clutching his mother's hand.

'So, if he wakes in pain, give him another dose,' the doctor said. 'I've another patient to see but I'll be back presently.'

Thomas woke about an hour later.

'Hello, darling,' Sarah said.

Thomas smiled a little, his eyes still closed.

'Darling, your mother's gone to heaven,' she said, whispering into his ear.

Thomas's eyes fluttered and a grimace came over his face. They saw him squeeze Emma's hand. After a few seconds, he released the grip, let out a sigh and fell back to unconsciousness, even without the medicine.

'Darling, darling,' Sarah cried.

'Da, Da,' Edward called.

Will rushed to the address the doctor had left with them. They were both back by the bedside within minutes. The doctor checked Thomas's pulse.

'He's extremely weak. But he's feeling no pain.'

An hour or so later, Thomas Edward Fraser Lovat took his last breath. Born on the day of his father's death, he would die on the day of his mother's, the day of his own son's birth just twenty-five years before.

Written off in Western thought as a series of coincidences, Pictish mythology would have a more elaborate story to tell around predestined rhythms and cycles of life.

By either story, the Son of a Jacobite was dead.

XL

S o, it came to pass that Edward Lovat, grandson of a Jacobite, had two sons by two wives. Both boys were of Highlander heritage, one doubly so. The destiny of one son was to be brought up in Ireland, the other in England.

The shared destiny of these half-brothers was that they would follow in their father's footsteps to Sydney Cove, arriving in the same year, 1837, albeit on two different ships at different times of the year. One would be a pioneer teacher, the other a pioneer priest, each contributing substantially to the early colonisation, some would say invasion, of Australia.

But these are stories yet to be told.

 Matador

For exclusive discounts on Matador titles,
sign up to our occasional newsletter at
troubador.co.uk/bookshop